As
High
as the
Heavens

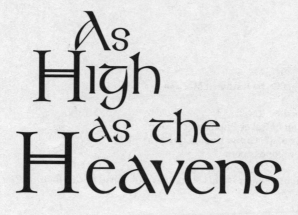

As High as the Heavens

Kathleen Morgan

Revell
Grand Rapids, Michigan

Published by Revell
a division of Baker Publishing Group
P.O. Box 6287, Grand Rapids, MI 49516-6287
www.revellbooks.com

A previous version of this story was published under the title *The Heather and the Thistle*.

Printed in the United States of America

Library of Congress Cataloging-in-Publication Data
Morgan, Kathleen, 1950–
     As high as the heavens / Kathleen Morgan.
        p.   cm.
     ISBN 978-0-8007-5816-5 (pbk.)
        1. Nobility—Scotland—Fiction. 2. Conspiracies—Fiction.
3. Family secrets—Fiction. 4. Scotland—History—16th century—
Fiction. 5. Highlands (Scotland)—Fiction. I. Title.
PS3563.O8647A83 2008
813′.54—dc22   2007037011

I will thank you, Lord, in front of all the people. I will sing your praises among the nations. For your unfailing love is as high as the heavens.

Psalm 57:9–10

January, 1568, Grampian Region, Scotland

"Och, help me endure this winter. And help me accept the life that fate—and my father—have decreed for me!"

As the sun's fading rays slanted through the birches lining the road to Dunscroft Castle, Heather Gordon bit back further entreaties—futile but instinctive after years of religious instruction—to a God who had long since ceased to care, and stepped back from the deep, stonecut library window. Usually protected from within by heavy iron shutters that could be firmly bolted against possible attack, the window stood unobstructed this day to catch the watery, winter light. The meager illumination, however, did little to brighten the gloomy, tomeladen room. If not for the view of rolling hills and distant mountains, Heather didn't know how she could've borne the sense of restless entrapment she always experienced this time of year.

She made her aimless way past the globe of the world and high-backed wooden settle covered with cushions to the bookshelves inset in the dark, wainscot-paneled walls. Ah, she thought, but she was so very weary of winter, and it was only mid-January. At least three months of cold, damp, and snow still remained here in the Grampians, the mountain range that formed a natural division between the Scottish Highlands and Lowlands.

If this year, though, were the same as all the years past, she'd have to endure only three more months and all would be well. Three more months, and she could once again accompany her father to Edinburgh to immerse herself in the heady charm and excitement that was Queen Mary's Court. Always before, such plans had indeed been sufficient to pin one's hopes and dreams on in the dreary days and weeks ahead.

But not this year. This year the queen no longer resided in Edinburgh. In truth, since her unwilling abdication last July in favor of her infant son, after the defeat of her and her third husband the Earl of Bothwell's forces by rebel troops at Carberry Hill, Mary was no longer officially queen.

There'd be no banquets or outings or dances led by the beautiful, carefree monarch this spring. Mary was imprisoned in Lochleven Castle, ensconced on its tiny island in the middle of Loch Leven, and her brilliant but illegitimate half brother, James Stewart, the Earl of Moray, had no intention of allowing her to rule again. The kingdom would survive with Moray now as regent for the infant king, but life as they had all known it would never be the same.

Expelling a deep sigh, Heather ran her emerald-and-pearl-beringed fingers along the row of leather-bound books, considering then discarding a number of titles before settling on a book of Scottish verses by William Dunbar. She pulled out the small, gilt-etched volume, opened it, and read a few of the poems. For a change, however, none of the compositions caught her fancy. With an even deeper sigh, she carefully returned the book to its spot and lifted her gaze to the next higher shelf.

Plato, Socrates, Aristotle. Gavin Douglas's translation of Virgil's *Aeneid* into the Scots language. Heather grimaced. Somehow, their stirring words didn't beckon today. Though she wished for a book thought-provoking enough to distract and help while away the hours until suppertime, when she hoped her father would be finished with his meeting with the Lords Fleming and Seton, and lesser noblemen George Douglas, John Beaton, and John Sempill, Heather wasn't in the mood just now for any heavy philosophical treatises.

Next to the ponderous tomes of the ancient Greeks and Romans sat yet another small volume, entitled *The Book of the City of Ladies* by Christine Pisan. Though Heather knew the writings of the famed French scholar and poet of the past century nearly by heart, she never tired of rereading her eloquent words in defense of women. Perhaps some of those declarations would soothe her restive spirit now. Perhaps, this time, she'd finally find the answers to what was really needed for a happy, contented life. Answers she'd of late so avidly sought and had yet to truly find.

Taking down the volume, Heather thumbed through the pages. The first words that caught her eye only plunged her heart deeper into the morass of confusion and resentment that had plagued her for the past year. *I considered myself most unfortunate,* she read, *because God had made me inhabit a female body in this world.*

Heather gave a snort of disgust and quickly reshelved that book as well. "God's injustice to women! As if, atop it all," she muttered, "I needed *that* reminder of yet another source of my discontent."

Just then the stout oak door swung open, ushering in a chill gust of air from the hall. Heather shivered, pulled her fine, crimson wool damask wrap about the shoulders of her tightly cinched, emerald green velvet gown with its high, stiff ruff collar, and turned. There, in the doorway, a preoccupied frown marring his strong, noble features, stood her father.

As dark as Heather was light, Lord Robert Gordon was a tall, robustly built man who, even in his fifties, carried himself with the athletic grace and vigor of a man a score of years younger. Well aware of the striking figure he still made, he dressed in the height of Court fashion, from his fine leather shoes with slashed decorations to his black knitted silk stockings and short trunks roundly padded with horsehair, to his ebony velvet doublet with its low, pointed waist, puff sleeves, and white linen ruff collar. Also in the current fashion, his graying, dark brown hair was cut close and short, as was his full beard.

Her despair and discontent dissipating in her renewed

swell of affection for her handsome, dashing father, Heather hurried over. "Is the meeting finished so soon?" she asked, barely masking her eagerness with what she hoped was a beguiling smile. "Ah, I pray so. Being relegated all afternoon to the confines of the library has long ago lost its appeal."

"Gae awa wi' ye!" Robert Gordon exclaimed with a chuckle, falling back on a more primitive form of speech to express his incredulity. "Have my ears finally failed me, now to hear ye complain of a few hours spent with yer books? It's past time, then, I send off for a new supply. Ye must surely have exhausted our meager offerings to speak now so disparagingly."

"Nay, Father. It's but the weather of late, and the time of year." Heather's smile faded. "And the fact it's the first winter I've spent without Mither too. No matter how close to my wit's end I'd become when the snow lay long on the ground and the cold kept us indoors, she used always to have some plan to pass the bleak, boring hours."

"Aye, that she did, lass." Robert's mouth tightened, and a wistful look flared in his eyes. "That she did. Though my bonny Margery has been gone all of eight months now, I, too, find some days without her harder to bear than others."

He stepped close and wrapped an arm about Heather's shoulders. "Come, lass," he said, guiding her back into the library's confines and shutting the door. "What I've next to say to ye will, I'd wager, win yer interest for a time. There's trouble afoot and much I must discuss with ye."

11

"Indeed?" Heather shot her father a worried look. Though she was well aware today's meeting had been convened hastily and with the utmost secrecy, her respect and loyalty to her father had precluded any queries or idle curiosity.

"Has this trouble, then, aught to do with this day's council with the lords and other nobles?"

"Aye, it does." He led her to two box-seated, panel-backed oak armchairs standing before the small hearth fire. "Sit, lass," he urged, "while I warm this frigid room a bit."

Heather settled herself on the farthest chair's green, blue, and yellow tartan-covered seat, snugged her shawl more securely up about her shoulders, and waited while her father knelt and added a few logs to the fire. It was strange, she mused, how cold the room had become in the hours she had waited. She hadn't noticed it before. Somehow, though, as she sat in tense anticipation of what was to come, her fingers suddenly felt like little blocks of ice and her cheeks and ears stung with what almost seemed like chilblains.

In the span of but a few minutes of prodding and poking, the feeble flames were coaxed back to their former intensity. Heat surged forth to bathe the little room in comforting warmth. Setting aside the iron poker, Robert Gordon then rose, walked over, and took the seat opposite his daughter.

Though Heather waited patiently for her father to speak, he failed to do so for what seemed an interminable length of time. Instead he stared down at his hands, hands that, as if they possessed a mind of their own,

12

ceaselessly clenched and unclenched in his lap. Finally, Robert Gordon cleared his throat, lifted his gaze, and fixed her with a resolute stare.

"What I next tell ye, lass, ye must swear on yer mither's grave not to reveal to a soul. Swear it now, or I can't tell ye a word more."

Apprehension plucked at Heather. This was far, far worse than she had imagined.

"Aye, Father," she said softly. "If it's of such import to ye, I give ye my word. I'll not tell a soul. But I'd like also to know why ye require such a solemn oath."

He averted his gaze, seemingly finding sudden interest in the fat, fluffy snowflakes beginning to fall outside the library window. For a moment Heather's gaze joined his. The ethereal beauty of the crystalline forms floating languorously past the windowpanes caught her up, holding her in thrall. How exquisitely beautiful they were, she thought, yet, conversely, how painfully deadly if one was ever caught unprotected outside in a storm.

Beauty and pain . . .

The bitter contrast evoked memories of the day her mother had summoned Heather to her deathbed. Margery had sent the servants from the room, then pulled Heather close. The sickeningly sweet smell of death had tainted the air, and only her deep, abiding love for her mother had kept Heather there.

"A word . . . with ye," Margery had whispered. "Of life . . . love . . . and a woman's lot."

Heather swallowed hard and nodded. "Aye, Mither?"

"I've always loved yer father. Who wouldn't . . . love

13

him?" Her mother's eyes misted with tears. "He was always so braw . . . so bonny."

Taking her mother's hand in hers, Heather waited.

"H-he never loved me, though. Leastwise, not as I wished him to." A fat tear rolled down Margery's cheek. "Aye . . . just as Rose's man never loved her . . ."

She clutched Heather's hand, as if afraid that letting her daughter go just then would be to surrender her to a similar fate. "Beware, my bonny Heather . . . beware of giving yer love to a man. They cannot help themselves . . . cannot help breaking yer heart and crushing yer spirit . . . aye, and even killing ye."

Disbelief, then horror, swamped Heather. Could it be? Had both her mother and older sister fallen prey to the same fate?

Rose had wed but two years ago. Donald Campbell had been every woman's dream—dashing and handsome, if a trifle shallow. Her sister had fallen wildly, passionately in love. After a brief courtship they had been wed. Rose had quickly become pregnant.

Donald, however, though he greatly valued the Gordon fortune Rose would one day inherit, put no such store in his vows of marital fidelity. One night, when his wife was only weeks from her childbed, he had become careless. Rose found him with one of her serving maids. In the terrible fight that ensued, she had somehow lost her balance chasing him and fallen down the stairs. Rose and her babe had died three days later.

Yet, though her sister's death had been a terrible blow, now to discover her mother's long-kept, devastating secret was an even greater shock. All these years, Heather

14

hadn't imagined her mother unhappy in her marriage, but then, when had she ever closely thought much on it? She had always been so engrossed in her books and, in her youthful naïveté, she had just assumed . . .

"Nay, not Father." Heather choked out the words. "Not Father."

"Aye, lass." Her eyes burning pits of agony, her mother managed a weak nod. "Even my braw, bonny Robert."

Beauty and pain . . .

The rich, tangy scent of wood smoke wafted by. The familiar odor only intensified Heather's awareness of the contrast between the now warm and cozy room and the sense of uncertainty and betrayal in the world outside. Uncertainty and betrayal so perfectly exemplified by a beloved father, an unfaithful brother-in-law, and the God who had allowed such a travesty of justice in the world.

As if for the first time, Heather saw her father with a new perspective. Saw him, in the rapidly waning light, as a man besieged by cares that had aged him in ways she had never before noted. Saw him as a man who, perhaps with the best of intentions, used others for his own means.

They cannot help themselves . . .

At the memory of her mother's sorrowing words, guilt at her own disloyalty, followed swiftly by a fierce resolve, flooded Heather. She was a woman in a man's world, and not even God would come to her aid. She had no other choice. Her father was all she had and, like her mother before her, she'd stand by him.

She would just never allow him, or any man, to pierce

the barriers she had been forced—in the aftermath of her sister's and mother's deaths—to build about her heart. The belated realization of their marital torment had been hard enough to bear. She'd not play the fool and risk that same pain and betrayal herself.

"Tell me, Father." Leaning forward, Heather took her sire's hand in hers and gave it an encouraging squeeze. "Ye know I can be trusted. Ye know, as well, that I'll do aught ye ask." She managed a taut little smile. "When everything's said and done, we are, now that Rose and Mither are gone, all that is left of the Gordons of Dunscroft."

He smiled sadly and patted her cheek. "Aye, my poor, bonny Rose and dear, sweet Margery. Well, it won't be long now, will it, before ye're wed?" His brow clouded in thought. "The ceremony's but five months away, isn't it? And once ye've wed that handsome son of Alastair Seton, ye'll soon see to bairns running about within these old walls again. Then I'll truly be content, what with my daughter and her husband and their bairns brightening Dunscroft once more."

She knew he meant well, knew he had done what any conscientious father would do, in betrothing her, as his now only child and heir, to Charles Seton. Of good stock and breeding, Charlie was also a younger son who stood greatly to gain in joining with the prosperous Gordons. And, if the truth were told, there were many men far less pleasing than Charlie. Indeed, in the few visits they had shared in the past months, Heather had found him to be quite pleasant and well-read. He seemed, if nothing else, a man who'd treat her kindly.

The fact that Heather didn't love him, or even find him particularly exciting, must never be permitted to influence her acceptance of the betrothal. Indeed, the fact she *didn't* love him was perhaps for the best. She'd make no errors clouded by love—neither those that broke the spirit *nor* the body. Still in her heart of hearts, Heather wondered if there wasn't—*shouldn't be*—more. More to a relationship between a man and a woman. More to life itself.

But such thoughts were far from the issue just now. What mattered was hearing what her father had come to say, and supporting him in whatever he desired. Heather turned to the hand that lingered on the side of her face, kissed it, then pulled away.

"Tell me, Father. Tell me and be done with it."

He leaned back then and sighed. "It's the queen. She must be freed from Lochleven."

"Aye, that she must." Heather frowned. Though she was well aware her father was part of a group of loyalists who had never accepted Mary's abdication, she had hoped he'd have allowed the younger, more hotheaded members of the faction to lead any plot to rescue the queen. It was beginning to appear, however, that that wouldn't be the case.

"What has that to do with me," she prodded when no reply was forthcoming, "or with the secret ye asked me to keep?"

"We can't rescue her with force of men. Lochleven is too well fortified. It would withstand us long enough for Moray to send a superior army against us. We must, instead, enter the castle by more devious means and spirit away Mary before they can sound the alarm."

"A wise plan."

Her hands outstretched, Heather leaned toward the fire to warm fingers again gone suddenly cold. The flickering light bathed her hands in red-gold hues, casting them into brilliant illumination, then shadow.

"It'll take a clever scheme, however," she said, "to fool Lochleven's chatelaine, the Lady Margaret Douglas, and her son William. They know the Gordons are loyal to the queen. We can't just float up to the castle and ask their permission to visit Mary."

"Nay, we can't," her father admitted. "In fact, we can't appear to be in any way involved in the queen's rescue. If the plot should fail, Moray's vengeance would be swift and harsh. But we *can* send a man the Douglases view as friend and ally into Lochleven to aid in Mary's escape. A man who, though they assume him loyal to their cause, is, in truth, loyal instead to the queen."

Her hands still spread to the fire, Heather glanced over her shoulder at her father. "Indeed? And who would such a man be?"

Robert Gordon smiled. "A man the exact double of that young fop Colin Stewart. Ye remember him from yer days at Court, don't ye? As luck would have it, the Lady Margaret dotes on him."

"A man who looks exactly like Colin?"

Heather turned to face her father. She was well acquainted with the handsome if dissolute Colin Stewart. For the past two years, he had been in attendance at Mary's Court the same months Heather and her father

18

were there. He had even for a time been a suitor for her hand, until her father had adamantly squelched that. His vast estates and noble lineage notwithstanding, Colin Stewart's conversion to the new church headed by John Knox had been more than the Catholic Lord Gordon could stomach.

"A man the exact double of Colin?" she repeated, forcing the memory of Colin Stewart's flattering if rather superficial courtship from her mind. "But how can that be? And how did ye come to know of this man?"

"It's a long story." An enigmatic expression shuttered his eyes.

"Well, I've the time to hear it, if ye've the time to tell it."

Her father grinned. "Ye've yer mither's blunt way of speech. I like that. Unlike her, though, ye know when to temper it with good grace."

Warmth stole into Heather's cheeks. Her mother, Margery Mackenzie, though of noble birth, had been a Highlander through and through. She had been as feisty and fiery as they came, leastwise until her unrequited love for Robert Gordon had finally crushed her spirit. Yet though Heather strove hard "to temper with good grace" her own tendency to the same bluff ways as her mother's forbearers, on occasion those inclinations escaped to betray her.

"I try, Father," she murmured, "to be all ye wish of me. Truly, I do."

"I know ye do, lass. As I know ye won't fail me in this, either." He sighed and settled more comfortably in his chair. "The man I spoke of . . . the double of Colin Stewart

. . . lives in the Highlands amongst Clan Mackenzies. He's more, though, than just an uncanny double for Colin. He is, in fact, Colin's twin brother."

"How is *that* possible?" The shock of such a revelation sent Heather's heart to pounding. "In all the times I spoke with him, Colin never once mentioned a brother. Indeed, he said his mither had died birthing just him."

"Aye, and that's what Colin and everyone else were led to believe. Times were unsettled then for Lord Stewart. He feared a clan uprising that might overthrow him. So he came to me for help. It was I who suggested he send one of his sons away to ensure, if the uprising succeeded, at least one would live to inherit."

"And the child was sent to the Mackenzies because they were Mither's kin and could be trusted," Heather supplied, her agile mind quickly picking up the thread of the tale.

"Aye." Robert Gordon cocked his head. "Yer Uncle Angus took the bairn and hid him with a trusted clansman and his childless wife. There he has grown to manhood, unaware of his true heritage, living the rough if wholesome life of a Highlander."

"But he's a full thirty years old now."

There was something amiss here, Heather thought. There was more to this than just a simple fostering of a helpless child until the danger passed.

"His father did indeed die in the uprising," she said, watching her own sire now with more care, "but Colin survived and was raised by his grandparents. Why, in all this time, hasn't this other twin been brought back?"

Something passed across Robert Gordon's face.

20

Something dark and furtive. Almost too casually, he lowered his gaze to flick a speck from his padded trunks.

"It seemed best not to complicate things," he finally offered. "Only one twin could inherit at any rate. Until now, it was decided that it was kindest to let the Highland-reared lad live out his life unaware of what he'd never have."

"And who made that decision for him?" Unease twined about her heart and twisted her gut. "Indeed, who was left of his real family to decide such a thing? Surely not Colin? And his grandparents died several years ago."

"Colin doesn't and must never know. It would be the ruination of our plans." Robert Gordon shrugged. "What does it matter anyway, at this late a date? What's done is done. Better to thank our good fortune that few know the truth of his existence. It'll serve our needs well in the rescue of the queen. And that, lass, in the end, is all that truly matters. The queen . . . *our* queen . . . and the ultimate welfare of our nation, matters more than the twisted path one man's life has taken."

"Aye, I suppose so," Heather admitted reluctantly.

Though the manipulation of the other twin didn't set well with her—and even more so because her father apparently had been involved in that decision—she had been raised to believe the good of the many must outweigh the welfare of one. It was best to face the fact that the less she delved into the reasons for this unfortunate sequence of events, the better she could accept it.

"It's sufficient that this man will well suit our plans," her father was saying, already moving on to his next point. "There *is* but one minor problem. His education,

21

I am sorry to say, has been sadly neglected. In truth, he has been raised as a common Highlander. It'll take some schooling to fashion him into a noble who can pass muster with that Douglas shrew and her brood."

Heather gave a wry laugh. "So, ye wish a man reared as an uneducated peasant to impersonate Colin well enough to worm his way into Lochleven?" She shook her head in bemusement. "And pray, how much time do ye imagine that task will take?"

"It doesn't matter. We've only three months left. By the beginning of May, when all threat of winter is surely past, we must strike. It'll be the best time of year for the queen to rally the support she needs to regain her throne." He paused for a moment. "And that's why we need ye, lass."

"Need me for what?" Heather asked, suddenly wary.

"Why, what else? To school the lad to appear the noble, of course."

"Me?" Her eyes widened in surprise. "Ye want *me* to journey into the Highlands in the dead of winter to teach some man who is scarce educated—"

She stopped. Her eyes narrowed.

"Can this man even read? It'll be nigh impossible to teach him if he cannot read."

Nervously, her father slanted his gaze from hers. "I can't say for certain. There's been little opportunity to question the particulars of his upbringing all these years." He glanced back and managed a wan smile. "But surely yer uncle saw to it that he was taught to read."

"Och, aye," Heather said with a disgusted snort. "And haven't I already seen many times over what attention to detail Uncle Angus puts into things? It'd be the greatest fortune if this man can even eat with knife and fork, much less wash more often than once a fortnight."

"It doesn't matter, lass." Her father leaned forward and took her hand. "We can't risk involving additional people in this plot, or word of it will leak out and we'll all be dead before we've the chance even to attempt Mary's rescue. It was why I offered yer services. Only a woman could well and quickly teach the manners of Court and the proper way a noble comports himself. And only a woman—if it can be done at all—could get a proud man to mold himself in ways foreign to his nature."

"So, ye mean to use me to manipulate this man."

Anger flared in Heather's breast. In some inexplicably painful way, she was beginning to feel as used and manipulated as this mysterious Highlander. Only a woman, indeed!

"I don't like it, Father." She shook her head, a frown on her face. "I don't like it at all."

"Neither do I or any other of us, lass," he said, patting her hand to soothe her. "I know it's most unusual—sending ye so far afield at a time like this. But ye'll be well chaperoned in that fine tower house of yer Uncle Angus. And ye can bring a serving maid, and even one of the cooks to keep ye in all the dainties ye're accustomed to.

"Why," he forged on eagerly, as if warming to his subject, "if ye've a mind for it, while all the preparations for yer journey are being made, we can take a short trip to Aberdeen to buy ye enough new books easily to entertain ye for the next three months."

When Heather remained silent and most obviously unconvinced, he squeezed her hand. "Ah, lass, lass, what choice do we have? And it's for the queen. In the end, we must all sacrifice whatever it takes to save the queen."

True enough, Heather thought in grudging agreement. They must all be willing to sacrifice for the sake of the queen. But to journey north in this weather, and deal with some potentially illiterate and most definitely unwashed Highlander . . .

Gazing at her father's pleading countenance, Heather knew she couldn't refuse him even this. She sighed her acquiescence.

"Well, a sojourn in the Highlands with Uncle Angus and Aunt Jean and some barbaric peasant wasn't quite how I envisioned passing the remaining winter, but I too wish to see Mary regain her throne."

When her father gave a small cry of joy and leaned forward to hug her, she lifted a warning hand. "I only said I'd do what ye asked. I can't promise what can be accomplished with this man in but three months' time."

"Och, dinna fash yerself, lass," her father, once again falling back into more ancient dialect, said by way of assurance as he took her into his arms. "Ye're a well-read, intelligent, and most bonny young woman. Ye'll win this man over like ye've won the hearts of so many others of his sex. Ye must be a wee bit patient with him at first, though. It'll all be so new to him. It'll take time for him to adjust, once he knows what is expected of—"

Heather went still, then pushed out of her father's arms. "He doesn't know about this? Have ye even asked him if he wishes to help us?"

Robert Gordon inhaled a deep breath. "He'll help, and no mistake. Angus is his laird. He'll do what Angus asks. Besides, the Mackenzies have always been intensely loyal to the throne. There's no reason to doubt his—"

"Ye presume much, Father, in making plans for this man's life without even first consulting him. It isn't right or fair."

His lips pursing in thought, he considered that for a moment. "Well, ye're most likely right, lass, but we also can't spare the time. First, I'd have to meet with him personally to gain his agreement, then return for ye. It's just as well I bring ye along, prepared immediately to embark on his lessons. The worst that can happen, for the price of yer journey, is that he refuses."

Heather eyed him wryly, then rose and walked across the library to stare out the window. Twilight had fallen, and the land was shrouded in a hazy, snow-muted light. The skeletal trees swayed and clacked their branches in the rising wind, until the frigid air swirling against the stout, stone walls finally found a chink at the window and surged triumphantly inside.

Awash in a sea of mixed emotions, Heather pulled her damask shawl more tightly to her. Not even an hour ago, she had stood at this very window and wished mightily for some event to rescue her from the days of endless boredom. Yet now that the opportunity was presented her, she wasn't so certain she wouldn't far prefer the safe, predictable existence that had always been hers. To journey far afield in such unstable times was frightening enough. But to set out on an undertaking that could well be life-altering for some mysterious man . . .

A man who, Heather realized with a small shiver, was the darkly handsome Colin Stewart's identical twin. Yet a man most probably as unlike his brother as any man could be.

What if he were content with his life as it already was? What if he were wed and had a family to protect and feed? How would he feel to be asked to join such a dangerous undertaking? An undertaking, at its heart, fraught with deception and manipulation?

Heather's fingers clenched in the shawl's warm, rich wool. It wasn't right what they planned for this man. Even if he agreed to an outward transformation to make him appear what he had, in truth, always been born to be, he hadn't any way of knowing what it might cost him in the end. And all because her father now sought to use them both—Heather included—as he had once used her mother and, in the doing, broken her heart.

Indeed, she thought with a ripple of presentiment, there was no way of knowing what her complicity in this deliberate trickery might cost her, either. It was, at the very least, a foolish, danger-fraught way of easing the winter's boredom. And, at the worst, a sorry solution to the gnawing sense that life should hold more for her than a loveless marriage to a kind if unexciting man.

With all her heart, Heather now wished she had never set such a course of events into action—even if only with a selfish, ill-conceived, and ultimately futile prayer.

2

Kintail Country, the Highlands

"Och, it's a cauld, nestie day, isn't it, Duncan, my lad?"

As the two men rode along, the dark-haired Highlander paused to settle his skittish horse, then shot his father a wry glance. "And is it any more so than what ye'd expect for the end of January?"

Just then a chill wind blew down from the towering heights of Beinn Eighe, surging across Loch Torridon to engulf the two men in a frigid blast of air. With his free hand, Duncan Mackenzie tugged his thick plaid more closely to him and gave a great shout of laughter.

"By mountain and sea, how I love this land! It's like a beautiful woman, one moment all soft and sweet-smelling as the heather on the hills and the next, as brash and prickly as a thistle."

Malcolm Mackenzie grinned at his son. "Yet even the

27

prickly thistle has its soft, silky down, if ye just take the time to find it. Like *most* women, not that ye've ever lingered wi' one long enough to discover that."

At the gentle reproof in his father's words, Duncan chuckled. "I'll give ye bairns to bounce on yer knee soon enough, Father. But the lasses are as bountiful and sweet as the highland flowers in summer, and I've yet to have my fill of them. Ye wouldn't wish me to wed one lass in haste, would ye, then find my true love in another?"

"Duncan, Duncan," Malcolm laughingly replied. "Have a care, lad. Ye can't play so fast and loose wi' the lassies, or fate will yet step in to punish ye for yer carefree ways."

"Indeed?" Duncan gave a disparaging snort. "And what punishment would fate deal me, do ye think, in retribution for my unwillingness yet to wed?"

"Och, who knows?" His father shrugged. "Mayhap it'll send ye a lass to love who won't love ye."

"Then I'll be verra sorry and repent my wild ways, and fate will take pity on me and give me the lass as my reward." He tossed his dark, windswept mane of hair from his face and grinned. "Isn't that the way of the lassies, Father? They like ye best when ye're brought low?"

"Well, I don't know about that. They do like to comfort and coddle ye, though." Malcolm cocked his head in consideration. "I can't deny that I like it verra much when yer mither takes it into her head to coddle me. It's verra, verra pleasant."

"Aye, so I've noticed," his son muttered dryly. "And I wish for that selfsame coddling myself, when the time is right. In the meanwhile, I've always treated the lassies with honesty and honor, and never made promises I'd no intention of keeping. Can I help it the good Lord hasn't yet chosen to send me the woman I must take to wife?"

"Nay, I suppose not. But yer mither and I are beginning to wonder where in this wide world are ye expecting the Lord to find ye a wife, if not from here in the Highlands? Unless, of course, ye're planning a wee trip sometime soon?"

Duncan laughed. "Not that I know of or wish to make, of that ye can be certain."

He turned his gaze back to the road ahead. It was a cold, dreary day. Though the recent snowfall had melted, the dampness and mud only made the weather seem even more miserable. The journey to their laird's tower house was but a half day's ride, yet the going had still been arduous in the treacherously slippery terrain. Duncan only hoped the unexpected summons was for something of import, to drag them out on such a wretched day.

"Have ye any idea why Angus Mackenzie wished to see us?" he asked, deciding it was past time to change the subject from his flirtations with the local lasses. "I've heard no rumors of a war brewing, or a renewed feud wi' any of the other clans, and it isn't time to pay our taxes. I must confess to a wee bit of curiosity over what our laird wants wi' us."

"As do I, lad. As do I. Whatever it is, we can't allow ourselves to be dragged into some extended commitment or an expedition that would call us too far afield. Yer mither can't care for our cattle by herself, what wi' her recurrent bouts of dropsy this winter. Though she'll most likely recover by spring, as she did last year, we can't always impose on our neighbor's generosity to stay with her."

"Aye, it's hard enough for most of us to get by each winter," Duncan agreed, "without having to leave home and hearth to stay wi' neighbors, or go off on some quest for one's laird." He paused, then laughed again. "Well, naught is served, I suppose, in fretting over what we can't hope to know until we get there. Besides, Angus is a fair man. We'll just point out that one of us must tend the cattle and the other, for the time being, must stay near to Mither. He'll understand."

"Mayhap it isn't a task he expects of *us* at any rate." Malcolm eyed Duncan slyly. "Angus has one marriageable daughter left—Janet's her name, isn't it?—and I've seen how she looks at ye at the *ceilidhs*. Mayhap Angus but wishes to discuss marriage terms wi' us."

"Janet Mackenzie?" Recalling the last clan gathering for song, dance, and storytelling, Duncan rolled his eyes. "The lass is as plump as a partridge, giggles incessantly, and can barely see to find her seat at table. Besides, she's but fifteen and barely out of childhood. Make no mistake. When I wed, I'll wed a woman, not a girl."

"That would be my choice as well, lad. I but broached the possibility to give ye fair warning."

"And I've been duly warned," Duncan muttered, then flipped the end of his plaid up to cover his head as a sleeting rain poured suddenly from leaden, lowering skies.

The temporary diversion from the dull winter routine of leading the cattle out each day to scrounge whatever dried grass they could find, then herding them back to the shelter of the sheds each night, had initially seemed most welcome. Now, though, with his father's teasing mention of Janet Mackenzie's love-struck interest—an interest Duncan hadn't failed to notice after her several awkward, childish attempts at trying to catch him alone and finagle a kiss—he wasn't so sure he even wanted to set foot in their laird's tower. He didn't wish to hurt the girl's feelings, feelings he had managed to spare the past few times only by the most clever and quick-witted of responses, but he was fast running out of excuses.

The rain became a downpour, quickly drenching them and their mounts in a numbing cold. Duncan sighed and hunched yet farther down on his horse, noting that his breath escaped now in a cloud of vapor.

Verra fine, he thought glumly. *At this rate, we'll be frozen clear through to the bone before we even reach Angus's tower house.* And, if he didn't mistake the situation, Janet would be first in line to strip him of his wet clothes and towel him dry.

Perhaps the easiest solution to the problem of seductive young lasses, the dark Highlander mused with rising resignation, was indeed to do as his father suggested. Find himself a bonny wife and settle down, once and for all.

"Och, I'm so verra glad ye're here, Cousin Heather," Janet Mackenzie enthused that same morning, high atop her father's tower house. "It's been the most dreary of winters, and there are so few women around of our social standing to talk with. But now ye'll be here for the next three months. Och, I can't tell ye how happy that makes me!"

Heather, trying her best to avoid the frigid rain sluicing down off the roof of the small, sheltered stairway, suppressed a grimace at the girl's well-meant but endless chatter. She exchanged a long-suffering look with Beth Erskine who, at thirty-eight, was Heather's oldest and most experienced serving maid.

Three months indeed, Heather thought. It wasn't enough she must endure this time in a dreary if passably comfortable dwelling in the isolation of the Highlands, attempting to educate some possibly illiterate savage. But now, in the bargain, to add Janet Mackenzie's generally quite mindless company seemed almost past the point of endurance.

For a moment, Heather seriously considered seeking out her father and informing him he'd have to find some other tutor for the Highlander. But only for a moment. Heather knew Robert Gordon had neither the time nor easy resources to procure an adequate substitute for her, especially here. And the resultant look she knew she'd see in her father's eyes, a look of hurt and disappointment, would be more than she could bear.

So Heather bit her tongue, forced a pleasant smile on her face, and nodded in agreement. "I, too, am pleased finally to be able to spend an extended amount of time with ye, Cousin. I've always wanted to discover the secret of that special appeal of the Highlands and now, mayhap, I'll finally have the opportunity."

"Well, ye'll soon discover one of our most dearly kept secrets," Janet said with an impish grin. "Father tells me

Duncan Mackenzie rides here even now, summoned for a private talk with him and yer father. And that braw lad," she added with a lusty sigh, "is the finest piece of man flesh in these parts. I mean to wed him, but Father says I must wait until I'm sixteen to take a husband. He's worth the wait, though, and no mistake."

"Indeed?" Heather feigned a detached interest, guessing that this Duncan Mackenzie was the Stewart twin. "Pray, what's special about this man to make him 'the finest piece of man flesh'?"

"Och, he's every woman's dream—tall, dark of hair, with the finest pair of green eyes ye'll ever hope to see, and so braw and big." Janet's mouth curved in dreamy ecstasy. "He's most comely to look upon too. And his voice . . . well, it's so warm and mellow it would melt the snow on the mountains."

"He sounds most pleasing." Heather shot Beth a covert grin. "Mayhap he'll stay and visit a few days, and we'll have the pleasure—"

"Look, look!" Suddenly oblivious to the pouring rain, Janet ran from the shelter of the stairway and over to the crenellated battlements that topped the tower. "Is it? Is it him?" She squinted out over the countryside.

Politely, Heather leaned as far from the stairway as she could and, for her efforts, was rewarded with a torrent of cold raindrops in her face. With a sputter, she leaped back within the relative shelter of the stairway.

"Who? Where?" she called out to her cousin.

"There." The girl pointed down the muddy road leading to the tower house. Just crossing the curving stone bridge that spanned a frozen stretch of burn were the mist-shrouded forms of two men on horseback.

"I'd know those proud, broad shoulders anywhere and the braw way he sits his horse," Janet cried. "It's Duncan. Duncan's here!"

Still seemingly unaware of the water streaming from the skies, Janet gathered her skirts, turned, and hurried to Heather and Beth. Her unbound, curly red hair hung in wet ringlets, clinging to her face and shoulders. Rain coursed down her cheeks and dripped from her nose.

"Come, I must prepare myself to greet Duncan. It isn't often he visits us. I want to impress him with how much more a woman I am now than when he last saw me. He's certain to need a hot bath, what with the discomforts of the journey, and I must hurry if I'm to set all aright before he arrives."

"Then I'll not disturb ye in yer preparations." Heather stepped aside to let Janet pass. "There'll be plenty of time to visit further, I'm sure, once ye've had yer fill of this Duncan Mackenzie."

Aye, Heather added silently, *let* him *bear the brunt of Janet's attention*. It was more than gladly relinquished. Three months. Surely she could bear Janet, Duncan Mackenzie, and the Highlands for three months.

The girl smiled, nodded, then brushed past them and scurried down the stairs. Beth grinned at Heather.

"I'd say ye've yer hands full with that one."

"And which one are ye speaking of?" Heather asked with a soft chuckle. "Janet or this Duncan Mackenzie?"

Beth cocked her head, her sparkling gray eyes gleaming

with mischief. "I haven't decided. Mayhap one, mayhap both. Either way, though, I'd wager ye're in for a rough time of it."

Heather had no interest in awaiting the arrival of the two Highlanders. She already knew, even without Janet's added verification, that Duncan would be handsome. She had spent enough time with Colin Stewart to have briefly fallen under that special influence of piercing, jade green eyes, chestnut brown hair, strong nose, and stubborn jaw to know whereof Janet spoke.

But she was equally aware, for all his fine education and airs, the most noble of the two brothers was self-centered, arrogant, and lacked any depth of character. How much less impressive could the Highland-raised brother be, reared in nearly total isolation from everything that truly mattered? In the end, what counted wasn't braw looks and trappings, but the heart and mind of the man. And, odds were, not much good ever came out of the Highlands.

Though her own mother had been of the Highlands, Heather nonetheless considered herself a Gordon through and through. And the Gordons, who had risen over the centuries to become the predominant power in the northeast of Scotland, weren't natives to the Highlands or indeed even to Scotland itself. Of Norman descent, they were one of many families welcomed into his kingdom by David I. Indeed, they chose to call themselves the House of Gordon, rather than Clan Gordon, distancing themselves in every way they could from their more Gaelic—and coarser—Highland neighbors.

Even before her father spurned Colin Stewart's suit for her hand, Heather had found him lacking on so many levels. But at least Charlie Seton, as plain as he was in face and body, seemed a good, decent man. Her father had chosen well in that, if nothing else.

"Ye should go down and be there to greet the Highlander," Beth said as she followed Heather along the corridor to her bedchamber. "Janet's love-struck aspirations don't matter a whit in light of yer needs. And I'd wager, once he has a chance to set eye upon ye, he'll not spare that girl another look."

Heather glanced at her maid. She had brought two lady's maids with her—Beth and Alison Gordon, a distant cousin. Of the two, however, Heather far preferred the plump, brown-haired Beth's solid common sense and dependable ways to the flighty, vain little Alison. Her advice was usually good, her opinions based on careful observations. This latest statement, however, was most unsettling.

"I don't care if Duncan Mackenzie spares me a look or not," she muttered. "I haven't come here to please his eye or win his heart. I wish but to teach him what he needs to know and then be rid of him."

"Yet why not use all yer fine attributes, be they of the mind or body, to yer advantage?" Beth persisted, opening Heather's bedchamber door and stepping aside to allow her to enter. "I'd say, men being men and Highlanders being more men than some, the day might well be won more because ye're a lovely piece of woman flesh than because of some appeal to his fine sense of justice or love of learning."

"Would ye now?"

Heather flounced over to the blazing hearth fire and bent to warm her hands. By mountain and sea, she thought with a shiver, but it was even colder in the Highlands than in the Grampians. Was there nothing about this frosty, gray land to recommend it?

"When one wishes to win, one uses every weapon at one's command." Beth shut the door and walked over to her. "Isn't this but a battle of sorts, before the final skirmish against the walls of Lochleven? And isn't the price worth it, if it results in the rescue of Queen Mary?"

"Aye."

Heather's shoulders slumped, and she flung herself into a tall, oak chair. She leaned back, gripped the well-worn arms, and expelled a frustrated breath.

"I just don't like being the bait used to lure this man to a fate he has no way of fully choosing. I'd much prefer to face him in all honesty and fairness, and . . ." Her voice faded. "Och, I don't know *what* I really want to do," she finally cried. "I just don't feel right about this!"

"Yet there's no other way, is there, lassie?" Beth supplied softly, moving to stand beside her. "Not and be true to yer father and his cause?"

"Nay, no other way." Heather sighed. "And I must be strong in this, for he depends—"

A knock sounded. The two women exchanged glances, then Beth walked to the door and opened it. Robert Gordon stood there, a frown on his face.

"Come, come, lass." He motioned for Heather to join

37

him. "The man we've ridden all this way to meet has arrived. Naught will be served with ye hiding in yer room. Ye must greet him sooner or later and, to my mind, the sooner the better."

Heather rose, smoothed the wrinkles from her blue, high-necked, and pearl-studded satin gown, straightened the long rope of pearls encircling her neck, and made her way to him. Forcing a bright smile onto her face, she followed her father out the door and back down the corridor.

"I but thought to give the man a time to rest and refresh himself, before forcing my company on him. Oftentimes, to appear overeager isn't the best strategy."

"True enough," her father admitted. "But while ye linger in yer room, Angus's daughter has lost no time welcoming the Highlander and seeing to his needs. Before he squanders all his time and attention on her, I want to dangle the true prize before him." Robert Gordon smiled down at his daughter. "It'll sweeten the pot, so to speak, when I present our plan to him."

Unaccountably, resentment swelled in Heather. Need her father be so blatant in his use of her physical charms to manipulate and tempt Duncan Mackenzie? Maiden though she was, she wasn't unaware of the power of women over men. She was also aware that many men found her attractive. Physical beauty, however, was frequently more a detriment than an advantage if one wished ever to be respected and valued for one's mind.

But her father, Heather also knew, didn't desire yet another philosophical discourse, leastwise not at a time such as this. He wanted action and results. In the end, it was probably also the best course with the likes of a man such as Duncan Mackenzie, and well her father knew it.

Subtlety and the finer points of the philosophers would make little impression on the Highlander. He was, after all, little more than a savage. An attractive woman would have a much more immediate and forceful impact. Yet Heather also wondered how she'd deal with the consequences of such a game, especially once her father was gone and she was forced into frequent and close contact with this simple, primal man.

Thankfully, she had at least the safety of her uncle's intimidating presence and the formidable shelter of his tower house to protect her. After all, Angus was this Duncan Mackenzie's laird. Surely that, if nothing else, would compel him to maintain some semblance of manners.

"What exactly do ye wish of me, Father?" Heather forced herself to ask.

"Whatever ye think proper, lass. I don't want ye compromising yerself. That was never my intent. But I also know how susceptible I was as a young man to the influence of a beautiful woman, and I wager this young Highlander will be the same." Robert Gordon halted before a door near the winding stone turnpike stairway that pierced the southwest corner of the big, L-shaped tower house. "Just go in and offer Janet yer assistance. Yer presence and pretense of hospitable concern, if I'm not too far off the mark, will be all that's needed."

"As ye wish, Father."

She knocked on the door. A male voice, muffled by the thick wood and stone walls, answered, beckoning her in.

For an instant, Heather almost imagined the voice had an urgent, pleading quality to it, then decided she was mistaken. She pulled down on the door handle, paused to shoot her father a determined smile, then opened the door and walked in.

The sight that greeted her as she turned from closing the door behind her took her breath away. A tall, mud-spattered man, nearly naked save for his knee-high leather cuarans and the sodden plaid he fought to hold to him, stood in the middle of the bedchamber beside a steaming, wooden tub of water. Before him, her back turned to Heather, was Janet, pulling on the other end of the plaid just as determinedly as the man strove to retain it. Off to one side by a kettle of water simmering over a roaring hearth fire was a young maidservant, a grin on her face and an avid look in her eyes.

At Heather's soft gasp, Duncan Mackenzie jerked his glaring gaze from Janet. A pair of striking green eyes, topped by straight, dark brows, locked with hers. Janet's earlier description of Duncan Mackenzie as the "finest piece of man flesh," Heather decided as her glance swung from his head to toe and back up again, was the most inapt and imprecise use of the language that ever was.

As well-built and attractive as his brother Colin had been, this Highlander, in many subtle and not so subtle ways, put his sibling to shame. His proud, strong forehead was crowned with a lush, wild mane of damp, deep chestnut brown hair. Though a day or two's growth of dark beard shadowed his ruggedly arrogant, chiseled jaw and the line above his firm, sensually molded lips, the fine, high-bred features nonetheless all but shouted out his breeding. His face was unmarred, perfect in a manly sort of way, save for his nose, which was straight but for a slight lump over the bridge, and a short, ragged scar beneath his left eye that curved down onto his high cheekbone.

It was his eyes, though, that pulled Heather back again and again. Somehow, they seemed greener, sharper, and more assessing than Colin's had ever been. They held hers captive with a virile, unflinching directness she found disconcerting. This wasn't a man easily led or intimidated, Heather realized with a tiny, foreboding shudder. And not a man easily swayed from whatever prize he sought, either.

After what seemed an interminable length of time, but was likely no more than a few seconds, Heather broke eye contact, finding surcease from his intensely personal perusal by moving her glance down his body. As compelling as his face was, the muscled swell of his neck and shoulders effortlessly drew Heather's gaze downward, past a generous tangle of dark, dense chest hair and bulging pectorals to a most impressive set of lightly furred, rippling belly muscles that quickly disappeared beneath two strong, long-fingered hands clenching a generous wad of plaid.

Heather forced her gaze upward, back to his.

There, in the gleaming jade green depths, she easily discerned his recognition of what, at least to him, must appear an unseemly feminine interest. At the realization, coupled with his almost feral, masculine regard, Heather flushed. This wasn't quite the scenario or reaction she'd

41

had in mind, not from him, and most definitely not from herself.

"Er, Janet," she forced out the words past a strangely dry throat, "my father thought ye might be needing a bit of help with yer guest. Is there aught I can do to assist ye?"

At the sound of Heather's voice the girl gave a strangled squawk, relinquished her hold on the Highlander's plaid, and wheeled to face her. "I-I don't think so," she stammered, her glance darting nervously about as if she were a child who had been caught with her hand in the honey pot. "I was just helping Duncan with his plaid before he stepped into his bath. He was filthy, soaked to the skin, and shivering so badly his teeth clacked when he arrived. I thought it best immediately to get him into a hot bath."

She turned back to Duncan and held out her hand. "Now, give me yer plaid like a good lad, and step into the bath before ye catch yer death."

Duncan's gaze swung from Janet's to Heather's. The merest hint of a smile touched his mouth.

"Nay, lass. Even a Highlander has his modesty."

"Och, Duncan," Janet tittered shrilly, "ye're a bold one, and no mistake. But ye don't fool me with yer saucy words, and ye'll not sway a fine lady such as my cousin, either. She's a noblewoman, born and bred, and isn't impressed with an uncouth Highlander such as yerself."

"Indeed?" He cocked a dark brow. "A fine lady, is she now? Well, I may be uncouth, but I well know what that gleam in her eye, as she ran her gaze down my body, meant. And I'd wager what she was thinking was as uncouth as any man's."

At his shocking audacity, Heather's eyes narrowed in anger. Before she could open her mouth to deliver a stinging retort, however, Janet clucked her tongue.

"For shame, Duncan," she chided. "Ye're a brazen one—though with good reason, seeing how all the lasses sigh after ye—but this is the Lady Heather Gordon of Dunscroft Castle, daughter of Lord Robert Gordon and my dear, departed aunt Margery Mackenzie, who was my father's sister. Ye must offer yer apologies, and quickly now, or risk offending my cousin."

"Must I now, even for speaking the truth of it?"

"Aye, ye must."

His even, white teeth flashed in a lazy grin. Then with an elegant bow and sweep of the hand not still holding his plaid in place, Duncan bowed.

"If I mistook the situation, my lady, I beg yer forgiveness. And if I didn't . . ." He straightened, lifting his massive shoulders in a mocking shrug.

Disgusting, rutting stag, Heather thought. Well, he'd not unsettle her, even if his apology had hardly been any apology at all.

"Yer guest is correct in supposing neither of us wishes to view his manly attributes. Come, Janet. Grant him his privacy. The promises men make are usually far, far grander than what they ever are in reality."

Duncan threw back his head and gave a shout of laughter. "Aye, get on wi' ye, Janet. It's as the Lady Gordon says, leastwise in all cases but mine. Indeed, she must know, to speak so knowledgeably. And ye've been raised to respect yer elders."

Janet glanced uncertainly from Heather to Duncan. "Aye, that I have," she mumbled. "But, at nineteen, she really isn't all that older than me, Duncan. And she isn't wed, so I can't fathom why ye'd think she's—"

"Enough, Janet." Heather held out her hand to her cousin, who quickly joined her. "It doesn't matter what he does or doesn't think. Time enough to talk with him later. In the meanwhile, yer maid can see to his needs." She shot Duncan a final, scathing look before turning and leading Janet away. "Not that any amount of soap, water, and clean clothes will make him more than he ever was."

"And what is that, sweet lass?" came a deep voice behind her, rumbling with barely contained laughter.

"What else?" Heather retorted, at the end of her patience. "An oafish clod with naught more than whey for brains!"

3

Heather had never been so angry in her life. *The unmitigated gall, the presumption of the man to speak as he did to me!* she raged as she strode with Janet down the broad turnpike stairs leading to the first floor library and main Hall. She had suspected Duncan Mackenzie would be rough about the edges, perhaps even noticeably lacking in proper manners, but never that he'd act so arrogantly toward his betters. And though in truth he *was* her equal, he didn't know that. His rudeness, in light of the current situation, was inexcusable—even for a Highlander!

Her father must be informed immediately. It would most likely change everything. It was one thing to tolerate the presence of an ignorant, simply raised man. It was quite another to endure such a bold, ill-mannered one.

Especially, Heather belatedly and quite reluctantly admitted, one who exuded such a powerful animal magnetism. One who was so finely wrought in face and form, even if in some wild, untamed sort of way. He frightened

45

her, threatened something deep within her. Even now, Heather didn't understand all that had passed between them when they had first locked gazes. All she knew was he was danger personified, yet a danger she was drawn to nonetheless.

Her father wouldn't be pleased to hear the truth. She knew he wished for Duncan to be attracted to her in order for her to more easily manipulate him to their plans. She doubted, though, that he wished, or even expected, his daughter to fall so quickly under such a crudely arrogant man's spell. Nay, Heather thought with a sinking feeling, he wouldn't be pleased at all.

Yet dare she admit to such a thing, dare put to words strange, roiling emotions she had yet to sort through or understand? It was more than likely she'd appear the fool, and for reasons, when exposed to the harsh light of reality, that were silly, inconsequential, and easily subdued. A brief instant of illogical attraction, of simple admission that the Highlander was a proud, powerful, appealing young animal, did not—and never would— make for the same kind of love-struck yearning Janet Mackenzie shamelessly evidenced.

At the realization, Heather's cheeks warmed in em- barrassment. She understood now the reasons for her cousin's reaction to Duncan Mackenzie. The lass, how- ever, was but fifteen years old. She, on the other hand, at the decidedly mature age of nineteen, was far more educated and worldly wise.

Relief filled her. The solution to her brief flare of fasci- nation with Duncan Mackenzie was simple and obvious. Look past the outward form and into the man—a man who had already revealed himself to be coarse, cocky, and far too outspoken for his own good. A man who, she reminded herself belatedly, she must mold into something he would probably never wish to be.

"Well, Father," Heather muttered beneath her breath as they drew up before the library where Robert Gordon and Angus Mackenzie were visiting prior to the supper meal, "ye've gone and done it this time. And I've most assuredly found the solution to my winter doldrums."

"What did ye say, Heather?" Janet inquired, shooting her a quizzical glance. "I didn't quite catch all the words."

Pasting on a falsely bright smile, Heather turned to her cousin. "Naught, Janet. I was but muttering to myself." She reached for the brass door handle, but Janet stopped her.

"Please, a moment more, before ye enter the library. About . . . Duncan."

"Aye, what about him?" Heather's smile faded into a thin, tight line and her hand dropped back to her side. "He was rude and far too full of himself. I can't say I care for him overmuch."

Janet exhaled a deep breath. "Aye . . ." she agreed slowly, "he *is* full of himself, and no mistake. But Duncan's really not a bad sort, once ye take the time to get to know him. He has a good heart, and he wouldn't hurt a soul. And, for all his manly blustering, he has never forced himself on a woman." She giggled. "Even if he weren't already so God-fearing, he has no need to. Eventually, all the lasses throw themselves on him."

"God-fearing indeed!" Heather rolled her eyes. "He's

no different than any other man I've known. Most of them, be they nobleman or commoner, have such inflated opinions of themselves that if they don't get their way, they turn quite nasty and dangerous." She placed a hand on Janet's arm. "Have a care with this man, cousin. Ye may not know him quite as well as ye think. Ye haven't, after all, the years of womanhood that lend the caution around men we all must eventually gain."

Anger flashed in the girl's eyes. "I may not have yer fine learning or advanced age, Heather Gordon, but I know Duncan's heart. And I tell ye true, he *is* a good man. Just because he's not some high and mighty nobleman doesn't make him less worthy of consideration and respect." She studied Heather closely, and the light in her eyes suddenly turned wise beyond her years. "But it's easier for ye to consign him to his proper place well beneath ye. That'll make for less difficulties in the end, won't it?"

Startled by the unexpected accusation, Heather's hand dropped from Janet's arm. "I don't know what ye mean. The man was rude and spoke to me in a way no gentleman speaks to a lady, and now ye upbraid *me* for being unfair to *him*? Truly, Janet, ye need to overcome this blind affection ye have for the man, before it's yer ruination."

"Must I now?" Janet tossed her curly red mane in a gesture of defiance. "Well, I won't stand here and discuss this with ye further, or I'll risk insulting a guest. Besides, I must help Mither with the final preparations for supper. Best ye hie yerself to the library. There, at least, ye'll find the quality of men ye're more suited for."

With that, the girl turned on her heel and flounced away. Heather stared after her, torn between outrage and amusement at her cousin's high dudgeon—and all in the defense of some Highlander's all but nonexistent honor. Well, there was nothing more she could say to convince Janet to walk carefully about Duncan Mackenzie. The girl was far too gone on him. But, in time, Heather decided, it might be wise to broach the subject of her daughter's infatuation with Jean Mackenzie. Perhaps her mother wasn't fully aware of the extent of Janet's hero worship of the big Highlander.

That thought in mind, Heather turned and entered the library. The most private room in the tower house with its thick oak doors and two walls lined with tall, sturdy wooden bookcases, it smelled of spice and pine logs snapping in the hearth. That many of the shelves were empty of books and decorated, instead, with small, bronze-bound chests, extra pewter ware, parchment scrolls neatly tied with ribbon, and an assorted collection of framed Mackenzie family miniatures was ample testimony to the fact that, though learning was evidently revered in the laird's house, money was lacking to buy sufficient books.

Her father and uncle were seated before the hearth, Robert Gordon lounging sideways across the length of a high-backed, oak settle made soft with cushions. Her uncle sat in one of the two chairs placed at right angles to the settle. At her entrance, both men glanced up and smiled.

She closed the door and made her way to the other chair. Only once she was seated did Heather note the pewter mug of warmed, mulled wine flavored with cinnamon and cloves her father dangled carelessly from his hand.

Heather frowned. In the past few years, her father had acquired the disturbing tendency of imbibing a little too freely of his favorite liquor. Though, as one of Queen Mary's trusted advisors, he'd had many cares and concerns of late—the queen's growing difficulties with her Lords of the Congregation, her marital problems, and the troublesome interference of the ever-present and vociferous Reformation preacher John Knox—still, turning to drink was never the best way to deal with things. Far better to engage him in stimulating conversation and distract him, Heather decided.

"So," she began, glancing from one man to the other, "have ye determined the easiest way to get this Duncan Mackenzie to help us? From what I've just seen of him, the man's monumental self-absorption will preclude the necessary transformation."

Angus Mackenzie, who had just raised his own mug of wine to his lips, choked on his drink. Heather turned to her uncle.

"Are ye all right, Uncle Angus? Should I come and clap ye on the back?"

"F-fine," he sputtered. "I'm fine. J-just give me a moment."

"I think ye startled yer uncle," her father said with a chuckle. "Yer most unflattering assessment is greatly at odds with the man he was, just before ye entered, extolling to the high heavens."

"Indeed?" Heather smiled grimly. "And precisely what

50

positive attributes does this Highlander possess, aside from a cocksure opinion of himself with the ladies?"

"Och, more than ye might realize, lass," Angus was finally able to reply. "He's a braw warrior, always at the forefront of any clan skirmishes. And he's a hard worker to boot. His father's cattle are some of the finest in this region, and they've one of the largest herds, too, and that with only the two of them to care for the beasties and bring them to market."

"From the way he talks," Heather muttered, "I'm surprised he could spare the time from his skirt chasing."

Angus laughed. "Och, Duncan manages that well enough, too, though most likely not frequently enough to suit his tastes, what with all the work he has to do."

"Well, be that as it may," Robert interspersed, pausing to take another deep swallow of wine, "I've yet to convince Angus of the grave necessity of keeping the secret of Duncan's birth from him, much less come to a decision on the best way to broach the subject of the plot to the lad."

"I, too, had misgivings about that—hiding his true heritage from him, I mean," Heather said, glancing at her uncle. "But Father assured me the secret must be kept until we've rescued the queen. Then time enough to tell Duncan, and no sooner."

"But the lad's as loyal as I to the queen," Angus protested.

Heather turned to her father, a slender brow cocked in query. Robert shook his head and sighed.

"Mayhap he is, Angus. But Duncan is too vital to our plans to risk him riding off in a huff, or deciding first to seek out his newly discovered kin. Once they meet him, the element of surprise in substituting him for his brother at Lochleven is lost forever. Nay, I'm verra sorry to use the lad so, but the queen's welfare must come before his."

The big, black-haired Scotsman eyed them both for a long moment, then sighed his acquiescence. "I suppose ye're right," he said, stroking his bushy beard with a great paw of a hand, "but I still don't like it. And his father, Malcolm, won't like it, either."

Robert leaned forward, suddenly tense. "Ye told Malcolm? I told ye not to tell anyone, Angus, not even his foster parents!"

"Och, dinna fash yerself, Robbie, my man." Angus held up a hand. "I haven't told them aught, save that the babe was an orphan when I first gave him to them. And, even then, I didn't lie, for his mither was already dead and his father died soon thereafter. I only thought it was finally time at least for Malcolm to know. Heather wasn't far from the mark in doubting whether Duncan would be willing to learn to play the foppish nobleman"—he grinned sheepishly—"present company excepted, of course."

"And why is that?" Robert relaxed and leaned back in his chair, sipping carefully from his mug.

"Because Duncan, like all Highlanders and especially the Mackenzies, is a proud man." Angus paused for an instant, a look of indecision in his eyes. "Ye'll pardon me in the saying, but we don't hold much with the prim and mincing ways of the nobility. I can't see Duncan—loyal subject that he is—agreeing even to pretend to manners he holds in the highest disdain."

In the wake of Angus's statement, there was a dead silence. Then a fire-eaten log crashed to the hearth. Robert Gordon began clicking his finger against the side of his pewter mug, and Angus shuffled uncomfortably in his chair.

"We must *all* compromise and sacrifice to save our queen, Uncle," Heather finally said, irritation at the Highlanders' contempt for noble ways threading her voice. "Do ye think I particularly relished traveling halfway across Scotland in midwinter, or leaped for joy at the idea of playing tutor to some big, lumbering lout of a Highlander, if ye'll pardon *me* in the saying?"

"Heather," her father interjected warningly, "no good is served insulting yer—"

"Nay, Robbie, let the lass speak her mind. I must accept blame for being the cause of her anger." Angus grinned at Heather, his teeth a white slash in a swarthy forest of hair. "Do ye know how much ye sound like yer mither, the saints preserve her, when ye get riled like that? It's good to see, lassie. Many are the times I've wondered if Margery passed on even a drop of her Highland blood to her bairns."

"Well, she did, and no mistake," Heather assured him, once more in control of her temper. "Mayhap I worded it poorly, but my point was that we all must be willing to do what needs to be done. Our selfish desires can't enter in, no matter how strongly they drive us. If this Duncan truly is the man ye claim him to be, then, with yer help, we should be able to convince him to do what must be done. But ye must be with us in this, Uncle, or I fear we'll never succeed."

Once again, Angus stroked his beard. "I'm with ye, but I don't have to like it, do I?"

"Nay, ye don't, Uncle," Heather replied softly. "But the victory, in the end, isn't so much in the liking as in the doing, is it?"

A knock sounded on the door. "Enter," Angus bellowed.

Janet's head peeked around the thick wooden portal. "Mither says for ye to come now to table, or she'll feed it all to the livestock."

Angus stood and set aside his mug. "Are Duncan and his father finished with their baths, then?"

"Aye." Janet swung the door open, taking great care not to meet Heather's gaze. "They await us, even now, at table."

"Then come." Angus gestured to Heather and her father. "It's past time we feasted on my bonny Jean's victuals. Afterwards will be soon enough to hunker down to the real purpose for yer visit."

Aye, Heather thought as she rose and followed the two men from the room. *We'll all hunker down and turn our efforts to winning over a certain pigheaded Highlander. Yet, despite my fine words to the contrary, I can't say I'm any more convinced that it's such a wise idea than I was before.*

Janet must have had the say on how the guests were situated at table, leastwise when it came to placing

Duncan and Heather across from each other, and her own seat snugged up next to his. For once, though, Duncan actually welcomed the talkative, adoring Janet's presence. It forced him to tear his gaze from Heather at least from time to time, and saved him from a blatant and discourteous case of staring.

Not that any red-blooded Highland male would've blamed him. Heather Gordon was the bonniest lass he had ever laid eyes on, and he had laid eyes on his fair share in this part of the Highlands.

Never, Duncan admitted as his gaze swept over her for the hundredth time as they all sat there, savoring first a fine lentil soup, followed by a haunch of roast venison, potatoes, and buttered kale, had he seen hair quite that fair shade of blond. It was, he thought in an uncharacteristic moment of poetic license, as bright as sunlight across the water, even if it was mostly snagged up beneath that silly little cap all covered with pearls. And her skin, it fair to glowed with health yet was, at the same time, almost translucent in its fragility.

Her eyes, sharp with intelligence, were a luminous, clear blue fringed by dark lashes and slender brows. Her cheekbones were regal, her chin delicate and held high with unconscious dignity. Her nose was slim, pert, with delicately flared nostrils, perfectly suiting her proud visage. And her mouth . . .

It took all of Duncan's considerable self-control to restrain his avid gaze from returning time and again to those full, elegantly molded, and most sensuous of lips. Lips she frequently, as she ate, licked with a small, pink tongue, moistening them until they glistened, making her mouth appear even fuller and more ripe.

Ripe . . . like a lush, sweet berry . . . a berry all but begging to be devoured . . .

By all that was holy, did she know what effect she had on him? Duncan wondered as he sat there in a rising agony of fascinated longing, battling unsuccessfully to keep from staring at her. More importantly, if she did know, did she even care? Yet then, why should she? He was nothing to her save a savage Highlander who, for some unknown reason, must share a meal with her this night. There was privilege enough in that, yet all the privilege to which he could ever dare aspire.

Yet aspire and strive he still would. Duncan knew no other way. There had always been a part of him, even from a wee lad, that dreamt of someday being a man of power and wealth. Perhaps it was why he labored so hard most days from dawn until dusk, why he did everything with such energy and devotion. And perhaps, Duncan realized of a sudden, it was also why Heather Gordon held such a mesmerizing appeal.

She personified his fantasies, what he had always aspired to, though such aspirations were, in truth, likely little more than hopeless illusions. She'd never, no matter how hard he worked, no matter how successful he became, be attainable. They were and would always be from two different worlds, worlds that never voluntarily met save in the most desperate of straits.

But, all that considered, something special had flared between them if only for an instant, when their eyes first met there in his bedchamber. Still, initial attraction and fulfillment of a desire could be two entirely different things. A woman as rich and bonny as Heather Gordon could have any man she chose.

Somehow, though, Duncan couldn't see Heather ever coming to him only as a casual lover. She wasn't that kind of woman. And, if the truth be told, for all his blustering bravado at times, he wasn't—and had never been—that kind of man.

At the realization, a fierce sense of possession, of resolve, flooded him. Being the man he was and the woman he sensed her to be, he would—he must—have Heather Gordon as wife, or not at all.

Even as Duncan took up the idea and examined it like some finely wrought sword for possible flaws, his father's words earlier today—when he had joked with his sire about fate—came back to him. *Mayhap*, Malcolm had said, *it'll send ye a lass to love who won't love ye.*

With an effort Duncan wrenched his thoughts from what now seemed a prophetically disturbing prediction. He was being an addle-brained lad to moon over Heather Gordon like this. And more than foolish to cherish any hope of taking her as a wife.

To distract himself from his increasingly unnerving preoccupation with the blonde beauty, Duncan turned to Janet. At the moment, however, the girl was chattering with her mother, who sat on her other side. Casually, Duncan scanned the table. His gaze careened into that of Robert Gordon.

To his surprise, the man had been watching him closely. Watching him watch Heather. Duncan went still, every muscle tensing for attack. His thoughts about Heather

57

had been far from chivalrous, and surely another man—especially the father of the woman in question—would sense that and be enraged. He'd have done the same, he admitted grudgingly, in a similar situation.

But, as Duncan held Robert Gordon's gaze, the older man quickly masked his thoughts and turned to Angus. Without another glance in Duncan's direction, or further indication he had even noticed the heated looks the younger man had sent his daughter, much less cared, Robert proceeded to engage his brother-in-law in conversation.

Duncan frowned. What was the man about, so casually to ignore another man's bold appraisal of his daughter at table? There was no doubt he had seen Duncan's brazen glances. In that moment their gazes had locked, Duncan had felt like a deer being stalked by a hunter. But why? And for what purpose?

He leveled another look at Heather, his eyes narrowing. Perhaps the answer lay with her. Did she play some clever game with him—a game for which her father had earlier given his leave?

Try as he might, Duncan was unable to catch her attention. Almost as if she didn't dare make visual contact, Heather assiduously avoided meeting his gaze. But did the effort spring from a maiden's shyness, he wondered, or from a guilty conscience?

He wouldn't know, couldn't know, until she—and perhaps her father—chose to play their hands. Somehow, Duncan thought, glancing back at Robert Gordon and deciding he didn't like the man, he doubted he'd have long to wait.

After the sweets were served, Angus rose and called for a private meeting with Duncan, Malcolm, Robert, and Heather. They adjourned once more to the library, where they took their place in the various chairs and a settle placed near the fire. After the laird's wife had refilled the goblets of claret some of the men had brought with them from supper, she adjourned, closing the door firmly behind her. For several minutes, all seemed to content themselves with sipping their claret or gazing into the fire. Duncan, though, sensed a rising tension— and a subject hanging heavy in the air that none really wished to broach.

"Well, there's no sense skirting about the reason I called this meeting by first spending the requisite time in inane conversational gambits," Robert Gordon finally began, leaping into the verbal fray without further preamble. He glanced at his daughter who sat beside him, smiled, then continued on. "I had Angus call for ye, Duncan, because the queen has need of ye."

Duncan went still. This wasn't what he had expected, though he had expected something of great importance.

"The queen?" he repeated, stalling for time in which to gather his wits back about him. "Queen Mary?"

"Aye, one and the same." Robert paused to take a swallow of his claret. "We, several friends and myself, mean to rescue her from Lochleven Castle. But we need yer help."

Duncan exchanged glances with his father, who was

sitting next to him on the settle. "If it's fighting men ye're seeking to help ye storm the castle this spring, then I'm yer man. Is it yer wish I raise an army of Mackenzies to aid ye?"

"Nay, lad." Robert chuckled softly. "Naught so bold or dramatic as that. We mean to enter Lochleven peaceably, and spirit Mary away right out from beneath her jailers' noses. That's where ye come in. Ye look remarkably like a man named Colin Stewart, a good friend and true to Lady Margaret Douglas, Lochleven's chatelaine, and her son, William. We mean to send ye into the castle in Colin's stead, and, when all are deep in their cups, ye'll free the queen and help her escape."

"Ye want me to impersonate another man?" Duncan frowned. "And who is he, that I look so much like him?"

Robert fingered the rim of his goblet. "He's a young nobleman, heir to Lord David Stewart's fine lands and holdings in Atholl. Why ye look so much like him is a mystery, though. I can only surmise it's some sort of miraculous coincidence."

"Miraculous?"

The older man grinned. "Aye. A miracle sent from God to save our queen."

"Well, God or no, it all seems too easy, too convenient."

Duncan tried to catch Heather's eye, but she kept her gaze downcast. Suspicion flared. A sudden surety sprung from some heretofore hidden place.

She knows something, he thought. *She's in league wi' her father in this. But how, and why?*

"Indeed? In what way does this all seem too easy and convenient, lad?" Robert inquired with a mild arch of a brow.

Duncan refused to be seduced by fine manners and calm words. They'd get to the bottom of this muddy pool here and now.

"How else? That ye would've known that two men who live so far apart," he replied, "are supposed exact look-alikes. I'm thinking there's more to this than what ye care to reveal."

"I keep naught hidden, lad." Robert smiled benignly. "I've known Colin Stewart for years and, in truth, had important dealings with his family. And ye know I visit Angus here in the Highlands from time to time. If ye recall, I attended a *ceilidh* last summer in which ye were present. It was then I noted yer striking resemblance to young Colin, though at the time I thought naught of it. These things happen, the rare occurrences of two unrelated people appearing as doubles. I've seen it before in my travels. Ye'd have noted it, too, if ye'd ever chosen to leave the Highlands."

Despite Gordon's glib reply, Duncan realized, there was something here that still didn't fit. Unfortunately, for the moment, he couldn't quite put his finger on it. Best to hear the man and know it all. Only then, with all the facts at hand, could he make an informed decision.

"I can't say parading around as some noble sits well wi' me," he said. "And if this Lady Douglas is such close friends wi' the man, I doubt I'd be able to fool her long enough to gain access to the queen."

"True enough, lad. As ye now are, ye'd fool no one." The elder Gordon took his daughter's hand and gave it a reassuring squeeze. "Ye need schooling in the ways of a noble and, more particularly, in Colin Stewart's special manner. That is why I brought my precious daughter with me. She knows Colin well, and is also knowledgeable in all it'd take to make ye act and think like a noble."

For the first time since they had entered the library, Heather met Duncan's gaze. In the depths of her glowing, blue eyes, he saw the confirmation of her father's words. And, seeing that confirmation, for a long moment he was too startled, too shocked to speak.

Could it be? Did Robert Gordon mean to offer his daughter to serve as a tutor? Did he mean for her to devote hours, days, even weeks to his training, in close quarters and intimate conversation?

At the consideration, it was all Duncan could do to master his excitement. If it were true, his shared resemblance with Colin Stewart wasn't the miracle at work here this night, but the great gift he was being offered in the opportunity to spend an extended period of time in Heather Gordon's presence. Perhaps fate had indeed stepped in this day, and that fate was smiling most kindly upon him.

"Are ye saying," he forced himself to ask, "that ye're offering yer daughter as my personal tutor?"

"Aye, if ye'll have her."

Have her? Was the man blind as well as daft? This was a gift to kill for!

"If ye say she's fit to teach me what needs to be taught, aye, of course I'll have her."

At his apparent doubt as to her abilities, Heather shot him a baleful glare then, clamping her mouth tightly, swung her gaze back to the fire. Duncan hid his smile of satisfaction. *Good. As hard as she tries to hide it, she isn't as docile or accepting of all this as it would first seem.*

"Heather is an extremely well-read, intelligent young woman." Robert contemplated the contents of his goblet momentarily before taking another swallow. "Ye'll be hard-pressed, I'd wager, to find her lacking in any subject."

"And, once again, I'll take yer word on it." Swiftly, Duncan turned his attention back to the older man, lest he reveal the extent of his pleasure with the situation. "How much time will this transformation require? And where will it take place? I can't leave the Highlands for any extended period of time just now."

"We haven't much time to spare, only three months at most. The plan is to rescue the queen within the first week of May. And as far as the place . . ." Robert shrugged. "It'll be best to do it here. It'll be easier to maintain the secrecy of the project as far from the queen and the court spies as possible. Angus has agreed to put ye up in his house for the interim. That way ye can have daily access to Heather and yer lessons."

Duncan met his father's gaze, then turned back to Robert, shaking his head. "Three months doesn't seem an adequate time to me. But, as before, I'll take yer word on it that yer daughter can teach me what I need to know by then. It won't be convenient, though, for me to stay here wi' Angus. My mither's ill and my father can't spare me for so long a time. I can't work our steading, then ride back and forth to here every day. It's a half day's ride each way, ye know."

Robert turned to Angus. "Can't ye spare a few men to help Malcolm in the time we require Duncan's presence?"

The Mackenzie laird considered the request, then nodded. "Aye. It'll be difficult, but it can be done."

"Well, difficult or not," Duncan growled, a plan forming in his mind, "I won't agree to this no matter if Angus can or can't spare the men. No purpose is served in inconveniencing all, when an alternate solution is readily available."

At his words, Heather jerked from her contemplation of the fire, her gaze slamming into his with a watchful, wary intensity. Duncan smiled. *She senses the trap about to be sprung. She's indeed canny and quick-witted.*

"And what solution would that be?" Robert Gordon asked, his eyes blank save for a light of simple curiosity. "It's the last thing in my mind to inconvenience any of us."

"We've a fine, large cottage." Even as he smilingly continued, Duncan's resolve hardened. "Yer daughter, if she's truly set upon doing her part to help free our queen, can surely endure three months there."

"I'll do no such thing!" Heather, speaking out at last, leaped to her feet. "It isn't seemly, nor are your quarters, I'm sure, aught close to what I've become accustomed. The lessons will be given here or not at all."

Duncan leaned against the settle's tall, wooden back, folded his arms across his chest, and shrugged. "Then I fear, sweet lass, further discussion is pointless. If ye won't budge from behind these walls, then yer father's plans for the queen's rescue will never see the light of day."

4

In the long silence that followed, Heather looked from her father to her uncle in outraged disbelief. "And what have ye to say to this?" she finally demanded, directing her gaze to Angus. "Ye're his laird. If ye command him to stay here, he must do so."

Next, she turned to her father. "And ye. Pray, inform this audacious lout that it isn't his to say, what I should or shouldn't do."

Robert Gordon and Angus Mackenzie exchanged glances. In that fleeting interchange, Heather found the answer to her demands. There'd be no help from either her father or uncle. In their minds, the queen's rescue took precedence over everything else. Everything . . . including propriety, physical comfort, and personal misgivings.

With that daunting realization, Heather's resolve hardened. Though her cause obviously lacked supporters, she had no intention of giving up without a fight. Even if she was ultimately forced to acquiesce to Duncan Mackenzie's offer, she intended to apprise them all of the terrible price, in the bargain, they forced her to pay.

"Are ye certain that ye've fully considered what ye two ask of me, in going to this man's house?" Heather looked first to her father then her uncle. "Where am I to sleep? In the common room with the farm animals and in full view of this man and his father? Indeed, how will I dress or bathe with any semblance of privacy? And what will Charlie say to our betrothal," she added, at last riveting an accusing gaze solely on her father, "when he hears his future wife spent three months in the rustic, unchaperoned company of other men?"

Her father's eyes widened. "Och, I confess that I didn't think of that." He looked to Duncan. "My daughter's right. It's out of the—"

"She doesn't have to sleep wi' the animals," Duncan replied with a long-suffering roll of his eyes, before sending a sardonic glance in Heather's direction. "Besides the common room—which, by the way, contains no farm animals save our terrier bitch—we've two separate sleeping chambers. One my parents share and the other's mine. For the duration, I'll gladly relinquish my chamber to the lady so she can not only sleep there but 'dress and bathe wi' some semblance of privacy.'"

"It's a fine, large cottage, lass," Angus chose at that moment to offer his smiling contribution to the conversation. "Duncan and his father have worked their steading well in the past years. Indeed, it's now one of the most prosperous holdings in all of Mackenzie lands. And Fiona—Malcolm's wife—keeps a spotless house. In the bargain, she's also an accomplished cook. Ye'll lack for none of the basic comforts."

"Aye, if I do say so myself," Malcolm Mackenzie finally spoke up, "we've a verra nice house. All thanks to Duncan, though. It was his especial hard work and clever business dealings which brought us such prosperity." He graced his son with a fatherly look of pride. "Aye, my Duncan has a fine head on his shoulders, that he does."

Heather shot Duncan Mackenzie—who hadn't budged from his infuriatingly self-confident, arms-folded-over-chest pose—a seething look. "I didn't mean to insult yer home," she said, forcing a smile for Malcolm Mackenzie's sake, "but surely ye can understand, as a noblewoman, the delicate position such an arrangement places me in. I'm to wed in six months' time. My betrothed, though a kind, understanding man, might not take kindly to my—"

"Then he'll just have to trust ye, won't he?" Duncan drawled lazily, his mouth twisting with what Heather could only view as derision. "Since ye do love him—don't ye?—what possible temptation could an 'audacious lout,' not to mention 'oafish clod with naught more than whey for brains' such as I present?"

At Heather's scandalized gasp, Malcolm and Angus broke into laughter. Robert Gordon, however, mottled with rage. He wheeled to face his daughter.

"Ye called him an oafish clod?" he demanded. "Lass, lass, I don't understand why ye've taken such an instant dislike to the man. Angus has assured me Duncan knows his manners and will treat ye with all courtesy and deference. And, though I admit our plans have taken a wee detour, I didn't realize ye'd become such a . . . a—"

"Peevish, scolding vixen?" Duncan supplied helpfully when Robert seemed suddenly at a loss for words.

"Aye," Robert agreed, seizing on the suggestion a bit too eagerly before catching himself. "Well, be that as it may, ye know what I mean, lass." He had the good grace to flush in embarrassment before hurrying on. "Ye said ye were committed to the queen's rescue. We must all make sacrifices—"

"Aye, that we must, Father," Heather muttered, controlling an urge to walk over and slap that smug, triumphant look off Duncan Mackenzie's face with the greatest difficulty. "It just seems, of late, *I'm* the only one making the sacrifices."

"Ye and yer father expect me to risk my life in impersonating another man so as to enter Lochleven. I'd say yer wee sacrifice, in coming to my home to teach me, pales in comparison."

At Duncan's accurate if unwelcome observation, Heather gritted her teeth, then turned to meet his unflinching gaze. "Aye, in comparison, I suppose ye're right." She paused, searching for the right words, even as she grudgingly admitted Duncan Mackenzie had won this first of what would assuredly be many battles between them. "I beg pardon if I offended ye and yer father in my reluctance to reside at your house. It wasn't that I doubted yer assurances of yer home's comforts, as much as I—"

"I know, lass."

His keen gaze knifed into hers. In that fleeting look, a sudden knowledge passed between them. A knowledge of the true reasons for Heather's fierce opposition to spending time with him in the relative seclusion of his home. A knowledge of her strong attraction to him. And that knowledge, though a rousing victory for Duncan, was an equally shameful admission for Heather. Shameful and forbidden yet, conversely, exciting in a way she had never before experienced.

At the realization, a small shiver rippled through her. A shiver of anticipation, of dread, and no small amount of fear. There was no way, though, to avoid the confrontation to come. With all her strength and courage, she must face the next three months and deal with Duncan Mackenzie as best she could.

"Then I suppose it's settled, isn't it?" Heather said.

"Aye, I suppose it is," Duncan replied, his expression suddenly shuttered, his voice devoid of emotion.

He didn't fool her, Heather thought, though all present might imagine he didn't care one way or another for the victory he had just achieved. Just below the surface of his outwardly indifferent demeanor, his true nature smoldered. It but awaited the right time and place to flare anew.

She had seen that look before. She was now an heiress, after all. Already, many men lusted after her fortune, even more than they lusted for her. Before, though, Heather had always known how to deal with them. Known and done so with the greatest ease, for she had felt no answering attraction for any suitor that she couldn't soon master.

But now, staring back at the dark and disturbing Duncan Mackenzie, Heather realized this time it wouldn't be so easy. Though she knew not why, she found Duncan Mackenzie the most exciting man she had ever met.

She could only hope, for her peace of mind at the very least, the heart of the man wasn't half as exciting as was his person.

"I don't like it, my lady," Beth Erskine murmured later that night as she helped Heather prepare for bed. "What can yer father be thinking, to allow ye to journey deep into the Highlands and so far from yer aunt and uncle's supervision in the bargain?"

She shook out a long-sleeved, woolen sleeping gown. Gathering it up, Beth slid it over her mistress's outstretched arms.

"And who does that Highlander think he is, to tell ye that ye can't bring along both yer serving maids and cook, no matter how small his house might be?" She frowned. "Nay, I don't like it at all."

"That's not the half of it, Beth." Heather pulled the sleeping gown down into place and fastened the high-necked collar closed. "Not only is Duncan Mackenzie an overbearing despot, but he's also a crude, brazen rogue." She shuddered. "And to think I must work in close quarters with him for the next three months!"

Beth eyed her wryly. "Well, he *is* one of the most braw, strapping young men I've seen in many a day. If I hadn't already set my sights on Tavish Gordon . . ." She finished the sentence with a besotted sigh.

"Ah, aye, the elusive Tavish," Heather said with a chuckle, choosing to ignore her maid's reference to Duncan's quite impressive physical attributes. "One would think that man had had enough of the single life after forty-two years, and be sick nigh unto death of sharing his sleeping quarters with all my father's fine horses."

"He has yet to find the right woman, he has told me." Beth walked to the four-poster bed and turned back the thick woolen sheets. "Well, I'll tell ye true. I've decided to be that woman. My Seamus has been dead all of six years now, and it's past time I take another man to husband."

"So ye think Tavish is the one for ye, do ye?"

Beth nodded. "Aye, that I do."

"Then mayhap I can convince my father to allow Tavish to accompany us to the Mackenzie's steading and serve as groomsman and personal guard for the time we must remain there." Heather grinned conspiratorially. "Think on it, Beth. Three months crowded together into a simple cottage. If the man doesn't offer for ye by the first spring flowers, he isn't worthy to be called a Scotsman."

A chestnut brow arched, and interest flared in a pair of gray eyes. "That's an intriguing thought," Beth agreed slowly. "But can ye get yer father to part with his precious head groomsman, even if only for a few months?" She made her way to the hearth, took up a set of iron tongs, and removed a brick she had placed there earlier to heat.

Heather gave an injured sniff. "That's the least my father can do, after what he has managed to entangle me in." Picking up the book she had been reading before supper, she began to leaf idly through it.

"I must confess," Beth offered as she returned from the hearth. "The few times I saw him, yer Highlander didn't seem all that crude or brazen, leastwise not to me." She lifted the bedclothes and slid the hot brick along the length of the mattress at the foot of the bed. "He but smiled at me, then stepped aside in a most gentlemanly fashion so I might pass. But there was naught offensive in his words or manner. Of course, mind ye, I'm hardly a lass in the first bloom of womanhood, nor as bonny as ye."

"For yer information, he's not my Highlander. And, secondly, he hardly treated Janet Mackenzie as churlishly, either," Heather muttered, "and she was single-handedly trying to strip him naked when first I met him."

Beth turned. "He was naked, was he? And does yer father know of this?"

"He wasn't completely naked." Heather rolled her eyes in exasperation. "He still had his kilt clutched to him. Though," she added with a wry chuckle, "Janet was trying her verra hardest to relieve him of that, too."

"And how did he appear?" Beth asked after she had extracted the brick from the bed and returned it to the hearth, then hurried back to her mistress. "Was he as well-made without his clothes as with them? Was he truly, as Janet put it"—she paused for a giggle and impish grin—"the finest piece of man flesh in these parts?"

Her maid's unabashedly shameless questions stirred memories Heather would've preferred to have forgotten. Memories of Duncan Mackenzie, standing there, his wild mane of dark hair damp, his face, arms, and legs mud-splattered, his magnificent body bulging with muscle and most attractively hair-roughened.

A hot rush of blood warmed her cheeks. Heather shook her head vehemently, inasmuch as to dispel the disquieting images as to visibly disagree with Beth's questions.

"I wouldn't know." She pretended sudden interest in laying aside her book and climbing into bed. "Ye, with yer wifely experience, would've been far better suited than I to assess such manly attributes."

Beth walked over and pulled the comforter up to cover her. "Mayhap, but mayhap not. Ye're a woman grown. Ye know yer mind and what ye like and don't like. And what I asked for was *yer* opinion of the Highlander."

"And what does my opinion of the man matter, one way or another?" Heather demanded, growing angry because she knew her cheeks still flamed red. "He's naught to me save as a student to be tutored, and as the key player in the plot to rescue the queen. One way or another, in three months' time I'll be well rid of him—and glad of it!"

"Aye, that ye'll be, my lady. One way or another." Beth stepped back, snuffed the single candle burning at the bedside and, in the dim, flickering light of the hearth fire, smiled. "Be rid of him, I mean. As for the being glad of it, well, that may well be another matter entirely. Aye, another matter entirely, if I'm any judge of affairs of the heart—and the prickly course that loving oft takes."

The weather the next day, though cold, was perfect for traveling. The mud from the previous day's rain remained frozen. The sun shone, gracing the land with its weak radiance, and the usual brisk winter winds failed to blow.

After only a sparse breakfast of porridge and hot milk, Heather, accompanied by Beth, Tavish Gordon, her father, Angus, and Malcolm, set out with Duncan Mackenzie shortly after dawn. They rode directly south for several hours before reaching the slate gray waters of Loch Carron, the impressive sight of the mountain range known as the Five Sisters of Kintail far in the distance. Finally, they took an old cattle trail east into yet more mountainous terrain.

Birch woodlands, their branches still devoid of foliage, filled the glens along the way. High on the mountainsides, the mighty red deer stalked the shadowed depths of pine. Occasionally, Heather caught a glimpse of a wild goat herd, a few newly born kids among them.

It was an exciting sight—the rugged beauty of the snow-capped mountains, the river-threaded broad straths and barren glens, the forests teeming with wildlife. It was a land as foreign yet savagely beguiling as the handsome Highlander who rode before her. Aye, savagely beguiling, Heather reminded herself grimly, and also as dark and dangerous.

A little past midday, they reached the last of the myriad, snow-covered hills separating them from the quaint stone cottage Duncan Mackenzie called home. The little dwelling sat in a secluded dell, sheltered by tall pines on the north and a rocky outcropping of mountain on the west. On the east, in a stand of leafless, ancient birches, was a small but well-built cattle byre.

From the south, the house looked down on a now frozen burn that meandered across the steading and through the cattle pens before emptying into a large pond at the base of yet another hill. Beyond lay a large, densely wooded forest. A faint wisp of smoke wafted gently from the cottage's stone chimney. In the now bright sunshine, the scene was both charming and welcoming.

"It doesn't appear so poorly, does it, lass?" Heather's father asked from beside her. "The steading and house are obviously well maintained and look quite prosperous. It won't be as bad as ye first imagined, I'd wager."

More for Duncan Mackenzie's benefit, who, at her father's comment, cast a quick glance over his shoulder, than because she truly felt heartened by the scene before them, Heather managed a brusque nod. "Aye, I'd imagine not," she replied. "But then, things aren't usually as bad as one fears, are they?"

Duncan eyed her for a brief moment more, then grinned and turned back to the road ahead. *The wretched, conceited rogue*, Heather thought, clenching her horse's reins so tightly her knuckles turned white. *If he, for even one second, thinks he's bested me . . .*

With an effort, she forced her attention back to her father. "Can't ye stay even one night? These Mackenzies are all but strangers to me, and I'm sure to feel more at ease after—"

"Lass, lass," Robert Gordon chided with a paternal smile, "ye've never lacked for skills with speech, not with strangers or even yer betters. Why, if I recall correctly, wasn't it ye who, when but a lass of thirteen, strode right up to our queen and introduced yerself before Mary gave ye leave, or ye were even properly announced?" He chuckled softly. "A lass of yer mettle will never lack for courage, no matter the situation."

Disappointment flooded Heather. She knew well enough by now what her father's true answer was when he hedged in such a fashion. "So ye mean to make Uncle Angus's tower house before dark, do ye?"

"It isn't for me to decide, lass." Her father smiled apologetically. "It's hardly polite of me to dictate the day's agenda to my host."

"Aye, I suppose not," Heather muttered. *Especially when it's evident ye've no wish to linger here a moment longer than necessary*, she added with an uncharacteristic bitterness.

"Ye've Beth and Tavish to keep ye company," Robert Gordon hastened to add, apparently noting the disgruntled tone of her voice. "And besides, there's Fiona Mackenzie to chaperone ye as well. Ye'll not lack for protection, if protection is even what ye're needing."

Aye, protection, Heather thought grimly. It was indeed a ludicrous consideration. Who or what had she to fear? Surely not Duncan Mackenzie. As overbearing as he was, it was equally evident he knew his place and his manners, at least when in the presence of his elders. He was no danger to her unless she allowed him to be.

Besides, she was no love-struck girl like Janet Mackenzie. *She* would never permit herself to act in such an addlepated fashion. It was bad enough she seemed to have lost Janet's friendship, and all because she had chided the young woman about the dangers of hero-worshiping Duncan Mackenzie. But then, to add insult to injury, Janet seemed to think she had ridden joyously off this morn in eager anticipation of spending months with Duncan in the relative isolation of his home.

Why, one would've thought Janet had imagined she had stolen Duncan Mackenzie right out from beneath her nose! And all because of some man whose physical comeliness warranted hardly more than a passing glance.

In the clearer light of a fresh new morn, Duncan Mackenzie wasn't anything special. There were plenty of men as big and strapping as he. Plenty of men with the most astonishingly broad shoulders and well-muscled bodies. Plenty of men who walked with an effortless, catlike grace that caught the eye and made the mouth go dry . . .

With a jerk, Heather realized where her thoughts were once more leading. She flushed, mortified with herself and unaccountably angry with Duncan Mackenzie.

His brother Colin, for all his ardent courtship, had never stirred her in such a way. Indeed, no man had ever affected her like Duncan Mackenzie had in the span of less than a day. Yet the grim truth remained. She didn't know this man or his heart and his mind. For all his fine looks and exciting manner, what if there was naught more? What if he was a dullard or, worse still, what if he thought little of women save for the selfish pleasure he might find with them?

That admission brought Heather back full circle, frustrating her all the more. She was no love-smitten girl and would never allow herself to be. If she ever gave her heart to a man, it would be because she admired his mind and was moved by his soul. Because he recognized her intelligence, her womanhood, and cherished it, wished to nurture it and bring it to even greater fruition. And, most of all, because she was totally convinced of his undying love.

That much Heather, at the very least, knew of herself. Though the knowledge had come too late to help her mother, Heather had seen the deep, soul-searing pain Margery Gordon must have lived with all the years of her marriage. And she had seen, as well, what wedding the wrong man had done for her sister.

Precisely because of those experiences, Heather knew she had set standards that few, if any, men could ever hope to meet. Standards Duncan Mackenzie most certainly didn't fit, whether as an illiterate Highlander or the nobleman he truly was by right of birth.

It was the God's honest truth, Heather well knew. Until the man ceased to affect her at any level, she must remind herself of that fact as oft as it took. Fine looks meant naught. A seductive pair of green eyes, a roguish smile, and an inexplicably compelling animal magnetism were scant reason to surrender one's heart and soul to another. Besides, three months was surely far too short a time to lose one's heart to a man.

It was all but a matter of time, Heather reassured herself as they headed down the hill toward the Mackenzies' cottage. Her unsettling attraction to Duncan Mackenzie would soon pass. Close contact in the ensuing months would quickly dispel whatever romantic notions he had stirred within her. All she had to do was get to know the man. Then her beloved logic and clearheaded thinking would return, just as they always had before.

She was a strange one, Duncan thought, watching Heather Gordon draw up before his home and glance about her. Her manner, though she took great pains to mask it, was one of trepidation mixed with curiosity, overlaid by a haughty demeanor he sensed was more a screen to hide behind than a true aspect of her inner self. How he knew this he wasn't certain, and that surety was most unnerving.

Did he perhaps desire for the woman to be attractive in every way, that he saw what he wished so desperately to see? The consideration gave Duncan pause. If it were true, he had never acted in such a foolhardy manner before—a manner that, in the bargain, was a danger-fraught way to risk one's heart.

Dismounting, Duncan strode over to Heather Gordon. Behind him, the others of their party began to follow suit, climbing off their horses to stretch stiff limbs.

"Here, lass," he said, lifting his arms to her, "allow me to assist ye."

She stared down at him for a long moment, her gaze cool, assessing. Then she shook her head.

"Nay. I'm a competent horsewoman and can well dismount on my own."

Duncan grinned and stepped back. "Have it yer way, then. I but wished to act the proper gentleman." He angled his head, a roguish smile on his lips. "It *is* what proper gentlemen do, isn't it? Offer a lady whatever she wishes?"

Heather grimaced, then gave a brusque nod. "Aye." She paused to slide down off her horse, then turned to him. "But a gentleman also knows when to back away and not press so hard."

Duncan's smile never wavered. "Then I trust ye'll see to that aspect of my education as well, lass."

"Ye can be sure of it."

Satisfaction filled him. He liked her spirit. For all her fine manners and breeding, Heather Gordon had grit and wasn't easily intimidated. She intrigued him in so many ways—her pale golden beauty, her sharp intelligence, her poise and proud spirit.

More than anything he had ever wanted, Duncan wanted to pull Heather to him and kiss her. He wanted to pierce her prim and proper reserve and see what lay beneath. Some instinct assured him a warm, passionate woman lay just beyond that haughty reserve. A woman, he realized with growing unease, he very much wanted for his own.

It was daft to consider such a thing. Why, he barely knew the lass and, all jesting aside as to his purported appeal to those of the feminine persuasion, he believed in the sanctity of marriage and in saving himself for the woman he would eventually take to wife. Besides, for what seemed the hundredth time in the short span of a day, Duncan reminded himself that Heather Gordon was so far above him in social standing as to be completely and permanently unattainable. Yet, in spite of it all, he desired her still.

That realization was the most disturbing one of all. Only a fool dreamt of what he could never have. Only a fool allowed unrequited need to gnaw at his innards until he died from the festering wound. Indeed, until this moment, Duncan had always prided himself on accurately assessing and resolving each situation to his advantage, and never, ever, being led to play the fool.

Even if it *were* to play the fool for the bonniest lass he had ever laid eyes on.

Stepping aside, Duncan, with a gallant sweep of his hand, indicated Heather should go ahead of him. "If ye please, lass, my mither and home await yer consideration. For yer sake, at least, I pray ye find both to yer liking."

Heather shot him a disdainful look. "Yer mither, I'm sure, I'll find quite suitable. Yer home, though, may well be a different matter."

As she headed toward the cottage, Duncan fell in beside her. "Well, it's no grand manor house, to be sure, but we find it verra pleasant."

In reply, Heather could only manage a skeptical sniff before they halted in front of Duncan's foster mother. A woman in her late fifties, she, like her husband, had red hair, though her gray-streaked tresses were a deeper shade of auburn. Her eyes were hazel, her body reed thin, and she leaned heavily on a gnarled wooden cane. Like many Highland women, she wore a plain, tan-colored homespun blouse and a long plaid skirt of brown, green, and yellow. Over that was added another long plaid that fell from her shoulders to her heels, belted at the waist and fastened on the breast with a large brooch of silver.

She awaited them on the immaculately swept doorstep of a large, drystone house thatched with heather and bracken. Besides the stout oak door, the front of the dwelling sported two paned glass windows, which Heather knew to be extremely rare for the Highlands. In the afternoon sun, the glass sparkled from what was obviously frequent and meticulous cleaning.

"My name's Fiona, miss," the woman said as she extended her hand and managed an awkward curtsey.

The effort to rise from the curtsey even with the aid of her cane, however, seemed impeded by some infirmity. Fiona lost her balance and tilted forward. With startlingly quick reflexes, Duncan grabbed his mother's arm, righting her. Fiona shot him a grateful, loving glance, then smiled at Heather.

"Ye'll be forgiving my poor showing, miss, if ye will," she explained, "but I've had a bout of dropsy for the past month that won't subside. The swelling in my legs makes them a wee bit cumbersome."

"Then it's best if ye take to yer house and have a seat," Heather said. "It's said to be the best remedy for the dropsy—putting up yer feet, I mean—besides the use of the leaves of the fairy fingers plant." She motioned to Duncan. "Help yer mither, will ye, sir? No purpose is served lingering out here when she's obviously ailing."

"Och, but it's not proper to lie about when guests have come to call," Fiona protested, pulling back when Duncan made a move to escort her inside. "I'll not have it said a Mackenzie shamed the clan by failing to offer proper hospitality."

"Yer hospitality is fine indeed, madam." Heather moved to take Fiona's other arm. "Rest assured neither my father nor I find aught to fault." She met Duncan's quietly assessing gaze and, with a sharp jerk of her head, indicated they should go inside.

He answered with a brief smile, then turned his attention to assisting his mother. With the greatest tenderness Duncan led the way, escorting her to a crudely hand-carved but well-made high-backed chair comfortably padded with cushions. Heather helped as needed, all the while marveling at how gentle even a big man such as this Highlander could be.

It was evident from the care he took, and the look of concern on his face, that he loved his mother. The realization startled Heather, though when she paused to consider it further, she knew her assumption was both unfair and unrealistic. Even uneducated, simple folk were capable of love and tenderness.

Perhaps it was just her eagerness, even need, to consider Duncan Mackenzie in a negative light that had motivated her deliberate misperceptions. If so, it wasn't right or fair. And it was most certainly beneath her to act thusly. Was she so afraid of him and his potential power over her that she must take such pains to view him so poorly?

Shame flooded her. With a fierce effort, Heather forced a heartfelt smile.

"Ye're a fortunate woman, madam." She knelt and shoved a footstool beneath the older woman's feet.

With a grateful sigh, Fiona settled back into her chair. "How so, miss?"

"Ye've a devoted son who obviously cares deeply for ye." Heather glanced up and met Duncan's intent gaze.

A look of surprise flared in the depths of his eyes. She smiled, her gaze not wavering from his. *It's the least I can do*, she told herself, *for my unkind thoughts. And it's also the truth, in the bargain.*

"Aye, that he is," Duncan's mother agreed. "And ye're a canny lass to see it, too." Curiosity brightened her eyes. "Is that why ye came here today then? Because ye and Duncan have fallen in love and wish to wed?"

5

For a long moment Heather stared at the other woman, both speechless and dismayed. It didn't help matters that Duncan Mackenzie stood there smiling with avid interest even as he awaited her reply. What was she to say that wouldn't offend the mother without encouraging the son?

She shot Duncan a scathing glance, then turned to Fiona. "It isn't so much a matter of a special affection," she began carefully, smiling all the while. "Leastwise, not in the manner of true love and all. Rather, I've come to assist yer son in a grand scheme to rescue the queen from Lochleven."

Fiona frowned in puzzlement. "A scheme to rescue Mary? And ye and Duncan are involved in it?" She lifted her gaze to her son. "And what is this, my fine lad? What have ye gone and gotten yerself into this time?"

Duncan grinned. "It'll all be explained in due time, Mither."

At that moment, Malcolm, accompanied by Robert Gordon, Angus Mackenzie, and Beth, walked in. Duncan looked up. He met his father's glance, then motioned Malcolm over.

"Yer wife seems verra interested in the reasons for this sudden gathering of visitors. Mayhap, while I offer the others some of our fine Highland hospitality, then show the Lady Gordon to her quarters, ye should share the details wi' her."

Malcolm nodded. Pulling over a stool, he sat and hurriedly began regaling his wife with the particulars of the plot. For the next few minutes, Duncan busied himself with settling in Robert Gordon and Angus—each with a generous cup of heather ale—before turning his attention back to Heather. As he did, Tavish Gordon walked in, having finally finished putting up the mounts. His arms were loaded with the first of the many bundles his mistress had brought along.

Duncan strode over and quickly relieved the big, sandy-haired Scotsman of a few of the bundles. "Best ye deposit these in the lady's new bedchamber. No purpose is served scattering her belongings about the house. Fortunately for Lady Gordon, my room is spacious." He turned to Heather. "If ye will, come along wi' us. I'm sure ye've a need to wash up and attend to whatever fine ladies attend to afore ye eat the midday meal."

For a fleeting moment, a look of defiance flared in her glorious eyes. Her soft, full lips pursed as if to utter some disparaging reply. Duncan tensed, a jolt of excitement shooting through him. By mountain and sea, how he loved it when Heather responded to him—in any way!

Then the fiery look died and her mouth went slack. "Aye, that would be most appreciated," she replied, her voice soft now, controlled.

Duncan scowled. What had he said to elicit such a sudden change in her behavior? Had his mother's innocent question offended her? Or, rather, he thought with a wild swell of hope, had it struck closer to home than she cared to admit?

He firmly quashed that consideration. *Ye're playing the fool again, Duncan, my lad,* he lectured himself sternly. *Even if the lass finds ye a wee bit braw, she isn't empty-headed enough to allow her emotions to rule her. Nay, and certainly not for a rough, baseborn man such as ye.*

She paused in the doorway to his bedchamber and looked in. "I'll give ye that much," she said. "It's indeed a spacious room."

"Aye, that it is," Duncan agreed with a sly grin. "But only because it once served as the stable for our goats and milch cow."

"Indeed?" Her nose wrinkled in distaste, but she was mannerly enough not to belabor her already low opinion of residing in his house.

"That was fifteen years ago, lass."

Though he was tempted to let her believe the transformation from stable to bedchamber had occurred only recently, Duncan didn't want her to think them crude and uncivilized. But only for his parents' sake, he told himself. What Heather Gordon thought of him didn't matter, but he'd not permit her to continue to harbor such low opinions of his mother and father.

"Once the cattle byre was built, we moved all the farm beasts from the house."

"Not *all* of them."

She walked to the far end of the room, where a large, rough-hewn worktable stood, and picked up the half-carved form of a wooden horse. Its proud, finely wrought head was flung back, with one front leg emerging in what was obviously the beginnings of a rearing stance. Her golden head cocked in sudden interest, Heather turned and held up the horse.

"Who worked this?"

Though Duncan dearly loved wood carving, he was also very sensitive about his artistic endeavors, well aware many thought them a frivolous and self-indulgent waste of time. "*I* did."

He strode over. Taking the horse from Heather's hand, he laid it back on the table and covered it quickly with an oil-soaked rag.

"I'll clean up this clutter just as soon as I can. There wasn't time—"

"It doesn't matter." She placed her hand atop his over the rag. "As difficult as it may be to believe, I wasn't complaining. I found the work verra beautiful and was but curious who the artist was." A wry smile touched her lips. "Mayhap it's a sad commentary on my narrow-mindedness, but I never thought ye capable of such talent."

Somehow, Duncan liked it better when he and she were at odds, rather than now, when she stooped briefly to treat him as an equal. Indeed, for someone of her standing to pretend admiration for his meager talent was to reach far beneath her. It was . . . Duncan struggled for the correct words for his sudden surge of confusing emotions . . . it was condescending, even belittling.

He pulled his hand from beneath hers and took several steps back. "Ye can't help how ye were raised, even as I can't help my upbringing. Ye needn't pretend to admire aught of mine, though. I like ye far better when ye're sincere in your contempt. Leastwise then I know what manner of woman I'm dealing wi'."

Heather jerked her hand from the table. "What manner of woman! How dare ye accuse me of insincerity!" Fire flashed in her eyes. "Do ye know what ye are, Duncan Mackenzie? Do ye?"

"Aye, I do," he growled, refusing to back down as she approached him with hands fisted at her sides. "Yer opinion of me, though, is much more entertaining, not to mention amusing."

"And since when does a man find utter scorn and loathing amusing?" She halted only inches from him and glared up. "Tell me that, if ye will?"

She smelled like full-blooming heather in spring, like the fresh-washed grass after a hard summer's rain. For an instant, Duncan wished mightily to pull her to him and bury his face in the shimmering, silky mass of her golden hair. He wanted to kiss away the hard, angry tightness to her mouth until it softened with longing, curved with laughter. By all that was holy, but she was as proud and wild as some graceful doe or free-ranging Highland pony. And Duncan wanted very, very much to tame her, gentle her to his needs.

Just exactly what those needs were, Duncan didn't know or care even to consider. At least not just now, with Heather Gordon glaring up at him, looking all but ready to strike him, and big Tavish Gordon, his arms once again loaded with bundles, staring him down from the doorway.

He had pushed her as far as he dared this day. The wisest course was to back off a bit. They had three months together. Time enough to prick at Heather until he discerned the true woman beneath the beauteous if volatile surface. Meanwhile, it was best to turn the tables on her as fast as he dared.

Duncan sighed, forcing an apologetic grin. "No man of sound mind would wish to anger or disgust ye, lass. If I've done so, I beg yer forgiveness."

"*If* ye've done so?" She stared up at him in outraged disbelief. "Truly, are ye so thick-witted ye haven't any inkling how churlish ye can be?"

He shrugged. "When it comes to the likes of ye, lass, mayhap I am." He cocked his head. "Do ye think there's hope for me? Tell me true while ye still may. For if there isn't, if ye're well convinced I'm a hopeless, dunderheaded fool, then there's still time to leave wi' yer father."

What was his game? Heather wondered, eyeing Duncan Mackenzie narrowly. No matter how hard he tried to play the role at times, some instinct warned he was hardly a dunderheaded fool. Yet that consideration was far more acceptable than the growing suspicion that he toyed with her for his own pleasure, or for some other equally despicable, if yet mysterious, reason.

"Nay," she replied softly, determined not to be bested

no matter his game, "I don't think ye're suddenly gone soft in the head, and especially not just because of me. I think, instead, for some perverted reason all yer own, ye enjoy tormenting me. I think ye resent a woman being set over ye, even if only for a few months, and to teach ye what ye don't know. And I think," Heather added, "that ye'd resent it no matter who she was, for ye don't like the thought of any woman stepping out of her proper place."

"And that proper place would be?" Duncan prodded, his eyes gone dark, his mouth grim.

Good, Heather thought in satisfaction. She had finally managed to pierce his arrogant facade, if only a wee bit.

"Where else?" she countered with an offhand shrug. "In yer bed or fat with child, squatting at yer hearth, cooking up yer next meal."

His mouth dropped for the briefest instant. Then he threw back his head and laughed.

It was a rich, blood-stirring sound and evoked an automatic if unwilling response. Heather chuckled. As much as she hated to admit it, Duncan Mackenzie could be the most infuriating yet endearing of men, and all within minutes of the other.

That realization caught her up short. Infuriating she could deal with. Endearing, though—especially in this wild Highlander—was quite another story.

"Ye know it's true," she hissed, suddenly and unaccountably so angry it was all she could do not to slap that smug look off his face. "Be man enough to admit it!"

"Och, I'll admit it," he agreed good-naturedly between

rumbles of laughter. "But, though I'm likely man enough to bed and get many a lass wi' child, I don't wish to do so wi' most of them. Ye, on the other hand, are far more to my taste."

Duncan paused to eye her closely and, as he did, Heather felt as if he saw clear through to her very soul. For the first time since she had met him, terror flooded her. *Curse the man*, she thought in an agony of conflicted emotions. He all but bespelled her when he looked at her like that. Yet the worst part of all was she didn't know how to fight back, how to temper such raw, animal magnetism.

It was best—and certainly wisest—simply to ignore him. "Well, I can't say I care one way or another what yer tastes in women run to." She dragged her glance from his and scanned the room instead.

"Then what of my tastes, when it comes to bedchambers? Is aught of it to yer liking?"

Caught off guard, Heather looked back to him. "Wh-what did ye say?"

A devilish gleam in his eyes, Duncan gestured to the room. "Is this to yer liking? Will it suit for the next few months?"

"Far more than ye'll ever suit," she ground out beneath her breath.

He feigned puzzlement, yet somehow Heather knew he had heard every word.

"What was that, lass? I didn't quite catch what ye said."

"Naught." She gave a sharp shake of her head. "It doesn't matter."

He shrugged. "Suit yerself."

Heather turned and motioned her maid over. "Come, Beth. Let us set this room aright while the men continue unloading our belongings." She shot Duncan a challenging look. "If that meets with yer approval, of course."

His sweeping appraisal of her was answer enough, even before he spoke the words. "Aye, yer plan meets wi' my approval," he replied, his voice gone low and husky. "That, and so much more. So verra, verra much more."

Duncan had no sooner left his bedchamber than Robert Gordon rose from the table and approached. "Come, lad," the older man said, a conspiratorial smile on his lips. "I've a wish to speak with ye in private."

The scent of the heather ale was heavy on his breath. Too heavy for the one cup Duncan had poured the nobleman and his laird before escorting Heather to her room. Then he noted the once full pitcher was empty.

Disgust filled him. The man was a drunkard. If his control over the spirits was so weak, he wasn't fit to lead such a dangerous, complex mission, much less be Heather's father.

At that realization, the last thing Duncan wished to do was to go off and speak with the man in private. Lord Gordon had yet to utter anything of consequence, much less anything worthy of respect. He was Angus Mackenzie's brother-in-law, however, and for that, if for nothing else, Duncan had no choice but to bear with him.

He glanced about the room. Angus was still at table,

deep in conversation with Duncan's father. His mother dozed in her chair, her legs propped on the stool, a light woolen throw covering her. None would most likely notice or even question his departure with Lord Gordon.

"As ye wish, my lord." He rendered Robert a perfunctory nod, then indicated the front door. "If yer words are few, the best place to speak privately is outdoors."

Robert pulled his heavy cloak more tightly to him. "It'll do, lad. This shouldn't take long."

Duncan arched a brow, opened his mouth for a retort about how he wasn't anyone's "lad," then thought better of it. Loosening his plaid, he flung it about his shoulders and led the way outside.

What was the man about? he wondered. Had he perhaps grown weary of the friction between Duncan and his daughter? Or, worse still, had he finally become angered with Duncan's overt interest in Heather? If so, it was long overdue, and Duncan knew it.

As soon as they were outdoors and well past earshot of the cottage, Duncan halted. "Well, what is it ye wish of me, my lord? If it's yer daughter, I know I've—"

"Aye, it's partly about Heather."

A frigid wind blew down at that moment, setting the skeletal tree branches to clacking and a powdering of snow to whirl up into the air. The rich, acrid scent of burning peat wafted by on the bitterly cold breeze. Duncan inhaled deeply, savoring the familiar smell. Robert Gordon's nostrils twitched with distaste.

He should try and hide his disdain a wee bit better, Duncan thought wryly. Even when sober, the man was far too transparent in his dislike for things beneath him. And most especially for all things of the Highlands.

"If it's concern for yer daughter's welfare, I can assure ye—"

"Dinna fash yerself." Robert held up a silencing if unsteady hand. "All I wished to say on that matter was to implore ye to give all yer attention, and yer best efforts, to Heather. Time is short. There's much for ye to learn if ye're to fool the Lady Margaret Douglas. She's a canny one, the old shrew is, and dotes on young Colin Stewart. She's the one ye must deceive, or all is lost."

"I'll do my best, my lord." Duncan paused, awaiting further comment. When none was forthcoming, he indicated the door. "If there's naught more, shall we return to the cottage and a warm fire?"

"Hold a moment." The older man grabbed Duncan by the arm. Duncan glanced down at the other man's hand, then back up at him. Robert released his arm.

"There's one other thing," he continued, irritation beginning to sharpen his drink-thickened voice. "The subject of yer reward, if ye succeed in rescuing the queen."

Duncan shook his head. "I don't expect a reward, save for that of the satisfaction of seeing Mary restored to her throne."

"And I say, temper yer overblown Highland pride long enough to accept what is offered, will ye?" A knowing look gleamed in Robert Gordon's eyes. "I've heard it said ye're an ambitious man. Two hundred pounds could go a long way toward fulfilling many ambitions."

Two hundred pounds. It was a year's wage for one of the gentry, Duncan thought, and nearly four times more than he and his father had managed to earn in even one of their best years. Two hundred pounds would go a long way in building up their prize herd of Highland cattle, not to mention in helping complete all the improvements still needed to make the cottage more comfortable for his ailing mother.

He shook his head and sighed, knowing it still wasn't right to accept money for something more honorable to do for free. "That's indeed a princely sum, my lord, but I can't accept it. It isn't right to take money in payment for rescuing the queen. A man shouldn't benefit in the doing of his duty."

"Many men will benefit, just as many will be ruined, if Mary regains her throne." Robert Gordon's lips thinned in displeasure. "Why shouldn't a man who risks his life above all others not share in the largesse? It'll be but a small token, to be sure, in light of what the queen will grant ye for yer bravery, but yer due nonetheless."

"It doesn't matter." Duncan clamped his jaw in obstinate pride. "I don't do this for hope of reward."

A hard, calculating light flared in Robert Gordon's eyes, dispelling, if only fleetingly, the mists of his drunkenness. "Don't ye? Well, mayhap not for any monetary reward, then, but some prizes of the flesh can be equally as sweet, even if far more fleeting. Like, mayhap, my daughter's fair flesh?"

A cold chill ran through Duncan. He stared back, silent, waiting.

"If ye won't take money in payment for saving the queen," Robert snarled, "then take it as a bribe not to breed my daughter. I've seen how ye look at her. I know what such looks mean. Take the money as payment for sparing my bonny Heather from yer sordid advances."

It was the drink speaking, Duncan told himself. No father—leastwise not one who truly loved his daughter—otherwise would talk so crudely about her as Robert Gordon had just done. And, nobleman or not, no man his age would dare taunt a man far younger than he or speak so disparagingly of his honor.

"It's past time we were returning to the house, my lord," Duncan growled, clamping down on his rising anger. "Afore ye say aught more that ye might regret."

"Ye're a haughty one, to be sure, for all yer simple ways. Far too haughty to speak so to yer betters."

As if to attack him, Robert lurched suddenly toward Duncan, lost his balance, and would've fallen into the snow if not for Duncan's quick response. He righted the ale-besotted man, then immediately pulled back.

"I find yer crude manner distasteful," he said, "especially when ye speak so poorly of Heather. Ye may not bear a good opinion of me or my intentions toward yer daughter, but ye should have more faith in her. Heather isn't some ill-bred strumpet. Her morals are of the highest caliber."

"So ye'll abstain from seducing her then, will ye, and solely because ye've the greatest respect for her high morals?"

Nay, Duncan thought with a sudden, painfully intense insight. *I'll want her all the more* because *I respect her. Because she's a woman worth risking everything for, and a prize beyond compare. Not that ye're capable of un-*

derstanding that, leastwise not in yer current state. And perhaps, just perhaps, never.

"If it's any comfort to ye, my lord," Duncan said instead, "yer daughter despises me. She'd never stoop so low as to couple wi' one such as me. Ye've naught to be concerned about."

"I want yer word on it nonetheless, Mackenzie. I want yer word ye'll not touch my daughter."

"I'll not force myself on her, if that's what ye're implying," Duncan muttered, shooting him a furious, seething look. "As hard as it may be for ye to believe, we Highlanders have our honor."

"Then ye'll give me yer word ye'll keep yer filthy paws off her, will ye?"

"Aye, but not because ye offer me money. I wouldn't ravish yer daughter any more than I would any other lass, be she noble or common." He dragged in an unsteady breath. "Now, ye're more than welcome to stand out here in the cold until ye freeze, but I'm going inside."

"And did I give ye leave, ye cocky young upstart?" Robert Gordon yelled after him as Duncan strode out for the cottage. "Ye overstep yerself yet again, ye do, to walk away from one of yer betters."

"Aye, mayhap I do," Duncan gritted under his breath, never once breaking stride as he battled a savage swell of disgust and rage. "If I truly were walking away from one of my betters."

Duncan's bedchamber was not only spacious but also surprisingly well appointed for a man of such obviously rustic upbringing, Heather decided. Though his bed was a simple boarded affair, consisting of a shallow wooden box standing on four short legs, at least the straw mattress was supported by the newer rope mesh rather than the old-fashioned, less flexible boards. It was also quite well made and roomy enough for both her and Beth to sleep in comfort.

A down comforter encased in a coverlet of fine, dark blue woolen broadcloth and two plump down pillows graced the bed. Beside the bed sat one of two large, carved wooden storage kists. The other large chest stood beneath one of the room's two oiled paper-covered windows. The second window shed its wintry sunlight onto the worktable at the room's far end. Two large, framed maps—one of Scotland, the other of the world—adorned the walls, and a high-backed, comfortable-looking wooden chair sat at an angle to the kist before the window. Dried rushes covered the packed dirt floor.

Though the bedchamber lacked the additional amenities Heather was used to back at Dunscroft Castle, it was apparent the Mackenzies were indeed relatively prosperous. She guessed Duncan's bedchamber was the least well-appointed room in the house, recalling the hardwood floors covered by a few simple, handwoven rugs, the large dining table and set of four high-backed wooden chairs, the tall cupboard filled with pewter ware, and several large kists she had seen in the main room when she had first entered.

It wouldn't be so unpleasant residing here for the rest of the winter after all, Heather admitted belatedly, her cheeks warming with shame at her earlier disparaging remarks to Duncan.

"Shall I unpack yer things"—Beth chose at that moment to interrupt Heather's rueful musings—"or would ye prefer I fetch a basin of water for ye to wash up a bit?"

"Aye, fetch me some water, if ye will, Beth." Heather turned slowly, surveying the room once more. "Before we can put aught of our things away, we must first impose on the Mackenzies' generosity in using one of their kists."

"Ye mean, impose on Duncan Mackenzie's generosity," her maid, with a twinkle in her eyes, corrected her. "It's his room, his kists, I'd wager."

Heather sighed in exasperation. "Och, aye." She managed a shamefaced smile. "I suppose I'll need to remember that from here on out."

"It's always said ye draw more flies with honey than with vinegar."

"Och, and won't the Highlander like being compared to a fly?" Heather laughed. "Well, now that I think on it, he *is* rather a pest and most vexing at times, just like a fly."

"And then at other times," Beth offered snidely, "he's most charming, not to mention verra braw and bonny."

Irritation welled in Heather. Whose side was Beth on—hers or Duncan's?

"Mayhap in yer mind. I can't say I care much for him myself."

Her maid laughed. "And sure, the moon-eyed looks ye cast him when ye think none are watching arise from yer utter disgust. Of course, of course. How *could* I be so slow-witted, and me, knowing ye so well?"

101

"Beth, hish!" Heather's glance swung to the open door. Fortunately, no one seemed to be standing nearby. "Someone—my father even—might overhear and take yer words to heart."

"And do ye seriously imagine ye've managed to hide yer infatuation with this Duncan Mackenzie from even yer father, much less from the man himself?"

Heather's mouth went dry. Her face flamed red. "I-I'm not infatuated with Duncan Mackenzie. I just find him . . . well, verra different."

"Och, and that he is," Beth chuckled, "when ye put him up against the kind of men ye've known until now. Of the nobility, I mean. My Tavish is a fine piece of man flesh himself, if I do say so."

With a despairing sigh, Heather walked to the chair before the window. She sat and clasped her hands in her lap. A few weak sunbeams pierced the oil paper panes, flooding the spot with light and setting her many rings to glinting brightly.

"Och, Beth. What am I to do?" she moaned. "What am I to do?"

"About what, my lady?" The maid quietly closed the bedchamber door, then joined her mistress at the window. "Ye've done naught wrong."

"Haven't I?" Heather blinked back tears of humiliation. "I've barely met the man and already I'm all but panting with lust after him. Then, in the next moment, I'm flying in his face, hurling insults at him, all but begging for a fight."

She lowered her head and buried her face in her hands.

"Och, what's the matter with me, Beth? I've never been so petty or mean-spirited before."

"It's simple, my lady." Beth squatted before her and laid a hand on Heather's knee. "Ye're attracted to the lad, and he to ye. Why, the passions ye stir, one in the other, are strong enough to feel each time ye're both in the same room."

Heather lifted her head and gazed at her maid in horror. "Don't say such a thing. Don't even think it! He's not the man for me. He's not!"

"Why, because he's a commoner and beneath ye?"

"Of course. Ye know it's impossible . . ."

At the recollection that Duncan Mackenzie was, in truth, no more a commoner than she, Heather's voice faded. The realization caught her up short.

Though Duncan couldn't be told the truth about his noble heritage until Mary was rescued, there was nothing to preclude his knowing afterwards. Then there'd be nothing to preclude her permitting—her father's consent notwithstanding—Duncan's subsequent courtship, *if* he truly was as attracted to her as she was to him. Yet even the remotest consideration of such events transpiring filled Heather with terror.

If she must wed someday, she wished to wed a man she didn't love. It was the only way to prevent the same tragic fates both her mother and sister had suffered. If she never gave her heart to her husband, she'd never crave what she might well never have—his love and devotion. It was her duty to wed and bear children to carry on the Gordon lineage, especially now that she was the only surviving child and heir. That much she would do and do so willingly.

But she refused to entwine her life and hopes and dreams around some man. All she wanted from a husband was to be left alone to pursue her life as she had lived it until now. A life filled with books, with music and fine things, with stimulating conversation and intellectual pursuits. What she didn't want, and wouldn't tolerate, was the sacrifice of all at the altar of an unrequited love.

Aye, Heather decided, it was indeed possible Duncan Mackenzie desired her. If her attraction for him was so obvious to Beth and the others, it was most likely equally obvious to him.

But he was nothing more than a crude, uncivilized savage—a savage who surely wanted only to bed her and nothing more. She *had* to believe that, though the longer she was with him, the more difficult it was becoming to cling to those earlier assumptions. Indeed, to believe anything else was to lay her heart wide open to unspeakable pain and rejection.

And he couldn't help who he was. It was part of his upbringing, the way of the Highlander. Indeed, it was said they loved nothing more than their fighting and reiving, their ale and wenching. It was also said they had no interest in more tender pursuits. They hadn't the time, nor placed much value, on loving.

They cannot help themselves . . .

"Aye," Heather replied finally in response to her maid's question. A fierce determination filling her, she rose and stared down at Beth. "Because he's a commoner, he can never, ever, be the man for me."

104

6

The midday meal consisted of two hastily dressed and roasted hens, some leftover venison haggis, fresh-baked barley bannocks, a round of hard cheese, and a mess of boiled cabbage. Dessert—for all Scotsmen were fond of their sweets—was a burnt cream pudding.

Though Heather had no cooking ability, she offered Beth's services to assist Fiona. Duncan, quite surprisingly, volunteered to fetch whatever ingredients were needed, set the table, then carry over the bowls of food. Heather, in the meanwhile, played the hostess, graciously serving her father, Angus, and Malcolm more heather ale.

Soon thereafter, Angus hinted broadly that he and Robert should depart. As Heather watched her father say his farewells to the others, freshened anxiety swelled in her. Once he was gone, her fate—whatever it was meant to be—was sealed.

"Ye must be brave, lass," Robert said when he finally came to his daughter. "It's a hard thing I ask of ye, and well I know it, remaining behind with strangers in a strange place. But ye do have Beth and Tavish." He managed a grin. "It wasn't easy giving up my head groomsman, ye know, but I did it for ye, lass."

"Aye, Father," Heather mumbled, blinking back the tears. "I know."

"Lass, lass, it's only for three months." He took her by the arms and pulled her to him.

Och, but he smelled so good, Heather thought, clinging to her father like one drowning. Smelled like home, calling to mind those once simple, happy times when she had been safe, cosseted, secure. But such comfort and the naïve belief life would always be so had fled, never to be cherished again. Now, all she had was herself. Her wits, her courage, and her determination not to be vanquished—neither by life nor by any man.

"Once it's over," her father blithely forged on in what Heather knew was a well-intended attempt to comfort her, "only three months later ye'll wed Charles Seton. Soon enough, all of this will be only a memory. A memory of a great adventure in which ye did yer verra braw part to save our queen."

She nodded numbly, then shoved back. For several seconds Robert stared intently down at her. Then a frown creased his brow, and he opened his mouth to speak.

Forcing a bright little smile, Heather immediately cut him off. She knew him well and knew, despite all his self-serving actions and complex, conflicting motivations, the soft spot he had for her in his heart. He was on the verge of rescinding his request for her to remain here and teach Duncan Mackenzie what he needed to learn. And if he did so, Heather wasn't certain she wouldn't leap at

106

the chance to return home. Return home, and ruin all the carefully laid plans to rescue the queen.

"Get on with ye." She punctuated the command with a wave of her hand in the direction of Angus Mackenzie and the horses. "The day draws on. Ye must leave or ye'll not reach the tower house before dark."

He laughed then, his relief immediately evident. "Aye, that we must." Her father paused a moment longer. "Ye'll be all right then, lass? Ye're sure?"

Nay, Father, Heather silently replied, *I'm not sure. Two days ago I could've given ye a better answer, but two days ago I hadn't met Duncan Mackenzie. Two days ago, I was yet untouched, still ignorant of what havoc desire can play with the heart and mind.*

But none of that is yer concern. Ye've greater problems awaiting ye and far larger schemes of life and death with which to deal. In comparison, my petty fears and romantic dilemmas pale, shrivel to insignificance—as well they should.

"Aye, Father," Heather said instead, "it'll all be fine." She laughed. "If only Duncan Mackenzie truly *can* be made to appear the fine gentleman in but three months' time."

At the mention of the big Highlander, something passed across her father's face. Something dark, angry.

"Don't imagine for a moment, lass," he muttered, lowering his voice for her ears alone, "even if ye can effect such a transformation, that the disguise sinks past that rogue's pretty face. Beware of that muddy-mottled rascal, I say. He'd like naught better than to ply ye with his

107

soulful looks and honeyed words, and for no reason other than to breed ye, then brag on it to all his friends."

Hot blood flooded Heather's face. She lowered her gaze.

"Father! Don't speak so . . . so—"

"So crudely?" he finished for her. "Well, it's the truth and can't be ignored. I've seen his kind before. Have a care, lass, is all I say. Ye've much to lose if ye give yer heart to him. He, on the other hand, only stands to gain. It's the way of things and will always be so, I'm verra sorry to say."

They cannot help themselves . . .

With a chilling rush, her mother's dying words washed over Heather. She shivered.

"Aye, Father." She lifted her gaze once more to meet his. "Yer words are true. I won't forget."

Robert Gordon smiled. "I know. Ye're not only a good lass but a sensible one. Ye're that Highlander's match and more." As if secretly pleased about something, he chuckled softly. "Och, what I wouldn't give to stay and watch ye humble that arrogant young stallion. It'd be worth—"

At that moment, Angus—already mounted—rode over. "Hoot mon," he cried. "Are ye planning to squander the entire day in farewells, then? The sky's taking on a rather ominous cast and may well bode snow before nightfall. If we don't depart soon . . ."

"Aye, aye," Robert agreed laughingly. "Even now I was just finishing with my daughter." He hesitated, then gave Heather one final, quick hug before heading off to his horse.

She watched him ride away, her brawny uncle at his side, her gaze never leaving her father until the two men finally disappeared over the hill. Already the clouds were beginning to obscure the sun, and the wind had taken on a bite it hadn't carried earlier. Heather clutched her warm, woolen cloak more closely to her. They'd be lucky indeed to make it back before—

"He warned ye against me, didn't he?"

Heather jumped in surprise, the unexpected sound of Duncan Mackenzie's deep voice startling her from her preoccupied thoughts. She whirled around, the hem of her cloak creating flurries in the snow.

"I-I don't know what ye're talking about. Not that it's aught of yer business at any rate, what my father and I said to each other."

Duncan gave a snort of disgust. "Don't play the fool wi' me, Heather Gordon. I saw the sly looks yer father sent me as he held ye. He thinks I'm some craven lecher and mean to bed ye sooner rather than later."

Once again, Heather's cheeks flooded with warmth. "And what if he did say it?" she demanded, suddenly weary of being fought over, much less considered some prize side of beef. "Would he have been so far off the mark? Would he?"

Anger flared in Duncan's eyes. "It's one thing to desire a comely wench. It's quite another to take advantage of her."

"It isn't honorable, is it?" she taunted, her hands fisting at her sides. "And ye, being an honorable man and all, wouldn't ever take advantage of a woman? Would ye?"

He stepped close, so close he all but towered over her.

Heather quashed the impulse to move back, refusing to let the Highlander intimidate her. He was quite imposing, though, and a fleeting image of him engulfing her in his arms filled her.

What would it feel like to be held close to him? To lay her face on his big, broad chest? To hear his heart thundering beneath her ear?

Somehow, none of the questions mattered. Somehow, Heather sensed with an instinct strong and sure, there was nothing Duncan Mackenzie could do to her that would be unwelcome or disgusting. In her deepest, innermost being, in spite of everything warning her to the contrary, she knew she wanted what he offered, wanted him. Craved what she was forbidden to desire and dared not take.

"It's true enough," he said, his voice a husky rasp. "I'd never take advantage of a woman. Never. My immortal soul is worth far, far more to me than some passing gratification of the flesh."

His mention of a religious faith took Heather by surprise. She hadn't imagined a man such as Duncan Mackenzie to be overly devout. He was too earthy, too blunt spoken, and too unequivocal about his interest in her. Then again, perhaps he was but trying a different tack to blindside and beguile her.

She smiled grimly. One way or another, he'd be sadly disappointed if he thought to win her with claims of saintly virtues. One could hardly be manipulated by something one no longer believed in.

"Yer words sound honorable enough," Heather said, steadfastly meeting his wary, watchful scrutiny. "But how honorable can it truly be, when an experienced man seduces some maiden who doesn't yet sufficiently know herself? Indeed, how honorable is it to manipulate a maiden's romantic dreams of true love, twisting them to a more carnal intent that ultimately serves only the man and never the woman? Where is there aught of honor in that?"

"Ye ask hard questions, lass." Duncan shook his head and sighed. "Yet why must *all* the honor lie wi' the man? Mayhap a woman should also consider her own honor, and not offer promises she has no intention of keeping. Mayhap ye shouldn't send me those hot, slanting looks, nor tease me wi' yer saucy words, nor . . . nor . . ."

As if realizing the turn the conversation had suddenly taken, Duncan faltered. Slowly, a flush crept up his neck and flooded his rough-hewn face. He closed his eyes for an instant, shook his head again, and sighed.

"Well, now, I've sure and stumbled into a dung hill and dirtied myself handsomely, haven't I?" he asked finally with a sheepish grin.

"Ye've only yerself to blame," Heather muttered angrily, refusing to concede him anything. "Ye were, after all, the one who started this sorry debate."

He chuckled and shoved his fingers through his windswept mane, sweeping the lustrous chestnut locks back from his face. As if drawn by some invisible thread, Heather's gaze lifted to his hair, lingered there a moment longer than was wise, then fell to his face. Duncan stared back at her, knowing even as did she, what she had once again done.

Ye shouldn't send me those hot, slanting looks, nor tease me . . .

A flood tide of guilt and shame swamped Heather. Frustration filled her. Fool, she berated herself. She was naught more than a silly fool. And yet *she* blamed and scolded him.

"I-I beg pardon," Heather said, forcing herself to offer an apology as bitter as gall. "Ye're right, of course, in wishing to share the blame equally with the woman. I don't mean to give ye false messages, or play the tease."

"I don't think they're false, lass. The messages ye send me, I mean." Duncan smiled sadly. "I but think ye don't sufficiently know yerself yet, or understand fully the implications of what ye offer. For my part, though, I'll endeavor to treat ye honorably during this time we must be together."

He turned then and headed back to the cottage, leaving Heather to stand there, suddenly aware everyone else had already gone inside. Everyone save Fiona Mackenzie, who was leaning on her cane in the doorway, a troubled look in her eyes.

Heather found Beth in their new bedchamber, apparently in the throes of unpacking. Still preoccupied and disturbed by her most recent verbal tussle with Duncan Mackenzie, Heather needed a moment to realize her maidservant had paused in her task and was now staring at the bed in horror. After grabbing up her harp from the midst of one parcel, Heather glanced in the direction of Beth's gaze.

There, in a nest made from two of Heather's fine silk gowns and several lawn chemises, was a most decidedly pregnant if scruffy-looking terrier bitch. A prick-eared, motley brown dog who had apparently decided it was time to give birth.

"Nay," Heather wailed and, well aware of Beth's fear of dogs, lunged at the panting, distressed little animal. "Not on my gowns. Not on my gowns!"

Her rescue attempts were rewarded with a sharp yip and a glancing brush of teeth, before she had the presence of mind to jerk her hand from harm's way. Bemused, Heather stepped back and glared down at the dog. At the same time Beth, with a terrified squawk, rushed from the room and called for help. To further add to the confusion, the terrier bitch chose that moment to deliver her first pup.

"By mountain and—" Duncan raced into the room. When he saw what lay on the bed, he slid to a halt.

"Cuini!" Hands on his hips, he glared down at the dog. "Did ye have to go and whelp on Heather's gowns?" Next, he turned to Heather. "I'm verra sorry about this. She's my mither's dog, actually, but chooses to sleep wi' me. It's natural for her to whelp where she feels most comfortable and secure."

"Cuini, eh?" Heather shot the once again straining animal a disgusted look before glancing back up at Duncan. "And is she queen of yer home, inasmuch as she is in name then? Ye didn't warn me, atop everything else, I must share a bed with a dog and her brood."

Duncan managed a lopsided grin. "Och, dinna fash

yerself, lass. Once she's done, she'll gladly make her bed wi' me again—wherever that might be."

"A distinct consolation, to be sure." Heather turned back to the bed. In a gush of fluid and blood, another pup emerged. Eagerly, Cuini began to lick and chew at the sac encasing the pup, until she finally had the membrane free. Then she commenced to gnaw on the cord.

Nausea welled in Heather. She swallowed hard and turned away.

"Ye haven't witnessed a birthing afore, have ye?"

Och, Heather thought, must she now also endure his pity? "Nay, I haven't," she snapped. "What of it?"

He shrugged, unperturbed by her show of temper. "Naught. But mayhap ye should step into the great room until it's over. I felt four pups. This could take a while longer."

Heather shot the terrier a quick look. Her heart sank. Her green silk gown would never be the same.

"I've work to do, if Beth and I are to have this room in order before bedtime. In the meanwhile, why don't *ye* attend to *yer* dog?"

"Ye don't mind me in yer bedchamber, then?"

"Aye, I mind, but since yer dog won't let me close to her . . ." She held up her right hand, which bore a slightly abraded mark where Cuini had snapped and briefly met flesh.

Concern in his eyes, Duncan grabbed Heather's hand in both of his. "Och, did she bite ye?" He leaned down, examining it, and stroked the pad of one thumb carefully along the length of the scrape.

His touch, gentle yet stirring, took Heather's breath

away. His hands were callused from work, the nails short, and the first three of his fingertips were stained, most likely, she mused, from recently rubbing some colored finish into a piece of carved wood. But, as work-roughened as his hands were, they were still the hands of an artist, a man born to a finer life than the one in which he had been inadvertently reared.

His fingers were long, tapering, his hands broad, finely veined, and covered with a sprinkling of dark hair. His wrists were strong, powerful, as were his muscled forearms. It was the lined expanse of his palms, however, as he cradled Heather's far smaller hand in his, that mesmerized her.

The mounded, muscled flesh bespoke great strength and courage. Bespoke a man firm in his resolve and vision. A man, Heather realized with a ripple of surprise, who, though he might achieve his goals in a different way, shared goals very similar to hers.

The revelation was astonishingly clear, though Heather was unsure from whence the surety came, or even the logic of it. So clear that, for an instant, she felt bonded to him. Felt as if they had melded minds—and that he had felt that joining just as keenly as she.

With a small gasp, she wrenched her hand free. "A-aye, she bit me," she replied, nervously looking back to the bed. "It was only a glancing strike, though, and my fault. I should have known better. The wee dog was all but whelping her first pup, and then to have this shrieking stranger looming over her . . ."

"Ye're kind to say so, lass." Duncan's eyes burned with a fierce, inner intensity. "Cuini is a fine, wee dog when she's feeling well. Ye'll see. And there's no better ratter around. I'd wager ye'll soon be fast friends."

"Aye, I'd imagine so . . ."

Distracted, Heather noted the terrier was bearing down on yet another pup. She hurriedly turned away.

"Go, go to yer dog," she urged, shooing him toward the bed. "And, if ye can, at least try and prevent her from tearing my gown. Though the dress might be ruined, there's still hope of salvaging most of the fabric for some other garment."

"Och, aye." Duncan grinned shamefacedly. "It's the least I can do. The verra least."

"Aye, the verra least," Beth Erskine agreed with the utmost distaste, eyeing the scene on the bed from the safety of the doorway. "Rescue the gown and get that vicious little dog out of our room, just as soon as ye can."

Cuini soon delivered a fine litter of four pups—one male and three females. After removing the soiled clothing from the bed and transferring the little dog and her offspring to a box made soft with clean rags, Duncan carried the animals from his former room. Heather and Beth finished their unpacking, and the rest of the day passed uneventfully.

After a light supper of bread, cheese, and the remainders of the dinner meal, Malcolm and Tavish remained at the big table to play dice, while Beth joined Fiona at the hearth to watch the older woman spin wool with a distaff and spindle. Heather found the process fascinating and lingered with the other women for a time too, watching as Fiona tied the wool to the distaff, then tucked it beneath her left arm. Next, Duncan's mother teased some fibers from the wool and fastened them to a notch on the spindle. Then she twirled the spindle. As it turned, it twisted the fibers into yarn. From time to time as she worked, Fiona paused to wind the yarn around the spindle before repeating the whole process again.

Finally, though, Heather and Duncan took to a smaller table set in one corner not far from the fire. Three tallow candlesticks, which stank most foully and dripped grease into a grease pan beneath the iron tripod candleholder, lit the area. By its flickering light Heather managed to see well enough to scribble a few notes on a sheet of paper as she began questioning Duncan as to his abilities, or lack thereof, in playing the nobleman.

"Ye must not take offense," Heather explained, her quill pen poised above her paper, "if I ask ye about things ye can't do. My questions aren't meant to prick at yer pride but only to ascertain where ye may be lacking when it comes to playing the noble. And especially," she added with a smile to soften what was to come, "in portraying a dandy such as Colin Stewart."

"A dandy, is he?" Duncan rolled his eyes. "Well, why should I be surprised? I've yet to meet a nobleman who wasn't more concerned wi' his clothing than wi' the man beneath them."

And mayhap that's because so few of them are as manly as ye, Heather thought, her gaze flitting briefly over Duncan's body before schooling it back to the paper that lay before her. He wore a loose-fitting shirt of pale homespun, deeply cut at the throat to expose his strong neck and a swath of dark, densely matted hair on his upper chest. His long, wide sleeves were rolled up to just above his elbows, accentuating the sinewy, athletic length of his lower arms.

His belted plaid was a simple affair, the tartan a muted one frequently used as camouflage on the hills and moors, of dark brown, purple, and blue. The full amount of woolen fabric was loosely pleated, belted, and the excess plaid flung over the left shoulder and was fastened with a silver brooch. Duncan wore the garment well. Indeed, the bulky amount of plaid only added to his already quite formidable aura of size and strength.

It was an ancient garment whose history harked back centuries to the first, long saffron shirts and woolen cloaks worn by the early Scots. Yet, though most Highlanders still clung to the old ways of dress, the more civilized nobility had chosen to adopt many of the affectations of the English Court. Affectations, she feared, Duncan might well balk at when the time came.

Those concerns, however, could be dealt with at a later date. What mattered now was the commencement of his education, an education that posed challenge enough in itself. She sighed and laid down her pen.

"As adverse as ye may be to the latest form of fashion," Heather began, trying to choose her words with the utmost tact, "ye must learn not only how to dress but also become intimately familiar with its proper use. Colin has impeccable taste and style. Even one error in appearance could alert someone ye're other than him."

Duncan's mouth quirked. "So, have ye made a note then, of how sadly deficient I am in proper dress?"

Heather shook her head. "Nay. One glance at ye each day will be sufficient to remind me."

"Och, what a prickly tongued wench ye are!" he said with a chuckle. "Is there naught about me, then, that ye find satisfactory?"

Aye, far, far too much, if the truth be told, Heather thought before firmly quashing that consideration. She took care, however, to hide any outward response by lowering her head to scribble a few lines on her paper.

"What did ye scribe there?" Duncan laid a finger on the paper, pointing to the still damp ink drying on the page.

"It doesn't matter." Heather looked up and forced what she hoped was a neutral smile. "And, fortunately for ye, during yer short stay at Lochleven, there should be scant occasion for yer lack of reading ability to be tested."

"And did I say I couldn't read?"

She frowned. "Well, one would assume that to be the case, considering ye asked me what I just scribed."

"Could ye read well in this light and upside down then?"

Exasperation filled her. "Nay, mayhap not. Are ye saying then that ye can read?"

He arched a dark brow, leaned back, and folded his arms over his chest. "And is that so hard to believe? That some crudely raised Highlander might possess a familiarity wi' books?"

"Nay, it isn't so hard to believe!"

Try as she might, Heather couldn't keep an edge of exasperation from her voice. Curse the man. Must he always bait her so unmercifully?

119

"Leastwise," she added, "of those in the Highlands more highly born. Now, if ye will, permit me to move on to other—"

"Ye've a most irritating habit of discounting people, ye know, a habit which may someday cause ye great grief if ye haven't a care."

"Fine." She slammed down her pen. "Fine." She shoved back her chair and rose to her feet.

Duncan eyed her calmly. "And where are ye going now? I thought we'd work to do."

"Och, we do, my proud, stubborn friend. But first, to lay the issue of your reading ability to rest, I'm going to my bedchamber to fetch one of my books."

"Suit yerself," he called after her, laughter rumbling in his chest. "But ye needn't go even that far, if ye wish. The chest along the far wall there holds some of my own books. Books," he added, "I've read many a time."

"Aye, I can just imagine," Heather muttered sarcastically as she changed direction and strode to the big chest. "Ye owning books, much less being able to read them. But ye wouldn't let it be, would ye, though I was willing to overlook that failing. Nay, ye wouldn't let it be," she said, pausing before the chest and lifting the lid, "and now yer pride will force me to shame ye before . . ."

As the contents of the chest came into view, Heather's voice faded. She went hot, then cold, then hot again. There, stacked in carefully arranged rows, were piles of leather-bound books, old and well-worn, but books nonetheless.

For a time Heather stared down at them, myriad emotions roiling within. One moment suspicion, tinged with determination to prove Duncan wrong, held sway. Then, in the next, shame, deep and soul-searing, seized her.

Overlaying it all, though, was fear. Fear that, in testing him yet again, she'd discover another facet to an already complex, intriguing, and infinitely compelling man. A man who, in the short span of days, had beguiled her like she imagined her father had beguiled her mother. Like Donald Campbell had beguiled Rose, perhaps even to the very day of her death.

But fear could be overcome, Heather reminded herself, if one just found the courage to face it. Indeed, she was making more of this possibility that Duncan Mackenzie could read than was necessary. His brother Colin was literate, prided himself, even, on being an avid student of the ancient philosophers. But such knowledge had done little to form his character for the better, or turn him from the shallow, silly ways of Court.

Squatting before the chest, Heather perused a few of the volumes. Her breath caught in her throat, however, when her gaze fell on a familiar title. Though the gilt lettering was faded, even completely obliterated in spots, she recognized the book nonetheless. *The Book of the City of Ladies* by Christine Pisan.

Heather smiled. So, she thought with grim satisfaction, Duncan not only claimed he could read, but he also claimed that he was familiar with all these books. What better way to test him than to discover the depth of his understanding of Christine's work?

Taking up the volume, Heather rose and returned to the table. Briefly, Fiona looked up from her spinning, cast her a quizzical look, then resumed her work. The rest of the cottage's occupants, save Duncan, however, scarce noted her passing.

She sat, laid the book on the table, then shoved it across to Duncan. He took it up, perused the title, and began to thumb through it.

"Do ye have a preference which chapter I read?" he asked, finally glancing up to meet her steady gaze.

"Aye." Heather paused, turning over the book's contents in her mind. "Pray, read chapter 37, where Christine speaks to Reason concerning the great good accrued to the world through women. I always find those passages most inspiring."

Duncan smiled. "Do ye now?" He thumbed through the pages until he appeared to find the appropriate chapter, then looked up. "That doesn't surprise me. Somehow, I imagined ye would."

He began to read. "My lady, I greatly admire what I have heard ye say, that so much good has come into the world by virtue of the understanding of women. These men usually say that women's knowledge is worthless. In fact, when someone says something foolish, the widely voiced insult is that this is women's knowledge. In brief, the typical opinions and comments of men claim that women have been and are useful in the world only for bearing children and sewing . . ."

His recitation of Christine Pisan's work was fluent, his inflections and emotional tone as he read moving and dramatic. Not only could Duncan Mackenzie read, Heather quickly realized, but he also seemed to understand and appreciate what he read. Indeed, she could almost believe he agreed with the great medieval writer's thoughts. But how could that be—a man in sympathy with the age-old lament of women?

Tears filled her eyes. It wasn't fair. Duncan Mackenzie was supposed to be some rough, uncultured Highlander, a man who was hardly a worthy adversary much less a man she could come to admire, even respect. Yet, at every turn . . .

"That's enough." She finally forced out the words in a choked whisper. "Ye've made yer point and more. Once again I was wrong about ye. I-I beg pardon."

He closed the book and lifted his triumphant gaze. When he saw her tears, though, his smile faded. Confusion darkened his eyes, then regret tinged with compassion.

The consideration of his pity was harder to endure than his arrogant comments and heated looks, Heather thought, so bewildered and miserable she could scarce bear it. Far, far harder. She shoved to her feet.

"I-I'm weary." Fiercely, she blinked back tears. "This is sufficient for one night."

In a swift move Duncan leaned across the table, grabbing her wrist before she could turn away. "Lass, dinna fash yerself. Ye didn't know. If it hadn't been for Father James when I was but a lad, I'd never have had the chance to learn to read. But ye couldn't have known."

"Nay, I couldn't have known." Heather twisted free of Duncan's loose clasp. "But it doesn't matter. Once again I've been a fool to underestimate ye. But I'll not do it again." She shook her head with a savage determination. "Nay, never, ever again!"

7

Duncan rose early the next morning to begin the day's chores with his father. Preoccupied with thoughts of Heather, he was taciturn and moody, replying only when asked a direct question. They worked for several hours, feeding the cattle, goats, chickens, and pigs, then cleaning out the manure from the cattle byre and other animal pens. By that time, Duncan's welter of emotions over Heather had grown to monumental proportions.

"Father," he finally said, sinking the tines of his pitchfork into the damp straw and dung of the last stall. He leaned on its long wooden handle. "Have ye e'er desired something ye knew ye couldn't have? Desired it more than ye e'er desired aught afore?"

Malcolm Mackenzie paused in his strewing of fresh straw in a nearby, already mucked-out stall. His brow furrowed in thought.

"I can't say I've e'er wasted the effort desiring what I knew I couldn't have. What purpose would it have served, save to make me miserable?"

"Och, Father." Duncan exhaled a weary breath. "Must ye always be so sensible?" He paused, deciding to take another tack. "And what of Mither? Were ye so certain she'd wed ye, when ye finally thought to ask her? What would ye have done if she'd refused ye? Would ye have so easily moved on to another lass and not given Mither another thought?"

"Hmmm . . . Now that's a hard one," his father said, frowning. "To be sure, there wasn't a more bonny lass than yer mither to be found. But though I desired her more than I'd desired any woman afore or after, I never thought I couldn't have her."

He chuckled, his brown eyes alight with memories. "Of course, my bonny Fiona led me a fine race nonetheless, even as she cast me saucy looks and whispered sweet encouragement. But surely ye're speaking of things other than bonny lasses, and—"

As if some sudden thought had struck him, Malcolm's eyes widened. He went silent. Then he dropped the armful of straw he'd just gathered and walked over to lean on the wooden poles separating the two stalls.

"Ye haven't gone and lost yer heart to the Gordon lass, have ye, lad?" A look of rising concern in his eyes, Malcolm stared up at his son. "Yer mither made some passing strange comment about ye two last eve, once we were abed, but I assured her ye were far too sensible a lad to yearn after some haughty lady. I told her true, didn't I, Duncan, my lad?"

Duncan gripped the pitchfork handle tightly and stared off into the distance. If the truth be told, what he felt for Heather was hardly sensible.

"She's like no other woman I've e'er met, Father," he finally replied, then sighed again.

"She's bonny enough. I'll give ye that," Malcolm agreed grudgingly. "But she's betrothed, soon to wed, and would never spare ye a second look if she didn't have to tutor ye to aid her father in his plot to rescue the queen. Indeed, if not for this plot, ye wouldn't e'er have met her."

"True enough," Duncan conceded. "But I have, Father, and now I want her more than I've e'er wanted any other woman." He turned, locking gazes with his sire. "Do ye remember that day we rode to Angus's tower house? That day we first met Lord Gordon and his daughter?"

"Aye." His father eyed him warily. "What of it?"

"Do ye recall how ye warned me not to play so fast and loose wi' the lassies, or fate would step in to punish me?" Duncan gave a rueful laugh. "Well, I think fate brought Heather Gordon into my life for just that reason. That it sent me a lass to love, but who won't e'er love me."

"Och, lad, lad." Malcolm reached over the poles to clasp his son by the shoulder. "Don't do this. Don't let yerself be tormented in such a way. She isn't worth it. No lass is!"

"No lass, Father? Ye can say that in good conscience, knowing how much ye love Mither?"

"It's different wi' Fiona." Malcolm released Duncan's shoulder and stepped back. "She's a Highlander, born and bred. We've always shared a common upbringing, understood each other and what we wanted from life."

"I feel the same wi' Heather." Duncan rested his forehead on the top of the pitchfork handle. "I know it makes no sense, Father, but I feel I understand her, that we

126

share the same dreams, love so many of the same things. I think now it's the reason I've never felt the slightest inclination to wed one of the local lasses. I've always wanted more from a mate than a warm, fertile body and a good cook."

"And what else is there to desire in a wife?" Malcolm paused, then laughed. "Well, that and a companion and friend, of course."

Frustration filled Duncan. As much as he loved and respected his father, there were times when he realized they didn't, and never would, share the same outlook on life. Realized that his sire, though he tried mightily to understand, never would—or could.

"What else, indeed?" Duncan shrugged. "A soul mate? A love which spans the barriers of culture, upbringing, and social class?"

Malcolm shook his head in puzzlement. "Truly, Duncan, there are times when I don't understand ye, and it distresses me. Distresses me sorely."

Aye, Duncan thought sadly, *it distresses me, too. Though I've never spoken to ye of these thoughts, Father, there are times when I feel so isolated, so alone in my hopes and dreams for the future, so discontent with the life the Lord has apparently given me. I feel like some traitor, wishing for more than life here can e'er hope to provide. It's why I work so hard, burying these thoughts beneath the exhausting burden of back-breaking labor, hoping against hope the nagging sense of emptiness will someday ease.*

But it hasn't helped, leastwise not for long. Indeed, the thoughts only worsen, until they've finally culminated in a physical form—the form of Heather Gordon. Yet I can't have her, any more than it seems I'll e'er fulfill my elusive, unrealistic dreams of a life of something bigger and better. And I feel so guilty, as well, that I can't seem to find a peace in just doing what the Lord wills.

He lifted his head. "It doesn't matter at any rate. I won't e'er have Heather Gordon. I must live wi' that and bear wi' the time I must spend wi' her. It'll be over soon enough, at any rate."

Malcolm managed a small, uncertain smile. "Aye, that it will. Three months will be over soon enough." His face brightened. "In the meanwhile, consider the local lassies a wee bit more. There'll be a *ceilidh* in two weeks' time. If ye let it be known ye'll attend, I'll wager all the lassies of marriageable age from miles around will come."

"Do ye think so, Father?"

"Och, of course, lad. Of course." Malcolm laughed, evidently relieved to be done with the discomfiting topic of Heather Gordon. "And ye know, as well as I, we've some of the bonniest lasses in all of Kintail."

Mayhap, Father, Duncan thought, the misery welling once more to drown him in the murky depths of despair. *None, though, will e'er be as bonny as Heather. And none, I sorely fear, will e'er complete me as I sense she would.*

Exhausted from the emotional as well as physical travails of the past day, Heather slept in late. About midmorn she rose and, while Beth and Tavish carried in several buckets of heated water for her bath, she had a light breakfast of tangy goat cheese, fresh bannocks, and a mug of cider. At long last, though, Heather was bathed, dressed, and sufficiently fortified to face Duncan Mackenzie.

Sweeping majestically from her bedchamber in a dark blue silk gown lavishly trimmed with lace, Heather glanced about for Duncan. He was nowhere to be found. She scowled in annoyance.

"He's out of doors," Fiona offered, noting her reaction, "helping his father care for the animals."

Heather marched over to one of the leaded glass windows and peered outside. The sky was overcast, the day gloomy. Though there were footprints in the freshly fallen snow leading from the cottage, again, Duncan was nowhere to be found.

"Most likely, by now, they're in the cattle byre mucking out stalls," the older woman once again offered helpfully.

"Well, I've already ruined one dress since my arrival," Heather muttered. "I'll not risk another traipsing out after him."

Fiona rose and hobbled over to join Heather at the window. "I don't know if Duncan, being a man and all, was sufficiently appreciative of what ye lost when Cuini whelped on yer dress."

Heather gave a snort of disgust. "As a matter of fact, nay, he wasn't."

"Well, then, I'd like to replace yer dress. It won't be so fine as what ye lost," Duncan's mother hastened to add when Heather turned a surprised gaze on her, "but, if I do say so myself, I'm one of the best weavers in Kintail. I could weave ye a good, warm tartan that we could sew into a fine woolen gown."

"Och, it wasn't yer fault—or Duncan's, for that matter," Heather said, feeling instantly guilty for her mean-spirited grumbling.

Fiona Mackenzie, from the moment of their arrival, had treated them all with the utmost hospitality and kindness. She couldn't help it her son was so maddening. He was, after all, a grown man and responsible for himself. She'd not, however, Heather resolved, place additional burden on the already ailing woman in trying to retaliate against Duncan's arrogant manipulations.

"It was my dog that did the deed," Fiona persisted. "Besides, our life here in the Highlands is far more rough than yers. Ye'll ruin more than one gown, I'm afraid, if ye persist in wearing such elegant if fragile cloth."

She had a point, Heather admitted, glancing from her silk to the other woman's sturdy tartan cloth skirt and long plaid covering her shoulders. Fiona's clothing was practical, sturdy, and warm, she added, noting, with a small shiver, that silk was a poor insulator against a room cool despite a roaring hearth fire. Why not take Fiona up on her offer? Perhaps Duncan would treat her with greater respect if she dressed more like his kind.

"That would be a wonderful idea," Heather said, managing a bright smile. "I wouldn't have ye do the work without assistance, though. Beth could—"

"Hish, hinny." Fiona raised a silencing hand. "It wouldn't be a fair replacement for what ye lost, if ye or yer maid assisted me. Besides, when it comes to my weaving, I can't say I'd take to much interference. Duncan says I'm quite protective of it, and I'd wager he's not far from the mark."

Heather laughed ruefully. "Ye'll never convince him, at any rate, that he's ever far from the mark." She sighed and shook her head. "Truly, I've never met a more obstinate man."

"I'd wager not," Fiona chuckled. "Ye're a bright lass. Ye bring out the fire in my Duncan. Still, though ye run him a good race, I can't help but wonder if ye haven't met yer match in my son."

"He's indeed a most unique man," Heather ventured tactfully.

The conversation, she sensed, was beginning to take a turn. She slanted Fiona a careful look.

"I know we've had our disagreements. I'm sorry for that. It isn't proper behavior, neither for the teacher nor the student."

"And is that all ye are to him, and him to ye, then?"

Heather's eyes widened. Beth's warnings had indeed been disturbingly accurate. Others had noted the deeper implications of her and Duncan's mutual animosity.

She looked to where her maid and Tavish sat across the room at the small table, apparently engrossed in an intense game of cards. Beth was so smitten with the big Scotsman Heather doubted she even realized two other people were in the room. There seemed little danger of them becoming interested in her and Fiona's conversation, much less overhearing it.

"I don't know what ye mean," she hedged, turning back to the older woman.

Fiona angled away from the window and leaned against the wall. Remembering her swollen legs, Heather almost suggested they go to her bedchamber to sit and talk. Then she reconsidered. The sooner this particular conversation ended, the better.

"Don't ye?" Fiona cocked her head and smiled. "My Duncan's verra attracted to ye. And, for whatever reasons ye might have, ye encourage it."

Heather flushed. "I-I do no such thing! He's just the most aggravating—"

"So, it's as I feared," the older woman cut her off briskly. "Ye're equally drawn to him."

She sighed and shook her head. "Lass, lass. What do ye expect to gain from this little game? Ye're a fine lady, and my Duncan"—she paused and sighed again—"well, suffice it to say, he can never be the man for ye."

So, Heather thought, Fiona was ignorant of her foster son's true heritage. If she had known, she wouldn't have spoken thusly, unless . . . unless she sought to protect his identity, not knowing the danger was past.

Heather was tempted to prod her further in the hope of ascertaining what Fiona truly did and didn't know. She quickly discarded that idea. What purpose would be served at any rate?

"I don't expect to gain aught, madam," Heather replied instead. "And if I play some game, I'm unaware of it. It isn't, after all, as if I'm experienced in this sort of thing."

"Ye've never had a man court ye afore?" Fiona gave a snort of disbelief. "Come, come, hinny. As bonny as ye are, ye can't seriously expect me to believe that."

"It isn't the same, I tell ye!"

Exasperation filled Heather. How could she make Fiona understand?

"Before . . . before Duncan, I didn't care. There were no men who . . . affected me . . . like Duncan does."

Fiona said nothing.

"Och, I feel like such a knotty-pated lack wit," Heather cried softly. "I don't wish to act poorly toward Duncan, truly I don't. But I also don't know what to do." She reached out and took Fiona's hand. "Help me, I beg ye. I no longer have a mither to speak of this with. And I don't wish to cause Duncan harm in any way. Truly I don't."

For a long moment, Duncan's mother eyed her closely. "The best course of all would be for ye to hie yerself back home posthaste," Fiona finally said. "That being impossible, considering the queen's plight and all, ye must gird yerself for the weeks and months ahead. Ye must, at all times, maintain the most reserved air wi' Duncan and speak wi' him only when necessary to teach him what he needs to know. The rest of the time, when ye aren't tutoring him, ye must take great pains not to spend wi' him. And, above all, ye two must not e'er be alone."

"Aye, that's the wiser course," Heather said, nodding in agreement. "It'll be hard, but if ye'll support me in this . . ."

"I will and gladly, hinny." Fiona's mouth softened. "I don't wish for ye to be hurt but, even more so, I don't wish for my son to suffer."

Heather nodded, and managed a wan smile. "Aye. It's best for the both of us."

Fiona straightened and turned to go. "Aye, it is indeed. But what is best," she muttered as she hobbled away, "isn't always what hot-blooded lads and lassies get."

Heather, her glorious blond hair snagged up beneath yet another cap, was squatting by the box holding Cuini and her litter when Duncan finally returned to the cottage. She had one puppy clasped to her, cuddling it closely. As the midday meal was nearly ready, he shot her but a passing glance, then strode to the pitcher and wash basin. In an effort to block out the freshened image of her, all soft, curvaceous woman, Duncan gripped the handle of the pottery pitcher tightly and poured out a generous amount of wash water.

After cleansing his face, hands, and forearms, he dried himself, then turned to his mother. "Do ye need any assistance, Mither? Wi' so many extra mouths to feed, I know ye must toil far longer than afore."

Fiona made a dismissing motion with her hand. "Dinna fash yerself, lad. Beth has helped me wi' the meal, and Tavish even fetched the potatoes and turnips from the cold cellar."

"And what of the Lady Gordon?" Duncan asked, of a sudden inexplicably angry with her, even as he struggled to remind himself she was a guest in their house. "Was she too afraid of roughening those fine hands of hers that she couldn't stoop to offer ye aid?"

"I didn't come here to cook and clean, Duncan Mackenzie," Heather snapped, drawing up at that moment behind him. "I came to teach ye how to act the noble. Ye seem determined, however, to squander what precious little time we have."

134

Duncan turned on his heel to confront her. "And how so, madam? Ye only arrived here yesterday."

"Aye, but today's half gone already and not even a second has yet to be devoted to yer tutoring." She shook her head, her mouth set in dour lines. "This won't do, I tell ye. It just won't do."

He stared down at her, fighting with all his might not to be taken in by the delicately carved profile lifted to him, nor the pale, creamy skin and slim, pert nose, or the full, finely molded lips. Saucy wench, he thought. If she imagined she was in charge, she was sadly mistaken. Though he had no intention of carrying through with the suggestion that had just now flashed through his mind, he couldn't resist the temptation to rile her a bit more before firmly setting her back in her place.

"Well, then mayhap if ye won't assist my mither," Duncan drawled with a sly grin, "ye can assist me wi' my chores."

Heather gaped in shock. "Are ye daft, man? How dare ye suggest I work outside in this weather, unchaperoned, and with the farm animals no less!"

"Ye wouldn't be unchaperoned. My father would always be about." Duncan shrugged, a twinge of shame finally forcing him to back off. "But suit yerself. I won't shirk my chores and load further work on my father's back. He's sixty, ye know, and well past his prime even for a Highlander."

"And what is that to me?"

"Naught, save ye could tutor me just as well in most things while we work as if we sat here inside."

"Ye're impertinent and crude to suggest such a thing."

135

Anger flashed in Heather's eyes. "Ye also, now that my father and yer laird are gone, seek to turn the tables to yer advantage. Ye're no man of honor, Duncan Mackenzie!"

"Mayhap not, but a little work never killed anyone." He cocked his head and considered her closely. God forgive him, but he couldn't decide if she were more exciting angry or when she looked at him with those hungry, needing, vulnerable blue eyes. "Though, of course, ye could be the first, if ye're truly as frail and fragile as ye make yerself out to be."

"I never claimed to be frail and—" Heather paused. A light flared in her eyes. "If yer father needs help so badly," she began again, nodding with sudden resolve, "I'll give ye Tavish to take yer place. That will free ye to work with me."

He should've known Heather would find some way to slither free of the little trap he had set. It had been a poor idea at any rate, engaging her in hard, filthy work that would've quickly reduced her to exhaustion and, hopefully, also taken the edge off her beguiling beauty. Truly, he must be getting soft in the head even to consider such a daft idea. Aye, soft in the head, Duncan admitted ruefully, gazing down at Heather, and he had a certain bonny blonde to thank for it.

"Well, if it would redeem yer low opinion of my honor . . ." He stroked his jaw, pretending to consider her offer.

"Och, aye. It would indeed," Heather cried a bit too eagerly. She turned to Tavish. "Ye understand, don't ye? I haven't any other choice. I *must* have sufficient time to tutor the Highlander. I wouldn't ask such a thing of ye otherwise."

"Dinna fash yerself, my lady." Tavish walked over and rendered her a small, stiff bow. "I'm not afraid of a little hard work." He shot Duncan a black look. "Especially aught any Highlander claims he can do."

Duncan chuckled. "Och, have no fear, Tavish, my lad. We won't work ye beyond yer puny abilities. Indeed, I haven't any intention of surrendering all my chores to ye. I couldn't bear being cooped up inside all day, even in the company of such a gracious teacher."

"It isn't for ye to determine the length of yer classes, Duncan Mackenzie," Heather warned. "It's for me to decide—"

"I'll give ye two hours in the morn," he cut her off with an upraised hand, "two after the midday meal, and two in the evening. That's six hours a day, more than most could bear, I'm sure." He grinned wolfishly. "And certainly more than ye'll be able to endure, dealing wi' the likes of me."

"Fine." Heather sent him a seething look. "Fine. Ye're most likely correct at any rate. Ye'd test the patience of a saint, and no mistake."

"Then we're agreed?"

"Aye," she muttered, "but from here on out I set the rules, not ye."

Duncan chuckled softly. "We'll just have to see about that, won't we?"

Heather's chin lifted, and a resolute look gleamed in her eyes. "Aye, we will indeed."

True to his word, Duncan began his first lessons after the midday meal. Yet, even with a pleasantly full stomach after a fine dinner of thick slices of smoked salmon, fresh-baked brown bread, boiled potatoes, and buttered turnips, followed by a fine quince pie that mellowed his mood considerably, Duncan was soon biting his tongue and clamping down on his rising irritation.

"A noble doesn't speak so . . . so crudely," Heather was struggling to explain. "Ye must change yer way of speech, and do so completely from this day forth. It *must* become second nature, or ye'll surely falter in a difficult moment and undo all our work—not to mention," she added in a more somber tone, "endanger yer life."

"And would ye have me begin to act the dandy from this day forth, too?" Duncan said through gritted teeth. "Must I also prance around and affect prim mannerisms, so as to make them second nature?" He grimaced and shook his head. "Nay, I can't do it. I'd surely become the laughingstock of Kintail, not to mention stir wonderment and talk over why I suddenly began acting thusly."

"Well, then at least agree to practice yer speech at all times when at home," Heather urged. "The mincing dandy can wait a time, until we're closer to leaving for Lochleven."

She was trying her best to keep her temper, Duncan well knew. She was trying her best not to react negatively, or begin yet another argument with him. He sensed that from the long pauses she took before she spoke, from the instinctive stiffening of her body in anger when he proved difficult, before she finally forced herself to relax and smile. Indeed Heather was, he admitted grudgingly, putting forth a far more admirable effort than he.

"Fine," he muttered, his guilt nudging him into a compromise he really didn't want to make. "I'll practice yer way of speaking while at home. But if one person here dares laugh . . ."

"And who would do so? They all know why ye do what ye do, why it's so important ye begin to change."

Duncan considered that a moment. "Who indeed?" He sighed. "Mayhap, in truth, the problem lies more wi' me."

"*With* me," Heather promptly corrected him.

He scowled. "*With* me," he repeated. "I can't say I care to change what I've grown up wi', though."

"*With*. Grown up *with*."

Duncan sucked in an exasperated breath. "Grown up *with*. I can only wonder what I'll be, once ye're done *with* me. Once this becomes second nature, it'll be equally hard to change back to the old way. Yet my friends, my family, will want me to."

"And ye fear ye might not want to?" Heather supplied softly. "That what ye learn, ye might wish to keep? That ye might never be the same man again?"

How did she know this? Duncan wondered. How could she cut right to the heart of the matter with such ease? Was it perhaps because they truly *were* so closely attuned, one to the other?

He had imagined it so, right from the start. Yet, conversely, he also feared the perception sprang solely from a love-struck longing that it be so. But now . . . now that same perception returned—even more strongly than before.

"Aye," he said, gazing deep into her eyes. "And if I'm no longer the same man, who *will* I be? And, more importantly so, will this man be accepted back in Kintail, and will this man e'er be happy again here?"

"*Ever*," Heather whispered, never breaking his intense glance. "Ye must . . . say *ever*, not e'er."

"Aye," Duncan replied slowly. "So I must."

His gaze fell to the table before them. Fell to rest upon the slim, delicate hand lying on the paper before her. With all his heart, he wanted to reach across that table and take up Heather's hand. Wanted to lift it to his lips and kiss it. Kiss it in gratitude for understanding him as she did, and for caring that such concerns distressed him.

But he didn't. He had no right to touch such a fine lady, much less presume such intimacies with her. And most especially not here, in the presence of his mother and Heather's maid and groomsman. At this moment, he was as grateful for the requisite chaperones as Heather must be!

"If the truth be told, it's my fear, as well," Heather offered when Duncan remained silent. "From the start— even before I met ye—I wondered what all this might cost ye in the end. And I wonder at and fear it still. I wouldn't have ye irreparably harmed, Duncan. It'd hurt me as much as it'd hurt ye."

"Would it, lass?"

His voice dropped to a husky whisper. *Duncan. She's finally called me Duncan.* The realization sent a fierce joy surging through him.

"Aye, I fear it would."

He knew he shouldn't ask the next question but, suddenly, Duncan needed to know. Needed to know at whatever cost, whatever the answer.

"Why, lass? Why would it hurt ye?"

She opened her mouth to speak. Then, as if recalling herself at last, Heather clamped it shut again. She shook her head, the soft, tender lines of her mouth hardening with determination.

"It doesn't matter, and well ye know it, Duncan Mackenzie," Heather said. "It's enough that I share yer concern and will take the greatest care that yer education not harm ye." She paused to glance down at her notes. "Now, let us continue with yer lesson. No purpose is served squandering valuable time discussing our innermost secrets."

And we dare not, either, Duncan thought, noting the attractive shade of rose now flushing her cheeks and washing her fair skin. *We dare not*, he realized with a sharp, bittersweet pang. *Yet, though we dare not, I wonder if such a decision is truly ours to make. And I wonder if, in the end, time itself isn't our enemy.*

A benevolent enemy who will lure us closer and closer in spite of ourselves, in spite of the well-intentioned efforts of others to keep us apart. Lure us to a fate we both fear and desire. A fate predestined by the good Lord Himself, long, long before we even met.

141

8

The next morning, Fiona began preparations for weaving the dark blue wool she planned to use to make Heather's dress. After the requisite two-hour lesson in mid-morn, and with several hours left before the midday meal and Duncan's next lesson, Heather soon found herself standing near the loom, watching in fascination. As the older woman threw the wooden shuttle between the two rows of thread, Heather stepped even closer.

Finally, Fiona paused in her work and glanced up. "Are ye of a mind, then, to learn weaving?"

Heather nodded. "It seems a fine craft. Not that my father," she added with a wry smile, "would deem it a proper one for a noblewoman."

"And have ye e'er done aught wi' yer hands, hinny? In an artist's fashion, I mean?"

"I've painted a bit in oil and tried sculpting a time or two. I also play the harp."

"Well, weaving requires the same dedication and attention to detail, not to mention an artful flair."

She began to work again, pulling the beater sharply

forward to pack the weft tightly together. Next, Fiona pressed a different treadle and threw the shuttle in the opposite direction.

"To make a plain weave, such as I'm doing for yer dress, every other warp thread is raised," she explained, "and the shuttle passed between the raised and upraised threads . . ."

The next hour passed quickly. Eventually, Duncan's mother seemed to relent of her earlier claims to being protective over her weaving, and offered to let Heather try her hand at the loom. When it was time to begin preparations for the midday meal, Fiona even allowed her to continue on when she left. With practice, Heather gained coordination and speed. By the time Duncan walked in with his father and Tavish, she had managed to add a good six inches' length of cloth to Fiona's earlier work.

Noting her at the loom, Duncan cocked a dark brow. He quickly washed up, then joined her, drying his hands and arms as he did.

"Ye make a most pleasing sight, lass," he said, "setting there, working the loom."

Heather shot him an arch look. "And, pray, why is that, do ye reckon? Mayhap because when I work thusly, I fit yer image of a good, meek, yet industrious wife?"

Duncan chuckled. "Och, nay. I'd wager ye'll never be meek, no matter who ye wed."

"But ye can see me as good and industrious then? Even being a noblewoman and all?" Heather asked with an impish grin.

He nodded emphatically. "Aye. Verra good and verra industrious."

She opened her mouth to deliver a witty comeback when Fiona's frowning gaze caught hers. Recalling her earlier agreement with Duncan's mother, Heather's smile faded. Curse it all. Once again she had forgotten her resolve to keep her distance.

Heather shoved the shuttle beneath the warp threads, and rose. "The meal's ready. I need to wash up."

Duncan studied her a moment, quite evidently puzzled at her sudden change of mood. Then he stepped aside.

"Aye, I suppose ye're right. We've time enough to talk further while we eat and then, afterwards, during my next lessons."

"Aye, during yer next lessons."

Without meeting his gaze, Heather swept past him.

"And what exactly will that next lesson entail?"

Nonplussed, she halted, hesitated a moment, then nodded in sudden remembrance. "Chess. I plan to teach ye how to play chess. It's past time ye begin to learn Colin Stewart's favorite game."

"Chess, is it, then?"

"Aye," Heather replied with a firm nod. "Chess."

The little entourage of Duncan, his parents, Heather, Beth, and Tavish drew up before a large, moss-covered stone cottage. In the encroaching darkness of the late afternoon of mid-February, lights already glowed from the large stone building that stood nearby. The sweet tones of a fiddle being tuned rose on the chill air, and the mouth-watering scent of roasting meat and baked goods wafted by.

As Malcolm and Tavish assisted Fiona and Beth from the horse-drawn wooden cart and helped unload the covered bowls of victuals Fiona had prepared as her contribution to the culinary part of the *ceilidh*, Duncan dismounted from his horse and walked over to Heather. She eyed his upraised hand for a fleeting instant before finally accepting his offer to help her down from her horse.

"My thanks," Heather mumbled, her heart racing and her cheeks burning when their bodies momentarily brushed as she slid off her horse. She stepped quickly back and made a move to go around him, never once meeting Duncan's gaze.

A firm grip on her arm halted her. "Heather, wait."

She froze and reluctantly lifted her glance to his.

"Aye? What is it?"

"We've never discussed what reason to give others for yer, er, extended visit at my home. There's sure to be interest and talk, though, once the clan learns of yer presence."

"And ye think after tonight," she finished for him smilingly, "mayhap the tongues will wag?"

"To be sure."

Heather considered for a moment. "Why not just tell them I'm Heather Mackenzie, Janet's cousin, visiting from somewhere south? I am half Mackenzie, at any rate. And that I've come to help yer mither this winter. All of that, in some manner or another, is true. That way it's not entirely a lie."

"Aye," Duncan replied thoughtfully. "No one has to tell a bald-faced lie, which suits me fine. Already, this plot requires enough deception as it is. And calling ye a Mackenzie isn't far from the truth."

"And what of Beth and Tavish?"

Duncan frowned in thought. "Friends of yer mither's, sent along to chaperone ye? That way, they can keep their own names and roles. It'll be easier for all if we don't change the whole story."

"Aye, it will."

His gaze swept down her body. "Ye look quite fine, ye do, Heather *Mackenzie*, in that gown and tartan cloak my mother wove for ye."

"It was most kind of her to make these clothes, not to mention take the time to teach me how to weave." Self-consciously, because she knew Duncan still looked at her, Heather ran her hands over the dark blue wool dress, smoothing any imaginary wrinkles. "It's so soft and warm, I don't think I'll ever wish to wear aught but Highland wool again."

"That plain garb also fits well with yer claim of being Janet's cousin, rather than the fine lady ye truly are." He offered her his arm. "Shall we join the others? It won't work—our little ruse, I mean—unless we share the plan."

She looped her arm through his. "Nay, I suppose not," she said with a chuckle, before stepping out at Duncan's side.

A few minutes later, with Duncan's parents and Beth and Tavish informed of the change of identity, the group entered the stone building. While Fiona, Beth, and

Heather deposited the food dishes on a long expanse of board set on trestles, the three men joined a gathering of other Scotsmen around a keg of whiskey. Soon, all three men were each lifting a wooden, two-handled quaich to their lips, drinking deeply of the beloved water of life. Not seemingly content to stop at one cup, Duncan, Malcolm, and Tavish quickly refilled at the keg.

Watching them, Heather frowned. Fiona, turning from the table just then, noted Heather's dark look.

"Ye can't keep a good Scotsman, be he High or Lowlander, from his *aquae vitae*, hinny. And ye might as well not even consider trying." She took Heather by the arm. "Come. Allow me to introduce ye to Dora Mackenzie. This is her and her husband Fergus's steading, ye know."

"Nay, I didn't know."

Heather plastered on her best social smile and followed Fiona across a room already beginning to fill with people. To her surprise, as she neared a small group of women standing beside the raised platform and the two fiddlers, Heather spotted Janet and Jean Mackenzie. When their gazes met, the red-haired girl scowled.

Och, verra fine, Heather thought in dismay. *She still holds a grudge then, does she?*

Fiona was quick to introduce Heather to Dora, taking great care, as she spoke, to make sure both Janet and Jean caught the modifications of the reason for Heather's presence in the Highlands. Instantly, understanding flared in Jean Mackenzie's eyes. Janet's mouth dropped, though, and only her mother's sharp elbow in the ribs silenced whatever comment the girl was about to make.

147

"We're verra glad to make yer acquaintance," Dora, a stout, ruddy-faced older woman with silver hair, said. "A new lass in these parts will stir the interest of all the lads, and even more so because ye're so bonny."

At the compliment paid her cousin, Janet shot Heather a scalding look. "Well, it'll do the lads no good in the end, will it?" she muttered. "Being as how she's only here for a winter's visit and all."

"Och, Janet, lass," Dora said with a laugh. "Don't be going and getting jealous. Ye've still a few years before ye can wed at any rate."

"True enough," Janet allowed, suddenly distracted as she scanned the room.

Watching her, Heather knew the exact instant she found Duncan. The petulant look vanished. Her eyes brightened with delight.

Janet turned to her mother. "If ye please, I'll leave ye here with Fiona and my dear cousin. I see Duncan over by the whiskey keg and would like to visit a time with him."

Jean smiled. "Of course, lass. Just be sure ye don't take a sip of Duncan's whiskey while ye're there."

"Och, Mither," Janet said with a girlish giggle. "Dinna fash yerself. Being near Duncan is intoxicating enough for me." Then, with a sly look at Heather, Janet turned and skipped off.

Foolish girl, Heather thought with a twinge of irritation, her gaze following Janet as she made her way through the crowd to Duncan's side. If she imagined her silly ways would ever intrigue a man like Duncan Mackenzie, she was sadly misled.

Yet the truth of the matter was that Duncan must someday wed, and soon if his parents had their way. A marriage to Janet Mackenzie would be considered by all as a definite step up in social class. The girl most likely knew it too.

Not that who or when Duncan wed should be of any concern to her, Heather well knew. One way or another, she, as Janet had so succinctly put it, was only here for a visit. All too soon, she must extract herself from this place—and Duncan's life—and go back to the only one she could ever live. No purpose was served in pointless dreaming or even more uncharitable jealousy.

Fiddle music rose on the air, faltered an instant as the two musicians found their timing, then swelled in a rousing tune.

> The king sits in Dunfermline toon,
> Drinking the blude-red wine;
> "Oh where sall I get a gude sailor,
> To sail this ship o' mine?"
>
> Up and spake an eldern Knight
> Sat at the king's right knee;
> "Sir Patrick Spens is the best sailor,
> That ever sail'd the sea."
>
> The king has written a braid letter,
> And seal'd it wi' his hand,
> And sent it to Sir Patrick Spens,
> Was walking on the strand.
>
> "To Noroway, to Noroway,
> To Noroway o'er the faem;
> The king's daughter of Noroway;
> 'Tis thou maun bring her hame."

It was the ancient ballad "Sir Patrick Spens," Heather well knew, a tale of the ill-fated journey of the knight to bring home Margaret, "Maid of Norway," the daughter of Eric of Norway and granddaughter and heir of King Alexander III of Scotland. It was, as well, the signal for the *ceilidh* to begin. All gathered around the fiddlers as they played and sang, some of the people actually joining in to sing the well-known and beloved ballad.

The songs went on for the next fifteen or twenty minutes before the *ceilidh*'s host, Fergus Mackenzie, finally called for the dancing to begin. Immediately, Janet, still strategically stationed beside Duncan, grabbed the big Highlander's hand and pulled him out to the middle of the wooden floor. Other couples quickly joined them as they lined up for a reel.

Heather turned back to Fiona. "I'm thirsty. I think I'll fetch myself a cup of cider. Would ye like one, too?"

"Aye, a wee cup would set well wi' me." Duncan's mother hesitated, then leaned close. "Ye must not begrudge Janet her time wi' Duncan," she said softly. "She loves him, ye know."

"Aye, and has set her sights on wedding him."

"Would that be such a terrible thing, hinny?"

Heather met Fiona's steady gaze. She should lie or at least dissemble a bit, Heather well knew, but then decided Fiona might as well hear the truth.

"Nay, not for Janet leastwise," she said, even as she knew that the girl would never have the kind of love she was seeking. Still, she sensed it might well be enough for her. "But for Duncan?" She managed a nonchalant shrug. "Well, it isn't my affair, one way or another, is it?"

"Nay, hinny, it isn't. And best ye remember that."

There was no reply Heather could give to dispute such a statement. Fiona was right.

"Well, I should be going to fetch our—" Before Heather could finish, a strapping, ebony-haired young Highlander grabbed her by the arm.

"Are ye dancin'?" Grinning broadly, the young man asked the legendary question.

"Are ye askin'?" Heather replied with the required response, knowing it'd be rude to refuse. Besides, she loved to dance.

The dark-haired Highlander—whose name was Geordie, he promptly informed her—swung her out into the middle of the floor. Though the more sedate court dances were the norm for ladies of her station, Heather had had Beth also teach her the lively country dances. And, being naturally light on her feet, Heather soon picked up the rhythm and steps.

Dance after dance, Heather was besieged by yet another man asking to be her partner. The attention, coupled with the wild abandon of some of the dances, was exhilarating. Only occasionally, as one set ended and before another began, did she have a chance to see how Duncan was faring. Countless young women, she noted with a jaded eye, were also taking their turns asking to dance with him. This went on for almost two hours, before Dora finally called for a halt in which to eat the fine feast set out on the tables.

Flushed and damp from her exertions, Heather quickly filled her plate then took a seat on one of the long, stout benches shoved against the walls. Hungrily, she dug into her mutton stew. After a few succulent spoonfuls of the savory dish, she paused to take a large bite of her buttered bread. At that moment, plate in hand, Duncan strode over and sat down next to her.

"Ye seem to have wasted no time making yerself the center of attention," he said without preamble. "It isn't wise, ye know, considering the talk that'll rise because of it."

Heather nearly choked on her bread. "Th-the center of attention!" she managed finally to croak out. "Whatever are ye talking about?"

Duncan rolled his eyes and shook his head. "In less than two hours' time, ye've danced with every unmarried man here and even a few of the married ones, for good measure. Yet still they clamor for another and another chance to twirl ye about the dance floor."

"And was I supposed to act the prim lady instead," Heather demanded, scooting around to glare at him, "and refuse them? I didn't think such behavior would be appreciated, considering the high value ye Highlanders place on hospitality."

"Highland hospitality doesn't extend to loose behavior in our women." His jaw tautened with anger. "Despite what ye may think of us, our women are well-bred and demure."

"And I'm not?" With the greatest difficulty, Heather clamped down on her outrage. "Is that what ye're saying?"

Slowly, a dark flush suffused his striking features. "Nay, I suppose I didn't quite mean it that way." Duncan glanced away. "I just meant—"

"I know what ye meant, Duncan Mackenzie," Heather snapped. "Ye're angry I wasn't clamoring with all the other lasses to win a dance with ye. Ye think it's yer due, being the strutting cock that ye are."

He swung back to her. "I am *not* a strutting cock! And ye hold yerself in far too high a regard, if ye imagine I care if ye dance wi' me—"

"*With* me," Heather automatically corrected him. "*With* me."

Clamping his lips shut, Duncan just glowered.

"Here now," Janet said, appearing suddenly before them, her own plate of victuals in hand. "I haven't seen either of ye for two weeks now. Move apart and let me sit between ye, so I can visit with ye both."

Glad for an excuse to put some distance between her and Duncan, Heather slid down the bench, not even pretending to want to talk further with either of them. She fixed her attention on her food. Out of the corner of her eye, though, she saw Duncan lean forward and glare at her again before manners forced him to turn back to Janet, who had immediately begun babbling away.

She didn't care, Heather told herself over and over. She didn't care what Duncan Mackenzie thought of her, and she certainly had no wish to dance with him—not now or ever. He *was* being a strutting cock, imagining it was his due that every woman at the *ceilidh* must swoon over him. She had every right to dance with whomever she wished. Indeed, she hadn't noticed any of the other women dancing too often with the same partner, Janet included.

Her fine plate of food, though, was ruined. It tasted

153

now like sawdust, flavorless and dry. Heather made a few halfhearted attempts to eat a few more bites, then gave up. She sat there with her plate on her lap until Beth, with Tavish in tow, walked over. Heather made room for them on the bench.

Her maid surveyed the contents of Heather's plate. "Ye're not eating. Doesn't the food suit yer fancy?"

"It isn't the food," Heather gritted out between clenched teeth. "It's that . . . that man!" She punctuated the last remark with a seething glance in Duncan's direction.

"Och, it's him again, is it?" Beth sighed. "What has he gone and done this time?"

"He accused me of wanton behavior because I danced with any man who asked me!"

Scowling, Tavish leaned over. "Shall I go and thwack him on the head for ye, mistress?"

Envisioning such a scene was most amusing. A tiny smile tugged at the corner of Heather's mouth.

"Och, nay, Tavish, though I'm grateful to ye for the offer."

"It's but a simple case of masculine jealousy," Beth observed calmly between bites of her roast venison.

"Jealousy!" Heather hissed. "I hardly think so. Or, if it was, it was only because I stole some of the attention from him."

"Be that as it may, ye aren't being fair or reasonable here." Beth paused to take a deep swallow of her cider. "Ye've been with him long enough now to know Duncan isn't a vain man, nor one who must find his value in the esteem of others."

"Well, it's still hard to believe he's jealous of the

attention other men show me," Heather grumbled, even as she finally faced the fact that Beth might be right. The consideration, though, she had to admit, was far from displeasing.

"Besides, when it comes to me, he surely isn't *that* uncertain of himself." She shook her head emphatically. "Nay, not Duncan Mackenzie."

"Isn't he?" Beth cocked her head, a mischievous light dancing in her eyes. "Mayhap ye're right. If he truly *was* that uncertain of himself with ye, it could only mean—"

"No more, I say!"

Heather leaped to her feet. Not sparing any of them a backward glance, she stalked over to where the plates were being scraped free of food into a big wooden tub. After cleaning off her own plate, she deposited it on a spare table. Then, taking up her cloak from a hook near the door, Heather threw it around her shoulders and headed outside.

It was a crisp, clear night. Heather walked a short ways to a stand of bare-branched oaks and leaned against the solid bulk of one of the trees. High above, the sky was a huge span of raven black, sprinkled with tiny, twinkling stars and pierced by a bright sliver of the moon.

She gazed at it wistfully. This night, the sky . . . it was all so calm, predictable, and comforting. Not at all like her life—or state of emotions—of late. And all because of that dunderheaded Duncan Mackenzie. Jealous, indeed!

"Ye shouldn't be coming out of doors alone," a deep

male voice intruded on her heated musings. "Especially after yer saucy behavior inside."

Ready for a fight, Heather whirled around, her hands fisted at her sides. Duncan stood there, his tall, broad-shouldered form backlit by the light glowing from the dance hall's windows. He hadn't even bothered to don his cloak, and stood there in shirt and belted plaid. He didn't, though, even for the sharp bite in the air, appear the least bit cold.

"And why would ye care?" she taunted, advancing on him. "What I do is my affair, as are the consequences of that behavior."

"Some of the men might take yer sudden departure as invitation to a passionate little tryst."

She came up to stand right before him. "Well, then I'm fortunate to have ye as my keeper, aren't I? Ye, of all men, would never suspect me of such conduct, would ye?"

"Wouldn't I?"

His face was shadowed, yet even by moonlight Heather could tell his mouth was grim, his jaw set and hard. Once more her anger rose. How dare he even think her capable of playing a wanton, much less imply it?

The possibility that he might doubt her hurt. Her anger faded in a sudden swell of confusion and sadness.

"Ah, Duncan, Duncan. Why are ye being so cruel?" Heather asked softly. "It shouldn't matter to ye what I do. Not that I'd purposely seek to hurt or shame ye or yer family. Surely ye know that, don't ye?"

He stared down at her for a long moment, then flung back his head and gazed up at the heavens, his big body gone rigid, his arms stiff at his sides. "By all the saints," he groaned, "I don't know aught about ye *or* me anymore."

Duncan lowered his head, his burning gaze—even in the darkness—searing clear through Heather. "Forgive me, lass, for my earlier unkind words. Never have I spoken like that to a woman and now to say such things to ye, of all women . . ." He sighed. "I'm a fool who doesn't even know what he wants anymore, save that I know I want ye badly. That I lie awake at night on my pallet and long for ye. That I can scarce keep from touching ye"—his hands went to clasp her arms—"whenever we're together. And when I dare consider kissing ye . . ."

As he spoke, Duncan pulled her close. Her breath caught in her throat. Her heart began an erratic thudding within her chest. Frantic thoughts roiled in her head—thoughts of flight, of calling for help. Yet even as they shot through her mind they were instantly muted, consumed by an ardent hunger to just once be held in his arms and have him kiss her.

"Aye?" she prompted gently. "What do ye think, feel, when ye consider kissing me?"

Lifting on tiptoe, Heather reached for him, grasping Duncan's face in both hands. She gazed deeply into his eyes.

"I've never been kissed by any man besides my father. I never thought, indeed never wished, to kiss another man save my husband. But since I first met ye, Duncan Mackenzie, the thought of kissing ye has been almost constantly on my mind."

"Has it, lass?" he whispered, his warm breath on her face as light as the brush of a butterfly's wing.

"Aye, Duncan. It has."

His hand moved, sliding up her back to clasp her neck, supporting, protecting, caressing it. "And if I kissed ye now would ye find offense in it? Would ye think me an uncivilized brute, an unprincipled savage?"

The deep, husky timbre of his voice vibrated along every sensitized nerve ending Heather possessed. A warmth washed over her, sweet, rich, thick as honey. And she ached for him. Ah, how she ached!

"Though my mind tells me I shouldn't want it so, my heart cries out with longing for yer kiss."

Heather gazed up at him then sighed. Her head lowered. Her hands slid from Duncan's face to rest upon the broad, solid expanse of his chest.

"But it's wrong, Duncan. I'm betrothed. I shouldn't want another man, leastwise not like I want ye."

A long, strong finger crooked beneath her chin. Ever so gently, Duncan lifted her gaze back to his. "And have ye ever considered that mayhap ye shouldn't wed a man ye don't want, lass? How can he possibly make ye happy?"

She smiled sadly. "In truth, I never thought to find happiness in a husband. I but thought to do my duty to my father and family. My happiness, I always believed, would be found elsewhere—in books, learning, and mayhap, eventually, in my children."

"That isn't right, lass." He smiled down in tender compassion. "A man and a woman were meant to find joy and completion, one in the other. They were meant, one in the other, to render support and sustenance in life's journey, in both good times and bad. Never have

158

I believed God gave woman to man solely to procreate the race, so that each might fulfill a duty."

Ah, Heather thought, the tears springing to her eyes, *but it's all so different for ye. Ye've no obligations, save to see to the care of yer family. But I, I've an ancient heritage, the weight of countless noble generations, to bear. I've heavy responsibilities as the Gordon heiress and my father's only child. I can't wed any man I please.*

Any man I please . . .

The words took Heather by surprise. Since her mother's and sister's deaths, she had never once considered the possibility of wedding for love. Indeed, she had chosen to avoid such a fate as if it were some leprous scourge. Yet, in the short time she had known Duncan Mackenzie, her thoughts had turned time and again to such considerations. He had, despite their verbal battles and the heightened tensions when they were together, become the man she'd have chosen, if she had ever had the right to choose.

An unwashed, uncivilized, illiterate savage indeed! He had never been the man she had first imagined him to be. He had, in truth, exceeded even the breeding of the family to which he truly was kin. He was his brother Colin's equal and more.

Perhaps that was what frightened her most. Duncan was everything she could ever want in a man. Duncan was the kind of man a woman could lose her heart to. Yet if he failed to love her as deeply, as passionately, in return . . .

A sudden remembrance shivered through Heather, and it was more bitterly cold than the chill night wind blowing through the glen. *They cannot help themselves . . . They cannot help themselves . . .*

For a fleeting instant, Heather's eyes slid shut. For a fleeting instant she fought a savage battle. Then she opened her eyes. She shoved back from Duncan.

"Yer words are fine, yer beliefs noble," Heather forced herself to say. "And mayhap, for ye, they are quite possible to attain. But they can't ever be for me. I wish they could, but they can't."

"Ah, lass, lass." Sadly, Duncan shook his head. "I thought ye were made of stronger stuff than this. I thought ye possessed more fire, more spirit, than to allow others to dictate yer life for ye."

"And what do ye know of me?" Heather cried, stung by what she imagined were his pitying words. "What do ye know of the events that have shaped me and my decisions, to judge me so?"

"Ye're right." He lifted his burning gaze to hers. "I don't know. Tell me of them. Help me to understand. Help me to help ye."

"And what makes ye think I need yer help, much less want it?"

With a muttered curse, Duncan reached out, encircled her waist with a powerful arm, and pulled her back to him. "What indeed?" he growled, wrapping his other arm across her shoulders to imprison her. "Could it be because ye want me as much as I want ye? That ye feel incomplete without me, as I feel when I'm not with ye?"

Heather struggled within his grasp. "Let me go, Duncan," she cried, sensing he was near the limits of his control. "Ye've no right—"

160

"I've *every* right," he cut her off, his voice gone ragged, raw, and savagely intense. "*Every* right to fight for the woman I want and need!"

Then he said no more. His head lowered. His mouth descended, claiming hers in hungry, demanding possession.

9

For a heart-stopping instant Heather stood there, frozen in shock. Shocked by his boldness. Stunned by the knowing, expert way Duncan's mouth moved over hers, by the feel of him—all hard-muscled, overpowering man—pressed so closely to her.

Never had Heather known such sensations, nor craved them as desperately as she craved them now. Yet even as her heart cried out for more, her mind pulled back. *Danger*, it whispered. *Beware, or ye are surely lost.*

"N-nay." Gasping, Heather wrenched her mouth from his. "Ye can't . . . ye must not—"

"Can't? Must not?" Duncan asked softly. "Why? Because I'm not worthy of ye? Because, for a crude Highlander to kiss ye might sully yer precious, highborn virtue?"

Caught up in a maelstrom of confusion and need, Heather shook her head. "Nay, it isn't that at all. It's just that—"

"Ye didn't like how I kissed ye?" he finished for her, his voice gone harsh, ruthless. "Well, mayhap I was a wee bit rough. It's no excuse, but I confess to having forgotten myself. For that I beg pardon and"—once more he lowered his head toward her—"promise to show ye my more gentlemanly side."

Even as his last words faded, Duncan kissed her again. Ever so softly his lips touched hers and, this time, Heather couldn't restrain the ardor of her own response. With a moan, she rose to meet him. Her hands, still caught between their bodies, crept up to his chest, clutching the coarse fabric of his shirt and his plaid's thick, warm wool.

Ah, but he was sweet. He smelled of fresh air, of pine and musky man. He tasted of rich, potent malt whiskey. And the feel of him, his hands gentle upon her, his body so tall and strong and proud . . .

He kissed her long and deeply this time, his tenderness and care bringing tears to Heather's eyes. Somehow, even in her moments of greatest anger with him, she had always known Duncan was capable of such ardent response, such exquisite sensitivity. He was a man who lived life with a deep passion, whether it was in his love of learning or in the living of dreams he committed to with a wholehearted zeal. Indeed, he was, in every way, the man—the only man—to whom Heather could ever give her heart.

Beware . . . beware of giving yer love to a man.

Like the sharp, swift thrust of a sword, her mother's dying words slashed across Heather's memory, leaving in their wake a deep, lancing pain. She pulled back from Duncan, resting her forehead on his chest. Her breath came in sharp little gasps.

Her greatest fear had finally found form and substance

in the braw, bonny Duncan Mackenzie. She teetered on the precipice of surrendering her heart to a man, a gift she had vowed never to give, even if and when she might finally be forced to wed.

Behind her, a door opened. Light flooded briefly onto the yard separating them from the stone building and the *ceilidh*. Momentarily, the bright sounds of fiddle music and happy voices filled the air.

"Heather? My lady, are ye there?"

It was Beth. Faithful, ever-vigilant Beth, who wouldn't allow her mistress to compromise herself or foolishly follow her heart.

Releasing her hold on Duncan's clothing, Heather leaned back against the strong barrier of his arm. "Let me go," she whispered. "We've been outside alone overlong, and well ye know it."

Duncan chuckled softly, but released her. "It'll never be overlong for me, lass. Spending time alone with ye, I mean."

Heather gathered up her skirts. "I must go."

"Wait." He grabbed her arm. "A moment more."

"And what more is there to say?"

"What we shared here . . . I'm not sorry nor will I apologize for it."

"Be that as it may, it can't happen again."

"Indeed? Pray, why not?"

The first faint tendrils of exasperation threaded through Heather. Must he be so thick-headed? Why must she always be the one forced to cause pain?

"Heather? Answer me, lass. Are ye out there?"

Concern tightened Beth's voice now. Heather winced.

"Aye, I'm here," she called. "A moment and I'll join ye."

She turned back to Duncan. "We can't settle what is between us this night, Duncan Mackenzie, and well ye know it."

"Then ye're asking for a time to sort it all out, is that it?"

He wouldn't be deterred. "Aye." Heather sighed. "Now, I *must* rejoin Beth."

His hand fell from her arm. "Aye, so ye must." Duncan stepped back. "Go. Rejoin Beth."

For an instant longer Heather hesitated, then turned on her heel and strode away. Duncan, however, apparently wasn't content to let things be. The sound of his deep voice, full of male pride and a most irritating edge of triumph, followed Heather as she walked away.

"I enjoyed kissing ye, sweet lass," he called after her. "Even in yer inexpericncc, ye show a surprising gift for pleasing a man. Aye," he repeated huskily. "A surprising gift indeed."

Duncan leaned forward expectantly. "Well, what say ye, lass? Do I finally have ye in checkmate?"

"A moment. A moment." Heather waved impatiently for silence. "Let me think."

She stared hard at the chessboard, considering myriad possible moves that might free her from checkmate. None, however, would work. Duncan, for the first time

165

since she had taught him the game almost a month ago, had finally beaten her and beaten her soundly.

The thought irritated Heather. She had always prided herself on being an excellent chess player. Still, in but a few weeks, a novice, a Highlander no less, had mastered the game well enough to defeat her. True, Duncan had a quick mind and an even quicker facility for games of strategy. It was true, as well, since first being introduced to the game, he had used every free moment not taken up by work or his other lessons to hone his skills.

Tavish, little more than a rank beginner, in less than two days had been the first to fall. Next Duncan had set his sights on Beth, who had learned years ago under Heather's tutelage. She had held out a while longer, refusing to admit defeat until the end of the first week.

But to have Duncan beat *her* so soon . . .

With a sigh of exasperation, Heather tipped over her king. "Aye, Duncan," she admitted with a rueful shake of her head, "ye do indeed have me in checkmate. I concede."

He grinned broadly. "Och, but I do love this game!" He paused, a look of eagerness in his eyes. "Do ye think we could play once more, afore bedtime?"

"It's *before*, not *afore*, Duncan," Heather corrected automatically. "And, nay, I don't think another game would be wise so late in the eve. This one took over two hours as it was. And now that ye've a taste for victory," she added with a smile to soften her refusal, "I won't go so easy on ye."

He threw back his head and gave a shout of laughter.

166

"Ye won't go so easy on me, will ye? And when, Heather Gordon, have ye ever gone easy on me?"

"Tonight, mayhap?" she asked with a saucy grin, which quickly faded when she caught Fiona scowling at them from her chair at the hearth.

"Ye don't like to concede defeat in aught, do ye, lass?"

Though he still smiled, suddenly the look in Duncan's eyes had gone intense, thoughtful. Heather swallowed hard, clamping down on the sudden tightening in her throat and fluttering in her stomach. When he looked at her like that, it was almost more than she could bear.

It was a look that pierced clear through to her soul. A look of such sharp intelligence, of such insight and tender understanding. It made her want to cry. It made her want to stand up, walk around the table, and beg him to take her in his arms, just as he had done that night at the *ceilidh*, now two weeks past. And it made her want to surrender, body and soul, to him.

But she couldn't—and wouldn't—not ever again. She had given her word to Fiona. She had given her word to her father. Indeed, she had given her word, in a sense, to Charlie Seton, even if their betrothal had been arranged long-distance and signed and sealed only by their fathers.

She knew Duncan had soon noted her renewed reserve after their return from the *ceilidh*. Noted it and, bless him for it, wisely chosen not to press the issue. But then he hadn't needed to. Every time he looked at her, every time their eyes met or they inadvertently touched during the course of his lessons, they both knew, both remembered. Indeed, there was no need for words.

Nay, Heather thought in silent response to Duncan's question, recalling her thoughts back to the present, *I don't like to admit defeat. But ye, in so many ways, have tempted me like I've never been tempted before. Each time I rebuild my defenses against ye, ye find some chink in my walls and undermine me yet again. And, each time, just because I don't like to admit defeat and because I've made my commitments to others, I lift myself up and fight anew.*

I only pray my strength holds out, even as ye wait patiently, like some wolf circling its prey.

Heather forced a smile. "Nay, I don't like to lose," she finally said in reply. "But who's saying ye're the master of me, just because ye won a single game?"

"Not I." Duncan chuckled. "Indeed, lass, I wouldn't ever wish to be yer master. Where would the fun be in that?"

She began to gather up the chess pieces and place them in their velvet-lined box. "Ah, then I understand ye at last, Duncan Mackenzie. Ye like the chase and lose interest when the doe falls beneath yer relentless pursuit."

"Nay, nay, lass." Duncan reached across the board and clasped her fingers around one of the ivory chess pieces. "That's not what I meant at all. I only meant to say I like yer spirit. Ye stir me—in mind as much as in body. And I verra much enjoy being with ye. Verra, verra much."

She shouldn't let his words touch her, nor allow him to rouse anew the memories of his kiss at the *ceilidh*. But he did, nonetheless. Indeed, everything about Duncan

Mackenzie touched her, and the more she came to know him, the more enamored she became with him.

"Ye're too kind to say such things," she murmured, pulling her hand from beneath his. Embarrassed, confused, Heather couldn't quite meet Duncan's gaze. "And I'm verra glad ye enjoy being with me." She looked up, once more in control. "It makes our lessons and time together so much more pleasant, wouldn't ye say?"

His gaze narrowed. His jaw hardened. "That isn't what I meant, and well ye know it."

Heather finished putting away the last chess piece, closed the box, and stacked it atop the chessboard. "Be that as it may, it's the only way *I* care to interpret yer words." She stood. "It's best ye place no further meaning on them, either."

Duncan leaned back in his chair, his glance now intent, wary. "If ye think so easily to wipe away—"

His voice faded as he fought to regain control. The fire in his eyes smoldered for an instant longer, then was banked. Finally, Duncan exhaled a deep breath.

"Have it yer way then. It doesn't matter at any rate. What will be, will be."

Once again, irritation filled Heather. The man was far too sure of himself, even if she *had* foolishly given him reason.

"Will it now?"

Once more, the fire in his eyes flamed hot and bright. Once more, he took up the challenge.

"Aye, it will. Just ye wait and see."

For the next five days, a storm swallowed the Kintail region. It snowed heavily. And the times the winds finally died and the snow ceased to fall, the land lay enveloped in a murky, ice-coated bleakness. The men ventured out only to feed and water the animals and bring in firewood. The rest of the time they spent indoors, warmly ensconced in the snug cottage.

Duncan continued to make great progress with his lessons. His thick Highland brogue all but disappeared. With each passing day, his speech became more refined. When it became apparent his mastery of chess surpassed his twin brother's, Heather began teaching Duncan backgammon, as well as several of Colin Stewart's favorite card games. There was, however, only so much time they could spend on lessons before both wearied of the effort it took to concentrate on anything other than their growing attraction for each other.

By the morning of the sixth day, everyone was edgy with the weather-enforced confinement. Luckily, at dawn the sun broke through the thick clouds and a warming wind began to blow through the glen. By mid-morn, though still cold, it was pleasant enough to venture outside. Eager for some stimulating physical activity, Duncan insisted that Heather, Tavish, and Beth join him for a game of curling on the frozen pond.

Skeptically, Heather eyed the four wheat straw brooms and a large, round, flat-bottomed rock Duncan had gathered and placed near the door. "I don't think I wish to—"

"Posh, lass," Duncan immediately silenced her. "It'll do ye a world of good to get out in the fresh air and use something more than yer brain for a change. Why, ye're growing positively pallid, cooped up inside all the time."

"I keep myself well entertained," Heather said in her own defense, feeling rather miffed anyone should intimate she was lazy or afraid of a little work. "Besides yer lessons and my reading, I'm learning to weave and am even trying my hand at a bit of cooking. I'd hardly say I don't get any exercise."

"Aye, aye," Duncan agreed laughingly. "Ye're most certainly not a slothful woman. The outdoors, though, is a fine teacher in its own right. And a mind not periodically stimulated by fresh air and exercise is a mind that can't function at its best."

"So, now ye're accusing me of becoming dim-witted, are ye?"

Duncan sighed and rolled his eyes. "Women!"

Grabbing up her warm cloak and the thick woolen mittens Fiona had knitted for her, he handed them to Heather, opened the front door, and gently but firmly ushered her outside.

The sun was bright, the snow sparkled as if it had been sprinkled with millions of tiny diamonds, and the air was crisp and bracing. Heather threw on her cloak and donned her mittens. Then, after a narrow look at Duncan, she headed out in the direction of the frozen pond. Beth soon followed, the two men bringing up the rear with the stone and four brooms.

As she walked along a path leading down to the pond Duncan had cleared earlier, Heather reluctantly admitted that he had been right. Getting out into the fresh air and sunshine would indeed do her a world of good. Already she felt revitalized, and eagerly anticipated the excitement of playing an ancient Scottish sport.

A thick layer of snow blanketed the pines, their overburdened forms drooping like an army of weary soldiers. The tang of peat smoke wafting from the cottage's chimney mingled with the clean, crisp Highland air. In the distance a mountain cat screamed. High overhead an eagle shrieked and soared.

It was indeed a grand and glorious day, Heather thought, glancing about her. A day overflowing with promise. A day that stirred the blood and gratified the heart. A day to share with good friends . . . and one very special man.

"For a lass who didn't even wish to step foot outside," Duncan observed, catching up with her at last, "ye're certainly keeping a lively pace. Dare I hope ye've changed yer mind and are now in agreement with me?"

Heather shot him a slanting look. "It's a beautiful day. I'll give ye that. The game, however, is quite another matter."

"But now ye're willing, leastwise, to try it?"

"Aye, I suppose so."

Duncan gave a shout of laughter.

"Well, don't go on so about it," Heather grumbled, even as his exuberant delight secretly pleased her. "It isn't as if ye've beaten me at anything besides chess, ye know."

"Nay, I suppose not." Duncan halted a few feet from the pond. "It's a good beginning, though."

"A beginning to what?" Heather asked, instantly suspicious.

172

"Why, to transforming ye into a braw, bonny Highland lass, of course."

Heather gave a snort of disdain. "Ye dream wild dreams, Duncan Mackenzie. I've no intention of becoming a Highland lass or even of ever returning to the Highlands, once these remaining months with ye are over. I'm a Gordon, born and bred, and my first duty is to my family and home."

He shrugged, apparently unperturbed. "Mayhap and mayhap not. Have ye forgotten that yer mither was a Mackenzie? That already makes ye half Highlander. Besides, ye shouldn't close yerself off to new possibilities or change. To do so shrivels the soul and limits the mind. Be open, lass. Live life. Experience all its great potential."

He gestured about him. "And *see* what is truly before ye. What the good Lord, in His infinite love, has done for ye."

"The *good* Lord?" Heather's mouth twisted in derision. "I long ago lost hope in aught *He* could do for me. Still, that failed hope does naught to lessen the beauty of this day, or the fine company I'm keeping." She laughed. "Indeed, I'm wondering if the fine weather and glorious scenery always brings out the poet in ye?"

"Only in the Highlands, lass," he said with a grin. "Only in the Highlands."

Aye, she thought, there was indeed something about being in the Highlands. Perhaps it *was* in her blood more deeply than she cared to admit. Or perhaps it was the fresh mountain air and the simple yet healthy life she had been living since her arrival. Or perhaps, just per-

173

haps, it was the exhilarating effect a certain handsome Highlander had upon her.

It didn't matter. One way or another her time here was limited. Already a full month had passed and only two remained. Then, only three months more after that, she'd be wed. Wed to a kind, well-born man, but a man who wasn't and would never be a man the like of Duncan Mackenzie.

As quickly as that thought struck Heather, she shook it off. "Well, are we going to stand here all day," she inquired with a forced brightness, "or do ye intend to teach me curling?"

"Och, aye . . . It's simple really. The object is to slide a stone down the length of the pond and come as close to a marker as possible. To move the stone along and control its direction, ye sweep the ice in front of the stone with the brooms."

"I take it there'll be two teams?"

"Aye."

"Men against women?"

"That wouldn't be fair."

Heather considered for a moment. "Fine. Then I choose Tavish."

Duncan eyed her, then shrugged. "Have it yer way. I'll warn ye now, though. I'm one of the best curling players in all of Kintail."

She laughed. "And ye don't like to lose at aught, do ye?"

He grinned. "Nay, I don't. But ye knew that already, didn't ye?"

Though his words and smile were lighthearted, there

was an added meaning in the look he sent her . . . a hot, piercing, determined look. He hadn't forgotten for a minute, Heather realized with a forbidden thrill, about the *ceilidh* or their kiss, or the things said between them that night. He hadn't forgotten and had no intention ever of allowing her to forget, either.

Beth and Tavish, talking and laughing, arrived at that moment. Grateful for the interruption, Heather turned to them. Already their faces were flushed and their eyes sparkled each time they looked at each other. Heather smiled. If she didn't miss her guess, her maidservant would leave the Highlands with a future husband in tow.

"Tavish is my partner. Ye're paired with Duncan," she informed her maid. At the crestfallen look in Beth's eyes, Heather laughed. "Come, come now. The way ye two moon over each other of late, it'd hardly be much of a game if ye and Tavish played together, and well ye know it."

She took three brooms from Tavish, handing one to Duncan, one to Beth, and keeping the third for herself.

"Lead on." She motioned Duncan forward with an impatient wave of her hand.

The next two hours sped by in a gleeful if frenzied melee, interspersed with frequent mishaps that sent one or more players tumbling to the ice as they raced up and down the pond. True to his word, Duncan maintained an overwhelming command of the curling stone, scoring point after point with only minimal assistance from Beth. Heather, however, refused to admit defeat.

She dove repeatedly in front of Duncan, her broom sweeping furiously before her. Most times, however, she succeeded in accomplishing little more than temporarily diverting his forward progress before he nimbly dodged and continued forward once more. In spite of Heather and Tavish's repeated dismal defeats, there was laughter, spills, and invigorating exertion. Before the foursome realized it, Malcolm was calling them to the midday meal.

Flushed, damp with perspiration, her cloak and much of her skirts a sodden mess, Heather followed Beth and Tavish back up toward the cottage. Duncan soon joined her.

"Ye look most becoming with yer red cheeks and hair all askew," he said, grinning down at her. "And ye played a most ferocious, if bumbling, game."

"Grant me but a few more weeks of practice," Heather replied tartly, "and then dare call me bumbling."

"With the natural talent ye displayed today, I'd be a fool to dare such a thing." Duncan's grin faded. "The spring thaw, though, will soon be upon us. The pond ice will thin rapidly and become unstable. I'd wager we'll have few opportunities safely to play again."

Heather pretended affront. "And isn't it so like ye to teach me a game ye know I'll never have the chance to master? Must ye always be the one who is best at everything?"

"Nay." His expression turned serious. "Indeed, the thing I want most to be best at seems the one thing I'll never achieve."

176

Heather's steps slowed. "And pray, what might that be?"

"Think on it, lass," was his enigmatic reply. "Then tell me if ye can't guess what I want most in the world."

There was something in his eyes, something deep and dark and intense, that should've warned Heather not to press further. Yet that look of yearning, mingled with a fleeting vulnerability, beckoned with an irresistible force. That a man could feel so deeply about anything intrigued her. What a man wanted deeply was always a good measure of that man.

Heather drew to a halt and turned to him. "Truly, Duncan. I don't know. I'd be most interested, though, in hearing what it is ye want most in the world."

"And why is that, lass?"

She smiled. "Why else? It'd help me to understand ye better."

"Am I such a mystery to ye then?"

"Aye, that ye are. Ye're not at all the simple Highlander I first imagined ye to be."

He glanced away, finding sudden interest in the distant, snow-capped mountains. After a long moment, Duncan turned back to her.

"Not at all the simple Highlander, eh?" He sighed. "I'll tell ye true, lass. It'd be far better for me if I were."

Unease twined about Heather's heart. Was he already beginning to regret this masquerade he was preparing himself for?

"Mayhap," she finally said, knowing she must make some sort of comment. "But then, I can't say I'd find ye as interesting, or that ye would've suited as well for the role ye must soon play."

"Aye, but when it's all over ye'll return to yer fine life, as I must to the only life I know." As he spoke, a haunted expression shadowed Duncan's eyes. "Yet, in all truth, will it ever be the life I'll want again? It's a bothersome question. A question that, of late, gnaws most mercilessly at me. It's a question, as well, that frightens me, Heather. It frightens me like naught I've ever known before."

10

Heather stared back at Duncan. It tore at her heart to hear him voice the same fears that had been hers since that January day her father had first revealed his plan to rescue the queen. It was bad enough she'd had to carry the secret with her all these months, a secret that had grown increasingly difficult to keep the longer she had come to know Duncan. But it was a secret she had still vowed to uphold.

Was there nothing she could say to ease his pain without revealing what she dared not reveal? His fears were justifiable. He cared for his parents; he was a man who took his responsibilities seriously. But he was also a man who seemed to need more than what a simple Highland life could ever give.

In the past, it was evident Duncan filled whatever free time he had with as much intellectual and artistic stimulation as could be found in such a remote and rustic place. He had his books, his wood carving, and now, Heather thought with a tiny smile, he also had his chess. But what if, after learning all she had to teach him, then pretending to the life of a nobleman for the brief time it took to rescue the queen, Duncan discovered a hunger for what had always truly been his birthright? What would he do then?

He was a man who straddled two worlds—the world of a simple Highlander as well as one of a Scottish lord. Would either world truly accept him, though, once he knew the truth? Duncan's twin might well hate his brother for his involvement in the plot to rescue the queen. He might also hate him for the possible threat to Colin's now sole right to the Stewart estates. Indeed, if Duncan *were* truly the firstborn of the two . . .

None of that mattered; none of that could be ascertained or resolved just now. All that mattered was Duncan. Duncan, who stood before her, his eyes shadowed with pain, his expression bleak and confused.

Impulsively, Heather reached out and took his hand. "Dinna fash yerself," she said, squeezing his hand in a gesture of comfort. "It'll all work out in the end."

He smiled sadly. "Ye're sweet to say so, lass. But already, since meeting ye I know my life has changed. And if, when it's all over, I lose ye—"

"Och, Duncan. Don't say it. Don't say it!" She tugged on his hand, attempting to pull him toward the house. "This isn't the right time for such words."

Duncan dug in his heels, refusing to be led away. "Will there ever be a right time, lass?"

A pair of penetrating green eyes locked with hers. A pair of eyes brimming with hope—and an unguarded look of love that took Heather's breath away. Panic rose to squeeze the breath from her lungs.

Frantically, she glanced around, seeking Beth, Tavish—anyone. To her dismay, everyone had already gone inside. There was no hope for succor, no rescue. She forced herself to meet Duncan's steady gaze.

"I-I can't say if there'll ever be a right time," she began slowly, choking back the response she truly wished to give. "Mayhap . . . when all this is over, but I can't promise ye aught. Though we seem to share much in common, there are yet things on which we differ greatly."

"Besides the difference in our social standing, ye mean?"

"Aye, that and the fact ye seem a God-fearing man, while I . . . I no longer bear any such reverent or loving feelings for God in my heart."

"And would ye care to tell me why that's so, lass?" He stared down at her, a troubled look in his eyes. "Surely ye didn't always feel such animosity toward the Lord?"

"Nay." Heather glanced away. "My mither was a kind, generous, deeply religious woman. If anyone deserved the Lord's favor, it was she. But He turned His back on her in so verra many ways, and she died in such pain. Such deep pain and despair. And, all the while, those who lived lives of selfishness and betrayal continued on, unscathed and indifferent."

She riveted her anger-bright gaze back to him. "I'll never forgive God for that. He's not fair. He doesn't care!"

Duncan took her hand. "Och, lass. Be assured that, with the Lord, no good is ever lost. And He *does* care. Indeed, His love's unfailing and as high as the heavens. Sometimes, though, it seems as if there's no reward for faithfulness, that all hope has died and there's little point in continuing on. Yet it's in those darkest times that the Lord is closest, bearing us up. All we must do is cling to Him and believe."

"Believe?" Her lips curled in derision. "And what is there to believe in? That the good reap pain and rejection and despair for their efforts, while the evil ones go through life untouched? That the harder one tries to love and serve God, the greater the trials?"

He sighed and gave her hand a gentle squeeze. "It may well seem so at times, that I'll grant ye. And man, being the weak creature that he is, always finds it easier to settle for less than to take the right turn, to choose ideals instead of baser things. Nonetheless, whichever path we choose, whether we believe in God or not, no one walks through life unscathed. A spiritual person, though, isn't destroyed or made worse by the pain. And even our weakness, our doubts and fears, can lead us closer to God if we let them."

Once more, anger welled, and Heather gave voice to bitter thoughts she knew she should've kept to herself. "Fine words," she muttered, looking down, "coming from a man who has never experienced a moment of weakness or been brought low by doubts and fears. Who has never lost someone more dear than life itself."

"And so I can't understand aught of what ye're going through? Is that it, lass?" Duncan released her hand. "That I'm one of those folk who, therefore, goes through life unscathed and indifferent?"

Frustration filled her. Och, now she had gone and done it for sure!

"Nay, I didn't mean it like that! I just meant . . ."

As she spoke, Heather forced herself once more to meet Duncan's gaze. To her surprise, there was no answering anger burning there. There was nothing but compassion and love, *such* love! Further words or attempts at explanation shriveled and died in her throat.

"Then what did ye mean, lass?" As if determined not to permit her to shy away from him or what seemed a rapidly disintegrating conversation, he grasped her by both arms. "That I've never been truly tested—neither my faith nor my courage? And that, until I am, all my fine claims to honor and integrity and trust in the Lord aren't worth much? Is that what ye really meant to say?"

Aye, that's exactly what I meant, Heather thought, going stiff and unyielding in his clasp. But she also knew she had already said far more than was kind or wise. Let Duncan have his deluded faith in God. *He* obviously needed it.

She, on the other hand, didn't need anything to do with God anymore. Despite Duncan's claims to the contrary, she had never felt God's presence in those dark days when her mother lay dying—a failing that hadn't been for want of trying. The long, fruitless, despairing hours on her knees had produced nothing, however, but cold-stiffened joints and an aching back.

Heather expelled a deep breath. "It's not my place to pass judgment on ye and yer religious beliefs. I beg yer pardon for my unkind words. Best, though, from here on out that we not speak—"

"Duncan! Heather! Dinner grows cold while ye two stand out there jabbering."

At the sound of Fiona's voice, overlaid with a thinly veiled anger, Heather jumped back. Immediately, Duncan released her. Like two sheepish children caught in a disobedient act, they wheeled about to face Fiona.

For a long moment the older woman, hands on hips, met and held Heather's gaze. Then, with a disgusted shake of her head, Fiona turned and hobbled back into the cottage.

Without another word or look in Duncan's direction, Heather followed quickly after.

"A word wi' ye, hinny," Fiona said. "In private, if ye please."

Heather glanced up from the book of Dunbar's poems she was reading and met Fiona's gaze. The older woman's glance was anything but warm. After three days of little conversation between her and Fiona save for what was absolutely necessary, Heather knew the moment of reckoning had finally arrived. Silently and without protest she marked her page, closed her book, and set it aside on the table. Then she rose and walked across the common room and into her bedroom. Fiona followed stiffly, her wooden cane tip-tapping across the floor, and closed the bedroom door firmly behind her.

Taking up the stool before Duncan's workbench and carrying it over to the window, Heather motioned for Fiona to seat herself in the more comfortable chair already placed there. "It's about Duncan and me, isn't it?

184

About that day ye found him holding me?" she asked as she settled herself on the stool. "It wasn't how it looked, ye know."

"Pish!" Fiona snapped, settling herself in the chair. "It was exactly how it looked, and well ye know it! Despite all yer promises to the contrary, ye can't stay away from my son. I should've known better than to trust the word of some scheming noblewoman."

"I'm not scheming," Heather protested hotly. "Duncan's a fine man, indeed, the finest man I've ever known. What woman alive wouldn't care for him?"

"I'm not concerned about other women," his mother cried. "I'm concerned what *yer* caring will do to him."

"And pray, exactly what do ye think I'll do to him?"

"Och, come, come now, hinny. Don't play the innocent wi' me." Fiona made a motion of disgust. "Ye'll break his heart, of course, then dance off wi' nary a backward glance."

"And what of my heart?" Heather climbed off the stool and began to pace to and fro. "Och, but then I've forgotten. I'm a scheming noblewoman intent on adding Duncan's heart to my collection of trophies, aren't I?"

"Aren't ye?"

Heather whirled around and rushed over to Fiona. She sank to her knees before the woman now glaring furiously down at her.

"Nay." She gave a fierce shake of her head. "I swear it. I'd never purposely hurt Duncan. He's a good man. In truth, he deserves far, far better than the likes of me."

Some of the tension eased from Fiona's lined and weathered face. "Then why do ye persist in leading him on?"

"Leading him on?"

His mother rolled her eyes. "Och, can ye truly be so dim-witted? Duncan's falling in love wi' ye. Do ye know how many times he's done that, counting this time with ye, in all the years I've known him? Do ye?"

"Nay," Heather replied softly. "How many times?"

"Once, lass. Once."

Stunned, Heather stared up at her. "I don't believe it. Especially not in a man as virile and handsome as Duncan. Surely some lass, at some time, has managed to capture his heart."

"Well, believe it or not as ye will," Fiona said with an indignant sniff. "But I know my son and know his heart. And I won't have ye breaking it, if I have to send ye and yer servants packing this verra day."

Tears filled Heather's eyes. She quickly glanced away.

"Ye can't do such a thing. The queen . . . the plot . . ."

"Ye and yer fine father can concoct another plot. Ye found Duncan. Ye can just as well find another look-alike for that fancy young lord."

Heather wiped the tears away and met the old woman's steely gaze. Fiona didn't know, didn't understand. But then, how could she?

"Nay, we can't," she insisted softly. "There won't be enough time, if a second look-alike even exists in all of Scotland."

"Then concoct another plan altogether. I don't care. I just want ye out of my house. Now. Today!"

"And what reason will ye give Duncan for my hasty departure?"

Fiona's eyes widened. She swallowed convulsively.

"I-I don't know. But I'm certain a sly lass like yerself could easily think of something. Besides, he'd accept it better coming from ye at any rate."

Heather's mind raced. She didn't wish to drive some acrimonious wedge between her and Duncan's mother. The older woman had treated her kindly, even generously, from the start. She didn't want her thinking badly of her, either. But her first loyalty lay with her father and Queen Mary. She must not forget that, though the remembrance was becoming more and more difficult with each passing day.

"Well," Heather began, forcing herself to utter words that filled her with loathing, "I won't lie to Duncan. If ye truly want me out of yer house, then tell him yerself. Have a care, though," she added, hating herself and the game she must play in order to win. "I don't think Duncan will take my departure happily. Indeed, if yer suspicions are true, who's to say he won't wish to return with me rather than remain here?"

She leaned forward, resting her arms on her thighs. "Indeed, have ye given any thought to that possibility, madam?"

This time, it was Fiona's eyes that filled with tears. "Och, ye cruel, h-heartless w-wench!" she quavered. "Ye'd steal my only child from me without an instant's hesitation, wouldn't ye?"

187

"Nay, it isn't my intention at all," Heather hastened to say, feeling instant remorse for her cold words. "But what choice do ye leave me, Fiona? Just as ye feel loyalty and love for yer son, so do I for my father. How can I let him down, or fail him when he needs my help so badly?"

"I never begrudged ye yer loyalty to yer father," Duncan's mother muttered, her gnarled fingers worrying the rounded head of her cane. "I just wanted ye to stay away from my son. Ye gave me yer word, ye did. Why, oh why can't ye keep it? He's naught to ye but some plaything wi' which to wile away the time until ye can return to yer fine lords. Yet when ye leave, it'll be Duncan who'll be devastated, not ye."

"How do ye know that?" Heather glanced down, her hands fisting in her lap. "Do ye truly think me so cold and calculating, so devoid of emotion, that I don't feel as strongly for Duncan as he does for me?"

"Then ye're saying ye love him? That ye'll toss aside all yer fine titles and elegant life, and come back to live wi' Duncan once the queen is free?" Fiona leaned forward, her eyes smoldering, intense. "It's what ye must do, ye know, if ye're to wed my son. Come back to the Highlands and care for him and the bairns he'll soon give ye, like a good wife should."

Heather's throat went dry. Her heart throbbed madly beneath her breast. Her clenched hands grew damp. Wed Duncan? Come back to live with him here? Care for him and the bairns she'd soon bear him?

Strangely, the consideration of such a life was most appealing. True, the life would be hard, filled with work, lacking in many of the comforts she had come to know and love, but somehow Heather knew it would also be a life both rich and happy. To wake up in the morn in Duncan's arms, to laugh and fight with him, to spend long winter eves playing chess or reading with him . . . And then, one day, to bear his children, to suckle them at her breast and watch them grow . . .

But to do so would be to turn her back on her father and her heritage, to risk all for the love of a man—a man who might ultimately betray her as her father had betrayed her mother, and her sister's husband had betrayed her.

Heather shuddered. It was far too much to risk, especially for a man she had known but a month.

"I care for Duncan," she said, meeting Fiona's searching gaze with a steady, direct one of her own. "I can't say I love him, leastwise not after only knowing him such a short time. But would I sacrifice all for the man I love?" Heather paused a moment, then smiled sadly. "I'd like to think I would, if I truly believed that man was willing to do the same for me."

"Yet ye aren't convinced any man ever would, are ye?" the old woman observed shrewdly. "Yer father certainly never struck me as the type to do so. Did he break yer mither's heart, then?"

Heather's eyes widened. An unwelcome heat flooded her face.

"It's impertinent of ye to ask such a thing. My parents' relationship is a private matter and will never be the topic of idle talk."

Fiona shrugged. "Suit yerself, hinny. I was but trying to understand the basis of yer unwillingness to commit yer heart and life to my son. I can't help ye, and him, if I don't understand."

"I never asked for yer help and I don't need it!"

"Don't ye?" She cocked her head. "Well, mayhap not. But I also won't stand by and watch ye make a muddle of yer relationship wi' Duncan, either."

"Are ye offering yer help then?"

Once again, Fiona shrugged, then stood awkwardly to leave. "Mayhap. Or mayhap it's but a warning. It'll all depend on ye."

I-I can't say if there'll ever be a right time . . . Mayhap . . . when all this is over, but I can't promise ye aught.

As Duncan mucked out the cattle byre that morn, Heather's words roiled repeatedly in his mind. And, as he worked, his emotions once again swung, as they had for the past three days, from great joy to utter disbelief to a gnawing frustration. Three days . . . and not another mention of the subject. Three days . . . and still he couldn't banish it from his mind.

Surely he had misunderstood her. Surely she hadn't meant there was hope for them, hope that someday something might come of their growing feelings for each other. Surely he had placed a deeper meaning on her words because it was what he had wanted so desperately to hear.

To take Heather as wife . . . such a consideration filled Duncan with wild dreams and even wilder emotions. Yet a more cautious, logical side of him warned not to presume anything when it came to a certain proud and headstrong beauty. If Heather Gordon was nothing else, she was a woman who'd give her love and devotion only if she wished to.

Besides, whether Heather returned his feelings or not wasn't the issue. The barriers of class and breeding still stood between them. And an even greater barrier had finally lifted between them as well. The barrier of Heather's estrangement from God.

Despite her protestations to the contrary, Duncan knew in his heart that Heather was a believer. Her anger against the Lord was far too powerful to rise from any other source than that of one who had once loved and lost. In his heart of hearts, Duncan also sensed that Heather longed for a reconciliation, if only she could find some way out of the darkness that currently enshrouded her soul.

God willing, he hoped he might be the person who could lead her back into the light of God's love. His mouth quirked in sad irony. Aye, he was a man full of hope. It would take more than hope, though, to overcome all the obstacles yet in his way.

All morn Duncan worked like a man possessed, tossing forkfuls of sodden, smelly straw into a rickety wooden cart, then laboriously dragging the cart from the byre through the mud to dump it in the steaming manure pile behind the building. More than anything he had ever desired, despite his misgivings and fears, Duncan found he wanted to spend every spare moment he could with Heather. It was, indeed, the only way he would finally ascertain her true feelings and discern exactly what her meaning that day had really been.

191

Finishing his morning chores a half hour earlier than usual, Duncan bade his father and Tavish a brusque farewell and headed back up to the cottage. As he walked along, the beauty of the day enveloped him. The sun was surprisingly warm, and the snow that had kept them closed up in the house for most of the past week had begun to melt with a vengeance.

Already, tender shoots of new grass were peeking through myriad slushy spots of snow. Their bright green contrasted with the delicate, drooping, white-petaled snowdrops that had bravely pushed their way up beneath the oaks and birches. The daffodils and yellow primroses, Duncan well knew, wouldn't be far behind.

Viewing the rebirth of the land after the dismal, bitterly cold winter, Duncan knew a joyous satisfaction such as he had never known before. It was oddly special this year, though. This year, the rebirth of life was mirrored in his own experiences, in coming to know and love Heather Gordon.

He should be shocked, so easily to recognize and admit to an emotion such as he felt for Heather. Never before had he felt anything for a woman—save for the filial love he had for his mother. Or at least nothing more than a distant affection or wry tolerance, he added, thinking briefly of Janet Mackenzie.

As he neared the cottage, his gaze snagged on the large wooden box he had constructed for Cuini and her brood. In the rapidly warming days of spring, he had daily carried it outside for several hours to sit near the steps leading to the cottage door. Inside, basking in the sun, was the little terrier and three of her four six-week-old pups. Puzzled by the surprising absence of one pup, Duncan paused to look around. The wee miscreant was nowhere to be seen.

He shrugged. Most likely Heather had the pup inside and was playing with it. She had taken a liking to Cuini and her babes over the past several weeks, and was frequently found sitting beside the box, watching them in fascination.

Heather, however, Duncan soon discovered when he entered the cottage, was also nowhere to be found. He frowned, the first tendrils of unease snaking through him. Where could the lass be?

He walked over to Beth, who sat with Fiona at the loom, and glowered down at her. "Yer mistress. Why aren't ye with her, wherever she is? Ye *are* supposed to be chaperoning her, aren't ye?"

There was no mistaking the implied reproof in Duncan's words. High color rushed to Beth's cheeks.

"She said she wished to sit outside on the stoop and watch the pups. There seemed no need to—"

"Well, Heather isn't there now and obviously isn't here, either," Duncan snapped, his ire rising apace with his growing concern. "And I just came from the cattle byre, so she also isn't there."

Beth's eyes went wide. She rose to her feet.

Fiona glanced from Beth to Duncan. "Now where has that headstrong lass gone off to now?" she muttered in disgust. "She becomes more difficult by the moment!"

Duncan spared his mother but a seething glance, then turned on his heel and hurried to the door. A pup was missing and Heather had gone outside to play with it, he thought as he leaped down from the steps, then paused to scan the area. Where might Heather and an errant pup possibly be?

It was a mite early for reivers to be in the area, filching whatever cattle they took a liking to. Unlikely but always possible. And if they had found Heather somewhere out of earshot of the house . . .

The consideration of what they might do to a woman as bonny as Heather turned Duncan's blood to ice. He broke out in a run, heading down the hill to where the trees thickened near the pond.

Halfway to the pond, Duncan finally caught sight of Heather. Her gown and cloak copiously dripping water, she staggered up the hill, Cuini's pup clutched to her. Her long hair had fallen free of its cap and hung in sodden hanks. Her lips were blue, and she shivered uncontrollably.

Duncan slid to a halt before her, took one look, and immediately gathered her up into his arms. "Little fool," he muttered, swinging around and striding back toward the cottage. "Ye fell in the pond, didn't ye?"

"Th-the pup," she said, her teeth chattering. "It w-went out onto the i-ice and fell through a m-melted hole. I-I tr-tried to reach it by l-leaning out from the b-bank, but then I sl-slipped and f-fell in."

She held the pup tightly with one hand, using the other to shove back the dripping hair falling into her face. "I-I was l-lucky the water wasn't over my h-head. I-I never realized how heavy long s-skirts are when w-wet."

"Nor how quickly and dangerously cold ye can get falling into a half-frozen pond."

194

By all the saints, Duncan thought, hefting her chill-racked body more tightly to him. She could have drowned, and no one would've realized it in time. In but a few minutes, Heather could have been gone from his life—forever.

The realization filled him with terror. He pulled her so close he could feel her trembling body through the wet clothes they both now wore. If he had lost her, just when he had finally discovered how much he loved her, needed her . . .

"Ye won't ever go down to the pond alone again—runaway pup or no," he growled, his voice, in his fear and anger, taking on a harsher tone than he wished. "And ye'll never, do ye hear me, *never* again go outdoors without either Tavish or myself with ye."

She stiffened in his arms. "And s-since when have ye become my n-nursemaid, Duncan Mackenzie? I'm quite capable of t-taking care of myself."

Foolish, headstrong woman!

"And I say ye don't know the dangers here," he snarled in return. "Soon reivers will stalk these hills and mountains, searching for sheep and cattle to steal. Many are outlaws living outside the control or protection of a clan. If they come upon a defenseless lass . . . well, there's no telling what might happen to ye."

"Then t-teach me how to d-defend myself." Heather turned in his arms to stare up at him. "There may come a t-time when ye and T-Tavish and yer father might be busy elsewhere. There may come a t-time when ye'll wish ye had m-my assistance. T-teach me, Duncan, so I c-can be of use then."

195

He halted. "Ye truly wish to learn how to use a bodice knife, how to defend yerself with it?" he asked, staring down at her in disbelief. By mountain and sea, but she never ceased to amaze him. "Ye'd be willing to fight, bloody yer hands, even kill someone if need be?"

Heather angled her head and looked up at him through her lashes. "And what's s-so strange about that?" Her voice now held a note of affront. "I m-may be more daintily raised than yer Highland l-lasses, but I'm still a Scotswoman. I'd f-fight to defend myself, my home and l-loved ones."

"Aye, I suppose ye would," Duncan said, a smile at last cracking the tense, hard lines of his face. "Ye've always been a fighter, ye have, Heather Gordon. I knew that from the first moment I saw ye."

"D-did ye now?"

"Aye, that I did." He stepped out again. "Yer knife lessons will have to wait a bit, though. First we need to get ye out of these wet clothes and warmed before ye take a chill."

"P-pish." Heather's laugh, racked as it was by her body-wrenching shivers, was unsteady. "D-dinna fash yerself on that account, D-Duncan Mackenzie. I'm as st-strong as a h-horse."

Though Heather was soon stripped of her wet clothes by her overwrought maidservant, roughly toweled dry and dressed in a warm nightrail, then tucked into bed with hot bricks at her feet, she nonetheless took a chill. By that night, her body felt as if it were on fire. Her throat was raw and scratchy, and a cough racked her body. She slept fitfully. By morn, her muscles ached and the fever rose. Heather began to drift in and out of consciousness.

Through it all, however, she imagined that Duncan was there, never leaving her side, bending over her when she cried out, his green eyes dark with concern. Even in her feverish haze that knowledge comforted her, that assurance he was near. She began to sleep. By the second night after the pond accident, her fever broke.

Chirping birds, the sounds of voices and activity in the common room, and the scent of bannocks baking finally woke Heather the next morn. She opened her eyes to bright sunshine flooding the room.

Heather stretched, gingerly easing the ache of fever-abused muscles, yawned, then looked around. Beside the bed, a tall, broad-shouldered man slept in a chair.

Duncan.

Heather smiled. So, her impressions hadn't been the product of a fever-besotted brain after all. He *had* been with her.

She turned, rolling to the edge of the bed, and took the hand resting limply on the chair arm. Squeezing it gently, she looked up at him, her heart swelling with gratitude and affection. *Duncan . . . ah, Duncan . . .*

He stirred, opening his eyes. When he realized she was awake, he smiled.

"Ye're better then, are ye, lass?"

"Aye, Duncan."

Heather's heart swelled with tenderness as she noted the dark circles smudging his eyes and the weary slump to his shoulders. He had lost sleep, been worried about her. Hot tears stung her eyes.

"How long . . ."—she swallowed hard and licked her dry lips—"how long have ye been with me?"

"It doesn't matter. We all took turns with ye, sponging yer brow, giving ye sips of water when ye were coherent enough to swallow. We were all concerned."

"Ye're all good and true friends." Heather stirred restlessly, tried to push to her elbows in an effort to sit up, and failed. "Help me, if ye please, Duncan. I'm as weak as a newborn kit."

"Aye, that ye are, lass." He stood, leaned down, and, grasping her gently beneath her arms, pulled her up in bed. "Suffice it to say, we were quite worried about ye."

He smelled of fresh air and wool. Of clean man and pine. She savored his scent, just as she savored the brief feel of his big, strong hands on her as he helped her to sit. She hunkered down against the pillows he had just fluffed behind her and smiled.

"I'm sorry to be such a burden. I know ye've many duties, and yer lessons . . ."

"Hush, lass." Duncan laid a silencing finger to her lips. "No one begrudges ye the time they spent with ye. No one."

She was tempted to ask about Fiona, wondering if the older woman had forgiven her at last. Then Heather thought better of it. If Duncan was yet unaware of the difficulties between her and his mother, it was better to let that lie. Besides, it was a problem best worked out between her and Fiona.

"I'll be back to my old self in no time. I promise." She managed an encouraging smile. "Why, we could even resume yer lessons after the midday meal. I'm certain—"

"Ye'll *rest* after the midday meal," Duncan was swift to correct her. "And I don't want to hear one word of protest from ye about it, either. Time enough to continue my lessons in a few days, *after* ye're fully recovered."

Heather opened her mouth to inform him yet again he wasn't her nursemaid, then thought better of it. It was hardly fair recompense for his solicitous care, immediately to begin arguing with him. She sighed, lowering her gaze to the fine, hand-worked coverlet.

"As ye wish."

A chuckle rumbled deep in Duncan's chest. "Ye're quite biddable, ye know, when ye're sick. I think I like that. Aye, I think I like that verra much."

"Do ye now?" Heather's head snapped up. "Well, don't come to expect it. Once I'm feeling more like my old self, I—"

"Ye'll once more be the saucy, sharp-tongued wench as ye were before," he finished for her. "But that's fine as well. I like ye saucy and sharp-tongued, too."

She arched a slender brow, inexplicably pleased. "Do ye now?"

Duncan nodded with vehement conviction. "Aye, that I do."

11

"Nay, Duncan. Ye can't go," Heather pleaded with frantic intensity two weeks later. "Ye can't risk yerself so close to the time we must depart for Kinross. It's too dangerous."

"Lass, lass," Duncan said, chuckling. "It's still nearly a month before our departure for Kinross and Lochleven Castle."

"I don't care. I say again. It's too dangerous." She took hold of his arm, her nails digging into hair-roughened flesh and its underlying muscle. Somehow, some way, Heather thought, her panic rising, she *had* to make him listen to reason. "If aught happens to ye, any hope for the queen's successful rescue is forfeit."

"Would ye send my father after the reivers alone then?" Duncan's expression darkened, and Heather knew he was finally at the end of his patience. "Or would ye prefer, instead, we ignore the five head of cattle that were stolen?" As if to put an end to their discussion, he wrenched free of the painful grip she had on his arm.

"They aren't worth yer life or the success of the plot."

"Mayhap to ye," he growled, casting her a troubled look. "They're worth little in comparison to yer great wealth, after all. But to us, five cattle are a small fortune."

Stung by his cutting words, Heather stepped back. "Ye've no call to speak to me like that. My concern is for yer safety, and not just because of the plot."

"Well, mayhap I was a wee bit harsh," he admitted, his face reddening. "But it'd help mightily if ye didn't berate me so. I'll be careful. I always am."

"Duncan's a braw warrior, lass," Malcolm added, walking up at that moment to join them. "And, if I do say so myself, I've another fight or two left in this old body."

Two crudely stitched leather bags hung over each of Malcolm's shoulders. In his arms, he carried two goat-skin-covered water flasks. He handed a flask and leather bag to Duncan, then walked to his horse. Duncan flung both over his shoulder.

After securing the articles, Malcolm immediately swung up on his mount. He shot his son an expectant look. Then, to give Heather and Duncan a moment more of privacy in which to say their farewells, he pretended interest in the distant mountains.

With a weary sigh, Duncan turned back to Heather. "It's time to go, lass. The longer we linger, the farther away the cattle and reivers get."

She stared up at him a long moment, countless emotions roiling within. Then, with a soft cry, Heather flung her arms about his neck, hugging Duncan close.

201

"Take care," she whispered achingly. "I don't know why, but I fear for ye greatly."

After a split second of quite evident surprise, Duncan pulled her close. "And is this sudden display of affection mayhap because ye've finally realized how irresistible I am," he asked with a grin, "and can't bear to be parted?"

At the hopeful, teasing note in his voice, combined with his heart-stopping smile, Heather couldn't help but smile in return. Then, remembering herself, she forced a stern look to her face and leaned back to glare up at him.

"All I've realized about ye, Duncan Mackenzie, is that ye're a big, blustering fool."

He pretended affront but didn't release her. "Well, it's said women like that sort of man. Tavish is as big and blustering as I, and he seems to suit Beth just fine."

"Aye, that he does," Heather agreed, momentarily forgetting her own concerns in her happiness for Beth. "Indeed, why not take him with ye?" she added, sudden inspiration striking her. "I'd feel much better if there were three big, braw men going after the reivers than just two."

"And who'd protect ye women then?" Duncan shook his head. "Nay, Tavish stays behind and no more of it."

"But I know how to use a bodice knife now," Heather protested. "Ye yerself said I was quite adept with it, and that after only a week's practice. I could protect Beth and yer mother, if need be."

"Tavish stays, lass."

To punctuate his statement, Duncan released her,

turned, and tied the water flask and leather bag to his saddle. Then, without even a backward glance, he swung up onto his horse. Only then did he again meet Heather's gaze.

"I must be going." He gathered up the reins.

"Duncan, a moment more." She reached up, laying her hand on his bare knee.

Duncan's glance fell to where her hand rested on his leg. A smile tugged at the corner of his mouth. Then he looked up.

"Aye, lass?"

"Take care of yerself. For yer sake . . . and mine."

He grinned, his eyes gleaming with a savage joy. "Aye, for yer sake and mine."

With a shout of laughter, Duncan wheeled his horse about and sent it galloping down the road. Malcolm shot him a puzzled look, then urged his own mount out after his son.

Heather stood there for a long while, watching until they disappeared at last into the morning mists. Try as she might, though, she couldn't shake off the sense of foreboding, of imminent disaster, pressing down on her like lowering clouds before a storm. She didn't know from whence the feelings came; she just knew she felt them. Only one thing comforted her—the hope that, whatever was soon to come, Duncan and his father would emerge from it alive.

The night was cold, the black canopy of the heavens strewn with sparkling, pristine bits of light. High up in one of the budding oaks, an owl hooted. In the dark shadows, feral eyes gleamed. The wind rushed down from the mountain, stirring the campfire into wildly leaping tongues of red and the sparks to flying into the air.

Duncan tugged his thick plaid more snugly to him and scooted closer to the fire. For good measure, he tossed a few extra sticks of wood into the flames, prodding them into place with a long branch. Then, to warm his innards even as the fire warmed his flesh, he tossed down another small cup of whiskey.

"Do ye wish me to top off yer cup again?" his father asked, leaning over to offer him the whiskey flask.

"Nay." Duncan wiped his mouth with the back of his hand and shook his head. "Two cups are sufficient to ease my sleep but not grace me with a headache in the morn. By the looks of the cattle tracks, we might well come upon the reivers on the morrow. If so, I'll need all my wits about me."

Malcolm nodded. "Aye, so ye will. I didn't count on there being six of them. Mayhap it'd be best to take a small detour across the mountain and fetch help from my cousin."

"And waste a full day each way if we did?" Duncan stroked his beard-stubbled face. "In the meanwhile, the reivers might well reach the coast, and we could easily lose the cattle once and for all." He sighed. "I don't like going up against six men any more than ye do, Father, but we've done it before."

"Aye," Malcolm agreed with a wry chuckle, gazing into the fire, "but the last time was ten years ago. I'm not quite as limber as I used to be."

Duncan grinned. "Ye couldn't tell that from all the complaining Mither does when she's feeling well, when ye take it into yer head to chase her about yer room."

"Och, my Fiona will make me feel like a lad of twenty to my dying day." Malcolm poured himself one last cup of whiskey, then stoppered the flask and laid it aside. "It's how ye must feel about the Gordon lass, I'd wager," he added, eyeing his son covertly over the cup he had lifted to his lips.

Och, here it comes now, Duncan thought. He was only surprised his parents had kept their counsel as long as they had about Heather's and his growing affection. Indeed, their concern and disapproval—especially his mother's—had become all but palpable of late.

He met his father's gaze squarely. "Aye, I suppose so."

Duncan hesitated, then decided his sire might as well know the full truth of it. He inhaled a deep breath before forging on.

"I love her, Father."

"I thought as much. And yer mither was convinced of it weeks ago."

"Was she now?" Duncan's mouth twisted in a crooked smile. "Well, it shouldn't surprise me. I've never been able to hide my true feelings from Mither. Leastwise not for verra long."

"She asked me to talk to ye about it, this infatuation ye have wi' the Gordon lass. She asked me to warn ye away from her afore it's too late."

Duncan made a small sound of disgust and shook his head. "It's already too late. I told ye. I love her."

"Och, lad, lad." Malcolm downed the contents of his cup and set it aside. "Didn't I warn ye to beware? What do ye hope to gain in loving a woman such as her? She'll never wed ye. It'd be too far to stoop beneath her, and—"

"Heather's not like that, Father." Angrily, Duncan cut him off. "Haven't ye seen that with yer own eyes, in the past months of being with her? And I think . . . I *hope* she is coming to care for me as much as I do for her."

"So, ye imagine true love will wipe away all the obstacles in yer path, do ye?" His eyes smoldering with anger, Malcolm leaned toward his son. "Well, Duncan my lad, life isn't that easy or that simple."

"It can be."

"Nay, it can't. I learned that the hard way, after yer mither and I wed and we tried to start a family."

Duncan shrugged and again began poking the fire with the branch. "And what was so difficult about that? Ye had me."

"Nay, we didn't."

Ever so slowly, Duncan laid down the branch and turned to his father. "What do ye mean, ye didn't have me? I'm yer son, a Mackenzie, and—"

"Ye may or may not be a Mackenzie, but ye never were our son, leastwise not by birth." Malcolm dragged in an unsteady breath. "Angus brought ye to us one night, after we'd tried for years to breed a child of our own and failed. Ye were but a wee babe, and Angus said ye were an orphan, that yer real mither died in birthing ye, and yer father soon followed her. He gave us no further information about ye, though, swearing us to secrecy.

206

And he demanded we never ask him about yer true family ever again."

The wind whipped up just then, sending the flames arching high into the night. A fire-eaten log split at its center, tumbling with a crack and shower of sparks into the campfire. And still Duncan sat there, shocked, speechless.

His father and mother weren't his birth parents? He may or may not even be a Mackenzie? And their laird had refused, for some unfathomable reason, to reveal the true story of his birth?

"Mayhap we erred in not demanding to know all there was to know about ye, lad," Malcolm said, "but we were desperate for a bairn. Yer mither, after all the years, was beside herself with sadness and longing. What did it matter to us whose bairn ye used to be? They were dead, after all."

"Did ye ever think it might matter to me?" Duncan demanded hoarsely, finally finding his voice.

Anger, frustration, confusion . . . all swelled in him, churning together so chaotically he suddenly felt sick to his stomach. "Why now, after all these years, have ye decided to tell me of this?"

Malcolm looked down, unable to meet his son's searing gaze. "Yer mither thought ye should know. She felt it might affect yer decision about the Gordon lass."

Duncan gave an unsteady laugh. "Och, aye. I'd imagine it might. It's bad enough I'm a common Highlander, but now I learn I don't even know who my real father was, or my real name, or even which clan I truly belong to."

"Yer given name is Duncan. That much Angus would tell us."

"A lot of good that does me," Duncan snarled, the bitterness welling within him. He shoved to his feet, staring down at the fire.

"What will ye do . . . about the Gordon lass, I mean?"

For a long moment, Duncan closed his eyes. Indeed, he asked himself, what *would* he do? He had been a fool ever to imagine there could be a life together for him and Heather. This newest and most startling of news but confirmed it. For all he knew, he might well be the offspring of some illicit love affair.

There was no way of knowing, unless . . . unless Angus Mackenzie could be brought to tell the whole tale. Duncan opened his eyes and riveted his gaze on his father.

"Heather Gordon isn't the issue here. The truth of my heritage is. And only Angus Mackenzie can tell me what I need to know."

"And what if, in the knowing, ye discover things even more hurtful than what ye know now? Let it be, lad. Fiona and I, we've been good parents to ye. No one need know any different. And, once the Gordon lass is gone from here, life can go back to the way it was. Ye'll see."

Nay, life can never go back to the way it was, Duncan thought bitterly. Now, atop it all, he was a man who didn't even know from whence he truly came. And that made him even more unworthy of Heather than he had been before.

Choking back a curse, Duncan turned and strode off into the night.

Three days later the steady, rhythmic clatter of morning rain on the thatched roof woke Heather from a restless sleep. She rose, bathed, and dressed, then helped Beth prepare a simple breakfast. Fiona's dropsy had flared up again, and the older woman soon took to her chair by the fire, her painfully swollen legs propped on a stool. Beth spent the morning playing cards with Tavish, and Heather, as she had for the past two days, commandeered a chair by the window, where she anxiously watched for any sign of Duncan and Malcolm's imminent return.

The mood in the cottage was quiet, somber, as it had been since Duncan and his father's departure. It was how it always was when Duncan wasn't about, Heather thought, struck yet again by the realization of the significant and positive impact the big Highlander had on the day-to-day attitude of all. Duncan was just so full of life and living, so strong and sure in all he did. A person would have to be deaf, blind, and daft not to be stirred by him.

Her thoughts couldn't help but turn again and again to the unsettling discussion they'd had about religion. And, though Heather had battled long and hard against the realization, she had finally yielded to the inevitable truth. Duncan was the man he was *because* of his spiritual beliefs, and not in spite of them. If she wished ever to spend her future with him, she would not only have to accept that fact but respect it.

If the truth were told, as they had spoken of her spiritual pain and his staunch faith, Heather had felt a renewed stirring of her own heart toward God. If the truth were told, she longed for some of Duncan's love and trust in the Lord.

Once, she too had loved and trusted Jesus with all her heart. Once her most favorite part of the day was bedtime when she would kneel to say her prayers, followed by her mother reading her a story from the Bible. They were practices that had filled Heather with such peace, comfort, and joy. Would times like those ever be hers again?

She stared through the leaded windowpanes, straining to see past the water sheeting the glass and distorting the view. It was such a wet, miserable day. She hated to imagine Duncan and his father out in the drenching weather, herding back the cattle they had surely rescued by now.

The mouthwatering fragrance of a fine venison stew wafted past. A stew rich with thick chunks of turnips and potatoes, cabbage and carrots, and succulent pieces of venison, all blended together in a savory gravy. Heather smiled to herself. It was a stew she had made without any help from Beth or Fiona. A stew made to welcome back Duncan and Malcolm, to fill their bellies, nourish their bodies, and warm their hearts.

She didn't know how she knew it, but somehow Heather felt certain the two men would return this day. Fiona had but laughed when Heather had announced that this morning, but it didn't matter. Nothing mattered save that Duncan return safe and whole . . . return to her.

The hours passed; the gloomy, waterlogged day drizzled

into an equally gloomy, sodden eve, and still there was no sign of Duncan and his father. Then, just as Heather finally gave up hope and began setting the table for the supper meal, a horse neighed close by outside. Heather dropped the pewter spoons she held, which fell to the tabletop with a clatter. She wheeled, gathered up her skirts, and hurried to the door.

"M'lady. A moment!"

Tavish leaped from his chair with such haste it toppled over backward. Grabbing up his sword, he stalked over to block Heather's path to the door. Sword in hand, he glared down at her.

"Ye haven't any inkling who might be outside. Permit me to go before ye, in case it isn't Duncan and Malcolm."

She opened her mouth to protest, then thought better of it. "As ye wish, Tavish. Though ye'll soon see it's indeed Duncan and Malcolm."

With an amused quirk of his mouth, the big grooms-man turned, opened the door, and looked outside. "Who goes there?" he cried. "Identify yerselves."

"I-it's me . . . Duncan," a voice called faintly back. "H-help me. Father . . . he's sorely wounded."

At her son's words, Fiona gave a cry and shoved awkwardly to her feet. "Malcolm!"

The older woman motioned frantically for Heather and Beth to follow Tavish, who had already hurried outside. "Make haste, I beg ye. Go, see what ye can do to help my husband."

Heather exchanged a quick look with Beth, then hurried after Tavish. In the light streaming from the cottage,

211

she could barely make out the form of a man riding astride a horse, holding the other man wrapped in a plaid and slumped over before him. Even as she flew down the steps, Tavish was drawing up beside the two men.

"Duncan, what happened?" she cried as she slid to a halt beside Tavish and looked up at the big Highlander. "Are ye hurt as well?"

"A-aye," he replied unsteadily, "but first see to my father." He met Tavish's glance. "Can ye hold him if I hand him down to ye?"

Tavish nodded. Heather signaled to Beth, who had just arrived.

"Come. Stand with me. We'll grasp Malcolm's legs while Tavish takes him by the arms. It'll be the easiest way to get him from the horse."

Beth joined her mistress. After a few tense moments, they had Malcolm down. He was unconscious.

"Can ye carry him into the house?" Heather asked her groomsman.

"Aye," Tavish said, gathering Malcolm up into his arms.

"Good. Then Beth and I will help Duncan to the house."

Tavish stalked off, carrying Malcolm's limp form.

Heather turned to look up at Duncan. "Come down."

He stared at her for a long moment. "Step back then. If my strength fails, I don't want to fall on ye."

"Swing yer leg over, then lean on yer horse and lower yerself to the ground." She signaled to Beth to move to

Duncan's right while she moved to the horse's head. "That way we can catch ye and keep ye on yer feet."

"Do ye really think so, lass?" Duncan asked, managing a weak grin.

Even in the meager light from the cottage, Heather could see how pale and haggard Duncan looked. Fear gripped her. Though his father might be more seriously wounded, Duncan's wounds—whatever they might be— were also severe. She whispered a quick, fervent prayer, then squared her shoulders and took hold of the horse's reins.

"We'll catch ye, and no mistake," she said. "Now, come down, I say."

Thankfully, though Duncan's dismount was awkward and slow, the horse stood quietly. As soon as his feet touched ground, Heather released her hold on the reins and grasped Duncan by the arm. He swayed unsteadily for a moment before finding his balance. Then, with Beth supporting him on one side and Heather on the other, he limped up to and inside the house.

From the open doorway to Duncan's parents' bedchamber, Heather could see that Tavish had already placed Malcolm on the bed. Fiona was standing over her husband, peeling away layer after layer of blood-soaked bandages—bandages that had done little to staunch the constantly oozing, gaping abdominal wound. Heather winced, then looked quickly away. Even with her limited knowledge of sword wounds, she knew such an injury was fatal.

Duncan faltered at that moment, and it was all the two women could do to keep him on his feet. Once he had steadied, Heather took a firm grasp of him about the waist.

"Beth," she then said, "turn back the covers on my bed and lay a sheet down to protect the bedding."

"N-nay," Duncan groaned in protest. "I can't take yer bed. My . . . my pallet will serve."

"And do ye think I care to minister to ye on my knees?" Heather chided softly, knowing she would only win this particular battle by turning his concern for her comfort against him. "Nay, my bed—*yer* bed—will be yer resting place until ye're healed. I'll hear no further word on it."

He lifted his head, eyed her briefly, enigmatically, then nodded. "As y-ye wish, lass. I haven't . . . the strength . . . to debate it just now."

"Or ever, Duncan Mackenzie. And it's about time ye realized that, too."

His mouth quirked. Before he could waste further strength on a reply, however, she urged him forward. Once they reached the bed, Heather sat him on the edge. Then, with Beth's help, she stripped off Duncan's ruined shirt.

Multiple superficial slashes rent his arms and torso. Painful though they might be, none were serious enough to so severely weaken a man as hale and hearty as Duncan. Puzzled, Heather met Duncan's gaze.

"M-my leg," he whispered hoarsely.

Reaching down, he lifted his kilt to expose his right thigh. A soaked, mud-stained bandage, apparently fashioned from the lower part of his shirt, was wrapped about a wound that had, from the looks of the blood already staining the blanket beneath him, pierced through the outer edge of his upper leg. To Heather's dismay, an odor of putrefaction already emanated from the bandage.

Steeling herself to what lay ahead, Heather turned to her maid. "Beth, fetch soap and hot water, a washcloth, bandages, heated oil, and some of Fiona's healing salve."

The maidservant nodded and hurried from the room.

Kneeling before Duncan, Heather quickly removed his sodden, mud-covered cuarans. Then she rose, reaching for the broad leather belt cinching his waist. It was testimony to Duncan's pain and exhaustion that he didn't protest or even question her when she removed it, and then his plaid.

After helping him to lie down, Heather covered Duncan with a light blanket, exposing only his wounded leg. By that time, Beth had returned with the necessary supplies.

"Cleanse and dress the wounds on his arms and chest," Heather said, immediately taking up a clean cloth and dipping it into the basin of steaming water Beth had set on the table beside the bed, "while I—"

"Nay, lass." Duncan halted her hand as it moved toward his leg. "Let Beth treat my leg," he said with firm emphasis. "In the meanwhile, I'd like ye to see if my mither needs help."

He meant to spare her the sight of his pain, Heather realized as she gazed down at him. Meant to spare her from the possibly revolting sight of his infected flesh, and what it might take to treat it. Perhaps, as well, he doubted she possessed the necessary skills to properly care for him.

In most other circumstances, in situations where she'd had time to pause and think it over, Duncan may well have been right. But though Heather had come from a formerly pampered existence, she had already faced the death of a loved one, stood by and watched someone she cared for suffer and waste slowly away. She would certainly not turn away now, no matter how difficult or painful.

"If ye wish for Beth to treat yer leg, I don't mind," Heather said, gently disengaging her wrist from his clasp. She handed the cloth to Beth. "But I won't leave ye, Duncan. I can't. I just can't."

For a long, poignant moment, he stared up at her. A look of wonder, then tender regard, darkened his eyes. Finally, he exhaled a deep breath.

"Come." Duncan extended his hand, palm up. "Come and hold me while Beth sees to my leg."

With a tremulous smile, Heather moved to the head of the bed, scooted onto its edge, and lifted his head and shoulders to cradle them in her lap. Then, taking both his hands in hers, she nodded to Beth.

"Get on with it."

The brown-haired woman bent to her work, quickly cutting away the filthy bandages to expose the gaping leg wound. It was a three-inch-wide sword thrust. As Heather had feared, the edges were swollen, the flesh a fiery red, and the bandage was stained with blood and pus. Beth's glance met hers. Heather knew she was equally distressed.

The maid dipped the cloth once more into the hot water, rubbed in some soap, then met Duncan's gaze. "First I'll wash yer leg, then move to yer wound with a fresh cloth. Are ye certain ye wouldn't like a dram or two of whiskey before I begin? It'd ease yer pain a mite."

"Nay." Fiercely, Duncan shook his head. "That'd take too long to work. Just do it and be done with it!"

Once more, Beth looked to Heather. She nodded, signaling for her maid to begin. At first, Duncan was relaxed, lying loose and comfortably in Heather's lap. But as Beth finished her washing of the rest of his leg, took up another clean cloth, wet and soaped it, then proceeded gently to cleanse his wound, he soon went tense in Heather's arms.

"T-talk to me," he ground out. "T-tell me what y-ye've been doing since I l-left. Aught if only to take my m-mind from the pain!"

Her heart aching for him, Heather gripped Duncan's hand the tighter and forced an encouraging smile. "It won't be much longer. Hold on. Hold on."

"T-talk to me." His eyes clenched shut and sweat beaded his brow. "I missed ye so, lass," he gasped. "And even in the w-worst of it, I held yer face before me, and f-fought mightily to come back to ye."

"And I was always with ye," Heather whispered, bending close until her lips were but a hairsbreadth from his ear. "Ye never left my thoughts all the while ye were gone. And I prayed. Och, how I prayed . . ."

"D-did ye, lass? It w-warms my heart to h-hear—"

Duncan jerked in her arms, his body arching in agony.

The breath hissed through gritted teeth. His eyes clamped shut.

Heather glanced down to where Beth still worked. To cauterize the still-oozing wound and hopefully destroy the last bit of infection, she had poured the gaping hole in Duncan's leg full of boiling oil. It was excruciating, Heather well knew, but it was the treatment used by the best physicians.

"Hold tight. Hold tight," she cried, clutching Duncan to her with all her might. "It'll be over soon. I swear it!"

Yet, in spite of all her intentions to be brave and strong for Duncan, Heather couldn't bear to see him suffer so. Tears welled, then coursed down her cheeks.

"Och, l-lass," Duncan moaned, gazing up at her with pain-glazed eyes. "D-don't cry. I'm not w-worth it."

"And if not ye, then who should I concern myself with?" she sobbed, her body shaking with her pent-up feelings and fear for him. "Ye're the finest, kindest—"

"H-hish, lass," he crooned, his body finally uncoiling from its whipcord tautness as Beth finished the liquid cautery treatment.

Gently, Duncan freed a hand from her clasp. He stroked Heather's cheek, wiping away her tears.

"I'm not so fine as all that. Indeed, I'm not even as good a man as I once thought I was."

Startled, she looked up, locking gazes with his. "Whatever do ye mean?" Heather asked, some instinct warning her to be wary.

A pained confusion, a bewildered torment, clouded his eyes. "The first night we made camp after we left here, my father told me . . ." His voice faded.

Though Heather sensed it would be better not to prod and poke at what was obviously an equally painful wound of his heart, she suddenly wanted—needed—to know. "What, Duncan? What did yer father tell ye?"

He looked away, then sighed. "It doesn't matter, leastwise not at a time like this. Malcolm . . . my father . . . sacrificed his life for me. That sword thrust—the one he took to his belly—was meant for me.

"Och, dear Lord, dear Lord!" he groaned, the cry wrenched suddenly from somewhere deep within him. Turning his head, Duncan hid his face against Heather. "H-he gave his life for me," he said finally, each word taut with agony, "and I was never even his son!"

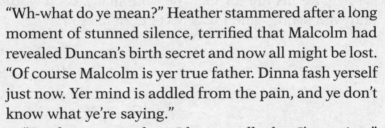

12

"Wh-what do ye mean?" Heather stammered after a long moment of stunned silence, terrified that Malcolm had revealed Duncan's birth secret and now all might be lost. "Of course Malcolm is yer true father. Dinna fash yerself just now. Yer mind is addled from the pain, and ye don't know what ye're saying."

"On the contrary, lass. I know well what I'm saying," he rasped thickly, tensing once more as Beth applied a marigold salve, then began to wrap his leg with fresh bandages. "My fath—Malcolm—told me I was given to them when my real parents died. All they knew was that my forename was Duncan. Our laird wouldn't tell them aught more."

"He's still yer father," Heather said, noting Duncan's hesitation now in naming Malcolm his sire. "What matters, in the end, is he was always there when ye needed him and was a good parent to ye."

"Aye," he admitted grudgingly, "I know it. I just . . . just need time to . . . to sort through it all." He glanced down as Beth finished tying off the bandage. "If it wouldn't cause ye trouble, could ye fetch clean water to bathe the rest of me, lass?" Duncan asked the maidservant. "I'm quite filthy"—as if to add credence to his request, he gestured to his torso and other arm and leg—"and would dearly love to feel clean again."

Beth nodded and smiled. "It's no trouble at all."

Duncan took her arm. "Would ye also see how my father fares? And if my mither has need of me?"

"Aye, if ye wish." She rose, picked up the basin of dirty water, and walked from the room.

As soon as Beth was out of earshot, Duncan turned back to Heather. "I had ample time to consider my father's words on the ride back. Indeed, it helped keep my mind off my wounds and the fact Father was slowly bleeding to death in my arms. Time enough to wonder if there might not be some connection between my mysterious true family and the fact that I supposedly share such a striking resemblance to this Colin Stewart."

Panic rose in Heather. *Och, not now*, she thought. *Not now.*

What could she say to him? She didn't want to lie to Duncan. But he was too clever, too insightful, easily to lead him astray.

Why, oh why, did Malcolm have to tell him? If only he could've waited another month. Then it would've been safe for Duncan to have known it all. But not now. And not from her lips.

There was no avoiding Duncan's piercing regard, however, or the trusting way he patiently awaited her reply. "Did ye think to ask yer father that question?" Heather asked in an effort to prevaricate.

221

"Nay, I didn't and, when I finally did, it was too late. He was unconscious." He took her hand, lifted it to his lips, and kissed it. "I thought ye might be able to share some of yer understanding on the matter, though."

"And why would ye think I knew aught?" She licked her lips, then swallowed hard. "Besides, uncommon as they are, such things do happen."

"Do they? I wonder." Duncan eyed her, then, as if a mask had fallen over his face, he smiled thinly. "Well, mayhap ye're right. Ye've seen and done far more than I have, considering I've never even left this part of the Highlands. If the resemblance doesn't concern ye, who've seen both of us, then I suppose I shouldn't let it concern me."

But it does, Heather thought glumly, *and for good reason. And I haven't fooled ye a whit, have I, Duncan? Och, Father, Father*, she beseeched her sire silently. *Why have ye placed me in such an untenable position and forced me to lie to Duncan? Didn't ye ever consider the sort of man he truly is—a man who won't be fooled for long?*

Thankfully, Beth returned at that moment, another basin of steaming water in her hands. Both Duncan and Heather looked to her expectantly. The maidservant placed the bowl on the small bedside table, then turned to them.

"Yer father is still unconscious."

"And his wound?" Duncan prompted, struggling to shove to one elbow. "Have they been able to staunch the bleeding?"

"Aye. It took cautery with a red hot iron, though. The heated oil wasn't enough."

With a deep, weary sigh, Duncan sank back against the pillows. "I thank the Lord for that." He grimaced and shook his head. "I fear it won't be enough to save him, though. The sword thrust he took to his belly . . ."

His voice broke.

"He's home, surrounded now by family and friends who care about him," Heather hastened to offer, kneeling beside the bed to take Duncan's hand in hers. She kissed it tenderly, then cupped it to her cheek. "If aught can be done for him, we'll do it, and no mistake."

Duncan managed a wan smile. "I know that, lass. I know that." His eyes slid shut, and he sighed once again. "Och, but I'm tired. The ride home seemed endless and it was so cold, what with all the wind and rain. I tried to keep Father as warm as I could, but it was nigh impossible . . ."

"Ye're both safe and warm now," Heather whispered. "And we're here for ye. Sleep now," she urged. "Ye'll feel better once ye take a bit of rest."

Ever so slowly, Duncan's lids lifted, and she was impaled by a pair of deep green eyes, eyes that smoldered with undisguised agony. "Will I, lass?" he asked softly. "Ever feel better, I mean? The only man I've ever known as father lies dying in another room, yet though I love him with all my heart, he never truly *was* my father. And, when my mither someday dies . . . well, then I'll have lost the final link with whatever family I'll ever know."

He gave a gruff, self-deprecating laugh. Then he slowly shook his head, his eyes closing once again.

"Aye, I've a lot to look forward to," Duncan whispered,

"as I watch my life as I've always known it tumble down about me."

Despite all attempts to halt the inevitable, Malcolm died in the gray hours of early morn. Just as his life had been lived, his strong body quietly accepted the final defeat, and he softly, gently breathed his last breath. Fiona, in a state of semi-shock, was at his side, her gnarled, arthritic fingers clasping her husband's hand.

When the realization that Malcolm was gone finally struck her, she gave a low cry, lifted his lifeless hand to her lips for one last, heartfelt kiss, then rose and hobbled from the room. Heather, who had left Beth to watch over the sleeping Duncan, looked up at Tavish. The big Scotsman's eyes were red and tear-filled, mirroring, she was certain, her own anguish and sense of loss.

Malcolm, in the few short months they had shared, had, like the rest of his family, become dear. Heather knew she'd mourn him for a long time to come.

She rose from her chair on the other side of the bed, bent, and leaned close to his ear. "I love yer son with all my heart," Heather whispered. "I'll do all I can for him, in the difficult times ahead as he comes to terms with the man he truly is. I swear it, Malcolm, on my word as a Gordon and a Scotswoman."

Puzzlement clouded Tavish's gaze as Heather straightened. "I must go and see if Fiona needs aught," she explained. "Then, when Duncan wakes, if his mither isn't able to do so, I must tell him about his father."

"It may be a time before Duncan wakens, my lady," the

big Scotsman said. "After ye've seen to Fiona, mayhap it'd be best if ye lay down for a few hours. Ye haven't slept all night. I can easily waken ye when Duncan calls for ye."

Heather smiled sadly. "Aye, mayhap I'll take a few hours' rest. Strange, though, but I don't feel weary. Leastwise not in body, though my heart is sorely weighted with sorrow." She paused, studying him. "Ye could use a few hours' rest yerself, my man."

She motioned toward the door. "Go, take to yer pallet."

"And then who will help ye with wrapping the body in its shroud and laying it out until time for the burial?"

"We'll need yer aid with it all, Tavish," Heather said. "It can wait a time, though, until Duncan has opportunity to say his farewells to his father. Until then . . ."

"Fine, fine," Tavish muttered. "Just be sure to wake me when ye've need of me."

"I will, Tavish. Have no fear."

She watched her groomsman stride from the room, then turned back to Malcolm. As was the custom, Heather placed coins over his closed lids and set a plate of salt on his breast to prevent swelling. Finally, after one long, heartfelt glance at Malcolm Mackenzie, she turned and left the room.

Duncan slept until early afternoon. Heather, who had insisted on being at his side when he wakened, had finally dozed off in a chair she had pulled close to the bed when he stirred, groaned, and touched her hand.

"Lass?" he ventured, his voice a rough rasp. "Are ye awake?"

Ever so slowly, Heather opened her eyes. Her head pounded, her eyes burned, and her throat was raw. She felt groggy and dizzy, all at the same time.

It was all she could do to muster the strength to nod, much less reply. "Aye, I'm awake."

In a painful rush of memory, reality returned. With an effort, she straightened in her chair.

"Duncan . . . there's something I must tell ye."

"My father's dead, isn't he?"

For a long moment, Heather stared at him. It was the moment she had dreaded, but he deserved to know, deserved to have the opportunity to pay his final respects before his father's body was prepared for burial. And there was no one else to tell him.

Fiona had fallen into a catatonic state shortly after her husband died, taking to her chair, where she clasped her arms about her and, with head lowered, sat there, silently grieving. So enmeshed in her own private sorrow, the older woman would've been of no comfort or assistance to Duncan.

"Aye, he is."

"When?" came the brusque, emotionless query. "When did he die?"

"Early this morn. He never regained consciousness."

Duncan struggled to shove to a sitting position. For once, however, his bruised and abused body wouldn't bend to his indomitable will. With an anguished gasp, he fell back against the pillows.

226

"By mountain and sea," he cursed in frustration, "must I lie here like some puling invalid while my father molders?"

Heather rose. "Pray, grant me a moment to fetch Tavish, and we'll help ye."

She hurried from the room and soon returned with her groomsman. Duncan was dressed in a clean linen shirt that came to just above his knees, and his legs were lifted to the edge of the bed. Then, with Tavish on one side and Heather on the other, they made their slow, halting way across the common room and into the other bedchamber. As tallow candles burned nearby, they helped Duncan to the bed, pulled up a chair, and assisted him to sit. Tavish hesitated, then walked silently from the room.

For a long moment, Duncan stared at his father. Leaning over, he next rested his forearms on the edge of the bed and took up the old man's hand. Cradling the long, limp fingers in the callused expanse of his own, Duncan closed his eyes and bent his head.

"Och, Father . . . Father . . ." he groaned. Tears seepcd from the corners of his eyes. His broad shoulders heaved with powerful, long-repressed sobs.

This was a private, personal moment, Heather thought. She shouldn't be witness to his pain, indeed, couldn't bear to see it.

She touched him gently on the shoulder. "Duncan, I-I'll be leaving ye now. Call for me when ye need me, but it's better if ye have some time alone with yer father."

"N-nay." He reached out, clasping her hand in a crushing grip. "I . . . I need ye now . . . here with me. Stay, lass. Please!"

He needs me. The words filled Heather with a bitter-sweet pang. He needed her and, though it was equally painful to stay, she knew she could no more deny him than to deny the ardently fierce emotions loving him stirred within her.

"Aye, Duncan," Heather whispered on a soft rush of air. "I'll stay with ye for as long as ye wish."

Pulling her hand from beneath his, she walked over, picked up a small stool, and brought it back to place beside his chair. Then, taking her place on the stool, Heather joined Duncan in his vigil.

A long while later, Fiona paused in the doorway. Her son sat motionless beside the bed she and Malcolm had shared for nearly forty years, head bent, his father's hand held tightly to him. And, next to him was Heather, her arm encircling Duncan's waist, her fair, golden head resting on his leg.

Two days later Malcolm was buried in a proper Christian ceremony. Afterward the somber group returned to the cottage. Fiona took to her room, and Duncan immediately limped from the house, leaving Heather, Beth, and Tavish to stare helplessly at each other.

The silence soon set Heather's nerves on edge. "Tavish," she said, rising at last, "see to the animals and other chores. After I help Beth get started on the supper meal, I'll come out and help ye."

"It isn't necessary, m'lady," the big Scotsman protested. "It'll take me a while, if Duncan doesn't return to help, but I can do all the work myself. Besides, it isn't fitting that ye soil yer hands with manual labor. If yer father was ever to hear—"

"Well, I certainly won't tell him if ye don't," she observed wryly. "And, indeed, it'll do me no harm and a lot of good to keep busy just now. Not to mention," she added, "it's the least we can do to help Duncan and his mither at a time like this."

Tavish didn't look at all convinced, but he nodded his reluctant assent. "As ye wish, m'lady."

Heather watched him leave, then turned to Beth. "A nice roast hen and a mess of cooked potatoes and carrots should make for a hearty supper, wouldn't ye say?" Not awaiting a reply, she walked over to where Fiona always hung her big white aprons. "If ye'd go out and catch a fat hen, I can begin peeling the potatoes and—"

"It'd be better if ye let me work on supper while ye seek out Duncan," her maidservant countered gently. "I'd wager he needs ye far more than I."

Heather paused, her hand on the peg holding one of the aprons. Hot tears sprang to her eyes. For a fleeting instant, she clenched them shut.

"I don't know what to say, how to comfort him," she whispered at last. "He's so withdrawn, so anguished and lost right now . . ."

"Ye, of all people, should understand what he feels. Have ye already forgotten how ye suffered when ye lost yer sister, then mither?"

"Nay." Heather shook her head. "I haven't forgotten."

"And what did ye need most from others at that time? Was it someone bustling about cooking and cleaning?

229

Or was it an understanding, loving friend to listen, to just be there with ye?"

Beth spoke true, Heather realized with a twinge of shame. It was just that she feared the part of Duncan's grief that encompassed his unresolved feelings about Malcolm's shocking revelation. To offer Duncan comfort just now, she feared, was to open herself to further probing on that thorny matter.

It would be far, far too easy to tell him all. It had been difficult enough, as she came to know and love him, to keep the truth from Duncan. How much more difficult would it be now, in his grief and desolation, if she dared seek him out?

Yet now, in his time of greatest need, purposely to avoid him was also a cruelty beyond comprehension. A cruelty that Heather feared she might regret to the end of her days.

With a bone-deep sigh, Heather released her grip on the wall peg. "Yer words have merit." She turned to face her friend. "I'll seek out Duncan and see if I can be of help. But only if ye're sure ye don't need any help with supper."

"Get on with ye," Beth said with an encouraging smile. She made a shooing motion toward the door. "Ye aren't that adept a cook just yet at any rate. If the truth be told, I'll have the meal prepared far sooner without ye than with."

"Och, and aren't ye the tactful one?" Heather shot back as she walked to the door and took up her cloak. "Mark my words. I'll be remembering that when next ye ask me to assist ye with some chore."

"Aye, I'm sure ye will," was Beth's laughing response as Heather opened and walked out the door. "I'm sure ye will."

The day was sunny. A cool but flower-scented breeze blew across the meadow. Heather hesitated on the door stoop but a moment, attempting to gauge in what direction Duncan had headed. Odds were he had taken the path leading to the pond and into the forest. Many times before, when he had needed some private time to himself, she had seen him stride out in that direction. Odds were he had gone that way this time, too.

She found him sitting on a fallen tree trunk beside the pond, gazing dejectedly into the water. Heather hesitated but an instant, then squared her shoulders and strode resolutely toward him. Her footsteps were muffled by the thick, damp padding of fallen leaves. Duncan didn't seem to hear her until she was but a few feet away.

When he did he leaped to his feet, his hand snaking to his dirk. Then, recognizing Heather, Duncan sighed and sank back onto the log.

"Ye shouldn't sneak up on a man like that, lass," he growled. "Some wouldn't pause in the slitting of yer throat before stopping to ask questions."

"And did ye think ye'd be in danger so close to yer house, and in broad daylight, no less?"

He looked up at her, his glance grim. "Don't ever imagine yerself safe anywhere or at any time. The reivers and outlaws who roam these mountains are not only desperate but bold. And if they, for even an instant, find yer guard down or sense a weakness . . ."

231

Exasperation filled her. Must he always be so protective?

"Yer warning has been heeded. Now, since I didn't come out for the purpose of discussing outlaws and their ilk, do ye think"—she motioned to the spot beside him on the tree trunk—"ye could scoot over a mite and let me share that seat with ye?"

Duncan eyed her wryly, then moved to make room for her. Heather gathered her skirts and sat, taking great care to keep her hem from making contact with the damp ground. Neither spoke for several minutes, pretending instead a sudden fascination with the wild ducks scavenging in the pond.

Sunlight gleamed on their dappled feathers, catching glints of ebony and chestnut and gold. The breeze snared in the fresh green foliage of the newly leafed-out trees, fought a brief battle for freedom, then rose to soar high above, the only vestige of its passing a soft rattling of branches and whisper of leaves. The pond shimmered and shook before them, then stilled, its surface now a glassy silver.

Heather could have sat there forever in the silent, budding forest, Duncan warm and big and powerful at her side, but that would only serve to comfort her. And it was Duncan whom she had come to comfort and support, if only she could.

"How are ye faring?" she began, tentatively feeling her way. "Is there aught I can do for ye in any way?"

He turned, gazed briefly down at her, then riveted his glance once more on the pond. "I live and breathe. I force food down to please ye and my mither. I do all expected of me, but this hole, this gaping wound within, near to sucks the life, and most certainly the joy, from me. And I can't say, at least at this moment, that I envision my life ever being happy again."

"It was how I felt," Heather said softly, "when my sister and then my mither died. Losing someone dear to ye is the greatest upheaval ye can ever experience in life. It turns yer world, as ye once knew it, upside down and inside out. It changes everything ye ever knew or trusted about life and living. And, for a time at least, it leaves naught in its wake save, as ye say, a huge, gaping hole."

Duncan clasped his hands before him and lowered his head until his long chestnut locks screened his face. "So what do ye do then, lass? I can't believe it's possible to endure this kind of pain for long, leastwise not without going mad."

"I wouldn't think so, either. I can't say, though, what would be best for ye, Duncan, save that mayhap if there were ever a time to turn to yer faith, it's now. Though ye no longer have an earthly father, ye still have a heavenly One who'll never, ever be far from ye."

He looked up, his mouth quirking in black humor. "Well, that's a surprise, coming from ye. Of all people, I never expected ye to say such a thing."

For an instant Heather tensed, then, remembering herself, forced her shoulders to relax. She laughed.

"Whether *I* believe it or not isn't the issue. What matters is that *ye* believe it and find comfort in the believing."

He sighed. "I confess I'm not so sure what I believe just now. I need time to sort it all out."

Heather reached over and took his hand. "No matter what ye do, stay close to the Lord. I'd have fared far better if *I* had."

"Aye, likely ye would have. Nonetheless, ye survived. Pray, share what worked for ye."

She paused, her thoughts flitting back to those days, weeks, and months after her mother had died. "I strove to fill the gaping hole with new experiences, with learning, and by involving myself with others," Heather replied after a time. "At first, it wasn't easy, and I did so with the greatest difficulty and by dint of much effort. But, eventually, I began to care again and even find some fleeting moments of joy in what I did."

"And now?" Duncan lifted haunted yet hopeful eyes to her. "How do ye feel now?"

Heather swallowed hard. Her heart commenced a wild pounding beneath her breast. Did she dare reveal the full extent of her feelings? Did she dare risk laying bare the secrets of her heart, secrets that now included a deep and abiding love for him?

She opened her mouth to speak, then clamped it shut as fear—and a lingering caution—overwhelmed her. To admit to her love for Duncan when he had yet to proclaim an equal affection for her was tantamount to surrendering all power, all control. It was exactly what her mother had done in loving her father, and it had broken her heart. It was what her sister had done, and it had cost Rose her life.

But, gazing now at Duncan, seeing the hunger and

pain burning in his beautiful eyes, Heather also knew she couldn't turn from him in his time of anguish. Though she feared the final yielding of her heart, she loved him too much to deny him whatever comfort she could give.

"How do I feel now?" She repeated his question, a bittersweet smile curving her lips. "Now, though I'll carry the loss with me for the rest of my days, I face life with renewed hope. Life begins and ends with people—family, friends, and those even more special. And, even, mayhap, also with God. I truly have been blessed. Unworthy as I am, I've finally found them all." Gently, Heather squeezed Duncan's hand. "Aye, I truly have been blessed."

He covered her hand with his. "Dare I hope I number at least as one of yer friends?"

"Ye're that, Duncan Mackenzie," she softly, achingly said, moved in that moment of poignant, soulful union past the point of reason, past all constraint and caution. "Ye're that and so verra, verra much more."

13

The next three weeks were strained, somber, and overlaid with a rising tension. Though Duncan healed quickly and was soon back at work caring for the farm animals, his usual warm, outgoing manner didn't return. What time he didn't spend comforting his mother or doing his daily chores, he used for solitary walks or studying several books on etiquette and Scottish history that Heather had given him.

She knew he was purposely avoiding her. She wagered she also knew why. Despite her protestations to the contrary, Duncan still suspected she knew more than she cared to reveal of the true story behind his mysterious background. He was most likely also hurt and angry at what he saw as her betrayal of him.

If the truth were told, Heather was equally angry. Angry at her father, angry at the situation that had forced her into withholding vital, legitimate information from Duncan. Ah, she thought, if only the queen's freedom wasn't at stake. If only she could foresee what Duncan's reaction would be to learning the truth about his heritage.

Perhaps then it would be safe to tell him, or leastwise convince her father to tell him.

She began to count the days left before her father's return. And, as time grew short, she tried once more to involve Duncan in his lessons. He was, however, less than enthusiastic.

"I don't see the point in practicing dressing like a nobleman," he growled one rainy morning near the end of April. "Ye can dress me properly the morn I'm to ride off to Lochleven Castle. By the time it's necessary to change again, I'll be long gone from there."

"True enough," Heather admitted, digging through her traveling trunk for a fine linen shirt, black hose, and a set of padded trunks. "But if aught should happen while ye're in Lochleven—ye tear an article of yer clothing or remove some part of yer attire to exercise, ye must know what each piece of clothing is called and how properly to dress yerself with whatever is lent ye."

She straightened finally, her arms laden with clothing, and turned to face him. "Besides, what if talk turns to the latest Court fashions? Colin Stewart is well known to favor the finest garb and prides himself on wearing the most up-to-date clothes."

"Ye mean he's a preening peacock, don't ye?"

"Well, aye, to some extent he is." Heather paused to consider the slight lump over the bridge of Duncan's nose and scar below his left eye. "There's naught to be done about yer nose and scar, I suppose," she finally said, "save to tell anyone who might ask that ye were set upon by thieves and soundly beaten."

"So now, atop it all, I must claim to an inability to

237

adequately defend myself." Sighing, Duncan dragged his fingers through his hair. "Och, is there no end to the indignities I must endure before this charade is finally over?"

The act of raking back his hair in exasperation drew Heather's gaze to Duncan's shoulder-length locks. "Er," she began carefully, deciding she might as well tell him all and get it over with, "there is yet one matter to be discussed, if we're to guarantee ye appear the spitting image of Colin Stewart . . ."

He followed the direction of her glance. "Och, nay," Duncan protested, as realization of her meaning struck him at last. "I can't, I won't, cut my hair."

"Duncan, ye must."

His eyes narrowed. "How short?"

Heather inhaled a deep breath. "Verra short. Colin wears his hair cropped close to his head."

"Fine, just fine," Duncan muttered. "And I suppose he also wears one of those prim little beards?"

"Nay." She gave a shake of her head. "Ye're in luck there. Colin is rather proud of his strong chin and jaw line, preferring not to hide it beneath some tuft of hair. Ye will have to take a bit more care, though," she added, eyeing his beard-shadowed face, "in shaving the morn ye must depart for Lochleven. Colin is quite fastidious in all aspects of his grooming."

"A preening peacock, to be sure," Duncan growled again.

She held out the hose, trunks, and shirt. "Well, be that as it may, it falls to ye to learn to dress exactly as Colin would. Do ye think ye can manage to garb yerself properly in these, or should I send Tavish in to assist ye?"

He shot her an offended look. "I don't need a nurse-maid."

Heather shrugged. "Suit yerself."

She watched until Duncan entered his room and shut the door, then turned and sauntered over to where Beth sat at the dining table, slicing carrots into a pot of water. She sat, took up another paring knife, and began scraping a long, fat carrot.

"He's a handful, isn't he?" her maidservant observed, never once lifting her glance from her task.

"Well, after all these months in the Highlands, I can't say I find the Court way of dress all that appealing myself." Heather smiled. "There's just something verra manly about a kilt and strong, bare legs."

Beth looked up then and grinned. "Aye, and even more so what they wear, or don't wear, beneath those kilts."

Heather flushed. "Beth! Have a care. Fiona might overhear."

"All the way from her bedchamber? I hardly think so."

"Well, I don't want to upset her, and she might not take kindly to hearing us speak so crudely of her son."

"And do ye think she's never heard a lass talk lustfully of Duncan or near to swoon at the sound of his deep voice?" Beth laughed and shook her head. "Even his mither can't help but notice what a big, braw man her son has become."

"Aye," Heather agreed with a rueful sigh. "A big, braw, pigheadedly proud—"

The rumbling, rhythmic beat of horses galloping down the road drew Heather up short. Her eyes widened. She glanced at Tavish. His hand on his dirk, the big Scotsman rose. At the same instant, the door to Duncan's bedchamber swung open.

"It's yer father, lass"—he walked from his room, dressed only in the form-fitting black hose and padded trunks—"along with Angus and several of his clansmen."

Though the thought of seeing her father again filled Heather with an exhilarating mix of joy and relief, she couldn't help but pause to inspect Duncan for a brief moment. As fetching a sight as he always was in his homespun shirt and belted plaid, Heather had to admit Duncan lent even the fashionably affected Court dress a decidedly rugged, masculine air.

His long, muscular legs bulged with strength, striking twin sculptures clothed in black. His broad chest and equally broad shoulders emanated a raw power few men could equal. And the sight of the dense thatch of hair covering his rock-hard pectorals and rippling abdomen all but took her breath away.

She would never grow tired of looking at him, Heather thought, even as she wrenched her gaze aside. Indeed, never grow tired of being with him, though their acquaintance last for the rest of their lives. Such dreaming, though, must remain a time more in its safe, hidden little place in her heart. First, there was a matter of the utmost importance that must, now that her father had returned, at long last be addressed.

With a resolute straightening of her shoulders, Heather gathered her skirts and headed for the door. Duncan

240

made a move to follow her. One quick glance at his half-clothed state, however, apparently made him reconsider. He backed into his bedchamber and shut the door.

There wasn't much time before Duncan changed and joined them. In the interim, Heather meant to speak with her father privately. Somehow, some way, she must convince him to tell Duncan the truth about his real parents, and tell him now, not later.

She opened the door and hurried outside. Robert Gordon and Angus Mackenzie were, even then, dismounting before the cottage. Heedless of the drizzle of warm rain, she quickly made her way down the steps and to her father. He greeted her with a big hug.

"And how is my bonny lassie?"

Robert squeezed her tightly, then released Heather and stepped back to survey her. As his gaze scanned her, a tiny frown formed between his brows.

"Ye appear well enough, though ye look as if ye've spent entirely too much time out of doors and"—his gaze slid down her body—"wherever did ye get that plain gown? It's such a drab wool and not fine at all."

"It's verra practical and warm, though, Father," Heather hastened to say, afraid Fiona, who had hobbled outside to join them, would overhear. "Duncan's mither wove it for me on her loom." She took him by the arm. "I need to talk with ye, Father."

"Do ye now?" he asked with an arch of his brow. "And I with ye, but first I've a need to see that strutting young cock ye've been tutoring these past months. See and speak with him, to determine if he's ready or not."

"Och, he's ready, and no mistake." Heather's gaze

241

skittered to the doorway where Duncan now stood, clothed again in his shirt and plaid. "First, though, I *must* speak with ye privately. It's verra important."

Across the expanse that separated them, Robert met Duncan's shuttered glance in his direction with a hard-eyed one of his own. "Verra important, ye say?" he muttered, never breaking gaze with the big Highlander. "And would this matter ye speak of have aught to do with Duncan Mackenzie?"

Somehow, Heather doubted her father's thoughts ran anywhere in the same direction as hers. "Aye, it has to do with Duncan. Will ye come away with me now? Please, Father?"

Reluctantly, Robert Gordon did so, allowing himself to be led to a large oak growing about fifty feet from the cottage. Well out of earshot of the others, yet still able to observe if any approached, Heather finally drew to a halt.

"Father," she immediately began, "I think it'd be best—"

"Has that lout made any untoward advances to ye?" Cutting her off, he cast a seething glance over Heather's shoulder. "If he has, the queen's plight or not, I'll have him flogged then thrown into Angus Mackenzie's dungeon, there to rot for the rest of his days!"

"Och, Father, it isn't that at all." Heather sighed in exasperation. "Duncan has always treated me with the utmost respect."

"Has he now?"

She returned his piercing look with a calm, steady one of her own. What her father might consider respectful most likely didn't include Duncan holding and kissing her, but what he didn't know wouldn't hurt him. Besides, Duncan's conduct with her wasn't the issue. His true paternity was.

"Aye, he has," she replied, a bit more brusquely than she had intended. "Now, if ye don't mind, I've another matter I wish to discuss."

When she paused, awaiting his acquiescence, Robert made an impatient motion. "Aye? What is it then, lass?"

"Malcolm was killed by reivers three weeks ago."

"I know. It was the first thing Angus told me when I arrived at his tower house yestereve. What of it?"

He was singularly callous when it came to the loss of a life, Heather thought. True, he hadn't been as intimately involved with Duncan's father as she had been, but some pretense at compassion wouldn't have cost him much. It disturbed her—her father's coldness—even as Heather realized belatedly that he had never shown much concern or sorrow for anyone else's plight, no matter how close he was to them.

Not even for the wife and daughter he had lost . . .

The realization was heart wrenching and rose from some hitherto tightly guarded place, but Heather struggled past it. What mattered now was Duncan, not a reality that had been there all along if she had ever cared—or dared—to face it.

Lifting her chin, Heather stared her father straight in the eye. "What of it?" she repeated softly. "Well, for one thing, the night before he was fatally injured, Malcolm informed Duncan that he wasn't his birth father. And, for

243

the other, Duncan now suspects I know far more than I've been willing to share about his true heritage."

Turning, Robert pounded his fist against the oak's thick trunk. "Of all the times for this to happen! Curse that old fool! Why now? Why was it of such import for Malcolm to tell Duncan now?"

"I don't know, Father."

Heather shot a sidling glance back to the cottage. Duncan stood there, talking with Angus Mackenzie. Every so often, though, he looked in her direction.

"It doesn't matter at any rate. What's done is done. But it's past time Duncan know the truth. No further purpose is served keeping it from him."

"And since when have I appointed ye to make my decisions for me?"

Heather's head snapped back in surprise. "I-I didn't mean it like that," she stammered, cut to the quick by his blistering look and hard words. "It's just that I've spent the past months getting to know Duncan and thought my insights and advice, leastwise where he's concerned, might be of some value."

"Indeed?" Robert's mouth twisted grimly. "And when did his interests suddenly become of more import than mine? When did his feelings become of more conse-quence than the welfare of our queen? When, I ask ye? When?"

"Never, Father." Stunned, bewildered, Heather took a step back. "But why should telling Duncan the truth endanger Mary or compromise yer needs?"

"Why?" He took her by the arm and pulled her back to him. "Because he's a lying, simpering, arrogant young

244

cock, and I don't trust him to do the honorable thing. Ye're naïve, lass, if ye imagine his kind would serve us a moment more if and when he discovered his true parentage. Pray, allow me to jog yer memory. The Stewarts are loyal to Moray, not the queen."

"That doesn't mean Duncan would turn against Mary. Ye can't know that for certain."

"Mayhap," her father conceded, "but are ye willing to risk it this close to the day of Mary's rescue?"

"Duncan's a decent, honorable man!" Heather cast a nervous glance toward the cottage. Luckily, Duncan was, even then, following Angus up the steps and through the front door. "He won't—"

Her father's grip on her arm tightened painfully. "Ye've fallen in love with him, haven't ye? Och, I should've known this would happen." He leaned down until his face was only inches from hers. "Has the bastard bedded ye, then? And have ye so quickly forgotten yer betrothed? Have ye?"

"Nay, Father, I haven't," Heather whispered in a pain-tautened voice. "And Duncan is far from a bastard, no matter how dearly ye wish it were so."

Suddenly, she couldn't bear to be near him. She wrenched free of his clasp.

"His conduct toward me has always been most noble and gentlemanly. Yer unfair words and crude accusations, however, leave much to be desired."

"Mayhap," Robert conceded harshly, "but ye've changed since last we were together. It disturbs me. Where does yer loyalty now lay, lass? With me and the queen, or with that pretty-faced young rascal?"

245

"My loyalties, and my conscience, haven't changed. I just don't see why—"

His mouth went hard and tight. "I forbid ye to tell him aught. Do ye hear me, lass? Do ye?"

"A-aye, Father. I hear ye."

Even as she spoke the words, Heather edged back. A fearful confusion filled her. She felt as if she were being torn asunder. Where *did* her true loyalties and conscience lie? No matter how much she owed her father, it wasn't right to manipulate Duncan so cruelly. It had never been right, but now, atop it all, her heart was involved as well.

There was more, besides, to consider. If she withheld the truth from him much longer, Duncan might never forgive her. Was that oft-regretted promise made to her father worth the potential loss of Duncan's respect and love? On the other hand, did she dare risk compromising, if not sabotaging, the success of the queen's impending rescue? And why, oh why, must it all finally rest on her shoulders?

Suddenly, it was too much to bear—that look of anger and suspicion on her father's face, the consideration of what Duncan would think and do when he finally discovered her complicity in the plot to hide the truth from him. With a choking sob, Heather turned and ran down the path leading to the pond.

"How has it been for ye, Duncan, my lad?" Angus inquired as his host poured out two cups of whiskey. Before the younger man could even reply, the Mackenzie laird quickly downed the contents of his cup, then shoved it back across the dining table for Duncan to refill. "These weeks since yer father died, I mean."

Duncan glanced up briefly, then poured out another dram for Angus. "It's a difficult time for all concerned." He corked the flask of whiskey and set it aside, then took the seat opposite the black-haired man. "Mither isn't doing well, what with the worsening of her dropsy and her deep and abiding grief over Father. I tell ye true, Angus. I fear for her health while I'm away attempting to save the queen."

"It won't be that long." Angus finished his whiskey in one gulp. "A week or so and ye'll be back, safe and snug in the Highlands. Then life can go on as it always has before."

"Can it, Angus?" Duncan worried his cup, considering how to broach the sensitive subject of his newly discovered identity with his laird. Finally, he threw all tact and caution to the winds.

"A few days before he died, my father—Malcolm—shared a secret with me," he forced himself to say. "A secret that ye, and ye alone, know fully. He told me—"

The front door swung open, and a florid-faced Robert Gordon stalked in. One glance at Duncan and anger flashed in his eyes.

Duncan's grip about his cup tightened. The man was spoiling for a fight, and no mistake. For Heather's sake and her sake only, though, he'd try and not allow his personal disdain for the man to influence him.

"Sit and rest yerself, m'lord." Duncan rose and gestured to one of the other chairs drawn up at the table.

247

"Would ye care for a cup or two of our fine Highland whiskey? After such a long journey, it would surely help to ease yer parched throat."

Perhaps Robert Gordon was undone by the congenial greeting, or perhaps Duncan's friendly if forced grin bemused him. He managed to clamp his mouth tightly shut, rendering his host nothing more than a curt nod of acquiescence before taking his seat. Duncan poured out yet another cup of whiskey, slid it over to Robert, then refilled both his and Angus's cups.

"To the success of Queen Mary's rescue," he then said, lifting his cup in a toast, "and to the restoration of her good and glorious reign."

Robert shot him a disgruntled glance and lifted his cup in salute. After quickly gulping down his whiskey, he shoved the cup across the table for Duncan to refill. *Best to humor the man*, Duncan thought as he poured out more whiskey, *and hope the liquor will at least mellow him*.

"Ye don't seem all that changed from the man ye were," Robert observed snidely over his cup, "if ye'll forgive my blunt words. I must trust my daughter's judgment, though, I suppose, considering time is short. Not much more can be done with ye at any rate."

From the corner of his eye, Duncan saw Angus shoot him a nervous, uncertain glance. He smiled grimly. No Highlander with any mettle tolerated any form of insult to his pride or honor, and Gordon had just stepped perilously close to impugning both. It would take more than Robert Gordon's inept efforts, however, to provoke him to anger.

"Though I've learned much of the ways of noblemen in the past months—enough, I'd wager, easily to pass for one," Duncan replied smoothly, "such behavior is far too affected to inflict on family and friends. I'd prefer, if ye don't mind, m'lord, to reserve such posturing when, and only when, it's needed."

Once more, Robert Gordon flushed with anger. "And I'd wager my daughter also taught ye it was acceptable to put on airs, too, didn't she?"

At mention of Heather, Duncan suddenly realized that she had yet to come inside. Unease filled him.

"And speaking of Heather, m'lord," he said, choosing to ignore the older man's barb, "where is she? It isn't like her to hide away when such illustrious guests, such as yerself and my laird, are present."

"The lass took it into her head to take a stroll," her father said with a disdainful shrug. "Dinna fash yerself. She'll be along shortly."

Duncan rose from his chair. "No offense intended, m'lord, but I think it's past time to fetch her. It's not wise to wander too far afield in these parts, and Heather can ofttimes forget to observe even the most minimal of precautions."

"Can she now?" A knowing smirk on his face, Robert stared up at him. "Or mayhap she but wished to keep some predetermined assignation with ye, instead?" He cocked his head. "Mayhap it's the true reason ye've suddenly grown so concerned for her welfare?"

"Foul-minded swine!" Duncan shoved back his chair with enough force to topple it over backward, leaped to his feet, and glared down at Robert Gordon. "Have a care for that filthy tongue of yers. It's one thing to push and prod at me. It's quite another to besmirch yer daughter's honor."

Robert blanched and reared back in his chair.

Angus leaned over and gripped Duncan's arm. "Get on with ye, lad. It's but the liquor talking. He doesn't know what he's saying. He's been drinking from his personal flask long before we even arrived here."

"I don't care." Duncan jerked free of his laird's hold. "Drunk or not, no man has the right to gainsay a woman's honor. No man—not even her father!"

"Nay, lad, no man does," Angus agreed with quiet emphasis. "But, as yer laird, I'm asking ye to let this lie. In the end, it's Heather and her safety that matters, not some paltry feud with her father."

He was right. As pleasurable a consideration as smashing in Robert Gordon's face might be, it was far more important to assure that Heather was safe. The barely leashed anger faded, replaced by a growing concern over Heather's increasingly prolonged absence.

Duncan turned to his laird. "Aye, Angus. What matters is Heather's safety. So, if ye don't mind, I'll leave the Lord Gordon to ye. At present, I've indeed far more important matters to deal with."

He strode to the door, but not before Robert Gordon, apparently having rediscovered his courage, fired one final, parting shot. "Keep yer hands off my daughter, Highlander," he shouted. "Do ye hear me? I'm warning ye. Keep yer filthy hands off my daughter!"

14

Ah, curse my father, Heather thought as she strode down the path leading to the pond, then kept on going until she entered the dappled shade of the oak and birch forest. *Curse him for his unreasoning hatred of Duncan, and his lack of faith in me.*

Wasn't it bad enough he had coerced her into leaving the safety of home and hearth to spend half the winter in the frigid Highlands, with total strangers no less, and that with nary a concern for how she'd manage or what hardships she might have to suffer? But now, after all these months, to return and immediately accuse her of immoral conduct. Why, it was past bearing!

It didn't matter that she *had* fallen in love with Duncan Mackenzie. It didn't matter if she truly believed it was cruel and unfair to keep the truth of his birth from him any longer. No matter her feelings for the handsome Highlander, Heather also knew her duty. Her duty to her queen and her duty to the Gordons.

She walked for a time—how long she didn't know—her thoughts centered on the dilemma of what to do about

251

her father. Finally, Heather drew up short, unnervingly aware of how far she had wandered into the forest and away from the cottage. Not a breeze reached this deep into the trees; not a bird chirped or leaf rustled.

Suddenly, Heather was overwhelmed with a sense of heavy foreboding—and a terrifying certainty that she was being watched. She turned, her glance searching the shifting balance of light and shadows.

"D-Duncan?" she croaked, struggling to discern who her unseen observer might be. "Is that ye, lurking behind some tree? If it is, I don't find yer game verra amusing. Come out, now. Come out, I say."

There was no answer. Fear prickled down Heather's spine. Her hands grew clammy, her throat dry. She withdrew the small dirk Duncan had given her, holding it out before her.

"Come, then," she said, fighting to hide the quaver in her voice. "Are ye such a sniveling coward that ye can't face a woman?"

"I don't know," a raspy, unfamiliar voice replied. "What do ye think, Jamie? Are we, or are we not, sniveling cowards?"

As he spoke, a big, burly man with scraggly brown hair stepped from behind a dense stand of bushes. Another man, shorter by a head but heavily muscled, followed quickly behind. Both were filthy. Both wore tattered shirts and frayed plaids, and looked as if they didn't possess a penny between them. Both, however, carried long wooden staffs and dirks shoved into their belts.

"Well, Jocko, my lad," said the shorter man, who was obviously Jamie. "I don't think anyone could fault us for admiring such a bonny lass from afar, do ye? It isn't as if we're e'en worthy of touching the hem of her skirts, after all."

Jock grinned, revealing several rotted and two missing teeth. "I don't know about ye but I, myself, was thinking of more than touching the hem of her skirts."

"Like mayhap," Jamie offered with a feral leer, "tossing up her skirts and seeing what secrets lay beneath?"

"Aye." Even as the big man agreed, he signaled for Jamie to fan out to his right in what Heather guessed was an attempt to encircle and entrap her. "Seeing and enjoying, if ye get my meaning."

Heather backed away. Frantically, she tried to gauge whether she could make it to within earshot of the cottage before the two men caught her. She had always been fleet of foot, but the two men—obviously outlaws—looked hardened and tough. Luck was as much with them, that they'd bring her down before she could reach help, as it was with her that she could successfully escape. It seemed the wiser course to face them rather than leave her back unprotected as she ran.

"Ye're fools if ye think I'll be taken easily." She waved her knife slowly before her. "I know how to use this, and use it I will."

"Och, and why would ye e'en wish to, my wee, bonny lassie?" Jock crooned. All the while, he moved in unison with his compatriot to maneuver until one stood to either side of Heather. "We mean ye no harm. A quick coupling in the leaves wi' each of us and we'll soon be on our way. Indeed, if ye don't wish for yer family or husband to know, none need be the wiser."

"But I'll know," another voice, deep with anger, rose from behind Heather. "And I can't say I find yer baseborn behavior at all to my liking."

"Duncan!" Relief flooded Heather with such a rush she felt almost dizzy.

He moved to stand beside her, a claymore in his hand. "Get behind me, lass. Now!"

For once, she didn't dispute his right to order her about and promptly did as told. From behind the broad, comforting expanse of his body, however, she peeked around to see the two outlaws' reaction. They didn't look at all happy or overly intimidated, though they possessed only dirks and staves and Duncan was armed with a claymore. Her grip about her own dirk tightened. It might take the two of them, after all, to rout the other men.

"Well, well," Jock said. "And what are ye to the lass? Her brother, or husband, or e'en lover, mayhap? One way or another, she looks woman enough to satisfy us all."

"What she is to me is hardly yer business," Duncan snapped, glaring murderously at the two outlaws. "And ye'll never get to her, save through me." He lifted his long claymore with a one-handed grip, his powerful arm muscles bulging with the effort to raise what was typically a two-handed sword. "Now, be gone before I strike ye where ye stand."

Eyes wide, the two men looked at each other. Then, with a mocking laugh and some covert signal, they simultaneously rushed him, staves held high. Uttering the Mackenzie battle cry, Duncan charged forward to meet them.

With a mighty slice of his sword, Duncan severed

Jock's stave in half. The act, however, left him open to Jamie's attack. The smaller outlaw swung his stave around, catching Duncan in the side.

Grunting in pain, the big Highlander staggered backward. Jock dropped one of his pieces of stave. He swung the other at Duncan's head. At the last second, Duncan ducked then kicked the onrushing Jamie in the gut.

With a choking cry, Jamie sank to his knees. Nonetheless, the momentary distraction was Duncan's undoing. Jock brought his stave down hard across Duncan's sword hand.

Numbed by the pain, Duncan dropped his claymore. Jamie scrambled to his feet and came up behind him. Swinging his stave in front of Duncan, he grabbed the other end and viciously slammed it against his throat.

"Duncan!"

Heedless of her own safety, Heather raced toward the two men. Even as she did, the smaller but brutally powerful Jamie began to throttle Duncan.

With a triumphant smile, Jock walked over. He picked up Duncan's claymore, turned, and approached for the killing blow. Yet, even as the breath was slowly forced from him, Duncan fought back with all his strength. Jamie, however, managed to hang on.

There was little time to consider the consequences of her actions. All that mattered was Duncan. Heather came up behind Jamie. Before Jock could discern her intent, she plunged her dirk into his compatriot's back.

Roaring in pain and surprise, Jamie dropped his stave. He leaped back and turned on her.

"Ye wanton she-fox!" he screamed, livid with rage,

255

then came at her, a look of murderous intent blazing in his eyes.

Released from the choking hold, Duncan fell to the ground. Jock, momentarily stunned by the sudden turn of events, hesitated, the claymore falling to his side. Not so for the wounded Jamie. He flung himself at Heather.

Only the quickest of moves saved her. She leaped to one side. Spinning around in a trick Duncan had taught her, Heather thrust out her leg. The burly little man tripped, tumbling headfirst into the mud and leaves.

At that moment Jock lifted his sword for the killing blow. It was too late. With blinding speed, Duncan rose into a crouch. He launched himself at Jock.

Both men went down. Jock's sword hand struck hard. The claymore sailed away.

Heather raced after it. Even as she reached the sword, gripped it with both hands, and heaved its massive length, Jamie climbed to his feet. He paused, though, when he saw the claymore in Heather's hands.

"Ye're no match fer me, lass," he rasped, "e'en wi' that big sword in yer hands. Ye haven't the strength to wield it."

In as much to hide her own uncertainty as to present a confident mien, Heather smiled grimly. "Mayhap not, but ye can't be certain, can ye, until ye test me? And ye've already had one taste of my blade. Do ye wish to risk a taste of another?"

For the first time, doubt darkened Jamie's eyes. He looked to Jock who, by now, was rapidly coming out on the losing end of the battle with Duncan.

"Ye're hardly worth the trouble." Jamie spat into the

leaves. "No woman is." Keeping an eye on the sword Heather held, he began to back away. "Let Jock have ye if he wants. If he e'en lives long enough to enjoy ye."

With that, Jamie wheeled about and fled into the forest. She watched until he was safely out of sight, then turned back to where Duncan still fought with Jock. The big outlaw was tiring even as Duncan's rage seemed to lend him an endless source of strength. It soon became apparent Duncan intended to give no quarter and might well beat the other man to death.

"Hold, Duncan," Heather cried, edging as close as she dared to the two men. "Let him go. Let him go, I say!"

Her plea was just enough to distract Duncan for an instant. Jock saw his opportunity for escape. He staggered backward, wheeled about, and fled in the same direction Jamie had gone.

With a cry of fury, Duncan set out after him. Jock, in his terror, was fleeter of foot. Still incensed, still fired with the lust for battle, Duncan stalked back to where he had left Heather.

"Little fool!" He grabbed her roughly by the arm and jerked her to him.

Heather's grip on the claymore loosened, and it fell to the ground.

"Have ye a death wish, then," he continued to rage at her, "to stroll into the forest alone after the countless times I've warned ye not to? Answer me!"

Taken aback by his anger, Heather gazed up at him in shock. "I-I'm sorry, Duncan," she stammered finally. "I was upset with my father and just meant to get away from him to sort out things. I didn't realize how far I'd walked until it was too late."

"Feeble excuses, each and every one!" He took her by her other arm and gave her a teeth-rattling shake. "It's so like a spoiled, pampered noblewoman to think only of herself. Ye're yer father's daughter, and no mistake."

Stung by his words, Heather wrenched free. Before she even realized what she was doing, she swung back and slapped him smartly on the side of his face.

"How dare ye," she cried, "accuse me of such insensitive, self-serving behavior! I told ye I was sorry and I am. Do ye think I wouldn't care if something happened to ye? On the contrary, it'd break my heart, it would."

He went still. "Why?" His voice had gone low and harsh. "Why would it break yer heart?"

Tears filled her eyes and clogged her throat. "Why do ye think, ye heartless wretch?" she whispered. She looked down, unable to meet his now intently searching gaze.

"I don't know, lass." Duncan crooked a finger beneath her chin, lifting it until Heather once more met his gaze. "I don't know, but I'd give my life's blood to hear it."

Heather opened her mouth to tell him. Then fear rushed in, choking back the words she was about to say. Tears welled and spilled from her eyes.

"I can't . . . I dare not say." She turned her head away. "Just let me go, Duncan. It's past time we were returning to the cottage."

His hand dropped from her face. He clasped her arm with a firm grip.

"Nay." A fierce determination burned in his eyes. "Ye'll

go nowhere until I have the answers I seek. And if ye won't answer me in words, then I'll make ye answer me in another way."

Her eyes widened. Panic twined about her heart. "What . . . what do ye mean to do?"

"Dinna fash yerself, lass." Duncan smiled, his mouth softening until it was full and ripe and sensuous. "I don't mean to finish what those two outlaws began. I only mean to kiss ye."

Before Heather could fathom the true intent behind his words, much less protest, Duncan's head lowered. He captured her lips in a deep, slanting kiss. She stood there a moment, stock still, dumbfounded at the sudden turn of events. Then reality returned.

With a muffled cry, Heather pounded on his chest, fought to escape him. In response, Duncan's arms encircled her body, dragging her yet closer. Not for a moment, however, did he pause in his relentless attack on her mouth . . . and her suddenly overloaded senses . . . and heart.

It was all too much, Heather thought, caught up in a whirling maelstrom of wondrous, melting sensations that coursed through her body. She didn't want this moment ever to end. It was too delicious, too mind-drugging, too heavenly.

Nothing mattered save that Duncan had come for her, fought for her, and now held her within the protective haven of his arms. Nothing mattered but the feel of his big, hard-muscled body pressed against hers.

She moaned softly, the sound caught somewhere between resistance and surrender. Then, in one sudden surge, all the fight drained away. Heather arched up to meet him. Her hands entwined about his neck.

A shudder rocked him. Duncan paused, then pulled away. He rested his forehead on her shoulder, his chest heaving now, irregular and harsh.

"Och, lass, lass," he rasped thickly. "Ye inflame me so, with yer sweet mouth and even sweeter body. We must stop this, and stop this now, or—"

"Or what?" Heather was quick to demand.

He lifted his head, staring deeply into her eyes, his gaze hot, hungry, and so very, very anguished. "I've wanted ye for so long now, indeed since the first day I met ye. Wanted to kiss ye, hold ye, love ye in the most intimate way a man can love a woman. Not that I could ever be worthy of ye, or that it was right to think of ye in such ways . . ." Duncan sighed. "But, after all these months of being with ye and working so closely with ye day after day, no amount of praying could long keep my thoughts from straying to ye."

"And do ye imagine my need for ye is any less than yers?"

For a fleeting instant, joy flared in his eyes. Then it faded.

"It makes me so verra happy to hear ye say that, sweet lass," he said. "But it doesn't matter. In but another week, the queen's rescue will have been attempted. Whether we succeed or fail, our time together is over. Ye'll return to yer life—as I must to mine—and they are lives that can never be joined." Duncan averted his gaze. "Especially now . . . now that my father—Malcolm—has died and I know that I was never who I imagined myself to be."

Heather clutched at his shirt. Her hands twisted in the coarse, homespun fabric. Och, how she wanted to tell him he hadn't a care in the world for who he was, that he was as noble in birth as she and that it would take more than some imagined difference in their social classes to keep them apart.

But she couldn't. She had given her word to her father. In the remote likelihood that Duncan prematurely knowing the truth might endanger the success of the plot, she still didn't dare risk telling him.

But, though she couldn't tell him all just now, she could give him her heart and her love. That gift might ultimately still be faint compensation for the great advantage of his true birth, but Heather knew now it was a risk she was willing to take. Perhaps she, in the end, would fall prey to the same entrapment of the heart as had her mother and sister, but she thought not, she hoped not.

Duncan was more than just a pretty face and a magnificently conditioned body. He was also a good, honorable, brave, and intelligent man. He cared for others, tried his very best to treat them fairly. He strove to live his life by the highest of principles. And though he made her laugh and cry, had even made her angry at times, whatever he did, whenever he was with her, Heather felt happier and more alive than she had ever felt before.

Though she might ultimately never wed Duncan and instead be forced to go to another, for this precious moment in time she was his. Heather lifted on tiptoe to brush her lips across his.

"I don't care what the world perceives us to be. I know

ye, Duncan Mackenzie, and ye're the finest man I've ever met or could ever hope to meet. Indeed"—she smiled up at him, her whole heart in that look—"if the truth be told, I love ye. Love ye with all my heart."

The expression in his striking eyes turned warm, tender. "I don't know what to say, lass. To hear ye speak such wondrous words . . . well, it boggles my mind and fills me with great happiness." He paused to brush a tendril of hair from her face. "But still I fear . . . I fear . . ."

"What, Duncan?" Heather prompted when he was slow to finish. "What do ye fear?"

He inhaled a shuddering breath. "I fear that, in the end, I'll still lose ye. There's yet so much standing between us—yer father, yer betrothal to another, my questionable heritage, and my obligations to the only woman I dare call Mither. And, though I want ye so badly I ache with the longing, I won't have ye any way save as wife."

"And when did I ever say I'd accept such an offer, if that's indeed what ye're offering?" Heather asked with an impish grin.

Her attempt at humor fell flat with him. "Ye know I can't make such an offer, lass. It'd be ludicrous."

She thought she knew why he imagined wedding her was an impossibility. That knowledge, however, still didn't do much to ease the sting of his rejection.

Heather gave a snort of disgust and began to turn away. "Pish, ye men are all alike," she muttered. "Ye hunt us as avidly as dogs on a scent. Then, when ye finally capture our hearts, ye immediately lose interest."

Duncan grabbed her by the arm, spinning her back around. "It isn't that way at all," he growled, anger darkening his countenance and tightening his lips. "I haven't lost interest in ye and never will. But I'm not worthy of ye and will never be. Would ye wish me to think only of myself?"

"Nay, Duncan." Heather jerked free of his hold. "I would wish, though, for ye to at least have the courage of yer convictions and be a man of yer word. Ye've yet even to admit if ye love me or not, and that after I've bared my heart to ye."

"Och, is that what this is all about then?" He gave an unsteady laugh and shoved his fingers through his hair. "Ye think I don't love ye and but play some game with ye?"

"Don't ye?"

"Nay, lass. I play no game."

Duncan reached out to draw Heather to him, but she stepped back. Confusion clouded his eyes.

"Och, lass, don't go and work yerself into a frenzy now. I love ye. But love isn't always enough."

"Apparently not!"

Och, Heather thought in dismay, *how could I have been such a fool? I've played right into his hands. Thank God Duncan's at least honorable enough not to take advantage of me. But the pain of his rejection, of loving him and not being loved as equally in turn, is almost past bearing.*

"Lass," he said, compassion gleaming in his eyes, "don't go on so. It isn't at all how ye imagine it to be."

"Isn't it?" Heather laughed, the sound high-pitched and strained. "Well, no matter. Naught was lost but a bit of my pride. And now it's past time we were returning to the cottage, wouldn't ye say?"

"Nay, I *wouldn't* say!"

In a swift move, Duncan took two steps, swung Heather up into his arms, and stalked off toward a fallen log about fifty feet away. For an instant, Heather fought to catch her breath. Then she began to struggle in his arms.

"What do ye think ye're doing?" she demanded, outraged. "Put me down, I say. Let me go!"

"Nay, I won't," Duncan said with a resolute shake of his head, "until we talk this out. Until I can convince ye, once and for all, of my true feelings for ye."

"I never said . . ." At the memory of her words earlier, Heather flushed crimson. "Well," she corrected herself hastily, "that wasn't what I meant, at any rate."

"Then exactly what *did* ye mean?"

"I meant . . . I meant . . . Och, I don't know what I meant!" Tears sprang to Heather's eyes and coursed down her cheeks. "Och, curse ye, Duncan Mackenzie," she wailed. "I don't know what I meant, and it's all yer fault!"

At the first sign of her tears, Duncan slid to a halt and lowered Heather back to stand on the ground. "My fault, is it?" He rolled his eyes. "I go to the limits of my endurance to treat ye honorably, and it's still my fault? Truly, lass, ye never cease to confound me."

Heather pounded his shoulder once with her fist, then, still sobbing, gripped his shirt and rested her forehead on his chest. "When it c-comes to ye, I c-can't help it," she cried, hiccupping between sobs. "Ye frighten me s-so."

"Och, lass, lass." Duncan encircled her with his arms and pulled her close. "It breaks my heart to hear ye speak such words. I don't wish ever to hurt or frighten ye. Indeed, I love ye so deeply that I'd sacrifice everything—even my honor, if need be—for ye." He leaned back, crooked a finger beneath her chin, and lifted her gaze to meet his. "Just tell me what ye want of me and I'll do it."

Heather looked up at him, saw the tenderness, the caring, the love burning in his eyes. A fierce joy swelled within her. Duncan truly did love her. Loved her with his whole heart and soul, loved her so deeply that he'd do anything for her. Surely, surely, it was safe to surrender her heart to him.

"Ye've given me all that I need," she whispered, hastily swiping away her tears. "Ye have for a long while now. The failing has never been in ye but in me, in my inability to accept ye for the man ye really are."

Duncan's brow furrowed in puzzlement. "I don't understand."

She gave an unsteady laugh. "Aye, I'd imagine ye don't. It's hard enough even for me to sort out."

He took her hand and led her to the log. "Sit, lass, and tell me what ye can. There's naught ye can say that will scandalize me, and so much I yet need to know about ye." He smiled, and the act softened his rugged features until Heather thought she'd weep again at the love and tender concern she saw there. "So much more I dearly want to know."

The rich scent of damp earth rose to mingle with the heady tang of mint and spice from the leaves of the nearby foliage. Heather took a seat on the log and inhaled deeply, willing the pleasant odors to fill her, strengthen her. Then she turned, as Duncan settled down on the log beside her, and met his steady gaze.

"My mother died of a broken heart," Heather began, "my only sister at the hands of a husband she'd fallen madly in love with, yet who had never, ever, been worthy of her . . ." For the next several minutes, she proceeded to recount what had finally led to her resolve never to allow her own heart to be ensnared by a man.

"Then, atop it all," she said, finishing at last, "my father was never the man I'd thought him to be, a truth I'd known all my life, even as I managed to deny it for so many years. What choice had I, at any rate? I'm a woman, not to mention a dutiful daughter, and dependent on him for everything." She paused, then sighed. "Mayhap ye'll find the reasons for my decision to avoid love cowardly, but there they are."

Duncan was silent for a long moment, a moment that stretched on for an agonizing eternity as Heather sat there beside him, fearing the worst. If he should turn from her now . . .

"I can't fault ye for what ye did," he said finally. "Ye were protecting yerself, yer heart, in the only way ye knew how. And I can also see now why ye took such an instant dislike to me," he added with a wry grin. "I must have seemed like just the sort of man to avoid."

Relief flooded Heather, making her head spin. She was thankful she was safely seated on the ground.

"Aye, ye did indeed. To make matters even worse, ye were the most devastatingly handsome—and well-built—man I'd ever seen, standing there that eve with but a wee piece of plaid to cover ye." She grinned and shook her head. "It took every bit of my self-control not to swoon right there on the spot."

Duncan chuckled. "Ye hid it well." He leaned over and kissed her on the cheek. "In fact, ye hid it so well and for so long, I began to despair ever of winning even yer friendship, much less yer heart."

"And I, in turn," she said, tracing a finger down his cheek and around his mouth, "fretted day and night that I was acting the foolish girl whenever I was around ye. Ask Beth, if ye don't believe me."

He leaned yet closer. "I'd rather kiss ye, I think, lass." His gaze darkened. "But only for a short while and only one kiss. We *must* be getting back before yer father comes looking for us. He suspects us as it is, and I don't wish to be forced to defend yer honor against yer own father, even as poor a father as he, in truth, may be."

"Nor do I," Heather said as she closed the remaining distance between them, "need to besmirch *yer* honor in order to test yer love for me. Leastwise," she added softly just before her lips touched his, "not today. Not today but soon, my love. God willing and we survive this plot to save the queen, verra, *verra* soon."

15

They left late the next morning, after the woman and man Angus had brought along to assist Fiona in Duncan's absence were thoroughly instructed in their duties, and Duncan had said his farewells to his mother. Fiona, however, refused to allow Heather to escape quite so easily. While the men were loading the last of Heather's belongings onto the packhorse, and Beth was busy retrieving Heather's riding cape and making one last check of their former bedchamber, the old woman approached her.

"A moment of yer time, hinny," she all but commanded, her gaze imperious and flint hard. "If ye think ye can spare it, of course, after all these months under my roof."

Heather nearly snapped back a tart refusal, but then thought better of it. Beneath the ill-mannered request lay something deeper, honest and heartfelt. Something that, Heather was certain, involved Duncan.

She forced a bright smile. "I can always find time to spare for ye, Fiona. Besides, even as ye approached me, I was intent on seeking ye out to say my farewells."

"Were ye now?" The older woman gave a disbelieving snort. "Well, then ye won't mind," she said, taking Heather by the arm and leading her around the corner of the cottage and out of sight of the others, "if we speak a moment in private."

"As ye wish." Heather drew up and waited patiently for Duncan's mother to begin.

Fiona hesitated but a moment. "Duncan told me what Malcolm had said. He also told me he suspected ye know more than ye're willing to say about his birth parents. Is that true?"

"It doesn't matter." If she refused to tell Duncan, she certainly wasn't about to tell his mother. "What matters, for the next week at least, is that we all focus on the plot to rescue Mary, and that it achieves a successful conclusion. Once it's over and Duncan has come through unscathed, there'll be ample time to deal with the issue of his true heritage."

"Then ye do know more than ye're willing to reveal."

Heather grasped Fiona's hand. "It'll do no good to upset Duncan now. Don't say aught to him, I beg ye. He'll know the truth soon enough. I swear it."

His mother eyed her intently. "I haven't much choice, do I? Believing ye, I mean."

"I wouldn't do aught to hurt Duncan. Do ye believe that at least?"

Fiona's lips tightened, but she gave a curt nod. "Aye, I suppose so. Ye love him, or so he tells me."

"That's true. I love Duncan with all my heart."

"Blessed Mither! I was afraid of that." The older

269

woman's shoulders slumped. "Well, be that as it may—and I'm not saying I give ye my blessing—no matter what happens at Lochleven, no matter what his true heritage and parentage are, Duncan will never be happy save in the Highlands. It's in his blood. Once it's there, ye can never take it away."

Somehow, Heather had always known that. It was just too painful to consider how she and Duncan could ever hope to make a life together here. She was, after all, the only heir to the Gordon estates.

"Aye, I know that."

Tears filled her eyes. Fiercely, she blinked them back.

A gnarled hand reached out and took Heather by the chin, gently turning her face until she met Fiona's searching gaze. "Ye truly *do* love him," Duncan's mother said, wonder now in her voice and shining in her eyes. "Ye truly do understand the problems facing ye both."

Heather nodded. "I'd like to think so."

"Mayhap I've misjudged ye, hinny." A thoughtful look gleamed in Fiona's eyes. "Mayhap."

"I wouldn't make any hasty decisions in that regard." Heather gave a soft, strangled laugh. "Ye can't yet know how all this will turn out. Even as much as I love Duncan, I can't be certain if our love will be sufficient to overcome all." She sighed. "I don't even know if, after all this is over and done with, we can ever be together."

"There are many obstacles in yer way, not the least of which is yer father," Fiona admitted. "Whatever happens, though, one thing is certain. He needs to come back. Ye must send Duncan back to me. No matter who he truly is, he must come back to the Highlands."

Inexplicably, anger filled Heather. Would no one allow her and Duncan the freedom to make their own decisions?

"And I say, Duncan must make that choice for himself," she replied, her voice gone low and hoarse. "That isn't for either of us to decide. When it comes to the matter of his life and destiny, it's his right to choose his own path, not ours."

"True enough." Fiona nodded in agreement, apparently not at all upset with Heather's impassioned protest. "But, more than aught he's ever wished, my son wishes to please ye, be wi' ye. Ye possess a great power over him. Ye can influence what he chooses ultimately to do. Have a care, hinny, that ye don't lead him where he doesn't truly wish to go. It'll destroy ye both, in the end, if ye do."

"I-I'll have a care."

Unsettled by the older woman's pronouncement, Heather backed away. There was no more that needed saying. Fiona's greatest fear had now become her own.

"I-I must be going." She waved vaguely toward the front of the cottage. "The others . . . they're waiting on me."

"Aye, so they are." Duncan's mother gathered up her skirts and headed back the way they had come. "And we don't want to keep them from their next adventure, do we?"

Nay, we don't, Heather thought as she followed Fiona. *In just five days' time, Mary must be rescued from Lochleven*

Castle. In just five days' time, Duncan must risk his life for the queen.

And, in just five days' time, Heather added, filled with an unnerving mix of fear and foreboding, she must decide, once and for all, whether there could ever be hope of a future with a certain dashing, devastatingly handsome, and decidedly wonderful Highlander.

The weather was mild, the roads dry, and the journey pleasant. Though Heather and Duncan, thanks to the ever vigilant Robert Gordon, had no opportunity for private conversation, they were content just to be near each other, to steal a secret smile or catch the other's gaze.

By the last day of April their little group finally entered the Tayside region. In the morning, they rode through a pelting rain. By noon the clouds had dissipated, taking with them the foul weather.

Blue skies appeared. The sun sparkled on the rain-soaked grass and trees, glinting in the drops of water like so many precious jewels. In the mists rising from the ground, the heady fragrance of flowers permeated the air. Riding alongside Heather, Duncan thought it was a glorious day to be alive.

To avoid undue notice of Duncan and any resultant unwelcome talk, Robert Gordon thought it best to wait until dusk before approaching the town of Kinross. Duncan's first inkling they were finally nearing the vicinity of Loch Leven was the cry of wild geese. Then, as they emerged at last from the trail winding through Blairdam

Forest, Heather pointed out the mist-shrouded shape of Benarty Hill in the east and the dark Lomond Hills on the left.

As they made their way along the shore to the west end of the broad loch, the cacophony of honking geese, nesting in the reeds and cattails along the lake's edge, rose in volume. Duncan exchanged a wry grin with Heather, then turned to gaze once again out upon the loch. In the fading light, the sun's final rays gilded the island castle in a rosy glow. With no small amount of concern, he noted how the loch's dark waters lapped to within almost a foot of the thick, high walls enclosing the castle. Save for the other option of swimming through the chill waters, access to and escape from the small but imposing fortress could only be made with the slow conveyance of a boat.

The castle's north and east walls sat at right angles to each other; the other two were multiangular. The small, five-storied keep was oblong, with walls of squared rubble that looked to be about five feet thick. At the keep's opposite corner, Duncan could just make out a tall, round tower. It was said Mary, the queen, resided there.

That reminder of why he was here, far from his beloved Highlands, filled Duncan with a fierce elation. His hands clenched around his reins. In but two days' time, on the second of May, he would join at last with several others within Lochleven Castle to rescue his sovereign.

But two days more, he mused, and all the past months of Heather's careful tutelage would come to fruition—or end in dismal failure. He could well imagine his fate if his deception was discovered within Lochleven's dank old walls. Perpetual imprisonment in the castle's dungeon or a summary beheading. Neither fate sat well with him, nor the additional consideration of the possible torture he might suffer in an attempt to extract from him the names of his co-conspirators.

As they rounded a curve of the loch, the town of Kinross at last came into view. Already, in the gloaming, lights burned brightly from myriad windows peeking from beneath steep, thatched roofs. Gray wisps of smoke from hundreds of cook fires curled up through stone chimneys into the darkening sky. It was a calm, cool, peaceful night. Duncan could almost imagine that he and Heather—husband and wife—rode toward home, to one of the many half-timbered houses in Kinross town.

But such an imagining wasn't reality. He and Heather weren't husband and wife. Life, at least for a time more, wasn't calm and peaceful. Instead, it reeked of intrigue and danger. That grim reality was hard to face, yet face it he must.

Life, as they had once known it, might well be changing. Changing . . . and not necessarily for the best.

All was in order for their arrival at Drummond House, a fine, brick courtyard dwelling on the outskirts of Kinross. Fat beeswax candles blazed from their perches overhead in the candle beams and from tall, brass tripods set on the floor. A small but cheery fire snapped and popped in the blue slate fireplace. The oak floors had been freshly waxed and polished.

Duncan scanned the parlor, overawed by its opulence.

Besides two long, high-backed settles, there were four box chairs and two stools. Situated between the settles and chairs were intricately carved, low oaken chests that also served as tables. Pewter plates decorated the fireplace mantel and, in addition to the hunting scene tapestries hanging on the wainscoted walls, an oblong, blue-and-red rug, swirled in some strange, complex pattern, covered the middle of the floor.

As fine as Angus Mackenzie's tower house had been, this house outdid it in every way. It was a most vivid symbol of the chasm separating a common man and the nobility, Duncan thought. He couldn't help but feel a twinge of envy for those fortunate enough to live such a life. It also brought most forcibly home the vast contrast between his upbringing and Heather's.

"It's a Turkey carpet," Heather said, coming up to stand beside him as he stared down at the big rug. "It was imported from the Orient and has been in the possession of the Drummonds for over twenty years now."

The Drummonds. Duncan jerked his attention back to their hosts, Patrick and Anne Drummond. Co-conspirators in the rescue plot, they had generously offered their grand and spacious home to the Gordon party. Several nobles also involved in the plot would arrive on the morrow to finalize the last details.

He managed a terse smile. "Ye've a fine house," he said, acknowledging the middle-aged couple. "Ye must be verra proud."

It took Patrick Drummond a few seconds to respond, so intent he was in staring at Duncan. His wide-eyed wife didn't reply at all.

"Er, aye," the man finally said. "It's a fine house indeed."

A door closed upstairs. Footsteps—two men by the sound of them—clattered down the long, wooden staircase. Duncan turned.

An older man with close-cropped hair, a thin mustache, and a pencil of a beard frosted with gray was followed by a much younger, plain-faced man of medium height, pale skin, and light brown hair. Both, by the way they carried themselves and the fine clothing they wore, were obviously also of the nobility.

As he caught sight of Heather, still standing with her back turned, talking to the Drummonds, the younger man's face lit with unabashed delight. "Heather!" he cried and hurried toward her. "Heather, my love!"

At the sound of her name, Heather wheeled about. Surprise, uncertainty, then dismay flashed across her face. She slanted a quick look at Duncan. He stared back at her, stone-faced.

For some reason, she couldn't seem to hold his gaze and quickly averted it. Gathering her skirts, she went to meet the younger man.

"Charlie, I—"

Before she could get another word out, the man she had called Charlie grabbed her hand, kissed it passionately, then pressed it to his breast. "Ah, lass, lass," he breathed, smiling ecstatically. "It's been so long since last I saw ye. I never thought much of yer father's plan to send ye away to the rustic isolation of the Highlands—and especially not for so long a time—but, looking at

276

ye now, I see it did ye no harm. Ye've a certain look—a glow, even—that ye never had before."

Blushing furiously, Heather pulled her hand from his chest. Tugging Charlie along to stand beside her, she turned back to Duncan.

"Er, Charlie," she began, glancing nervously from one man to the other, "this is Duncan Mackenzie, the man who is to impersonate—"

"It's quite evident who he is to impersonate, lass," Charlie laughingly finished for her. He grinned and held out his other hand to Duncan. "I don't know if anyone has told ye this or not, but ye're the spitting image of Colin Stewart. If I didn't know better, I'd wager a year's income from our sheep farms that ye're his long-lost twin brother."

Duncan went still. "I didn't know Colin Stewart had a twin." He turned to Heather. "Why didn't ye ever tell me that? Or did ye instead prefer, for some private reason, simply to omit that wee detail?"

Heather blanched, then looked to her father, who had moved to stand before the fire and talk with Patrick Drummond. Luckily, he had overheard Duncan's question and moved quickly to come up behind his daughter.

"It's but a figure of speech," he offered smoothly. "Isn't it, Charles? Colin Stewart is, and always has been, the sole heir of the Stewart fortunes. He has no siblings."

Charlie laughed good-naturedly. "Och, aye. I didn't mean aught by my ill-conceived remark, my good man." Once more he extended the hand he had let fall when Duncan had turned to Heather. "One way or another, allow me to offer my welcome and profound respect for yer courage and loyalty to our queen. It'll be quite a feat, indeed. That old curmudgeon Lady Margaret Douglas isn't easily fooled. I wish ye good fortune in finding the opportunity to spirit Queen Mary out of that moldering old fortress."

For an instant more, Duncan eyed the possessive clasp Charlie had on Heather, then took up his other hand and shook it. "Aye, loyal I am," he ground out, "but I can't speak to my courage. I but do what must be done." He paused, arching a dark brow. "And ye are . . . ?"

Confusion momentarily clouded Charlie's expression. Then understanding dawned. "Och, aye." He gave a wry laugh. "Pray, forgive my poor manners. I suppose the introductions *did* become waylaid, didn't they?"

"Aye, they did," Heather interjected. "And the poor manners are mine, not yers," she said, shooting the young man an apologetic smile before focusing her attention back on Duncan.

Somehow, Duncan knew what was coming. There was no doubt whatsoever in his mind that he wouldn't like what he next heard. He forced himself to stand there quietly nonetheless.

"Duncan," Heather said, meeting his steely gaze with a resigned but steady one of her own, "this is Charles Seton, son of Lord Alastair Seton. Charles is the man I told ye about . . . my betrothed."

Behind her, Robert Gordon coughed behind his hand, the sound suspiciously like that of a muffled laugh. Duncan's gaze swung to meet his. Blatant triumph gleamed in the older man's eyes.

The first day of May dawned bright and sunny. Duncan rose, washed and dressed, then went downstairs. Though sunrise had come and gone over an hour ago, after last night's upsetting meeting with the Setons, he hadn't slept well in the strange, if finely appointed bedchamber, and awoke groggy and ill-tempered. Heather had told him a light breakfast would be served for several hours in the great chamber. If luck was with him, Duncan would have an opportunity to steal a few moments to speak privately with her.

She was alone in the room, just finishing her bowl of porridge at the long dining table. When Heather saw Duncan she flushed, rose, and pretended sudden interest in shoving in her chair. Duncan, guessing her intent to grab her bowl and hurry from the room, strode quickly over and barred Heather's way.

She paused, ever so reluctantly lifting her glance to his. "Aye, ye wanted something?"

He didn't like the defensive look in her eyes, nor the edge to her voice. It smacked of evasion, as if she were hiding something.

"Ye know I do, lass," he forced himself to reply as civilly as possible, when what he wanted most to do was grab her and shake the truth from her. "I want to know when ye plan to tell young Seton about us."

Heather backed up against her chair. "I hardly think that's of much import just now, what with only one day left before ye must depart for Lochleven. There are far greater issues—"

"Not to me there aren't!" Duncan took her by the arms and pulled her to him. "Have ye changed so quickly, back to the fine lady ye once were, that ye now regret what we had, the words of love ye spoke to me?" He gave her a gentle shake. "Have ye, lass?"

Tears flooded her eyes, eyes, Duncan now noted, smudged with shadow as if she'd had an equally sleepless night. He leaned closer, staring intently down at her.

"Talk to me, Heather," he commanded softly. "Tell me true what's in yer heart."

Instead of answering him, she struggled to escape. "Och, let me be, Duncan. I don't wish to hurt ye, but I'm so confused. Charlie's a dear, sweet man, and last night, after ye stormed up to bed, he took me aside, told me he loved me."

"And now ye must weigh the relative value of his love against mine, is that it?" With the greatest of efforts, Duncan clamped down on his pain and rising anger. "If so, I can't see why ye struggle so long in yer dilemma. Seton's worth shines far brighter than mine."

"Don't say that!" With a sharp movement, Heather twisted free of Duncan's hold. "It isn't that at all. But I can't so easily toss all I've ever known aside. I'm my father's sole heir now. I have commitments . . ."

"Yer father spoke to ye last night, too, didn't he?"

Frustration filled him. What chance did he have against all the power and influence stacked against him? Indeed, he was a fool to imagine even for an instant that he had ever had any chance to win Heather's hand.

Yet to lose her so quickly, after less than a day back in her own world, not only wounded him deeply but also stung his pride. He had thought she cared more than that for him, that she valued what they had shared more than so easily to toss it aside. But now . . . now he wondered.

"Ye don't understand!" Heather gripped his arm, her fingers digging into his flesh. "Aye, my father was actively involved in inviting Charlie to join us here. I confronted him about it after I left Charlie last night. He doesn't care for ye; he admitted it and felt I should meet with Charlie before I made up my mind. But it doesn't mean I can't think for myself, nor make up my own mind who I'll take to husband. I just need some time . . ."

Duncan gave a snort of disgust. "Och, how fickle is yer heart, how shallow the love ye once professed for me, that ye now attempt to weigh it like some mess of vegetables bought at market."

"I'm not weighing it!" Heather cried, anger flashing now in her eyes. "But I don't wish to hurt Charlie or my father, if it can be helped. I love ye, Duncan, but it's no excuse to treat others callously."

At her fervent avowal, some of the pain ebbed. "What do ye wish of me, then, lass?" he asked with a weary sigh. "I don't want to lose ye. It'd tear out my heart to do so. But I fear . . . I fear . . ."

"Aye, it's the same for me." She reached up, stroked his face with a light, lingering, tender touch. "I need some time, Duncan, and today isn't the day to work it all through. The morrow—and all that must then come to pass—hangs heavy enough on me." She smiled wanly. "Pray, let us first get through tomorrow. Until ye come

281

back safely to me, I can't think so verra clearly about aught else."

He took her into his arms, holding her close, and rested his chin upon her head. "I'll come back to ye, sweet lass, and no mistake. Alive and well, or ye won't have to make a choice between Seton and myself at all."

By noon that day all the nobles involved in the plot had arrived. They met in the great chamber soon thereafter, taking their places around the long dining table. Heather, her participation essentially completed, was coerced to take in the town with Seton, leaving Duncan to stew impotently for the next several hours in a roomful of men. Until suppertime, no effort was spared in outlining in great detail the people to contact once within Lochleven, the timing of when to spirit Mary away, and where the horsemen awaiting the queen would be waiting along the shore.

Duncan learned that only fourteen-year-old Willie Douglas—the foundling son of Sir William Douglas, Lady Margaret's oldest legitimate son from her marriage to Robert Douglas—and George Douglas, another of Lady Margaret's sons, would actually aid him once he was in Lochleven. While Duncan, in the guise of their good friend Colin Stewart, kept Lady Margaret and Sir William sufficiently entertained and distracted, young Willie was to steal the castle keys from his adoptive father Sir William during the feast celebrating Willie's return to the island. He had only recently been forgiven and taken back into his father and grandmother's good graces, after having been banished subsequent to Mary's first failed escape attempt, of which he had played a part.

"The queen has been notified today is the day of her deliverance," Robert Gordon then informed him. "George Douglas has sent, via his mother, a pearl earring of Mary's. It's a signal to her that the time is ripe for escape. Yer first task, after settling into yer role as Colin Stewart, will be to find a private moment with George Douglas. He'll apprise ye then if there are any last-minute changes to the escape plan."

Duncan nodded. He had been given artistic likenesses of all at Lochleven—the queen included—to study. He hadn't a worry that he'd quickly and easily identify the key players there, friend and foe alike.

"The journey back across the loch still concerns me," Duncan said. "It'll put us all in the open for some time."

"There's naught to be done for it." Robert smiled. "Besides, Willie has orders to lock in the castle inhabitants once he, ye, and the queen reach the outside, then throw the castle keys into the loch. It'll buy ye all some extra time for escape, even after the theft of the keys is discovered. And if ye happen to meet with any resistance while attempting to reach the loch, we're counting on yer added brawn to hold them off for however long it takes for Mary and Willie to make it to and through the castle gate."

It seemed like a sound enough plan, Duncan thought. Once more, he nodded.

"It'll have to do then."

Robert Gordon paused to scan the faces of all the men present. "Do any of ye have aught more to offer? If not, I can smell supper cooking. We need to adjourn this room so the table can be set for the evening meal. And, if we hurry, I'd wager we'll have just sufficient time to wash up before Anne Drummond calls us back to table."

Alastair Seton chuckled. "After that pronouncement, Robbie, I doubt any of us would dare bring up another point. Besides, once supper's done, we still have several more hours of testing this man's"—he indicated Duncan—"knowledge of all things vital before we can take to our beds."

The others, John Beaton and John Sempill among them, quickly added their agreement. As they rose to depart, however, Robert Gordon stayed them with an upraised hand.

"A moment more, though, if ye will. Pray, indulge me with a cup of fine Rhenish wine to celebrate yet another recent change in plans."

The table's occupants glanced at each other in surprise, then sank back into their chairs. Robert rose, poured out seven cups of wine from a swan-necked, silver flask on the sideboard, and carried them back on a silver tray. After he passed a cup to each of the men, he raised his own in toast.

"Earlier today," he said, his smiling gaze meeting Lord Seton's, "Alastair and I agreed that the union of our two families was long overdue. Though the wedding date of our two children was originally set for three months hence, we've jointly decided little purpose is served in postponing it any longer. To that end, I invite ye all to the wedding of my daughter, Heather, and Charles Seton"—his glance swung to lock with Duncan's—"in two weeks' time."

16

Duncan crept through the sleep-shrouded house, moving with catlike stealth along the hall from the third floor where he had been bedded, down the stairs, and along the second-floor hall to Heather's bedchamber. It was the first opportunity he'd had since breakfast to speak with her. Most coincidentally, Charlie Seton had seen to it that she had stayed away all day and late into the evening, supposedly visiting some family friends who lived in Kinross.

Robert Gordon's hand was in that feeble ruse, Duncan well knew. A ruse to keep Heather and him apart as much as possible until the plot was commenced and done. Robert Gordon, who, Duncan thought, gritting his teeth in silent frustration, had also seen to it that his daughter wed before she had opportunity to break the betrothal herself.

But that would never be. The older man's self-centered manipulations would end this very night. If not for the queen and her rescue attempt on the morrow, Duncan would have straightaway taken Heather back with him to the Highlands. Such an act, though, would've been as selfish and self-serving as anything Robert Gordon had ever perpetrated.

Duncan had told her in the forest, that day the outlaws had tried to take her, that he loved her so deeply that he'd sacrifice everything—even his honor—for her. And he skirted perilously close to impugning that honor—and hers—in paying her a late-night visit in her bedchamber. He had never imagined, though, that events would force him to act in such a manner.

What if, after even this desperate measure, Heather still turned from him? Yet what choice was left him? Duncan wondered as he paused at last outside Heather's door. There was no way of knowing what other devious plans Robert Gordon had up his sleeve to keep him and Heather apart until she was at last wed to the Seton lad.

Not surprisingly, the door to her bedchamber was locked. Duncan grimaced in irritation, briefly considered knocking to waken her, then thought better of it. Though he knew Beth slept below stairs with the other servants of Drummond House, he didn't think it wise to risk awakening Heather's father, who he knew slept across the hall. Better to climb in through her bedchamber window if it was open or, if it wasn't, tap on it.

As luck would have it, Heather had drawn the window open to cool the room. After negotiating the maze of tree branches that spread just above and outside her window, Duncan leaned forward, shoved the window open wider, and swung into the room. He landed with a soft thud and glanced about. In a corner shadowed from the moonlight streaming in through the window, Duncan could just make out a bed. Heather slept, undisturbed, therein.

He hesitated but a moment, his courage momentarily failing him. If he left now, Heather wouldn't be the wiser. And that, perhaps, would indeed be the best for the both of them.

What gave him the right to force a life-changing decision on her? If God meant for them to be together, He would make it happen, wouldn't He? And if He didn't, then it wouldn't.

But what if Charlie Seton and Robert Gordon had found some way to change Heather's mind, to go against the will of God? Did he really want to know that, tonight of all nights, when he was about to risk his life on the morrow? Perhaps it was best to keep his illusions for a time longer. Nothing could really be acted on, one way or another, until Mary was free of Lochleven Castle.

Still, if he quailed now, he'd always wonder if their love was truly meant to be, or if he had squandered it because of his cowardice and inaction. He'd always wonder—and always curse himself, too.

Squaring his shoulders, Duncan strode over to the bed. He leaned down and took Heather by the arm, shaking her gently.

"Lass? Lass," he whispered, "wake up. Wake up, I say."

She mumbled something, turned toward him, and dozed on. Duncan squatted, shook her again.

"Heather, wake up. It's Duncan. I must talk with ye."

Lids, thick with long, lush lashes, lifted. For an instant

Heather stared at him, her gaze confused, unfocused. Then recognition dawned.

"D-Duncan!" she croaked in a sleep-thickened voice. "How did ye come . . . why are ye here?"

He pulled her to a sitting position. "Through the window. And my reason is quite apparent. I wished to speak with ye this eve." He managed a wry grin. "However, considering ye've been out all day and most of the eve with yer betrothed . . . well, this is the first chance I've had to talk with ye."

Heather brushed the long tangle of hair from her face, rose, and took up her bedrobe draped across a nearby chair. She hastily put on the garment and fastened it closed before glancing back to Duncan.

"It isn't proper for ye to be here. Couldn't we talk in the morn?"

Duncan gave a sardonic laugh and rose to stand before her. "Och, so now that we're back with yer own kind, it's time to stand on formalities again, is it? Last time we were alone ye hardly gave a care for proprieties. And now, now ye can't bear to be unchaperoned with me!"

"It isn't a case of bearing or not bearing to be alone with ye," she whispered, outraged. "It's a case of my father sleeping just across the hall, and my betrothed and his father resting upstairs."

"Aye," Duncan snarled, his anger rising apace with his anguish, "and how would it look if I were caught in yer bedchamber?" He stepped back, his hands fisting at his sides. "It'd be too humiliating, wouldn't it, to admit I had just cause to be here."

Heather stared up at him, then sighed and shook her

head. "Och, Duncan, Duncan. I don't wish to fight with ye. And I'll never be ashamed to admit to my love for ye. I just don't wish to cause others pain in the doing."

"It's too late for that," he growled. "Young Seton's in love with ye. Even a blind man can see that."

She looked away. "He's a dear, sweet man. But I swear I've never pretended to a deeper affection for him than one of brother and sister."

"Well, he hardly sees *ye* as a sister, and make no mistake!"

"And don't ye think I know that?" Heather turned back to him, her eyes blazing. "He's as adamant as my father that our wedding date be moved up." She cocked her head, studying him closely. "Ye do know of my father's intent to see Charlie and me wed in two weeks' time, don't ye?"

"Aye," Duncan said through clenched teeth, "I know. Is it yer intent, as well?"

She stared up at him. "I can't believe ye asked that. Do ye discount my love for ye so quickly, that ye'd think I'd so easily throw ye over?" She gave a snort of disgust. "Truly, Duncan Mackenzie, but at times ye can be so addlepated!"

A fierce, wild hope swelled in Duncan. "Then ye still love me? Ye still wish to be my wife?"

"Y-yer wife?" Heather's eyes grew wide. "Ye . . . ye never said ye wished to wed."

"And do ye imagine me so disreputable, that I'd tell a lass I loved her and then not wish to wed her?" Duncan shook his head. "Truly, lass. If ye believe that, ye don't know me as well as ye think."

289

She closed the distance between them and put her arms about his neck. "Then say it," she urged softly. "Ask me to wed ye, to become yer wife."

Taken aback by Heather's sudden boldness, for a fleeting instant words fled Duncan. Then reality struck. Heather not only still loved him but wanted him to propose to her. All his earlier misgivings fled. Somehow, some way, they *would* make a life together.

He grinned. "Will ye wed me, Heather Gordon, and be my wife?"

"Well, I don't know . . ." Heather said, pretending indecision. A mischievous quirk to the corners of her mouth, however, gave her away.

Chuckling softly, Duncan swung her up in his arms and twirled her about the room. "Say it, lass. Say aye or I'll turn ye about until ye're too rattled to tell up from down and right from left."

"D-Duncan!" Heather gasped. "Have a care or ye'll waken the entire household, servants included."

Ever so slowly and gently, he lowered her until her feet again touched the floor. "For a lass who just proposed to a man," he replied with a teasing grin, "ye've gone suddenly quite shy. Is this what I'm to expect once we're wed?"

"Nay." Pressing close, she hid her face in the curve of his shoulder. "But if only ye knew how long I've dreamt of this night . . ."

"I knew, sweet lass," he said, his heart pounding in his breast. "I was there in that verra same dream, hoping, wanting the same thing."

She lifted her face to his. Unshed tears, like so many

priceless jewels, glittered in her eyes. "Truly, Duncan? Truly?"

"Aye, truly." He covered her mouth with his, taking her lips with a gentle but uncompromising possession. "Truly and forevermore."

After a time, sated and breathless, they parted. Heather gazed up at Duncan through eyes made hazy with delight. "That was indeed magnificent." She sighed in contentment.

A chuckle rumbled deep in his chest. "Aye, I am a rather braw kisser, aren't I?"

She slapped at him playfully. "Och, and aren't we puffed up with ourselves, now that we've gotten what we wanted?"

Duncan leaned down and, yet again, kissed her. "I have ye, don't I?" he said, his voice a husky rasp when he finally drew back. "That'd make any man a wee bit puffed up, to have such a bonny lass as yerself for his own."

"Would it now?" Heather shrugged. "Well, I wouldn't know or care. I'm quite content with ye and want no other."

"Fine words. Let's see if ye, in all honesty, can still say them fifty years and nine or ten bairns from now. That'll be the true test of yer love."

In all honesty . . . the true test of yer love . . .

Inexplicably, Duncan's words stabbed at Heather's heart like no amount of guilt and agonizing over her burdensome secret ever had. How could she say she loved him, how could she hope to build a life together, on the treacherous foundation of lies and deception?

She couldn't. That reality, at least, could be denied no longer. Vow or no, she couldn't keep the secret from Duncan a moment more.

Wordlessly, Heather extricated herself from the warm haven of Duncan's arms, walked to the chest-high clothes cupboard, and opened it. Extracting a small, paper-wrapped parcel, she turned and made her way back to him.

"Here," she said, handing him the package. "I meant to give this to ye on the morrow, but mayhap it'll have more significance now."

Duncan frowned in puzzlement but undid the small parcel. Inside, finely wrought in silver, lay a representation of the Scottish thistle surrounded by a wreath of heather.

He looked up. "What's this for?"

"It's the clan badge of the Stewarts, the Scots thistle is," Heather explained. "Colin's inordinately proud of his own silver thistle brooch—a family heirloom—and wears it nearly all the time. I had one fashioned by a silversmith to look exactly like the one Colin wears."

"Down to the last little detail, ye've spared no effort in assuring I'll appear like Colin." Duncan smiled. "My thanks. I'll wear it gladly on the morrow."

Heather swallowed hard and forced herself not to break eye contact with him. "There's an even greater significance to that brooch than just serving as part of yer disguise."

He looked at her, his gaze guileless and infinitely trusting. "Aye, lass?"

"Ye always suspected that I knew more than I was willing to share about yer true parentage, didn't ye?"

Duncan's smile faded. Every muscle in his body tautened.

"Aye, that I did."

"My father made me swear not to tell, even before I first met ye. Even then, though, I protested that it wasn't right to keep such a thing from ye. Still, he was adamant and, to my shame and growing distress as I came to know ye, I kept the secret."

"Until now." He eyed her narrowly. "Why do ye finally see fit to tell me now?"

"Ye asked me to be yer wife." She forced herself to meet his suddenly hard, unflinching gaze. "I can't keep any secret from ye again."

"Tell me what ye know then."

The request was little less than a command, but Heather chose not to take offense. Duncan had a right to be angry. Until now, she *had* temporarily sacrificed his welfare for the sake of her father's and the queen's. She only hoped that once all was revealed he could put her knowing, if necessary, deception behind him. It was the only hope they had, if they ever wished to go on with their lives together.

"Ye were born a Stewart, not a Mackenzie," Heather said softly. "And, as ye may have also suspected, ye've always been the twin of Colin Stewart and never just some uncanny double. Hence," she added, her smile

293

rueful, "the additional significance of the Stewart clan badge I gave ye. It belongs as much to ye as to Colin."

Duncan looked away. "So, Colin's my brother, is he?" he finally replied, his voice low and drained of all emotion. "And ye and yer father would have me betray him and the people he considers his friends?"

"He and his friends support Moray, not the queen!" Heather cried. "In times such as these, sometimes it's necessary to pit family members against each other. Indeed, even Mary's stepbrother turned on her, didn't he?"

"Did ye ever once think, though"—his surprising calm as deceptive as that of the calm before a storm—"what the act might cost me in terms of my future relationship with my long-lost brother? Even if I don't ruin Colin in the doing, what will he think of me? Do ye truly imagine he'll ever welcome me home after the morrow?"

Heather hung her head. "I'm ashamed to admit that I never thought of that. I only worried over the unfairness to ye."

"Ye didn't worry overmuch, though, did ye? Ye managed to wait until the night before Mary's rescue to tell me."

When Heather remained silent, Duncan heaved a deep sigh. "Well, there'll be time enough to delve more fully into all that later. Just tell me this. What happened to my mither and father?"

Relieved to turn the conversation away from her personal failings in the matter, Heather finally glanced up at him. "Yer mither died birthing ye. Yer father, the Lord David Stewart, soon followed her in attempting to put down a clan uprising. Before that happened, though, he called on my father for aid. It was my father who suggested sending one of ye away into the safety of the Highlands to my mither's kin, the Mackenzies."

"I should've known yer father's hand was in this somewhere." As he spoke, Duncan strode to her wardrobe, opened it, and began digging through her clothes.

"What are ye planning to do?" As she watched him, unease filled Heather.

"What else? Wake yer father and demand that he tell me the rest of the story. Unless," he sneered, shooting her a dark glance, "ye know it all."

Heather shook her head. "Nay, I don't know it all. What I do know, I've told ye."

Duncan finally seemed to find what he was searching for. He pulled out a blue silk gown, turned, and walked back to her.

"Here, put this on. Ye're going with me."

Shivering now, Heather took the gown from him and hurried over to the dressing screen. Slipping behind it, as swiftly as she could, she dressed and then slid a pair of soft shoes onto her bare feet.

His expression just as dark and foreboding as when she had left him, Duncan awaited her. There seemed no point in further pleas for understanding. Heather stalked to the door, unlatched it, and swung it open.

"Let's be quick about this, if ye will. We've both got a long day ahead of us."

With a tight-lipped scowl, Duncan brushed by her and headed directly across the hall. Just as he was raising his fist to pound—not knock, Heather wagered—on her father's door, she managed to reach his side and grab his arm.

"Allow me," she whispered. "Odds are my father's a lot more likely to answer the door at this hour if he hears and sees me first."

Without a word, Duncan lowered his arm. "Have at it, then."

She tapped lightly on the door, then leaned close and called out in a low but insistent voice. "Father? Father, it's Heather. I must speak with ye."

There was a grunt from inside the room, the slap of bare feet on the wooden floor, then the sound of a latch being lifted. The door creaked open. Robert Gordon, tousled of hair and bleary of eye, peeked out.

"By all the saints, lass," he croaked. "It's surely past midnight. Whatever's the matter, that ye must disturb my sleep?"

Duncan stepped around Heather and all but shoved the door into his face. "*I* am the matter. And it's past time ye told me all."

Muttering an oath, Robert staggered backward. Duncan strode in, Heather in his wake. She turned quickly and shut the door.

Her father stood there in the long, linen shirt he slept in, his spindly legs and knobby knees poking out from beneath the voluminous sleeping garment making him look so much like an indignant crane. His expression, by turns bewildered and then outraged, only added to his rather droll pose. There was nothing droll, however, in the blistering words he turned on Duncan.

"Ye overstep yerself, my good man," he snarled, "to

presume to enter my bedchamber at this hour and make any sort of demands. If ye weren't so vitally important to the rescue on the morrow, I'd call for the constable to clap ye in irons."

"But I am, aren't I?" Duncan was quick to snarl back. "And so ye'll tolerate my audacity, won't ye?"

Robert made an impatient motion. "Be quick about it, then. It's come to the point I can barely tolerate being in the same room with ye."

"Indeed?" Duncan smiled grimly. "I wouldn't have thought ye'd speak thusly to one of yer own kind. And I *am* one of yer own kind, aren't I? A nobleman, a Stewart, I mean?"

The older man's gaze swung to Heather. "Ye told him then, did ye?"

She refused to make protest of innocence or quail before him. "Aye, Father, I did."

"Fool!"

"Rather, I'd say the fool was ye, m'lord," Duncan interjected. "Ye were the one who thought to keep the truth from me until it suited yer pleasure to tell me—*if* ye ever meant to tell me at all. But now I know, and ye'll tell me all, or I'll walk from this room and never look back."

It was a bluff, Heather knew. Duncan would never desert the queen in her hour of need. But she wasn't so sure her father knew that.

"What do ye want of me?" Robert snapped. "I'd think ye'd have already learned enough from my traitorous daughter."

Stung, Heather lashed back. "Ye'd no right to keep it from him. It was dishonorable and—"

"Enough, lass." With an upraised hand, Duncan silenced her. "It doesn't matter anymore." He riveted the full force of his furious gaze on her father. "Who's the firstborn of the two of us?"

Robert hesitated, eyed him nervously, then wet his lips. "Ye are. It was why ye, instead of Colin, were secretly taken away and hidden in the Highlands. That way if yer father failed to subdue the uprising, at least the true heir would survive."

Did Gordon tell the truth, Duncan wondered, or was this yet another prevarication from a man he suspected had lived much of his life twisting reality to suit his own means? One way or another, it might be difficult at this late a date to find many who *did* know the actual facts. But what if he really *was* the Stewart heir? It changed everything, he thought, glancing at Heather. *Everything*.

"So now Colin has gone all these years imagining he's the heir." Duncan gave a snort of disgust. "What a fine kettle of fish ye've now forced the both of us into. It makes me wonder if ye ever intended to tell me the truth, or just to let my brother continue to imagine he was not only the heir, but the sole child as well."

"Or, even more to the point," Heather added, "why ye waited all these years to reveal the secret. Until you fashioned the plot to free the queen, there surely could've been naught to compel ye to keep Duncan in hiding all this time. The uprising against the Stewarts ultimately failed, and no harm ever came to Colin because of it.

Why didn't ye bring Duncan back from the Highlands soon thereafter?"

Two accusing pairs of eyes glared at Robert Gordon. He smirked and shrugged.

"I had other things of greater import to occupy myself with and, after a time, saw no further reason to amend the wee oversight. Ye grew and flourished there in yer Highland home. And I had done all that yer father requested. I had seen to yer safety, fulfilled my vow to him. It wasn't my responsibility to continue to meddle in Stewart affairs, so I didn't."

"A fine and true friend, ye were," Duncan muttered. "Or *were* ye, even from the beginning? This smacks more of revenge than of loyalty, if ye ask me."

"Be that as it may," the older man replied, "time passed, and then one day the queen was betrayed by her brother. And, when I concocted the plot to rescue Mary using ye as the decoy, I certainly couldn't risk telling ye the truth then. The Stewarts are loyal to Moray. He's the man in power, the man of the hour. I couldn't be certain that, once ye knew the truth of yer birth, ye wouldn't turn to his side."

"So ye thought first and foremost to use me to yer own purposes."

"Aye," Robert replied defiantly. "For the sake of our queen, I'd do that and more."

Duncan gave another snort of disgust. "As if ye've ever done aught for another, save when it served to yer advantage."

Rage suffused the older man's features. "I don't have to stand here and suffer yer insults, ye arrogant pup. Ye've gotten what ye came for. Ye have yer answers. Now fulfill yer end of the bargain and be ready on the morrow. In the meanwhile, get out of my room."

"A moment more, *m'lord*," Duncan said. "Ye said earlier today that my brother was to be apprehended and held incognito until after I returned from Lochleven on the morrow."

"Aye, what of it?"

"Where is he now?"

Robert eyed him suspiciously. "If ye mean to free him, it won't—"

"I don't wish to free him," Duncan said, cutting him off. "I but wish to speak with him. He is my brother, after all. It's past time I meet him."

"And what purpose would that serve?"

"What's it to ye? I don't have to justify my actions to ye."

"Nay, I suppose ye don't." Robert gave a bitter laugh. "Ye'll regret it, though. Colin won't like learning his older brother has returned from the dead."

"Where is he, Gordon?"

Robert smiled thinly. "Below stairs in a locked and well-guarded room."

"Take me to him then."

"As ye wish. One thing, though. He can't learn where he is or who is holding him. Such knowledge would endanger us all."

"Not to mention," Duncan added sarcastically, "ye'd most likely then be forced to kill him."

"More the reason not to tell him aught, wouldn't ye say?" Robert gestured to the door. "Now, if ye don't mind,

I must dress. And I don't need ye gawking at me while I do so."

When Duncan looked about to trade another insult with her father, Heather took hold of his arm. "Come. We can await him just as easily outside as within this room."

Duncan paused to shoot Robert Gordon one parting, disdainful look, then silently followed Heather from the bedchamber. Once outside with the door shut behind them, however, he turned the full force of his rage on her.

"Hie yerself to yer own bedchamber," he said. "I don't wish or need for ye to accompany me below stairs. What I have to say to my brother, I prefer to say in private."

"But ye might need me to—"

"I'm not the imbecile ye and yer father seem to imagine I am. But ye risk much if Colin recognizes ye." He turned Heather around to face her bedchamber door. "And I tell ye true. I've had about all I can stomach of ye and yer kind this night."

Heather whirled about, tears of anger flooding her eyes. "Ye can be as cruel and pigheaded as my father. Do ye know that, Duncan Mackenzie?"

"Duncan Stewart," he corrected her, his own eyes glittering with frigid wrath. "Now, hie yerself to yer room and do so quickly."

"When can we speak next then?" Her tear-clogged voice rasped hoarsely in the silent hallway. "We must speak, must work this through."

He gave an uncaring shrug. "On the morrow mayhap. Or, then again, mayhap never. It'll all depend on many things, the least of which is will I even return alive from Lochleven."

301

17

After a sleepless night that had finally ended in total exhaustion at dawn, Heather woke early the next afternoon. As soon as the realization of the lateness of the hour struck her, she sat up in bed, an anguished cry on her lips.

Duncan!

Was it already three, when he was slated to ride out for Lochleven? Had she missed her last chance to speak with him before he left?

As her feet hit the floor a wave of nausea washed over her, followed swiftly by a pounding headache. Heather sat there for a moment, breathing deeply, before summoning all her willpower to rise and stagger across the room. There, in the polished metal mirror hanging on the wall over the clothes cupboard, she saw her swollen face and eyes, the pale, haggard complexion, the haunted expression.

Shoving a hank of hair aside, she grimaced, then stuck her tongue out at her watery reflection. "Och, verra good," she muttered in disgust. "Today of all days when it's vital

302

ye appear yer best, ye instead look like ye've just been dragged from the pit of some dungeon."

Irritation filling her, she glanced around, hoping Beth would leap from some corner and come to her aid. But Beth was nowhere to be seen, most likely downstairs somewhere, thinking she was doing the best by her mistress in letting her sleep.

Briefly, Heather considered going after her maid, then decided against that. By the time she dressed and found Beth to come up and help her repair the damages last night had wrought, Duncan might well be gone—if he hadn't left already. Besides, in her present condition there was little Beth could do for her at any rate.

After quickly cleaning up, Heather grabbed a simple, pale green silk gown. Her glance snagged on the farthingale propped on the floor beside the cupboard. After a fleeting consideration, she decided against taking the time to don the whalebone hoop that would extend the skirts of her gown outward into the currently fashionable cone shape. Indeed, if the truth were told, she had eschewed that cumbersome piece of equipment after only a few days at the Mackenzie cottage. And she couldn't say she had missed it once since then.

A few minutes more and Heather was out the door and hurrying downstairs. To her relief, she found Duncan in the parlor, a cloth about his shoulders. Beth stood behind him, scissors in hand. For a long moment Heather lingered in the doorway, gazing at them as she gave her rapidly racing heart a chance to ease.

Then, shoulders squared, she marched into the room.

"Good day, Duncan, Beth," Heather said, hoping the slight quaver in her voice wasn't noticeable.

Duncan gave a start and turned in his chair. The glance he sent her, however, was anything but warm or welcoming.

Beth shot her a quizzical look, her brow quirking as she scanned Heather's appearance. "Don't say one word," Heather warned between gritted teeth as she walked over and took the scissors from her maid. "Not one word."

"Do ye wish for me to stay and assist ye?" Beth fought to hide a grin that twitched at the corners of her mouth.

"Aye, pray do," Duncan said.

"Nay, please go," Heather promptly contradicted him. "And close the door behind ye, if ye will."

The maid looked from a scowling Duncan to her resolute mistress, then shrugged and walked from the parlor, making a great show of closing the door behind her. Heather stared after her, then turned back to Duncan.

"Well, do ye plan to finish me off with that"—he eyed the scissors Heather had clenched in her hand—"or are ye going to complete the cutting of my hair?" As if either option were equally acceptable, he turned in his chair and presented his back to her. "One way or another, I've but an hour or so left until I must depart for Lochleven."

"After how ye treated me last night," Heather muttered as she moved to stand behind him, "mayhap I *should* finish ye off."

"And precisely how did ye expect me to react, when ye finally told me the truth ye'd been keeping from me all these months?"

304

She grabbed a handful of his hair and began hacking at it with the scissors. Long, wavy locks of chestnut brown, like so many leaves tumbling from the trees in autumn, began to float languidly to the floor.

"Don't play games with me, Duncan *Stewart*. Ye know what I'm talking about. Ye were inordinately cruel and rude, not to mention particularly hard-hearted as well as heartless."

He gave a disparaging laugh. "Cruel and hard-hearted and heartless was I? Well, then I'm in good company."

"I know ye're hurt, angry, and even feel betrayed." As she scissored away at his hair, Heather forced down her own renewed swell of hurt and anger. "But can't ye see that I was in an untenable position, having to choose between ye and my father? As selfish as he is, I still love him. Yet, in the end, I still chose ye. I went against my father's wishes. I told ye the truth. Doesn't that count for aught with ye?"

"Do ye know what my brother said to me last night?" Duncan chose to reply instead. "Once he'd mastered himself and overcome the initial shock of meeting a man who was both brother and twin, he demanded I prove my loyalty to him and the Stewarts by helping him escape. When I refused, he called me a baseborn traitor and bastardly rogue, not worthy ever to call myself a Stewart, much less his brother." He laughed again, but this time the sound was bleak and bitter. "So, once again I'm a man without a family or home. I'm also a man who, in the end, I fear neither side ultimately will wish to claim."

"Ye can't know that for sure." As she spoke Heather's

hands flew, brushing, then cutting his hair until, beneath Duncan's lush mane, a neat, close-cropped, and well-shaped head began to appear. "It was never Colin's right to disown ye or deny ye what's legitimately yours. Ye're the firstborn, after all. And once Mary returns to power—"

"And what if she doesn't?" Savagely, Duncan cut her off. "What if, even if the rescue plot succeeds, she can't regain her throne? What will become of me then?"

"If we're discovered, ye'll be an outlaw just like the rest of us."

"An outlaw." He sighed in exasperation. "A fine choice indeed—either to be a man without a family or an outlaw. Somehow, whether the queen's freed or not, I fail to see what I gain."

"Ye'll still have me." Heather set aside the brush and scissors and stepped back.

Duncan turned. "Will I, lass? I suppose, to yer way of thinking, that'll make up for everything else I've lost."

His words slammed into Heather like a fist into her gut. "It might if ye truly believed I didn't willingly betray ye. It might if ye truly believed I loved ye."

He gave a despairing grunt and shook his head. "Aye, if I could truly believe that, no matter what happens, ye'd stand by me. Have ye given it much thought—the kind of life ye'd have with me, I mean? Stewart though I may be, I fear I've lost my only brother. Atop that, there's no guarantee I'll regain title to my ancestral lands. And that's the verra best that might happen."

Och, Duncan, Duncan, Heather thought, gazing down at him and feeling as if, bit by bit, he was shredding her heart into tiny pieces. With his shorn hair he looked so much like Colin now. He'd fool even Lady Douglas. *But, even if he and his brother stood side by side, dressed exactly alike, I could still pick out Duncan without hesitation. He is, and always will be, the man of my heart.*

"I don't care what life holds for me, just as long as we're together," Heather, stirred by her thoughts, proclaimed. "I love ye. I want to be with ye. Isn't that enough?"

"For some, aye, it might be." He stared up at her, his tormented gaze searing clear through her. "But ye've been raised to a far different kind of life than I. It's past time we both faced the reality of our situation. My way of life, and what I might be able to give ye, most likely won't improve. And ye need to be sure ye haven't let yerself fall in love with me because ye imagined I'd one day become the nobleman ye always knew me to be."

His words, even as they fell from his lips, stabbed through Heather with the brutal force of a blade most cruelly used. It took all of her willpower not to slap him or burst out weeping.

"So, ye think, do ye, that I offered my love to ye fully aware I might gain a fine name and family?"

He was no better, in the end, than her father or her sister's husband, she thought, her anger rising apace now with her pain. He held her in no higher esteem than they had held their wives, imagining her capable of guile and coldhearted manipulation. Indeed, she was no more than some skulking cur to Duncan, ready to turn at any moment and bite him.

Heather backed away, her horror and disillusionment growing with each halting step she took. "But then, how could ye think otherwise? Ye were never able to overcome yer disdain for those of the nobility, were ye? And, because of that, ye never really knew me. Ye never understood what really mattered to me. Indeed, I wonder now if ye were ever even capable of a true and lasting love."

Anger flashed in Duncan's eyes. He shoved back his chair and rose.

"Have a care who ye accuse of what, madam. It wasn't I who withheld information. It wasn't I who couldn't help but make all decisions based on prior, secret knowledge." Duncan gave a bitter laugh. "And yet ye dare accuse me of not understanding, of not being capable of a true and lasting love!"

"Ye'll never forgive me for not telling ye sooner, will ye?"

To Heather's dismay, tears sprang to her eyes. Fiercely, she blinked them away. Atop everything else, he wasn't going to make her cry. She'd had her fill and more of weeping over heartless, self-serving men.

"I was afraid of that," she gritted out past clenched teeth, "and, in my cowardice and indecision, I hesitated too long. But ye're just as wrong, in yer unbending, sanctimonious refusal to forgive me. Ye're just as wrong in failing to see any other motive for my actions, save of manipulativeness and self-interest."

"But that's the way of the nobility, is it not?" he countered with a snarl. "And are ye not yer father's daughter? His loyal, obedient daughter?"

"Aye, I'm loyal and obedient." Heather's hands clenched

at her side. "But I'm also honorable, and I try to follow my heart and always do the right thing."

"Do ye now?"

"Aye, I do."

There was no point in continuing this conversation further, Heather realized. A smothering sense of futility, of defeat, engulfed her. After last night, their emotions ran too high. Duncan's impending departure for Lochleven only intensified everything they now felt and said. Better to give him a time to cool his temper, to allow him to reflect on what had happened, and pray that he finally came to understand.

She sighed. "It's past time ye dressed. Ye must depart soon."

"Aye."

"Do ye wish me to come down when ye're ready to leave and bid ye farewell?"

A fleeting look of some softer, more tender emotion flashed in his eyes, then was gone. Savagely, Duncan shook his head, his features now set in an expression as hard as stone.

"Nay. It'd be better if ye didn't. If I'm to play the part of my brother convincingly, I need all my powers of concentration about me. I don't need yer memory as distraction."

He spoke true, Heather well knew, but his words hurt nonetheless. "Suit yerself," she choked out. "I wish ye Godspeed then, and a safe and successful outcome. If ye can still believe aught I say, believe that."

"And believe me when I say that I'm grateful for all

yer efforts in preparing me these past months. It was a sacrifice for ye, I well know, but deeply appreciated."

His words, to Heather, sounded suspiciously like a final farewell. She couldn't bear the implications of such a parting. Her eyes spilling over with tears she could no longer staunch, she fled the room, never once looking back.

George Douglas lost no time in seeking out Duncan. As the rowboat approached the landing at Lochleven Castle, a handsome young man with blue eyes, dark, wavy hair, and a ruddy complexion hurried over to offer his hand in assistance. Before the boatman even had a chance to tie the vessel to a mooring, Duncan had leaped out.

He took George's hand in greeting rather than in help. "What a glorious day for a feast!" Duncan proclaimed, forcing himself into the role of his grandiosely preening brother.

Pausing, he pretended concern over a smudge of dirt on his snug black hose. "Och, I haven't even met with yer sainted mother yet and already I'm soiled. Ye really must see to it that yer men keep the rowboats more tidy."

Eyes wide, George stared at Duncan in admiration. "Aye," he finally managed to stammer out, "I'll have a talk with the boatmen forthwith. But first, allow me to escort ye into the castle. It's a warm day. I'll wager ye might like a cool swallow of ale."

They began to walk up the short, grassy embankment toward the castle. As soon as they were far enough from earshot of the boatman, George lowered his voice.

"By all the saints, Duncan. If I didn't know the switch had been made, I'd swear ye were yer brother. Not only are ye his spitting image, but ye sound and speak exactly like him."

"I had a good teacher," Duncan muttered dryly.

His hand rose to finger the silver thistle that now lay pinned to his doublet. Freshened pain at the memory of Heather's betrayal battled chaotically with a fierce yearning to see her, hold her once more.

Fool, he berated himself. *Stupid, simple-minded, love-struck fool.*

"Aye, I'd heard that Heather Gordon tutored ye." George grinned. "Now that's one bonny lassie. I was once a suitor for her hand, ye know, before her father finally decided on Charlie Seton."

"It seems every noble of any repute has been Heather Gordon's suitor at one time or another." Shoving aside further distracting thoughts of Heather, Duncan glanced up at the guards walking the castle parapets. "Be that as it may, before we draw any closer, tell me now. Are the plans still as they were, or have any last-minute changes been necessary?"

"Just one. Once he stole the castle keys from my brother, Lochleven's laird, ye were originally to leave the feast with Willie and, if needed, act as guard to him and the queen. Now, ye're to remain behind for about a half hour to keep everyone distracted so the keys' theft isn't noticed. Then, and only then, are ye to join them at the castle gates where ye'll all escape together."

Duncan frowned. He knew George wasn't staying for the feast, having pled prior commitments so as to be available to help the queen escape Kinross once she reached the shore. But there was something about this new change that didn't feel quite right.

"And who will now guard the queen if someone discovers their escape?" Duncan asked. "Surely not young Willie?"

"All I know is other arrangements have been made to see to Mary's safety."

"Even so, a half hour's a long time. Do ye really think it'll take that long to free Mary from her room and get her down to the front gate?"

George shrugged. "It may. Hence the need for ye to meet them there. If the keys are missed before Willie can get her to the boats . . ."

"Aye, I know." Duncan sighed, quashing his earlier misgivings. "All will be for naught."

"Not to mention," the younger man added with a sudden touch of black humor, "our heads may take quick leave of our bodies."

"That would be preferable to torture and languishing in prison," Duncan muttered. "But we won't dwell on such dismal consequences. We've a mission to complete, and complete successfully. The sooner we embark on it, the better."

"Well spoken, Colin," George said, clapping him on the back as they walked through the front gate of Lochleven. "But first, before our cup or two of ale," he added, noting his mother standing on the steps of the keep, "ye must pay yer respects to the Lady Margaret."

Duncan's glance lifted to where Lochleven's chatelaine awaited. He plastered what he hoped was an

312

appropriately delighted smile on his face. There was no time left to worry over unexpected changes at any rate. The first true test of his disguise was upon him. He uttered a quick, fervent prayer and strode out alongside George.

"Whatever is the matter with ye, Colin?" Lady Margaret Douglas asked later that evening, a worried look in her eyes. "Ye've been unusually quiet for a time now. Is the feast not to yer liking? Is there aught that disturbs ye?"

Duncan ground his teeth in frustration. Aye, he thought, clasping his wine goblet so tightly his knuckles went white. There was much that disturbed him. Willie Douglas had surreptitiously appropriated the castle keys nearly a half hour ago. Since then, as the minutes ticked away and he waited for his predetermined time to take his leave, Duncan had sat there in agonizing dread that the theft would be discovered. But neither Lady Margaret, of course, nor any of the others still at table, was privy to that. So the charade, at least for a time more, must play on.

"Nay, naught's the matter, m'lady," he said, turning to the older woman on his right. "I was but enjoying a brief respite by listening to the other conversations at table. Besides which," Duncan added, faking an inebriated, slightly lopsided smile as he lifted his goblet of wine, "the excellent vintage served this night has set my head to throbbing and addled my thoughts."

Lady Margaret giggled and laid her hand atop his.

"Not so much that ye won't find yer way to yer proper bedchamber, I hope? I'd gladly escort ye there, and even turn back yer bed covers for ye, but then the servants' tongues might wag and their tales cause a scandal." She patted his hand with an intimacy Duncan found disturbing. "They can't truly understand the special relationship we share, can they?"

And neither would they want to, he thought grimly, taking in the older woman's appearance. Though she may have once been the beauteous mistress to Queen Mary's father, and borne him the bairn who'd someday be the Earl of Moray and Mary's half-brother, the years hadn't been overly kind to Lochleven's chatelaine.

Even in the best of times, it was said Lady Margaret was a stern, dour woman not given to great sentimentality, save for a favored few, his brother Colin included. And her attempts to slow the ravages of time with kohl-lined eyes, red-ochred lips, and skin whitened with ground alabaster, bordered on the ludicrous to a man who preferred his women fresh-faced and free of artifices.

But Heather wasn't here right now, and they might never be together again, Duncan reminded himself, if he didn't extricate himself soon from the cloying, strangely possessive presence of Lochleven's chatelaine. He took another swallow of his wine, then lowered the cup and nodded with all the solemnity he could muster.

"Nay, they can't, m'lady. And what would it matter if they did? They'd still be wrong at any rate."

She leaned back, withdrawing her hand, but a self-satisfied, predatory smile hovered on her lips. "Ye speak true, dear Colin. Indeed ye do."

Time to be gone from here, Duncan thought, before he gave away his distaste for the woman and the dissolute life his brother apparently was leading. "By yer leave, m'lady. I've a need to withdraw to my bedchamber." He made a vague motion toward his head. "The headache doesn't ease. And there's always the morrow."

"Well, though this gathering will be far less pleasant without yer presence, I give ye my leave." Lady Margaret nodded her permission. "And, as ye say, there's always the morrow. And mayhap even later . . . this verra night?"

Duncan shoved back his chair and stood. "Aye . . . mayhap later this verra night." He turned to the laird. "I beg pardon, m'lord, but my head throbs too fiercely to be good company much longer."

William, in the midst of a rousing tale, paused and frowned, but after a quick glance at his mother, sighed in resignation. "So be it, Colin. The night is drawing on, and all of us must soon be abed at any rate. Ye must give me yer solemn oath, though, that, on the morrow, ye'll spare me a few hours for a chess rematch. I vow it was only a lucky move of yers, the last time we played, that won ye that prize mare of mine."

"And now ye wish a chance at winning the horse back, do ye?" Duncan inquired, well aware that was where the laird was heading.

"Aye, of course, lad." William grinned broadly. "And, since ye're still a guest in my castle . . ."

"I've no choice but to acquiesce to yer offer," Duncan finished for him.

William feigned an ingenuous shrug. "If ye wish to call it that, then so be it."

315

"Then I'll most certainly need my rest." He bowed. "I bid ye good night, m'lord."

"Good night, Colin."

With a final, parting bow to Lady Margaret, Duncan turned and strode from the Great Hall. The cool night air was a welcome relief after the stifling confines of the stone chamber. The sudden sense of exhilaration sent his pulse to pounding and his blood to coursing through his veins.

If all had gone as planned, the queen and Willie Douglas would be awaiting him just inside the locked castle gates. It would take but a few minutes more to use the stolen keys. Then they'd soon be out on the loch, paddling their sovereign to freedom.

In the distance, frogs croaked from the rushes at the lake's edge. Water slapped against the pier. Some night bird called out, the sound sweet and melodious. But, even as Duncan drew near the front gate, he neither saw nor heard any sign of two other people waiting in the shadows.

Unease twined within him. He quickened his pace, crouching low to avoid notice by the skeleton crew of guards walking the parapets overhead. Yet, when he made the gate there was no one about. He tried the iron bound portal. It was locked.

For a fleeting instant, panic filled him. What had gone wrong? Was Willie, even now, still struggling to free Mary and bring her here? But George had said other accommodations had been made to provide them with help in negotiating Lochleven's corridors and courtyard. But if that help had failed to protect the queen and ensure her escape, the danger was great that all their plans would come to naught. Surely, now that the party had likely begun to wane with Colin's departure, the laird would soon notice the keys' theft.

Duncan hesitated a moment more, torn between the urge to search the castle for sign of Willie and the growing certainty that he had been purposely left behind. Such a dastardly trick would suit Robert Gordon well, he thought with a sick, sinking feeling in his gut. That last-minute change of plans, requiring him to remain at the feast after the keys were stolen, had never set well with him. Now, his worst fears seemed to have come to fruition.

It would be quicker to climb to the parapets and see if he could catch sight of a boat crossing the lake. The two guards walking sentry, Duncan well knew, had been gifted all eve with sufficient ale to muddle their senses. They'd pay little heed to a guest taking a bit of night air.

As it was, both guards must have decided it was time to imbibe a bit more of their ale. On his way to the parapet walk overlooking the loch and Kinross, he passed the men hunkered down in the sentry shack. They paid him scarce notice.

Far across the loch, Duncan could just make out a boat drawing near the beach. As he watched, two people, one a woman from her long skirts and manner of walk, climbed from the boat and disappeared quickly into the trees. Choking back a savage curse, Duncan gripped the stone wall and clenched shut his eyes, his mind racing.

"Foul-hearted traitor," he muttered softly, thinking dire

317

thoughts of what he'd do when he got his hands next on Robert Gordon. "If he thinks to trap me here, hoping I'll become a suspect in the queen's escape, as surely will all in this castle after tonight, he's sadly mistaken."

There could be only one reason, aside from the older man's quite evident hatred of him, for the despicable treachery. Gordon meant to assure that Duncan would never again be a threat to his plans to wed his daughter to Charles Seton. He had been a fool to fall so neatly into Gordon's little trap.

Aye, a fool once, but a fool no more, he vowed. If he remained in Lochleven, he might eventually be able to convince them he was innocent of any wrongdoing in the queen's disappearance. But if he failed, he would lose the chance at avenging himself on Robert Gordon, not to mention meeting again with Heather before she wed. And that failing—never again to see or speak with Heather—more than anything else would be beyond bearing. He had to escape, and escape soon, or all would be lost.

Duncan scanned the dark, lapping waters of the loch beneath him. It was said William Wallace, during the Wars of Independence, feared the great harm the English, who were then garrisoned in Lochleven Castle, could do to Scotland. His sword tied to his neck, he swam across the loch and captured the garrison's boat. Then, joined by his men, they crossed the loch once more and stormed the castle, taking it into Scottish possession.

He glanced down wryly at the fine clothes he now wore. If William Wallace could swim this loch, so could he. But William had done so garbed only in his shirt.

He, on the other hand, would have to cope with the encumbrance of fine hose, padded trunks, a high-necked ruffled shirt, and tightly fitted doublet. Well, at least not the doublet, Duncan thought as he unfastened it and pulled it from his body.

After removing the silver brooch Heather had given him and tucking it safely away, Duncan tossed the garment aside. He shot one final look over his shoulder in the direction of the guards. The two soldiers were still engrossed in finishing off the remains of the jug of ale. The time was ripe for an escape.

Duncan turned back, climbed atop the parapet and, after an instant's hesitation, dove toward the loch. His form was perfect. He cut through the water's surface with a precision honed by years of practice.

A few seconds more and Duncan broke the surface again, gasping, his body aquiver with the shock of the icy water. Yet it was water no worse than that in the burns and lochs of the Highlands, he reminded himself, before doggedly setting out across the lake. His long, effortless strokes quickly carried him to his destination.

The queen and her young warden were nowhere to be seen. It must be well past midnight by now. If all had gone as planned, Mary had already met up with George Douglas, John Beaton, and Lord Seton, and was even now on her way out of Kinross.

As Duncan neared the shallows on the far shore, the waning moon disappeared behind some clouds. Only a few lights flickered in the windows of the half-timbered houses of Kinross, dimly illuminating the way into town. As angry and determined as he was, though, the night could've been pitch black and he would've found his way to Drummond House. If naught else, Robert Gordon's foul, traitorous scent would've led him there—as surely as if the darkness had already burned away into broad daylight.

Climbing from the loch, Duncan paused to squeeze what water he could from his sodden shirt and now ludicrously dripping trunks. As he did, a stealthy movement in the trees, a subtle rustling of leaves, warned him he wasn't alone. His hand snaked to the dirk he had hidden at his waist, but it was already too late.

Something thick, hard, slammed into the back of his head. Everything went black.

"Bumbling fool!" a voice, Robert Gordon's voice, pierced the fog that Duncan awoke to. "Did ye have to thwack him that hard? He'll be out to midday at this rate, and I dare not tarry overlong in Kinross."

"Ye told me he was a mean one, and no mistake," a gruff, unfamiliar voice replied. "I wasn't about to take any chances wi' him. Besides, it was but a wee tap on the head, it was. I can't help it, can I, if the Highlander has such a dainty skull?"

Duncan groaned, opened his eyes to a dimly lit room, and attempted to shove to his elbows. Something jerked him back. His head hit the floor, and the unexpected impact set his temples to throbbing fiercely. He closed his eyes and turned away.

Something rough and prickly stabbed into the side of his face. Straw, he thought. The stench of human

320

excrement and things damp and moldy wafted by. A prison cell or dungeon. Curse Robert Gordon. Was there no end to the man's duplicity?

"Ah," Gordon's voice rumbled with relief, hovering directly over him, "our fine young cock wakens at last." He ground his foot into Duncan's shoulder, pinning him to the floor. "Listen and listen well, ye arrogant cur," he growled. "Ye may have thwarted my first plan to teach ye yer place, but ye won't escape me this time."

"It'll do ye no good, Gordon," Duncan rasped, fighting to throw off the man's foot. For the moment, though, he was too weak and dizzy to succeed. Finally, he gave up.

Glancing around, he noted the smoky torches dimly illuminating the tiny, windowless room, the acrid, pitch-scented air, and the four armed men standing on either side of Robert Gordon. Undeterred, Duncan still struggled to rise. Chains clanked and tugged. For the first time, he realized he was firmly anchored to the floor.

Rage scorched through him. With bleary, burning eyes, he locked gazes with the older man.

"Indeed ye were a fool to imagine ye could ever best me." Duncan managed a defiant, mocking smile. "Did ye seriously think some puny castle could keep me in?"

Robert removed his foot and leaned back, his lips twitching with amusement. "Well, mayhap I *did* misjudge ye. It would've been better, it seems, to have found some way to betray yer impersonation once ye reached Lochleven." He sighed and smiled. "But ye were so vital to our plan to amuse and distract Lady Douglas and, more especially, her son while the keys were stolen . . ."

321

"So, ye meant to sacrifice me all along."

Duncan cursed his stupidity. He should've known and made sufficient contingency plans to avert the inevitable confrontation with the older man.

"Or was this newest treachery of yers just recently devised, after ye realized that Heather and I had fallen in love?"

Gordon's mouth tightened in anger. He turned and motioned for the guards to leave the room, then squatted beside Duncan.

"Ye're right. I couldn't have ye interfering in my plans for my bonny daughter. Charles Seton, not ye, is the man for her." He paused, a hard, brittle light springing to his eyes. "But nay, none of what I'd planned for ye was just recently devised. For nearly all yer life—and yer brother Colin's as well—I've sought some way to ruin ye both. It's the true reason why I kept ye in the Highlands all this time, when I could've easily brought ye back to live with yer brother on the Stewart estates. And why I watched with undisguised glee as Colin became a spoiled, spineless fop not worthy of any decent woman or of any discerning man's regard."

"But why? What did Colin or I ever do to ye?"

"Och, it wasn't ye or yer brother," Robert said with an unsteady laugh. "It was yer father. We were the best of friends for years, and then he stole the woman who had always been meant for me."

Duncan frowned, his thoughts racing. The woman who had always been meant for Robert Gordon? "My true mither?" he asked at long last. "Are ye speaking of her?"

"Who else? She was mine, and mine alone, Fia was. And then he took her away." He laughed again. "So I had to punish him, I did. I bided my time, inveigled my way back into his friendship and trust, and awaited the perfect opportunity. Unfortunately, David didn't live long enough to discover the fullest fruits of my revenge. Not that it hasn't still been verra, verra sweet, indeed, mayhap even *more* sweet because it *has* been so long in coming. I've had all these years to fully savor it—the final and complete destruction of David Stewart through his only heirs."

It explained so much, Duncan realized, even as he struggled to fathom the depth of Gordon's hatred and need for revenge. The impact it'd had on his own and Colin's life so far notwithstanding, he also understood now why Heather's mother had died of her unrequited love for her husband. And why, as well, Gordon had suffered few qualms in using his daughter to his own purposes, even to dangling her as a prize before a man he hated and meant ultimately to destroy. His claims to the contrary of his love for Duncan's mother, the man was, and had always been, incapable of loving anyone but himself.

"Ye're mad, Gordon," Duncan snarled. "And more the reason to get Heather as far from ye as fast as I can. She deserves far better from life than ye'll ever give her."

"And ye're the one to give her the happiness she deserves, are ye?" Once more, the merest hint of a smile twitched at the corners of Robert Gordon's mouth, and a look of triumph glittered in his eyes. "After the way ye treated her the eve before last, and how ye parted yesterday? I think not, my good man."

The memory of Heather standing there with tears in her eyes as he accused her of all manner of self-serving, manipulative acts flooded Duncan. Remorse filled him. He had been cruel that eve, and even crueler still just before they had parted and he had ridden off to Lochleven.

But she had also said she loved him. Surely love didn't die so quickly, or with such an easy death as a few harsh words could cause.

Or did it?

"She'll choose me still," Duncan gritted out the defiant reply, his voice reverberating with more bravado than he suddenly felt. "See for yerself. Fetch Heather from her room. Do it now. Hear the truth from her own lips, if ye dare."

The smile hovering on Gordon's lips spread into a malicious grin. "Och, and if I could, don't ye think I would, if for naught more than to crush that overweening pride of yers once and for all? But alas, I can't. My daughter isn't here."

Duncan went very still. "What do ye mean, she isn't here? Where could Heather have gone, considering I left her less than a day ago?"

Robert Gordon gave an uncaring shrug. "Where else but with her betrothed? The plot had commenced and Lord Seton had his own part to play. No matter the outcome, there wasn't any reason for Charles to linger here a moment longer. And, believe it or not as ye will, it was my bonny daughter who suggested the long overdue visit with her beloved Charlie and his family."

324

As if something supremely amusing had just struck him, Robert paused, then chuckled. "Ye know her as well as I. Surely ye must understand, above all others, why she seemed to need a time to renew old acquaintances with young Seton before their imminent wedding."

With a snarl of animalistic rage Duncan jerked up, straining at his shackles, fighting to get to the other man. "There'll be no wedding!" he cried. "Not if I have aught to say about it!"

"And what, indeed, can ye say or do about it, my proud if foolish young man?" Robert Gordon asked softly. "This cell, those shackles, are as far as ye'll get for the next month or two. And, when I finally free ye, if I choose ever to do so, it'll be too late. Too late, at the verra least, for ye to interfere in Heather's wedding to Charles Seton. And even, mayhap, if I have aught to do with it, too late, as well, for ye to salvage aught of that fine life and heritage that ye no longer even deserve.

"Nay," he said, his features taking on a hard, frigid resolve, "far, far too late to do aught more than tuck yer tail between yer legs and slink off to that hovel ye call home in the Highlands. Aye, the Highlands, where ye've always belonged and will never, ever, rise above."

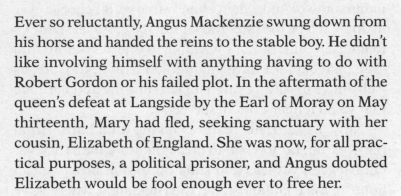

18

Ever so reluctantly, Angus Mackenzie swung down from his horse and handed the reins to the stable boy. He didn't like involving himself with anything having to do with Robert Gordon or his failed plot. In the aftermath of the queen's defeat at Langside by the Earl of Moray on May thirteenth, Mary had fled, seeking sanctuary with her cousin, Elizabeth of England. She was now, for all practical purposes, a political prisoner, and Angus doubted Elizabeth would be fool enough ever to free her.

It was, the big Scotsman well knew, the end to all their hopes of restoring Mary to the throne. It would also be the end to their lives, if Moray ever discovered the names of the men who had plotted against him and for the queen.

But there was yet one deed left to be done—and he would do it gladly—before he could hie himself back to the safe anonymity of the Highlands. Squinting in the glare of the setting sun, Angus looked up at the imposing brick structure that was Drummond House. Bathed in the rays of the setting sun, Robert Gordon awaited him in the doorway, his smile of welcome frosty and forced.

"Well, where's the lad?" Angus demanded without preliminaries as he climbed the steps to stand before the nobleman. "I can't say I've much taste for any involvement in this shameful treachery of yers, but if it's the only way to gain Duncan's freedom, for his sake and his sake alone, I'll swallow my displeasure."

"If ye ever wish to see him freed at all," Robert growled, his smile fading, "ye'll also mind yer tongue. It matters not to me if he rots below stairs. He's been a thorn in my side even before the first time we met. For that matter," he added, grimacing as if at some unbidden memory, "he remains so to this day."

"This has gone too far, ye know," the big Highlander said. "Yer obsession over losing Fia to David Stewart, and yer need to punish him through their sons well past the grave."

Surprise widened the other man's eyes. "And how long have ye known about David's and my wee feud?"

A grim smile touched Angus's lips. "Since even before ye wed Margery. Though ye've a fatal propensity for underestimating most folk, I'm not quite the country bumpkin ye've always taken me for. Unfortunately, my efforts to turn my sister from wedding ye fell on deaf ears. She loved ye too much to listen to reason, that ye weren't and likely never would be over Fia. Still, though I failed to save her, I won't fail this time. Ye'll give me Duncan or suffer the consequences."

Robert lifted a graying brow. "And those consequences might be?"

"I'll expose ye as the leader of the plot to free the queen."

He chuckled softly. "Och, aye, and risk bringing yerself and yer family down in the doing?"

Angus shrugged. "My chances of successfully escaping into the wilds of the Highlands are far better than yers, Gordon."

For a long moment, he watched the play of conflicting emotions in the nobleman's eyes. Anger, then growing fear. Frantic scheming, then rising indecision. Finally, though, all were banished by a defeated resignation.

"I've accomplished all I set out to do," Robert Gordon muttered at last. "He's not worth further thought, much less effort."

"I can take him out with me then?" the big Highlander asked. "No strings attached?"

"No strings. However, I'd suggest waiting until dark and garbing him in a hooded cloak." Robert opened the front door and motioned Angus inside. "Though it's rumored Moray finds Colin Stewart's accusation that his long-lost twin was the man responsible for Mary's escape ludicrous, it's possible his spies are still out and about."

"I'm surprised ye didn't turn Duncan over to Moray yerself. That would've put an easy end to yer dispute with the lad."

Robert paused in the entry area to shut the door. "As ye already intimated before, exposing Duncan would've risked exposing me and the other conspirators. Otherwise, I'd have done so long ago. My enmity with his father notwithstanding, the cur kept sniffing too long and hard at my daughter. He had to be stopped, one way or another, before he ruined Heather's marriage to Charles Seton."

Angus turned. "Am I to assume that's no longer a problem? Duncan ruining all yer fine plans for yer daughter?"

"It has all been taken care of, ye can be sure."

"Well, then it's for the best, I'd wager," Angus said. "Any lass who'd choose to do her father's will—especially the will of a father such as ye—over the call of her heart wasn't the woman for him."

"To yer backward Highland way of thinking," Robert agreed, his voice dripping with sarcasm, "I'm certain it must seem so. But then, ye and yer kind have always allowed yer passions to govern ye overmuch."

For a split second Angus's eyes narrowed, then he laughed. "Mayhap. Mayhap, indeed. But I'd still prefer to be governed by my passions than to tether my heart to petty, self-serving concerns, soul-rotting reprisals, and devious machinations. Now"—he gestured toward the stairs that quite evidently led down beneath the house— "if ye've said all ye need to say, I'd like to see Duncan."

"He's in the fourth room on the left." Robert Gordon pulled out a long, rusty key and handed it to Angus. "Give me an hour to depart Kinross. Then ye can free him."

Angus lifted an auburn brow. "So, ye don't wish to face him, do ye?" He took the proffered key.

"We've naught more to say to each other. I don't wish ever to see that strutting young cock again."

The laird of the Mackenzies shrugged. "Suit yerself." He smiled wryly. "If the truth were told, though ye well

329

deserve it for what ye did to him, I can't say I'd care to watch Duncan kill ye at any rate."

Footsteps, heavy and hesitant, sounded on the stairs. Duncan groaned and turned—or at least as far as his chains would allow—onto his side. Was it suppertime already? He didn't care. Food, what little was ever served, had long ago ceased to matter. Let his jailer, for all he cared, eat the tasteless swill.

The footsteps grew nearer, pausing finally outside his door. A key probed at the lock. The latch rattled. With a creak of rusty hinges, the thick oak door swung open. Seconds ticked by with unrelenting slowness, and still the visitor neither spoke nor moved.

Duncan lay there, his body burning with fever, too weak and weary even to pretend interest in whoever stood so overlong now in the doorway. Then the visitor—a man by the sound of him—walked farther into the room.

"Duncan?" a strangely familiar voice ventured. "It's Angus. Angus Mackenzie. Are ye awake? Speak to me, laddie."

It took a moment for Duncan's befuddled brain to sort through the words and grasp their meaning. Then comprehension, joyous and pulse pounding, surged through him. Oblivious to the chains jerking at his arms, the shackles gouging into his wrists, Duncan swung around.

"A-Angus?" he croaked, his own words sounding foreign, rough with disuse. "Is . . . is it truly ye, man?"

The big, burly Highlander stepped close, knelt, and placed his hand on Duncan's arm. "Aye, lad. It's me and no other."

Duncan blinked, attempting to focus through the haze of smoke and dim light. "Why? Why did ye come?"

"Why else, lad?" A chuckle rumbled in Angus's chest. "To take ye home, of course."

"Home?"

The word sounded like heaven itself. Home, Duncan thought with a bittersweet longing. Home . . . the Highlands.

"Aye, home."

Suddenly, Duncan's eyes burned, but whether it was from the smoke of the poorly wicked torches or from a swell of tears, he didn't know. "Nay, Angus," he whispered thickly. "It's not possible. Gordon hates me and surely means to see me dead. He won't permit ye to take me from here."

"Och, lad, lad," the Mackenzie laird chided, taking first one of Duncan's wrist shackles and unlocking it, then the other, "in the end, Gordon had little say in this. Once I finally discovered where ye were, I was determined naught would stand in my way. Besides, with a wee bit of persuasion, whatever his reasons for keeping ye here, they easily disappeared."

Duncan shoved to a sitting position, tossed the shackles aside, and leaned forward, cradling his suddenly throbbing head in his hands. *Whatever his reasons . . .* The words reverberated in his head. *When I finally free ye, if I choose ever to do so, it'll be too late. Too late . . . for ye to interfere in Heather's wedding to Charles Seton.*

331

He looked up, meeting Angus's worried gaze. "What day is this?"

"Thursday."

"And the date," Duncan demanded hoarsely. "I beg ye, Angus. What's the date?"

"June. June fifteenth," Angus replied, eyeing him warily.

"Six weeks. I've been here almost six weeks." Duncan clutched at his head, grinding his fists into his eyes. "Ah, curse Robert Gordon. He has done exactly what he'd always planned. He has won."

"I don't understand, lad." Angus gripped Duncan's shoulder and gave him a gentle shake. "Ye're speaking gibberish. Explain yerself. Tell me what ye mean. I can't help ye if I don't understand what ye need of me."

"Ye can't help, no matter if ye understand or not," Duncan groaned. "It's too late. Heather wed Seton over a month ago. There's naught anyone can do now."

"If she wed the lad, then so be it. She wasn't worthy of ye."

A frustrated rage scorched through Duncan. "Don't lay the fault at Heather's feet," he said through gritted teeth, glaring up at the older man. "I didn't come for her and, after how we last parted . . . well, suffice it to say I can't blame her for turning from me."

"Then what will ye do? Ye're free. Will ye come back with me to the Highlands?"

The Highlands. Though he couldn't claim true kinship with Angus or any other Mackenzie ever again, Duncan knew he'd still be welcomed, still be accepted there. And, Stewart though he truly was, he didn't care if he ever claimed his birthright or saw his dissolute brother again. Indeed, he never wanted anything to do with anything remotely related to the nobility.

"Aye," Duncan said, suddenly eager to be gone from here, "I'll come back with ye to the Highlands. It was always my destiny. And I've found the good sense to admit it at last."

Heather stood by the library's deep, stone-cut window, gazing down the birch-lined road leading up to Dunscroft Castle. Sunlight glinted off the wind-rattled leaves, touching them with a sparkling radiance. The rolling hills shone like so many huge, emerald green gems in the aftermath of the recent rain, and the distant mountains beyond stood tall and strong, majestic in their mighty splendor.

"How beautiful this place is," she murmured, "yet still it pales to the beauty of the Highlands."

But then, she added wistfully, *everything pales in comparison. Everything . . . and all because of one ruggedly handsome and most compelling of men.*

"Ye must forget him, m'lady," Beth said as she intently stitched the hem of her own wedding dress. "If he can't dredge up aught of forgiveness or understanding, he isn't worthy of ye."

Heather turned. Beth sat at the long table placed against the far wall, her back turned.

"Ye can't know for certain he hasn't forgiven me. No one can, unless they hear Duncan's denial from his own lips."

"And pray, how long will it take before ye give up that foolish little dream?" Beth glanced over her shoulder, sternly meeting Heather's gaze. "It's over seven weeks since ye two last parted, and there's been nary a word from him. Even a lass as love-struck as ye should be accepting the truth by now."

"I'm not love-struck!" Stung by her maidservant's jibe, Heather lifted her chin in defiance. "But I'm also not so certain Father told me the truth when he claimed to have waited well into the next day for Duncan to return from Lochleven, and that he never did. Think on it, Beth. What if something happened to Duncan? What if they caught him and he languishes in some dungeon? Or, worse still, they've killed him!"

"I liked Duncan verra much, until he treated you so unkindly. Nonetheless, I don't wish to think him dead or imprisoned. But, if he is, what can ye do about it? Ride to Edinburgh and demand he be released? Ye'd implicate everyone in the plot if ye did."

"Och, and don't ye think I haven't thought of that time and again?" With a frustrated toss of her head, Heather strode to the chair set before the hearth and flung herself into it. "It's the one and only reason I haven't gone seeking Duncan all these past weeks."

"As if yer father would permit ye to do such a thing," her maidservant said with a disgusted snort. She returned her attention to her gown. "Since the time ye refused to wed young Charlie and he brought ye back from the Setons, he hasn't let ye out of his sight for nary a day."

"I should've slipped away when he left last week."

Heather's lips tightened mutinously. "It's been like being in prison these past weeks, and all because I can't bring myself to wed a man I don't love."

"Ye spoiled all his fine plans, m'lady. Ye're no longer his loyal, biddable daughter. He doesn't know what to do with ye anymore."

"Father needs to let me find my own happiness in my own way, that's what he needs to do! But he won't. I see that clearly now. He won't ever do aught save what serves him. And he won't let me go to Duncan. Not now or ever." In spite of her best efforts, the tears began to flow. "Och, Beth, Beth. I don't know what to do anymore, where to turn."

"Aye, it's certain he'll never give ye to Duncan." With a sigh of resignation, Beth laid down her sewing, rose, and hurried over to her mistress. "Now, dinna fash yerself," she crooned, taking Heather into her arms. "All will be as it should. Ye must just give it a wee bit more time."

"But what if I n-never see D-Duncan again?" Heather sobbed. "I l-love him, Beth. I can't bear it if I d-don't know what has become of him. Och, I must know. I must!"

Beth grasped Heather by the arms and pushed her back. "Even if, in the knowing, it breaks yer heart?" she asked, scanning her face. "Even if, in the knowing, it shatters all yer newfound hopes and dreams?"

Heather stared back at her. "Aye. If I don't seek him out, if I don't know, I'll wonder all my life. I'll curse my cowardice and inaction to my dying day. I must try. Duncan . . . our love . . . are worth the risk."

Her maidservant smiled. "It does my heart good to hear ye say that. I feared for ye after Rose and yer mither died. Feared their mistakes in loving would cripple ye for the rest of yer life."

A sad smile lifted Heather's lips. "It may still. If he lives, Duncan may yet reject me and break my heart."

"But if ye don't try, if ye don't open yerself to loving—with all its inherent risks—ye won't ever find a true and lasting happiness." With an ineffably tender look in her eyes, Beth reached up and stroked Heather's cheek. "In the end, it's loving—and only loving—which makes us whole and satisfies us down deep to the marrow of our bones."

Love . . . It was indeed worth the risk, Heather thought. Love of a man such as Duncan Mackenzie, love of life, of honor, of family and friends. In the end, though, the source of all love was God.

She had known that truth as a child and young woman. She had rediscovered it when she had come to love Duncan. And she had accepted it once more, at long last, because to do otherwise was to turn her back on everything that truly mattered.

No one walks through life unscathed. As if he were there right now, Heather heard Duncan speak those words yet again. *A spiritual person, though, isn't destroyed or made worse by the pain. And even our weakness, our doubts and fears, can lead us closer to God if we let them.*

A spiritual person . . . A God lover . . .

Heather smiled sadly. With all her heart, she wished to be that sort of person again. A person like Duncan, whom she'd never forget and always—always—love.

Good, brave, and honorable Duncan. A man she might never see again or, even if she did, she might well have lost forever. But a man, nonetheless, next to the Lord, who had gifted her as no other.

"Aye," Heather murmured, dragging her attention back to the present moment, "down to the marrow of our bones." She turned her head, kissed Beth's palm, then took it and clasped it to her. "If anyone would know the truth of that matter, it'd be ye. Ye've had two great loves in yer life, haven't ye, first with Seamus and now with Tavish."

"Aye, that I have." Beth gave a wry laugh. "Though even I must admit the thought of wooing the formidable Tavish Gordon was quite daunting. Many a lass before me had tried and failed."

"He but awaited the right woman, and ye were that woman."

"But I didn't know that. And there was many a time I stood there, quaking in my shoes, before I gathered the courage to approach him."

Heather sighed, shook her head, then released her maidservant's hand. "As I quake now, contemplating the difficulties ahead of me. If Duncan *is* still alive and refuses to forgive me for my part in keeping the news of his brother from him . . ."

As if a sudden thought had struck her, Beth frowned. "Och, aye, Colin Stewart. I'd nearly forgotten to tell ye the latest news from Edinburgh."

"And that news is?"

"Colin Stewart has been imprisoned in Edinburgh Castle's dungeon to await sentencing for his part in Mary's escape from Lochleven. Rumor has it Moray desperately

337

desires a scapegoat. Because of that, Colin will most probably be executed."

Heather went silent and still. It wasn't fair. Colin was but an unwitting pawn, used first by one side to assure the queen's rescue and now by the other so that Moray might vent his rage at being bested, if only temporarily, by those loyal to Mary.

And Colin would most assuredly die. Her father and the other lords involved in the plot didn't dare speak up for the unfortunate young man. To do so would implicate them, with equally fatal consequences.

But to stand by and watch an innocent man die . . .

"I need to find Duncan, *if* he still lives," she said, filled with a fierce resolve. "Will ye help me, Beth? Help me find a way to escape Dunscroft? Help me find Duncan?"

"Aye, ye know I will. And so will Tavish." She paused. "What exactly do ye intend to do, m'lady?"

"What else?" Heather gave a wry laugh. "For starters, journey to the Highlands. If Duncan escaped Lochleven, I'll lay odds I'll find him there."

Duncan sat on the stoop outside his mother's cottage, throwing scraps of meat from the deer he had just cut and dressed to Cuini and her pups. The pups—wiry, gray-and-brown balls of boundless energy—had grown strong and healthy. Already they rivaled their dam in agility and aggressiveness, if their speed at catching the bits of meat he tossed their way were any indication.

The summer sun felt warm upon Duncan's face. The scent of grass and wildflowers was sweet. After a fine midday meal, his belly was full. With very little encouragement, Duncan mused, it'd be very easy to lean back against the house and doze a bit.

He had been home two weeks now. Though he hadn't regained all the weight he had lost when imprisoned those many weeks in the bowels of Drummond House, his mother's hearty Highland meals had leastwise quickly rejuvenated him. His racking cough and fever were gone. Long hours spent outdoors in the fresh, invigorating air and bright sunshine had restored most of his color. And the care and concern of his mother and friends had been a balm to his tortured soul.

Though he wasn't fully healed—and wouldn't be until the loss of the woman he loved, not to mention the still festering wound of Robert Gordon's treachery, a treachery he now realized extended far past what he had tried to do in separating him and Heather, finally eased—Duncan knew now he'd survive. He had only to endure and permit the peace and joy of being home to soothe him until, one day, the pain would disappear forever. In the meanwhile, he was loved and needed here, where he had always been meant to be.

It wasn't enough, Duncan well knew. Without Heather at his side, it would never be. But, reality being what it was, it was all he had. And, this time, he was determined to find whatever acceptance he could in that.

"So, ye imagine true love will wipe away all the obstacles in yer path, do ye?" his father had angrily demanded that night before they had fought the reivers. *"Well, Duncan my lad, life isn't that easy nor that simple."*

"Nay, Father," he softly said now in reply, his mouth

curving into a sad, bitter smile, "I suppose it isn't, though ye couldn't convince me of that at the time, could ye?"

He had been a fool in so many things. He had believed he could best any and every obstacle that stood in his way—winning Heather's heart and hand, overcoming the will of God that had ordained he remain in the Highlands and live a simple but far more fruitful life—when he imagined he was destined to achieve far greater and more noble things—and, aye, even helping to put Mary back on the throne of Scotland. Yet, in the harsh light of reality, Duncan was forced to admit he had failed in or been wrong about each and every one of those aspirations.

In the long weeks of his imprisonment, he had thought many times about taking his life and putting an end to the tormenting admission of his failures. There was nothing, Duncan now knew, worse than being held in some small, dark, dank cell, with no idea when or if you'd ever be freed. Alone and afraid, with nothing but futile, impotent regrets to contemplate hour, after hour, after hour.

There was nothing worse for a man raised to love the outdoors and fresh air, who had before always found his honor in service to others and his glory in unfettered freedom and an ever-beckoning sense of boundless opportunity. Yet, even in the blackest moments, Duncan had refused to give in to that most tragic of all despairs. Through it all, he had always known God was near and wouldn't forsake him. And, armed with that heart-deep certainty, Duncan had, in turn, refused to forsake God.

In the end, he had come to the realization that he was actually grateful for the experience—of both his failures and his incarceration. Both, at long last, had opened his eyes and forced him to examine, to compare, and finally to put his lingering doubts to rest.

Duncan thanked God for that gift, though a gift well-disguised and hard won. But then, he admitted wryly, the Lord had always been prone to teach him in such a manner, more often than not cloaking His most important lessons within the garb of hardship and suffering.

Strangely—or perhaps not really so—he seemed to learn best, or leastwise remember best, when the lessons came with difficulty, exposed to the light of day in layers of ever-deepening complexity and meaning. In the end, what mattered most wasn't how fast he learned, but that he learned and that the significance permeated to the depths of his soul. What mattered was that he finally saw the path the Lord had always intended for him to take and that he took it, when settling for less would've been so much easier. Easier, but also such poor recompense for all God had given him and wished for him to give back in return.

Those long weeks of his imprisonment, weeks in which he hadn't known from one moment to the next if he'd live or die, had forced him to consider many things. Things like what truly mattered in life, and what were but superficial trappings easily discarded. He'd had his taste, however brief, of the so-called nobler form of living and had found it shallow, frequently immoral, and bitter as gall. Life's true satisfaction—leastwise for him—would never be found there.

His foster parents had lived a full, rich, and satisfying existence. True, living off the land had been hard and they'd had their fair share of disappointments. But their innate optimism, courage, and unshakable trust in the Lord, combined with their undying love for one another, had always carried them through. Indeed, hadn't they, after repeated failures trying to start a family of their own, taken him in—an orphan of unknown heritage—and showered him with love all his life?

Love, optimism, courage. And, above all, trust in the Lord. All traits that were, to Duncan's way of thinking, ennobling, no matter what one's true birthright. And traits, as well, that assured the attainment of great things, even if only in life's simple, day-to-day existence.

Perhaps one day, he might seek out his real family if only for the sake of understanding his true heritage. Someday, too, he knew he'd wed, even if the woman would never be Heather. And, someday, his children might wish to know of their ancestors and their true birthright.

But not now and not soon. After what he had done to Colin in impersonating him, Duncan doubted his brother would be eager to open his arms in welcome. But perhaps someday, he'd seek him out and beg his forgiveness . . .

In the meanwhile, he'd mourn the loss of his bonny Heather and the few, glorious weeks and months he had shared with her. He'd mourn her but go on, living out his life with whatever shreds of honor were left him. There was no other choice, no other way.

His only solace was time. Time . . . the soothing balm

that would eventually deaden the pain, heal the wound, but leave a scar that would remain with him to the end of his days.

The sun beat down. A gentle breeze caressed his face. Duncan's lids lowered, and he leaned back against the house, surrendering at last to the seductive allure of sleep. Whatever life held, it was too much to deal with just now. Perhaps in time, but not just now.

The warm sun. The soothing breeze. The solace of home. They were all sufficient, and more, for now.

Sometime later, the sound of Cuini's sharp, yipping barks roused Duncan from a deep slumber. He sat up with a jerk, irritable and lethargic, and glared at the small dog.

"Must ye raise such a ruckus? If ye want the hare, just go after it and allow me . . ."

As his glance turned in the direction the little terrier was staring, her hackles up, her body stiffened in defense, Duncan's voice faded. There, backlit by the setting sun, were the forms of three horsemen riding down the road toward him. As Cuini continued her barking, Duncan's hand instinctively slipped to his dirk.

He lifted his other hand to shade his eyes from the sun's blinding glare. Though he couldn't make out the faces, he could tell his visitors were male—a strongly built man and two lads. They weren't dressed in Highland garb, however.

For a fleeting instant, apprehension that Moray had discovered his involvement in the plot to free Mary and had sent men to take him back to prison filled him. Then, abruptly, Cuini ceased her barking. Her tail began to wag, and she whined in eager anticipation.

Duncan's pulse quickened. His throat went dry. There was only one other person, aside from him and his mother, who could elicit such a joyous response from the little dog.

And that person was Heather Gordon.

19

"I don't like that look on Duncan's face," Beth muttered as they neared the cottage. "He doesn't appear at all happy to see us."

"And quite understandably," Heather muttered back from the side of her mouth, all the while fighting to quash her pain and disappointment over Duncan's quite evident displeasure at their visit. "He mayhap imagines . . ." She paused as a fresh wave of misery washed over her. "Och, it doesn't matter. We're here and here we stay until I tell him of his brother."

They drew up before Duncan and dismounted. Tavish and Beth hung back, pretending sudden interest in unloading the traveling bags each had tied to their saddles. Heather, after a moment more to fortify herself, squared her shoulders and strode up to stand before Duncan.

He looked thinner, his features careworn, indeed, even a bit older, but that could at least partially be attributed to his clipped hair. A fierce longing to reach up and run her fingers through the rich brown and now nearly two-inch-length curling locks flooded her. But Heather tamped it firmly down. She sensed such an action, at least at this moment, wouldn't be warmly received.

"Why have ye come?" Duncan's gaze as he scanned her—and the man's garb she wore as disguise—was narrow and cold. Briefly, his glance lifted to Tavish and Beth, then returned to her. "And why did yer father and husband permit ye to travel here without a better escort, much less come to me at all?"

"My father didn't have a chance to 'permit' me to do aught," Heather snapped, stung by his rude demand. "He wasn't home and, even if he had been, I wouldn't have asked. I'm done trying to live my life to his standards. And as far as a husband goes, I have none, so I didn't need his permission, either."

Something flickered in Duncan's eyes but passed so quickly Heather couldn't discern its origins. In the next instant, Duncan had grabbed her by the arm and was pulling her along with him.

"Come. Now," he growled. "I wish to speak with ye in private."

She opened her mouth to inform him she wasn't some horse to be led, then thought better of it. Far better that whatever passed between them be done in private. Both their emotions ran high just now. Nothing was served making a public display.

As soon as they rounded the corner and reached the back side of the cottage, Duncan halted. "Well, spit it out, then. What do ye mean, ye have no husband? Ye were supposed to wed Seton nearly six weeks ago."

Heather stared up at him, refusing to be intimidated by his furious glare. "Well, I didn't wed him, ye dim-witted lout. I love ye and will never love another. Or have ye so soon forgotten or by now don't even care?"

He gave a snort of disbelief. "Och, and sure ye love me. Is that why I haven't heard aught from ye in the past two months? And did ye even care what happened to me after I escaped Lochleven Castle?"

"And why didn't *ye* seek me out after ye escaped?" Heather shot back, refusing to give ground over a failing that was solely his. "Ye're surely bright enough to have discovered where I lived and have come to me. It isn't as if it's easy for a young woman to travel about Scotland alone, ye know. Not to mention, my father had me all but under lock and key in our home since I refused ever to wed Charlie."

That comment apparently gave Duncan pause. "Well," he finally replied, his tone more subdued, "it wasn't as if I could seek ye out, either. Just as soon as I returned from Lochleven, yer father had me thrown into a cell beneath Drummond House."

The blood drained from Heather's face. "I can't believe he'd do such a thing."

"Well, he did, and no mistake. I was there for six weeks, until Angus Mackenzie finally came for me."

She searched his face and saw the truth. "Nay, Duncan," Heather whispered. "Nay . . ."

When she swayed for an instant, he took hold of her other arm to steady her. "It wasn't yer fault, lass. I never meant to imply it was."

"It doesn't matter." Heather looked away, unable to meet his gaze. "All those weeks and I thought ye'd turned from me, couldn't forgive me, and I didn't try even once

347

to discover what had truly happened to ye." She lifted her tear-filled glance to his. "Och, if I hadn't been so proud, so afraid ye were truly no better than my father and my sister's husband . . ."

"There's fault aplenty on both sides, lass."

His grip on her tightened. For a brief, heady moment, Heather was certain Duncan meant to pull her to him and kiss her. Then, with a sigh, he released her.

"Why did ye come then, lass? Since it's now evident ye didn't know the true reason for my lack of communication with ye all these weeks, ye must have another reason for this visit. Pray, what is it?"

At the renewed reserve in his voice, disappointment flooded her once more. The barrier of her betrayal stood between them still. Heather wondered now if it would ever fall.

"It's yer brother, Colin," she forced herself to reply. "Moray holds him responsible for Mary's escape or, at least, Colin's the only man Moray can pin some form of charge on and make it stick. Even now yer brother languishes in the dungeon of Edinburgh Castle, awaiting sentencing and most probably execution."

"So, I must presume no one believed him. How convenient for yer father and the other conspirators. And how convenient, as well, for me."

"Ye don't mean that."

"Don't I?" He met her shocked gaze with a hard one of his own. "It was never my idea to involve my brother in this sorry mess. Let yer father go to Moray and tell him the truth. Let *him* inform the regent that it was Colin's twin who was responsible, and not Colin."

Heather sighed and shook her head. "And do ye truly expect my father willingly to implicate himself and the other conspirators, and all for the sake of one of Moray's allies?"

"I suppose that would stretch the limits of Robert Gordon's generosity, wouldn't it?" Duncan asked with a bitter twist of his lips. "So what would ye have me do? Give myself up instead?"

"Nay, I wouldn't wish for ye to sacrifice yerself. Moray would only torture ye, then kill ye, once he had the names of the others from ye. I only thought . . ." Heather paused, swallowed hard, then continued. "I only thought that ye might want to know about Colin. He isn't an evil man, ye know, just wild and lost after all these years without a true mither and father. Indeed, despite the relative inequity of yer upbringing, I'd say ye fared far better in the end than he."

"Yet now ye ask me to give it all up, to risk everything."

"Nay, Duncan." She reached out to him. "I would never ask ye—"

He grasped her hand and held her back from him. "Aye, ye would and just did. Ye knew that, once I heard, I couldn't turn my back on my brother. How could I? All politics and misunderstanding aside, he's my kin, my family, and a family stands together in its hour of need."

A wild hope and fierce joy filled her. "Does that mean ye'll go to him, help him?"

Duncan gave a bitter laugh. "Aye, though I haven't any

great hope of aught good coming of this. It'll most likely be, in the end, the ruination of us both."

"We'll find a way," Heather vowed, her voice husky with a joyous resolve. "Moray won't win this time. Sly, clever man that he is, he's no match for the two of us."

"There's no 'us,' lass," Duncan warned, his gaze narrowing. "This isn't yer battle."

"Isn't it?" Heather twisted free of his hold. Her chin lifted. "It was a Gordon who brought this misery down on yer house. It's only fitting a Gordon aid ye in its successful solution."

"Nay." Duncan shook his head with a savage intensity. "I'll not risk ye in the bargain. It's out of the question!"

"Is it now?" Heather grinned up at him in defiance. "And how will ye stop me? In coming to ye I've disobeyed my father. Most likely he'll disown me, once he discovers what I've done. And, since I also haven't a husband to command me otherwise . . ."

"Yer father won't disown ye. Ye're still his only heir. And I doubt ye'd disobey yer husband in this, either, if ye had one."

She angled her head, her lips curving in a smile. "Mayhap, and mayhap not. But, in the meanwhile, can I take that statement as yer acceptance of my aid?"

"Aye," Duncan said, exasperation gleaming in his eyes and threading his voice. "But I tell ye true, lass. If ye persist in such headstrong willfulness, I don't know if ye'll ever find a man to wed ye."

"Then mayhap I don't ever wish to wed at all," Heather countered, giving a proud toss of her head.

It was finally Duncan's turn to grin. "Aye, mayhap ye don't, at that."

They waited until midnight to leave their hiding place in Edinburgh Palace and creep stealthily through the long halls to the Earl of Moray's bedchamber. Thanks to Heather, who had learned a few secret nooks and crannies in the palace when she had spent time there with Queen Mary, and to Duncan's special talent for scaling walls and entering rooms through outside windows, less than half an hour later Duncan was standing in the earl's grand bedchamber.

James Stewart slept in a huge feather bed, his mouth loose and slightly agape, snoring softly. A beeswax candle burned near his bedside, casting a dim, flickering light on the regent's face. Duncan passed quickly by the bed, crept into the antechamber before the door, and gagged and bound the manservant sleeping there. Then he unlocked the bedchamber door. Heather hurried in.

She shot a quick glance at the manservant. Though he lay facing the wall, she feared the repercussions if he should happen to recognize her.

"Cover his eyes," Heather whispered, motioning toward the servant.

Duncan pulled the pillowcase free of the pillow, then drew it over the man's head. "Stay here," he whispered back. "It'd go just as badly for ye if Moray recognized ye."

"Aye." She gave a quick nod. "Now, hurry, and speak

to the man. The longer we tarry, the greater the danger becomes."

He smiled grimly, then turned and strode back into the main bedchamber. James Stewart slept on, apparently oblivious, Heather realized as she watched from her hiding place, to what was transpiring in his antechamber. As Duncan drew up at the bed again, he withdrew his dirk. Sliding it up beneath the slumbering regent's chin, he paused, then gently shook Moray awake.

"M'lord?" The softly spoken words echoed in the night-silent room, easily reaching Heather's ears. "Wake up, but have a care for the dirk beneath yer chin. If at all possible, I wouldn't have ye impaling yerself."

Moray gave a small start. His lids fluttered open, fought momentarily to focus in the dim candlelight. Then his eyes widened.

"Y-ye!" he croaked, staring up at Duncan. "How did ye escape yer cell? Only this eve I visited ye, and yer chains looked strong and solid."

"Well, then, I'd venture to say I'm either some foul spell caster or not the man ye imagine me to be," Duncan replied. "Now, tell me true, m'lord. Which of the two do *ye* think it is?"

Fear and confusion, followed by a cynical assessment, flashed in James Stewart's eyes. "Ye're another man altogether, aren't ye? Now that I look closer, I see the subtle differences. Ye aren't Colin Stewart, that much I'm certain. But ye look enough like him to be his . . ."

Moray's voice faded. Sudden realization flared in his eyes.

"Colin tried to convince me there was a twin. I didn't

352

believe him, though I'd heard the rumors that David Stewart had fathered twin boys, not just one. But he died so soon after the birthing, as did his wife, and when only Colin was ever seen . . ." He paused, scanning Duncan's face. "Then the rumors were true. And ye're the twin."

"Aye." Duncan shoved the tip of his dirk a fraction higher, pricking the soft skin beneath Moray's jaw. "And I can't have ye falsely imprisoning and mayhap even executing my brother. He's innocent of all involvement in Queen Mary's escape."

"Is he now?"

"Aye, he is. Didn't I just say that?"

"And are ye, then, taking the blame instead?" Moray's lips thinned into a hard little smile. "One of ye must, ye know. My mither assured me Colin visited her the eve of Mary's escape, then disappeared from Lochleven soon thereafter."

"I was the man who dined with the Lady Margaret that night." Duncan's mouth lifted in a grim smile. "If ye don't believe me, ask her about her offer to turn down my bedcovers and tuck me into bed that night. Only I could know that, and certainly not my brother, who wasn't even there."

Rage exploded in the regent's eyes. "Smarmy cur! How dare ye speak so of my mither? I'll have yer head on a—"

"Not before I have yers skewered on this wee dirk, m'lord," Duncan was swift to counter, twisting his dirk's tip a bit deeper until blood began to ooze from the puncture site. "And I didn't mean to insult yer mither, only to give ye some way of ascertaining the truth of my words, *if* ye still had a need to do so."

"I-I believe ye," Moray gasped. "Now . . . can ye . . . remove yer dirk? I won't . . . call for help. I swear it!"

Duncan pulled back his dirk but kept it close. "I've little time to bandy words with ye. Since ye say now that ye believe my brother is innocent, only one thing remains. Ye must pardon him and set him free."

"And are ye offering to take his place in the dungeon instead?"

"Nay." Duncan gave a harsh laugh. "I risk enough in coming here this night. I won't surrender myself to the likes of ye."

"Then why should I let Colin go? Someone must pay for Mary's escape."

"Ye'll give me yer word and scribe, then seal it, or I'll kill ye where ye lie," Duncan hissed, bringing his dirk up beneath Moray's chin once more. "If my brother can't live, neither will ye!"

"F-fine, fine." Moray pushed the dirk hastily away. "It'll be done as ye ask. But first, I've one question more."

"And that is?"

"Which of ye is the firstborn?"

At the question, Heather sucked in a breath. *Duncan,* she silently cried out to him, *beware. Moray's clever and calculating. He asks ye that for a purpose, and the purpose may well serve only him.*

"Colin, of course," Duncan lied. "Colin's firstborn."

Moray smiled. "That is good. If it had been ye, though I freed yer brother, I'd have confiscated all yer estates when I declared ye outlaw."

"It won't matter, one way or another." Duncan stepped back. "Outlaw or no, ye'll never find me once I leave ye this night. And, with Colin's pardon, ye'll have no right to our lands."

"Nay," Moray agreed wryly, rubbing the tender spot beneath his chin, "now I suppose I won't. A shame, though. Yer ancestral lands would have fattened my coffers considerably."

Duncan motioned toward the writing table set near the window. "Time's passing. Hie yerself to yer table and scribe out my brother's pardon."

"As ye wish."

Moray climbed from his bed. Clothed only in a long white nightshirt, he padded over to the writing table. A few minutes later he laid down his quill pen, capped the inkhorn, and began to wave the paper to and fro to dry it. After melting the sealing wax, Moray folded the letter, dropped a sufficient glob where the paper ends met, and affixed his signet ring's imprint in the center of the hot wax.

"I hope this will suffice," he said, finally turning to hand the letter to Duncan.

Duncan took it. "It'll suffice as proof, in the case ye ever try and go back on yer word. It wouldn't be a wise move on yer part, if ye did. I got to ye once. I can do so again."

Moray's mouth twisted. "I believe ye could. No man, no matter how high he rises, is ever truly safe if someone wishes him dead."

"And the higher a man rises, the more others have reason to see him dead."

"It's a two-edged sword, to be sure."

Duncan pointed toward the bed. "Now, it's past time ye were taking yer rest. Hie yerself back there."

Without protest, the regent rose and walked to bed.

"Lie down on yer stomach," Duncan then ordered, "and put yer hands behind ye."

Moray eyed him calmly. "Ye needn't trouble yerself. I won't give the alarm."

"Lie down, I say. Now!"

Meekly enough then, the earl did as ordered. Duncan soon had him bound and gagged. He then rolled the man over.

"Farewell, m'lord," he muttered, staring down at him. "I wish ye good fortune in ruling a kingdom ye so unfairly took from yer sister. I'd wager, though, that the yearning to rule far outstrips the inevitable reality of the experience."

He turned and strode to the anteroom. Heather took one look at his impassive face and quickly unlocked the bedchamber door. The way was clear. They were soon hurrying down the back hallways and stairs of the palace. Finally, though, Heather halted, pulling him into a small alcove.

"What is it, lass? We dare not tarry here overlong."

"Do ye wish to try and free yer brother? I don't trust Moray overmuch."

"He'll let Colin go. As sly and conniving as he is, Moray isn't heartless. And he knows now that it was me who helped free the queen, not my brother."

"Ye're certain, then?"

"Aye, I'm certain."

Heather hesitated a moment longer, weighing her next words carefully. "And do ye not have a desire to see Colin, and speak with him one more time? When he hears what ye risked in getting Moray to free him . . ."

"It doesn't matter." Duncan sighed and shook his head. "Ye heard Moray. He'll declare me an outlaw. I can never hope now to claim my rightful place beside my brother, or demand my fair share of the wealth and lands our father left us."

"That he left *ye*, Duncan Stewart," Heather reminded him gently. "Ye are and always will be the firstborn, the rightful heir."

He smiled sadly. "Duncan *Mackenzie*, lass. I can't be aught more than that ever again, and long hope to keep my head on my shoulders."

"Does that disturb ye, that ye must turn yer back on yer true heritage?"

"Nay, not anymore. At long last, I am who I want to be, and it pleases me. Pleases me greatly."

She took him by the arm. A warm satisfaction filled her. If nothing else good came of all this, Duncan was finally at peace with himself. For that, at the very least, she was happy.

"Then come," Heather said. "No more can be done here. The sooner we're gone from Edinburgh, the better."

"Aye," Duncan agreed fervently. "The sooner, the better."

By dawn, they were well into the Pentland Hills southwest of Edinburgh. In a thick stand of ash trees, Duncan finally reined in his horse. A puzzled look in her eyes, Heather drew up beside him.

"Why did ye stop? If ye imagine I'm too tired to go on, ye're sadly mistaken. The way I'm feeling just now, I'd wager I could ride the rest of the day."

"Could ye now?" He stared at her, his heart in his throat, dreading this moment now that it was upon him but knowing it must be faced, nonetheless. "And exactly where should that ride lead—north to the Highlands or south to the Grampians and Gordon lands?"

"I'll go," she said softly, "wherever the man I wed wishes me to go."

"Will ye now?"

That wasn't the answer Duncan had expected. His stomach gave a sickening lurch, then plummeted.

"So, ye've made up yer mind for Seton then, have ye?"

For a long moment, Heather stared at him. Then she laughed.

"Made up my mind for Charlie? Hardly. It's ye I speak of, ye silly man. Ye do still wish to wed me, don't ye? Or was yer proposal that night in Drummond House but a passing fancy?"

Duncan's eyes widened. His jaw dropped, and he swallowed hard. Surely . . . surely he had misheard.

"Aye," he finally said, fearing it was all some dream and he'd soon awaken to a grim and most disappointing reality. "Of course I still wish to wed ye. Despite all that passed between us in Kinross, I'll never stop loving ye, Heather Gordon. Not in this life or in the hereafter. But"—he held up a silencing hand when she opened her mouth to speak—"I can't offer ye aught but the life of a simple Highlander. Surely ye must realize that, after what I said to Moray."

"Aye, I realize that, Duncan."

She stared back at him, her eyes luminous, high color in her cheeks. At that moment, he thought he had never seen her look more beautiful.

"And will ye still wed me," he forced himself to ask, "even if I wish to take ye back to the Highlands? Will ye go with me even there?"

A broad, joyous smile lifted her lips. Happiness glowed in her eyes.

"Most especially if ye take me back to the Highlands. There's no other place in this whole wide world I'd rather live."

"Truly?" Och, but it hurt to breathe, Duncan thought, and his heart would surely burst in his chest, it was beating so hard. "Truly, lass?"

"Truly, Duncan."

With that, he threw back his head and roared out the Mackenzie battle cry.

Watching him, Heather felt her heart soar. For a fleeting instant her thoughts took wing, flying back to that wintry January day when she had stood at the library window, gazing down the birch-lined road leading from Dunscroft Castle. Almost unconsciously, she had spoken what she had imagined was an ill-conceived and totally pointless prayer, a prayer she had soon regretted when it had seemed to set about a course of events that had ultimately taken her to the Highlands.

But now, at this precious, achingly poignant moment in time, she was glad—so very, very glad—that she had uttered that prayer. Even in her darkest times, though she thought she had, she had never totally given up on God. He had been there all along, dwelling within her, down to the very marrow of her bones.

Thank Ye, Lord, Heather thought, lifting a swift, fervent, and ever so grateful prayer. *Ye are faithful. Yer love is unfailing and as high as the heavens. I will sing Yer praises forever!*

"Come then, sweet lass," Duncan said just then, his beloved voice raw and clogged with unshed tears. "Come. It's past time we were heading west. For the Highlands. For home."

"Aye, my love." With one final glance heavenward, Heather reached over to take Duncan's hand and bring it to her lips for a brief, tender kiss. "Aye, it is indeed."

Dear Readers,

I hope you enjoyed *As High as the Heavens*. Though the plot to rescue Mary, Queen of Scots, from Lochleven Castle happened almost exactly as depicted in the book, Heather and Duncan's involvement was, of course, fictional. Willie Douglas and his brother George were actually the only ones responsible for sneaking Mary out of Lochleven, right out from under the noses of Lady Margaret and Sir William. There were other conspirators—Gordon, Seton, Fleming, Beaton, and Sempill—on the outside also involved in the plot, though. I hope you didn't mind my literary license in adding a few fictional characters (including Robert Gordon) to that plot.

I'm considering a possible spin-off story about Duncan's twin brother, Colin. He'll need a lot of "reformation" to become a proper hero, of course. In the hands of the right heroine, though, we all know that such things are possible. Email me via my website at www.kathleen morgan.com and let me know what you think about a story for Colin. There's also a spot there to sign up for a semi-annual newsletter, featuring news about me, chances to win free books and other goodies, plus a way to keep you posted when a new book is in the stores along with other information that might be of interest to you.

Next in line is a Christmas novella that will be yet another spin-off story of my popular Brides of Culdee Creek series. It'll be out sometime in the fall of 2008 and be entitled *One Perfect Gift*. And, as time goes by, you can learn even more about *One Perfect Gift* by subscribing to my email newsletter or periodically checking my website.

Blessings,
Kathleen